T0356665

WHAT COMES AFTER

ALSO BY KATIE BAYERL

A Psalm for Lost Girls

WHAT COMES AFTER

KATIE BAYERL

NANCY PAULSEN BOOKS

NANCY PAULSEN BOOKS
An imprint of Penguin Random House LLC
1745 Broadway, New York, New York 10019

First published in the United States of America by Nancy Paulsen Books,
an imprint of Penguin Random House LLC, 2025

Visit us online at PenguinRandomHouse.com.

Library of Congress Cataloging-in-Publication Data
Names: Bayerl, Katie, author.
Title: What comes after / Katie Bayerl.
Description: New York: Nancy Paulsen Books, 2025. | Audience term:
Teenagers | Summary: "Cynical sixteen-year-old Mari has only ninety days to remember
how she died and to finally make peace with her mother or risk spending eternity adrift
in a vast nothingness"—Provided by publisher.
Identifiers: LCCN 2024038792 | ISBN 9780399545283 (hardcover) |
ISBN 9780399545290 (ebook)
Subjects: CYAC: Future life—Fiction. | Mothers and daughters—Fiction.
Classification: LCC PZ7.1.B38 Wh 2025 | DDC [Fic]—dc23
LC record available at https://lccn.loc.gov/2024038792

Manufactured in the United States of America

ISBN 9780399545283
1st Printing

LSCH

Edited by Stacey Barney • Design by Suki Boynton
Text set in Garamond Premier Pro

To my Ella B,
who helped with nearly every draft ·

WHAT COMES AFTER

AFTER

I DIED ON a Saturday in early October, four weeks before my seventeenth birthday, thirteen minutes *after* I was scheduled to begin the SATs.

Cause of death: trauma to the head.

Further details: unknown.

I've been told that some memory loss is normal. I've also been told that, contrary to what I'd always understood (perhaps even hoped), death does not equal The End.

The last thing I remember clearly was sitting in my guidance counselor's office—a full sixteen hours before I bit the dust, according to the sequence of events I've been given. I can still see the soft twist of Ms. Crawford's mouth as she told me there was nothing more she could do. I remember, too, the sinking sense that despite months of valiant effort, I'd hit a dead end. (No pun intended.) As I left the guidance suite and traced my way through Brookline High

School's empty hallways to its inner courtyard's crush and clamor, I felt more alone than I'd ever been. More helpless. For once, I saw no path out.

I didn't kill myself, if that's what you're thinking. They've assured me my wounds—most notably, a massive blow to the back of the head—weren't self-inflicted. It was most likely an accident. Possibly, an attack.

The rest—the how, the why now, the why *me* of it—is a bit of a black hole.

I do recall one bit, though. I'm not sure what you'd call it. A memory? Feeling? There's no sense of time or location. Just a rush of adrenaline, the itch of a shout. Then, a stampede of emotions. First, shock. Then, terror. Now, disappointment, confusion, rage, regret. And finally, joy.

Yup. The last one surprised me too. I thought dying was supposed to be the saddest thing imaginable, but in my final moment—if that's what this was—I felt all my burdens lift, and for a tiny sliver of a second, I was the happiest human alive.

Or, you know, dead. As it were.

The feeling was extremely fleeting. I opened my eyes and discovered: A ceiling. Spotless, white. Not regulation hospital tile, but far from heavenly. The mattress I lay on was decidedly thin. I blinked a bit, trying to make sense of it. Where *was* I?

Then, I saw her.

My mother looked like she did the last time I'd seen her, six months ago, April, but makeup-less and more subdued. Her blue eyes widened, setting off an unpleasant stirring in my limbs. (One, two, three, four. Yes, all four still intact.)

"Mari." Two pale hands reached for me, and the machine beside me let out an unsubtle screech.

Fun fact: Faye Novak, aka "my mother," kicked the bucket six weeks before me. Walked out in front of a bus, no explanation. I got the news on a swamp-thick morning in late August. My aunt Jenny delivered her ashes a few days later, then sat on the tiny sofa in my one-room apartment, waiting politely for me to cry. She was too late for that. I took the box, tucked it in a dark corner below the sink, offered to make us some coffee.

My mother was gone. Life carried on. For a while anyway.

Except now here she was, my dead mother, sitting on a simple chair pulled tight against my bed, machines bleeping all around, those baby-doll eyes brimming with regret. I felt a sudden, urgent need to flee.

At this point I became aware of the others. Their cries rose from the beds around us, some squeaky, confused, others low with anguish. Faye, meanwhile, just sat there, staring at me, expecting me to *do* something, *say* something. When her heart-shaped lips began to quiver, I understood: I might be dead, but my troubles weren't over, not even close.

"Where the hell are we?" I finally found the courage to ask. "Is this . . . ?"

"No." She shook her head.

She quickly brought me up to speed on a few details about death that had surprised her too. "Death isn't the end of things like we thought, baby. It's not exactly upstairs-downstairs, either, like other folks believed. Or maybe it is for them." The majority of souls have gone elsewhere, she explained, or perhaps to multiple elsewheres, sorted according to their deeds and beliefs, leaving the rest of us—the nonbelievers and agnostics, the spiritually muddled and decisively secular, plus all those who (like me) never once took seriously the concept of an *after*—in this in-between place. For us, this next phase is where the real work begins.

"It's our last chance to get things right," Faye said, "here, in Paradise Gate."

AN EXTREMELY BRIEF HISTORY
OF PARADISE GATE

Imagine it: A small-time bureaucrat, a self-help guru, and a tech developer pass over the threshold into the vast, eternal abyss. It's an ugly place. Gray. Profoundly lonely.

After a brief eternity[1] of wandering a realm that many describe as ennui made concrete, the three drift into a common orbit and immediately begin to gripe.

This is awful!

This is miserable!

It's meaningless and depressing!

How can any soul escape a despair such as this?

By then, they'd heard rumors of a lucky few who—poof!— had mysteriously released their anguish and gone on to a much better place. Such successes, however, were rare and the process murky. While the three knew instinctively that their goal should be to *move on*—transcend the eternal soup—they didn't yet know *how*.

What if there was a more transparent process? they mused.

"Something more efficient," proposed the bureaucrat.

"... and psycho-spiritually uplifting," envisioned the guru.

"... with some truly kick-ass tech," offered their code-savvy friend.

And because they had an eternity to work out the details, they did.

---

1. Ten days? Ten eons? Unclear. To a soul adrift, time is slippery.

Cut to today: approximately eighty cycles[2] into the future. The trio's dream: realized. The Powers That Be, as they now call themselves, have designed a functioning colony for secular souls, which, as far as anyone knows, remains the only such refuge in the vast misery known as the In Between.

Welcome, friends, to Paradise Gate. We wish you an efficient stay.

---

2. That's twenty years for those new to our system. One cycle = three months; or, ninety days.

AFTER

DAY 0

MURMURS BUILD AND groans erupt as, one by one, my dead peers take stock of our new situation. Their shocked expressions cause my own anxiety to kick in, a scream caught high in my throat.

Is this real? Is it a prank? A punishment?

Whispers fill the room.

What are all those machines? What are they planning to do with us? (To us?)

Dozens of beds line the bright, windowless ward. In them, bodies. Some old, many older. A few teens like me. All shapes, colors, and genders. No kids. We're in some sort of processing center for the newly dead, all of us outfitted in loose white pajamas (tunic, bottoms), and hooked to a tangle of sleek monitors. A few, like me, are accompanied by visitors—predeceased family and friends dressed in more normal clothes. No one appears ill exactly, or injured, though the navy-robed attendants keep assuring us that we have all definitely bit the dust. They smile pleasantly as they pause at bedsides to scan our screens.

"Yes, sir, you're dead. Yes, ma'am, you still have a body. A replica. No, we have not made a mistake."

It's a lot to take in.

A youngish attendant sweeps toward me, smiling blandly as he prepares to clamp a device onto my wrist. I look at Faye in alarm. "To keep track of your vibes," she says matter-of-factly.

"My wha— Ow!"

The device's light turns a bright crimson, which, from the attendant's frown, I gather isn't good.

Faye's been explaining the mechanics of everything (or what she understands, anyway; she's never been one for details)—how our souls left our bodies and passed over a threshold when we died. How, in the past, that was the end of it: Unaffiliated souls like ours might wander the expanse for an eternity, unable to shake free of their unprocessed angst. ("Which is terribly unfair, don't you think? Baby, did you know that a third of all Americans identify as nonreligious? And more than a billion people globally? We deserve decent afterlife opportunities too, right? Thank goodness for the Powers That Be!") I murmur something noncommittal because, really, I'm not sure I should be thanking anyone for what happened next. Apparently, the Powers erected a giant soul-scooping net that drags newly deceased souls out of the void and onto a dock where they are hooked into their grid, scanned briefly, and, if deemed salvageable (by whom? and by what measure?), uploaded into a giant shared simulation.

"It's like virtual reality, except not a game," I overhear a visitor tell her companion. "A place where we can clean up our act and play out our unfinished business."

My groaning neighbors go quiet as the visitor describes what we'll find outside the ward—a highly organized community, well-equipped homes, plentiful opportunities to learn and grow and maybe even get a massage from time to time. "If you earn it!" he says with a cheerful finger wag. "But more importantly, at the end of the ninety-day cycle, if you've done the work and resolved your angst, you'll be invited to ascend."

"Ascend where?" someone asks.

"The Ever After."

Everyone goes quiet, chewing on this for a moment. From their gauzy expressions, I assume that my neighbors are drawing on the usual stock imagery (clouds, harps, etc.). Personally, I still want to hear more about the gray drifting place. Because the idea of spending *ninety days* in whatever this place is with, of all people, my mother isn't something I can consider. Especially after Faye mentions that her bungalow sprouted a second bedroom this morning. "Can you believe it? We're getting another shot, baby! The Novak girls, reunited!"

Oh, hell nope. I throw back the sheets, ready to start a riot when I hear that.

Faye hops to her feet a split second after I do, her smile sucked away as she glances nervously at the attendants and a security camera winking down from above. Her pale face grows paler, fingers fluttery. She waves at me to lie back down, begs me to give her a chance—"Just wait, sweetie. Things will be better this time. I promise."

I crumple back onto the bed. I'm too dead for this. Too over it.

Promises. Uff. I fold myself neatly between the sheets and tell Faye to calm herself, sit.

She follows my order like an obedient pup.

"You're sure you don't know how you died?" Faye whispers a few minutes later. "How you hurt your head?"

I shake the head in question.

"Do you think someone hit you? Were you feeling okay before it happened?"

"I said I don't know." I add extra bite so she'll drop it. I literally woke from the dead less than an hour ago. A case of mild amnesia seems like the least of my problems.

When a navy robe hurries over to check a machine that's begun bleeping behind me, I take a deep breath and smile bravely. "Excuse me? Ma'am?" I ask. Maybe if I ask politely, she'll double-check my numbers or give me a test (I'm excellent at tests) and send me to a different afterlife. Maybe she'll realize this is all a mistake, that I don't belong here, with my mother, that this whole situation is just a little bit insane.

But the attendant swivels, her attention caught by a clatter across the room.

A middle-aged white woman stands atop her bed, ripping at her tunic. "I don't belong here! I'm telling you, I did everything right! I meditated daily! I was on the board of *three* local charities! Why won't anyone listen?"

An attendant speaks in low tones, to no effect.

"No, no, no! The service here is unacceptable! I want to speak with God. Immediately. Not a manager. *God.*"

"But, ma'am, we don't . . . more importantly, *you* don't— It says right here you didn't believe in any deities?" The room has gone hushed, all of us listening as the attendant points to his tablet. "Could this be an error?"

The woman's eyes turn to slits. "You know who I mean. The Big Boss. You must have one. Take me to her. Now."

The attendant smiles generously, pausing to press something on his screen while simultaneously attempting to explain the situation (i.e., no gods here, no "bosses" either, not in that sense, just a bunch of souls creating the best afterlife they can under a rather complex administrative structure), but the woman only grows more agitated the more he talks. Soon she is shrieking, hurling pillows. A siren blares, and a pair of guards crash into the room, making a beeline for her bed. Swift flip and the guards have her sideways. They carry her from the room plank-style as her shouts escalate into howls.

The doors slide closed, and the ward goes still, silent but for the machines' steady bleats. My neighbors exchange trembling glances. Only the attendants appear unaffected. The one nearest me leans in to check my monitor. She frowns at something, typing. "You had a question, miss?"

I shake my head, clear a frog from my throat. "Nope. I'm good. I'm fine. Everything's . . . fine."

The attendant smiles. "That's the right attitude. Keep thinking positive, dear."

A buzz sounds overhead. The initial assessment period has concluded. We're hurried from our beds, herded into a line at the far end of the ward. Faye, clinging to me, is whining something about second chances. I swat her away so I can peer through the crack in the doorway, but there's no sign of the guards or their yowling prisoner.

Another buzz and the lights blink. For a moment, the whole

ward seems to wobble. "Just a glitch," an attendant says cheerily. "Nothing to worry about."

More unanswered glances.

Faye and the other visitors must take their leave now. Faye makes another play for my hand. "Baby, listen to everything they tell you, okay? Just . . . do what they say. Promise?"

I push back her touch, then momentarily regret it (where are they taking us, exactly? when will I see her again?), but before I figure out how I want to handle Faye or any of this, we're being whisked down the hallway and my doll-faced mother is gone.

IN A LARGE room with faux-wood paneling, we're told to find a pillow and sit. A few older folks balk before discovering with delighted murmurs that their joints move more freely than they have in years.

I find a cushion in a middle row, near an exit door. More groups file in from other doorways, until there are at least a hundred of us, possibly more, huddled and waiting for whatever comes next.

Eventually, the front wall breaks open, revealing two figures on what appears to be a live two-way screen. They smile broadly, introducing themselves as the co-chairs and founders of Paradise Gate, aka the Powers That Be.

"Wherever you've been, whatever your burdens, we assure you that you're in good hands now," says a portly man in a collarless button-down. Screen name: Chairman Ted.

The woman—willowy, white-haired, unironic genie pants (screen name: Lady Lu)—pipes in. "Yes! Yes! We're here to help *you* find your best eternity! Join us and together we will manifest our brightest inner selves."

Oh boy. I side-eye my neighbors to see if they're hearing the same thing I am. These are the folks responsible for our eternal outcomes? But around me, the others lean forward on their pillows, listening intently. A few actually smile as the Chairman guy goes on a meandering monologue about his own past (boring) and the slightly more interesting story of how he, Lady Lu, and a third guy conceived Paradise Gate.

"Our mission from day one has been to provide secular souls with a clear path to redemption or, as we prefer to call it, *actualization*. In developing our program, we scoured the metaphysical theory and borrowed several helpful concepts from more traditional spiritual systems—"

"And self-help!" cries Lady Lu. "Don't forget self-help."

"Yes. Hmm. That too." Chairman Ted smiles broadly into the screen. "The short version of this long story, friends, is we've designed a unique, streamlined system for healing the past and achieving inner tranquility, and we're pleased to inform you that we've been wildly successful. Our settlement, still technically in a pilot phase, currently serves approximately seventy-five thousand souls per cycle and boasts impressive ascension rates. A majority who enter our program graduate within the prescribed ninety-day term."

"Excuse me?" Someone in the front raises a nervous hand. "Where do the others go? The ones who *don't* graduate?"

Chairman Ted pauses, squinting into the room. "Ah, well, we don't want to frighten you on your first day, do we?" He taps his belly. "No, let's focus on the positive for now. According to our research, success is twenty percent aspiration and sixty percent perspiration, which means, if you follow our program, we're eighty percent certain you'll succeed!" The Chairman chuckles while the rest of us remain silent.

"Our model isn't for everyone," offers Lady Lu more solemnly. "We don't accept pedophiles, sociopaths, or neo-Nazis, for starters—"

"Because!" interrupts the Chairman. "Because the truth is, we can only help those willing to work. We provide the tools and . . ." He glances significantly at Lady Lu.

"And the results are up to you!" she chirps.

"The clock is ticking now, friends. Think of this as the push you've always needed."

"Your last chance to become your best *you*!" coos Lady Lu.

By now, my dead stomach has sunk all the way to the floor. I need to go back. Start over. Fix whatever error in the script landed me here, dead at sixteen, in what feels like a terrible infomercial.

The Chairman stands taller. "Whatever reservations you may be experiencing, set them aside, right this second. Your job from here forward is to trust in the process."

A bell chimes and Lady Lu raises her hands, encouraging us to do the same. "Trust in the power of *you*."

BEFORE

———

SEPTEMBER (1 MONTH EARLIER)

LOOKING BACK, THERE were likely signs that my life would unravel. Choices, turning points, forks in the path. Take this route, and your life will turn out okay. This one, and you will wind up desperate, then dead, mere months before high school graduation with a wall of regret so high you can't even remember what's on other side.

But here's the thing: Who had time to worry about *signs* and *what-ifs* when the present was so consuming? Not me. I preferred to follow my nonnie's advice—*chin up, eyes ahead*. With my view fixed on the horizon, I still had a shot at survival.

Chin up, Bunny. That's what Nonnie said when I, as a fifth grader, became obsessed with melting ice caps, noxious gases, and crumbling democracies, with cows crushed in factories, rampant disease, one in five children living in poverty (in America!). Big concerns for a child, yes, but I liked to keep an eye on things.

Nonnie said it was one thing to *know*, another to let knowledge consume you. When she caught me spiraling, muttering about starving orcas, a planet on the brink, she'd pull me close, chuck me gently beneath the chin. *Come now, Bunny, you know what to do.*

And I'd take a deep, slow breath and stretch to my fullest height.

Chin up, eyes ahead, we'd say together.

And, as if by magic, the world became more bearable.

It's a motto that served me well, long after Nonnie's passing. It was still doing the trick on that quiet August evening when, at age sixteen, I tucked my mother's ashes into a corner beneath the sink and sent an apologetic Aunt Jenny on her way.

"I'll be fine," I insisted when Jenny explained (again) why I couldn't come live with her. (Pending divorce, property dispute, extremely messy living situation, etc., etc.) I lifted my gaze as Nonnie'd taught me and told Jenny that I understood. It was no problem. I'd done fine on my own these past four months. No need to change anything on account of my dead mother.

"I'm okay," I insisted. "Really. I promise."

I blinked back a small burst of worries—what would we tell my caseworker? would the state cut off funds if they discovered our ruse?—squashed all the questions down where they belonged. After all, I'd been through worse, hadn't I? Nights in shelters, that stint in a group home I'd rather forget. I'd weathered bigger losses too. (Yes, bigger than a dead mother.) With Faye gone for good, I told myself I'd be better off. It was all in my control now, order within reach. If I planned carefully, budgeted diligently, there was no reason I couldn't be happy.

If it all sounds a bit cold, calculating, perhaps it was. But I'd chosen a path and I intended to stick to it.

Of course, I didn't say all of that to Jenny. I gave my aunt just enough info to settle the worry line on her brow and get her back out the door.

Faye was harder to get rid of. She'd pop up, corner of my eye, over there by the radio. Now she wavered by the door. I'd glimpse her at the far end of the grocery aisle, that unmistakable sciatic hobble, or just beyond reach on a tightly packed train. Blink and her soft lines melted into someone else.

Was it a ghost? My mind playing tricks? Likely the latter. I was tired. I hadn't been sleeping right. The landlady's cat wasn't helping. Yowling half the night, scratching at my door. Once, I awoke to find him perched by my head, watching.

I cursed Faye. She was the one who'd insisted on feeding him, who'd always had a thing for strays. *Oscar isn't a stray,* I'd reminded her. *Look how fat he is! He has his own human.* A human who gorged him some days and forgot about him the rest, it's true. And okay, yes, sometimes I worried about Oscar too, but as Nonnie used to say, *We can't solve the whole world's problems.* A wise woman, my grandmother. Unfortunately, her wisdom had left no imprint on her elder daughter. Faye had coddled that old tabby, crooned to him, and now, in her absence, Oscar expected me to do the same. He spun around my pillow, kneading, seeking. Another spin, and his puckered bumhole appeared by my mouth.

Nope. Uh-uh. I jumped up, swatted Oscar toward the door, cursing loud enough to wake the dead. In the shadows, I swore I heard Faye laugh.

THE FIRST WEEK of my junior year arrived just in time. I'd enrolled in six classes (two APs), plus I had community service and my job at the grocery store. Homework filled all remaining gaps. After a full day, I'd come home late, hit the books for as long as my eyes could stand it, spend five hours tossing and turning. Then: early alarm, lightning-quick shower, and I was off for another round.

My guidance counselor, Ms. Crawford, caught the yawn that slipped one morning.

"Everything okay at home, Mari?"

Her gentle eyes probed, but I stopped them short.

"I'm fine," I said. "I promise."

And I was.

The hardest part, it turned out, was money. I was bringing in $342 a week, plus a monthly stipend from the state that went straight to rent. I kept a small cash reserve under the sink for food, train fare, and school fees. Brookline High was public, but most of my peers were wealthy, and everything—from lavish field trips to non-optional prom fees—seemed designed for them. For someone in my situation, that didn't leave a lot of wiggle room. So when my landlady showed up late one night, whining about the water bill, I began to sweat. Technically, it was an illegal sublet, no formal lease, so she could demand anything she wanted. Old Mrs. MacAfee was a little unhinged, if you ask me. Or maybe it was age that made her chant the same questions, over and over. *Did you shut the faucets properly? Do you think there could be a leak?* That night, I managed to convince her that the water issue wasn't in my unit, and got myself into bed.

The next morning, I stepped outside, toast wedged between

my lips, and a sharp rap sent me skyward. Several heartbeats later, I found the old lady peering owlishly from an upper window, knuckles pulled back from the glass to mime a faucet. I mimed one back. Yes, I'd turned it off.

"Batty old witch," I muttered, giving her the finger beneath my sleeve.

Oscar, as if agreeing, pressed hard against my leg, purring hopefully. "You little fucker," I said more softly, dropping him a bite of my toast.

I made it to the train stop, belly rumbling and out of sorts. The street-level platform was empty—a train had recently departed—so it was just me and a transient girl who perched on the platform each morning, singsonging: *Hello? So sorry. Can you help me? Can you spare any change?* Today her cup was empty.

It really pissed me off how few of these rich Brookline commuters stopped to help her. I didn't have much, never did. *You can't solve the whole world's problems,* Nonnie said. Still, the principle of it. I reached in my pocket for my lunch money. As I did, I caught another wisp of Faye on the breeze.

The girl looked at me quizzically with her strange amber-toned eyes.

"Are you okay?" she asked. Like those eyes could see straight into my head.

I shoved a dollar in her cup. "I'm great!"

Jesus. Why did everyone keep asking me that? "I'm totally freaking *fine!*" I told her, more harshly than necessary, before moving myself to the far end of the platform to wait for the incoming train.

AFTER

———

DAYS 1–5(ISH)

BEING DEAD IS surprisingly exhausting. After approximately twelve hours in that creepy intake center (a few more tests, two flavorless meals, plus an overview of rules that I was too overwhelmed to absorb), I was put in a windowless van and shipped out to the residences. We drove for what felt like hours, stopping occasionally to eject one nervous soul, then another. Through the van doors, I caught glimpses of buildings, mostly one-story. Bland little housing developments, perfectly paved roads, oddly angled trees.

My stop was last. I don't know why, after all I'd been told, I still hoped for another outcome, but as soon as the van doors swung open, I spotted Faye framed in the little bungalow's front entrance, waving frantically.

"Baby!" she cried. "Welcome home!"

The van peeled off, leaving me no choice but to follow her inside. Once she'd given me a brief tour of our digs—small living room, smaller kitchenette, two simple but separate bedrooms (thank the Powers!), I immediately crawled into bed. That's where I've been ever since, listening as Faye rattles about in the living room and periodically taps on my door, asking what I need.

The answer is simple: *Not her.*

On the third day, after I hear the front door shut—Faye gone to class or something—I drag myself from the bed to the sofa. The house is a lot nicer than I'm used to—gentle blue and cream tones; everything neat and new and vaguely modern. The overall effect is pleasant, I guess, if you're into houses with no personality, but its pristine surface becomes less substantial the closer you look. The TV has only four channels, I discover; the flimsy coffee table threatens to tip at the slightest touch.

I curl up on the oddly firm sofa in the pajamas I was given on arrival. (Some good news: Dead bodies don't seem to sweat or stink. So far, mine hasn't required a bathroom either.) I skip past Channel 1—a fiery lecture from the Chairman on the value of routines—to Channel 2—an inspirational talk show—to Channel 3—a strangely lit, aggressively edited "documentary" about the terrors that await beyond the grid. No thank you. The final channel is rerunning a marathon of *Dead Like Us*, a heartfelt family drama that feels like eating marshmallows for breakfast. I hate-watch seven episodes.

I should be doing something else—off taking classes like Faye so I can rack up points on my wrist device thingamajig, as she keeps urging me to do. During intake, they explained that the device tracks our moods as well as our activities, the inputs (e.g., take classes) and outputs (e.g., acquire food and clothes) operating like a sort of currency. The old me would have been out the door on day one, earning points and taking care of business. But current me, dead me, can't seem to care. Or move.

Faye says many souls go through a period of postmortem depression; she's been asking around, carrying back unhelpful bits of advice like a morbid little magpie. *Has your daughter tried visualizations? Cold rinses? What about jumping jacks?* The trouble is, each time Faye opens her pretty mouth, my thoughts go blank and I'm even less inclined to move.

That is, until I witness Faye attempting to cook.

She catches me off guard one evening (day five? day six?), stepping soundlessly into the kitchenette while I'm wrapping up a marathon session of *The Dead and the Restless*. I hear her rattling around in the cabinets, banging objects on the stove. The sounds grow more violent, and I turn to catch her standing over the sink with a can opener in one fist and a twist-top jar in the other. That's when my resolve unravels.

Fun fact: Dead people are even more bent on eating three squares a day than the living. Not for biological reasons, obviously. These replica bodies don't *need* food. (Or poop, apparently.) They're more like digital pets, responding to positive and negative behaviors via a system I have yet to fully comprehend. Our bodies aren't exact replicas either, I've realized, more like factory models with the wear and tear of life scrubbed clean. Faye's sciatica is gone, as are my ear piercings. My nails are smooth and cuticles won't tear, despite my best attempts. There are other, more unsettling differences too. Faye complains of feeling a little too cold no matter how many shawls she layers atop her muumuus. My own body feels oddly muffled except for the moments in the night when I awake with a rush of noise in my ears, every cell screaming. Still, we're expected to treat these bodies like real ones, go through the motions of a normal life. Mealtimes and a sleep schedule provide "existential stability," according to the Chairman and Lady Lu, whose pep talks fill every commercial break.

I've yet to feel inspired by these so-called spiritual leaders, but watching Faye alligator-wrestle a can opener somehow ignites me.

"Stop! Just . . . let me." I hit pause on my show (spoiler: every-one's dead) and slug across the living room to the kitchen. Faye hands me the jar with a grateful smile.

A bad habit I have: stepping in where my mother falls short.

Another bad habit: thinking it will make an ounce of difference.

It turns out the Chairman was right about one thing. There is a kind of comfort in routine. I release the sauce from the jar, pull out two pots, a box of spaghetti, and a round thing Faye insists is an onion (I sniff it; smells real), while Faye clings to the edge of the counter like a dog awaiting a treat.

We make an odd pair. Even now, I can see it, like I'm watching us from afar. Me: half a foot taller, lines broad where hers are delicate. Her eyes bright and skin fair against my warmer tones. More than one person has asked if I'm adopted. (I'm not.) I know nothing about my father, and it's never mattered, except in those moments when I wonder if he's the missing piece to this equation, the answer to why Faye and I never completely add up.

While I set the water to boil, Faye natters on about the change-over of advisers at the place where she takes classes and some new mindfulness technique that keeps putting her to sleep. Eventually, she pauses, seeming to notice that I'm still in the room. She's quiet for a moment, taking me in slowly, like she's had a new thought.

"Have you remembered anything else?" she asks nervously.

Okay, not new, then. My cause of death is currently Faye's second favorite topic, after herself. She seems to think that if I can remember this detail, it will somehow unstick me from my current paralysis.

"Could it have been a car? I saw on the feed that cars are responsible for eighteen percent of unintentional deaths."

"It wasn't a car accident."

"How do you know?"

"Because (a) I didn't drive. And (b) I was an excellent pedestrian; I always waited for walk signals." I give her a pointed look.

"Okay, well." She rearranges a set of votive candles on the countertop. "Have you tried retracing your steps? Visualizing where you might have been?"

I grunt, reaching for the "onion." (I have never in my life or death seen an onion this round, this smooth.) I begin to chop.

"Don't you *want* to remember, Mari?"

I slice, then dice in the other direction, chopping the "onion" into tiny, nearly transparent bits. It's amazing how this trick works. With my hands busy chop-chop-chopping, I don't have to think about the irony of our current situation or the messy circumstances leading up to my death or the bright flare of red on my wrist, foretelling an even more frustrating future. Most importantly, I don't *feel* . . . anything. Chop, chop, chop. Nothing to see, folks. I'm just here to cook.

Faye tucks her head and fusses with her candles, and for the briefest of seconds, I feel bad about being so cold. Then I remember: She brought it on herself. If it hadn't been for Faye's "free spirit," we both might have had a fighting chance at normal. If I'd had a mother who took her role seriously, who behaved like an adult, we might have even been happy. But that's not what she did, and it is not how things went. It took a long time for me to accept this plain truth: Faye isn't a good mother. Once unwrapped, a fact like that can't be put back in the box.

While the sauce simmers, we sit at the table, silent.

"Mari, I think it's time for you to go to the Center. Maybe we could go tomorrow."

I take a sip of water, examine my fingertips against the glass. Ten perfect, unbitten moons.

"My adviser says it's normal for a girl your age to need some adjustment time. Given the shock of what happened, he thinks maybe even a week. Mari, you've been here for eight days!"

Really? Eight? More time has slipped by than I thought.

Faye twists her pale hands around her glass. "Don't you feel ready yet? If you'd just give it a try—there are lots of souls your age at the Center and all types of activities and—"

The stove timer goes off. I get up to check the spaghetti.

She's been working this angle for a few days, dropping glossy brochures with smiling dead folks on my pillow, leaving more pamphlets splayed on the couch. The truth is, I'm starting to consider it. At this point, I'd consider anything that got me out of this house.

But another part of me can't—won't—give in to Faye. Not again.

"Mari . . ." Her lip does its signature wobble. She sneaks a not-subtle glance at her wrist, tipping it so I can see her own tracker's burnt-orange glare. "Mari, I . . . I don't want you to end up . . . You know, I *might* not—"

I clunk the pot down before she can say the rest. I know how long she's been here (forty-five days more than me) and how little progress she's made. Does my own wrist device flare a bit redder each time she brings it up? Yes. But I won't let her manipulate me so easily. My face a careful neutral, I scoop spaghetti onto both plates while Faye considers her next move.

"You're a good kid, Mari. You don't have to turn out like your screw-up mother. With a little work, there's no reason you shouldn't be fully actualized by midterm."

I sit down heavy and twirl my fork through loose strands of pasta.

She strokes the side of the table, not yet touching her food. "There's something else, baby. I hate to put this on you, but rent's gone up now that there's two of us. I'm doing my best, but my points aren't what they should be and—"

"Wait. You're paying *rent*?" If they explained this during intake, I missed it.

I look around at the little bungalow in all its cheap detail. It's a big step up for us in a way, but still. It's a freaking *simulation*.

"Nothing's free, honey. We're expected to earn points to feed the system, pay our keep. I really wish I could cover both of us, but my first month was rocky and I got behind on some things . . . and then you arrived so unexpectedly. So tragically, really. Are you definitely sure you don't know how—"

"No!" I slam down my fist, making the whole table rattle.

Faye goes quiet, then glances again at her wrist. I get it now: the brochures, the wheedling. She's not really worried about me. Faye's in debt, in over her head, again. She needs me to go to the Center, do whatever it is that will earn us points.

Here's the thing: I can't compensate for my mother's problems (history has proven it), but I also can't become indebted to her or caught up in any more of her drama. I won't let something like a rent bill pull me back in.

"I'll take care of it," I tell her after a moment of consideration. "I'll cover my own half."

"So you'll go? To the Center?"

I make the mistake of looking up then. Faye's eyes are two enormous oceans of blue, a tide so strong it tugs across the table, making the last bite stick in my throat.

I swallow hard.

"Fine. Yes."

Faye clasps her hands, her whole face gone electric. "Oh, baby! Yay! You won't regret this, I promise."

But I'm starting to think it's the only thing my tired soul is still capable of feeling. Regret.

Thanks to our sponsors, including the Center for Postmortuary Progress, where your end is our beginning.

Do you feel stuck? Confused? Do your existential woes weigh extra heavy? Don't despair! Every soul needs time to process life's residue. The good news: You don't have to navigate the next phase alone. The Center for Postmortuary Progress provides seminars and self-paced online modules addressing all your terminal needs. Best of all, our courses pay for themselves! Let us show you how to double your karmic intake and discover your best afterlife!

This cycle, check out:

- Death and the Afterlife 411: Essential Knowledge for Postmortem Success
- Unpacking Your Baggage: Clear Out the Clutter and Find Your Truest Self!
- And a brand-new elective: Moving On and Grooving Up: Dance Your Way to a Brighter Eternity

The Center is the only authorized provider of therapeutic self-actualization programming in the realm. Our certified instructors are trained in an interdisciplinary, metaphilosophical, fully secular approach to redemption. Results are not guaranteed.

AFTER

DAY 9

WE LEAVE FOR the Center absurdly early the next day, my second Monday in the afterlife. Faye wears a ridiculous pink polka-dotted muumuu, and I'm in the same white-tunic-PJ getup they provided at intake. I insist on walking (bus full of dead people? no thanks), and after a brisk twenty minutes, we arrive in Paradise Gate's downtown center: a tidy green park ringed by a cluster of dull gray buildings. Faye marches right up to the largest, dullest one and pauses with a dramatic sweep.

Really? This is "the Center" that everyone's been going on about? I was prepared for a temple built of crystals and woo, but it looks more like the sort of place you'd go to clear a parking ticket.

A trickle of people flows up the wide steps, their faces as calm and expressionless as the colorless sky above. They are a range of ages, sizes, and colors—just like the folks in the intake ward—but these souls have swapped their tunics for a mix of business suits, robes, and high-end yoga gear. I look down at my own attire and feel a vague but familiar unease.

Forever the new girl. Forever out of sync.

Faye reaches for my hand. I want to push it away, but the truth is I'm nervous. Also? I've always had a thing about revolving doors. As we reach the top step, Faye squeezes my palm like she remembers.

Deep breath. We plunge in, and several anxious seconds later, the door spits us out into a cavernous lobby. Massive burbling fountain. Giant gleaming portraits of Chairman Ted and Lady Lu. On either side, rose-colored banners insist: YOU'VE GOT THIS! YOUR ETERNITY BEGINS TODAY!

Faye pulls me toward a wall of scrolling screens. At first glance, I think it's some kind of arrivals or departures board—which, in a way, I guess it is. "The ascended," Faye says, pointing to the long rows of names. "You'll be on here soon enough."

I pause to scan more closely. Faye has told me my grandparents were part of one of the earlier cohorts to pass through the settlement. (Pop-Pop a firm atheist, Nonnie a "recovering Catholic.") Today, those cohorts are looked on as heroes, having carved a path for all of us.

Their names appear at the top of the screen: *Novak, Joseph A. Novak, Margaret C.* I rise on my toes to meet them. Nonnie and Pop-Pop's house—my home from first grade through fifth—was the last place I remember being truly happy. Nonnie's rules, like her love, were firm and consistent, and Pop's culinary skills were rivaled only by his ability to listen.

As their names slide past my fingers, I make a quick vow: If my grandparents are in the Ever After, then that's where I need to get. ASAP.

Faye pulls open the door to the main office, and together we scoot up to the counter.

"Can I help you?" croaks an old lady with glossy curls and a lipsticked smile.

"I'm here to register," I tell her. "For classes. Or support. Or whatever you call it."

I mark the blinking surveillance cameras in the corners above.

From all of the talk show snippets I've caught and the brochure pages Faye left scattered around the bungalow, I've gathered that the Center is more or less basic training for the newly dead. There are core courses everyone takes, with electives depending on your situation and interests. Faye, who bombed her midterm shortly before I arrived, recently enrolled in a more intensive program at one of the Center's satellite locations.

The receptionist—her nameplate says DORA—smiles wider. "You've come to the right place, hon." Her gaze flicks to my wrist. "And just in time, from the look of things."

Before I can cover my device's decidedly red glare or feel more than a quick flush of embarrassment, Dora turns her attention. "And you are . . . ?"

"Faye Novak. Mari's mother."

Dora looks from pale, petite Faye back to dark-eyed, big-boned me. "Will you be registering too?" she asks politely.

"Oh, no. Not me. I'm already enrolled—at the West Quadrant campus. I hit fifty days last week!" Faye beams, like it's a matter of pride.

"You don't say!" Dora breaks into another generous smile, but not before peeping the unhappy orange on Faye's wrist.

While the two of them chat about new course offerings and the latest self-purification strategies, I fill out the blue form (Physical Condition at TOD), the green form (Mental Condition at TOD), the yellow form (Emotional Condition at TOD), and the pink form (Sense of Humor Inventory).

Once I figure out that TOD means "time of death," the first three forms are easy to complete. I was an average sixteen-year-old, no happier than the rest, but no basket case either. I carried a lot of responsibility for someone my age, but I knew how to focus on what mattered and, more important, steer clear of trouble. I liked rules, liked school, the order and predictability of it. Grown-ups called me mature; my peers mostly ignored me, largely by design. I'd learned over the years how to linger below the waves of their complicated social dynamics, to blend in just enough to go unnoticed. *You're good at adapting,* Ms. Crawford once noted before I turned the subject back to my preferred territory: grades and tests.

On a scale of 0 to 10, how would you rate your mood on an average day? I circle the 5, which seems like a safe bet. Not an outright lie, but also unlikely to raise alarm.

I read through the forms, checking off everything that sounds like the normal, middle-of-the-road choice. I only dip into the lower numbers on a question about sleeping habits. I figure if this tracker thing is working, they already know about my insomnia.

The Sense of Humor Inventory is the easiest. It's a series of puns, jokes, and ironic statements, none of which are remotely funny. I check "not funny" on all but one: *According to official tallies, the most common last words among humans are "Oh, sh*t."* I have to be honest and choose "mildly humorous" for that one.

Forms complete, I hand them off to Dora, who sorts them into their color-coded baskets, skimming the pink survey before pressing a button on a massive intercom. "Franny, send me Larisa."

She holds out a scanner wand, and I place my wrist beneath it, wait for my device to bleep. **Eternity begins with a single step,** says my screen. **Enjoy 500 bonus points for registering!**

Maybe it's my imagination, but the red light softens just a shade.

Dora replaces the wand on its rack and turns her attention back to me. "So," she says.

"So," I say back.

"So, what was your fate?" she says in a gravelly tone I read as compassion.

"My fate?"

"Was it illness? An accident? Or . . . ?" Her plucked brows lift in a question, sending an uncomfortable tremor all the way to my chest.

Faye takes the bait. "It's a total mystery! She was fine one day, massive head injury the next, and no one knows how or why! She was a good kid, too, a real shining star, perfect daughter, ranked at the top of her class—"

"Hang on, that's actually—"

Faye waves away my fact-checking.

"—not true," I finish. (I made honor roll a few times, no better than most of my classmates.)

Faye, who is too absorbed in her performance to worry about details or the beep emanating from her wrist, lowers her voice dramatically. "My guess is it was stress related. Mari always worked so hard. She had so much discipline, and potential. It's tragic, really."

"Mmm." Dora takes another long look at me, clucking gently. "Truth is? After sixty-some cycles sitting at this desk, I'm not so sure I believe in tragedy."

My chin retracts. It's like she said she doesn't believe that garbage stinks. How can someone not believe in tragedy? It's one thing to not give in to it, to not wallow in it or use it as an excuse to generate more of the same, but how can you not believe tragedy exists? Maybe if I told her a little bit about the things I've been through recently, she'd take her words back. But before I can object, the door swings open and in walks someone who looks even more irritated than me.

The girl in the doorway scowls. "I'm Larisa. I'll be your afterlife ambassador. Or whatever."

Her dark eyes shift from my simple bun to loose pajama bottoms, pausing briefly at the *Get Blessed!* logo peeking through my unbuttoned top. (Faye lent me a T-shirt in case I experienced one of her cold flashes.) The girl doesn't know what to make of me, and I have to say, the feeling's mutual. With black hair lopped jaggedly above the ears and a striped purple jumpsuit, she looks like she's stepped off some sort of goth chain gang. She's shorter than me, slimmer than me, a lighter shade of skin. She appears East Asian, or possibly mixed. Her sharp gaze tells me she doesn't give a crap what I think she is, so quit trying. I'm okay with that.

"Speaking of excellent students, Larisa has been ranked at the top of her cohort since arrival. She recently hit thirty days and has made a name for herself as one of our hardest workers," Dora proclaims.

Really? This girl? I look more closely at Larisa, who simply grunts. "You ready for your tour, newbie?" Without waiting for my response, she tosses a "C'mon" over her shoulder and disappears through the door.

I step away from the counter, considering. I could skip all this (do I really want to deal with prickly peers? in the afterlife?), go back to the bungalow, and catch the next episode of *Dead Like Us*, or—I glance at my wrist, thinking of my grandparents noshing on warm pancakes without me—

I know what I have to do.

"Good luck, baby!" Faye shouts as the door whips shut behind me.

I run to catch up with my extremely rude afterlife ambassador. She leads me to the end of the hall, where she takes a left, then a right, another right, a left, a U-turn, five more turns, until I've lost the ability to trace my way back.

The halls are eerily quiet.

"Class is in session," Larisa explains. "We're expected to be productive at all times. Loitering: frowned upon." She demonstrates with a pinched brow. "But you and I have this tour to take care of, so we're good. Plus, I earned an extra self-study period anyway."

At the next turn, she gestures toward a glass atrium dotted with fake plants and old people waving smoking wands of incense. Another classroom window reveals a cluster of women kneeling on a pebble-strewn floor. "Electives," she says vaguely.

I try to make sense of the last one—it looks excruciating—and I feel Larisa attempting to do the same with me. "So what did you tell her?" she finally asks.

"Huh?"

"Dora. You must've said something 'cause she only gives me the toughest cases. I don't blame her either. The other ambassadors could scare off a lot of people with all their *enthusiasm* and shit. Oops." Her wrist bleeps, and she stamps her foot. "Dammit." She stamps again.

I step back slowly.

"Points off for cursing," she explains to my raised eyebrow. "Expressions of explicit anger and aggression are strictly taboo, especially around the newbies. Might shock your freshly hatched spirit or something. Don't worry, it's not that many points. Not like if I punched you."

I take another, larger step back. Wow. This girl. Also, "We just passed a door marked EXISTENTIAL ERADICATION. I don't think we need to worry about curse words being the shocker?"

Larisa's face shifts. I'm not sure, but I think I catch the flicker of a smile. "Well, they won't help my karmic savings, that's for sure." She squints more closely at me. "Seriously, what'd you do in there? Temper tantrum? Sullen silence? Tearing up of surveys?"

I shake my head. Make a scene? Me? This girl has me completely wrong.

"Then did you put something wacko on the forms? Are you severely withdrawn . . . or a misanthrope? Promise, I won't judge. I dislike most people too."

Larisa seems weirdly cheerful about the last bit. I'm almost sorry to disappoint her. "No. I don't *dislike* anyone. I mean, aside from . . ." Another shake of my head; no need to get into my mommy issues now. "Dora didn't even read my forms, just glanced at the pink one and called for you."

"Ah." Larisa nods gravely. "The humor survey. You're a not-funny chick. I see."

"It's not *me* who's not funny. Those jokes were terrible."

Larisa shrugs. "Dead-people humor. You'll get it eventually. Or"—wry smile—"not."

We resume our tour, traveling down another hallway, where Larisa points out several eternal rest rooms ("For naps," she clarifies with a chuckle), a string of meditation carrels, and a doorway leading to the self-observation deck. She shows me a giant auditorium reserved for ascension ceremonies and a glossy-floored Youga™ studio—"It's like yoga, but all about *you*." To this, she offers a decisive eye roll.

"I thought this place was secular," I say.

"It is."

"Well, then what's with all the talk of karma, ascension, and whatnot? Isn't yoga technically religious?"

"Technically, sure. But not everyone who does yoga is religious, right? And we can all understand *karma*. Around here, we use a lot of traditional concepts minus the god stuff. It for sure gets weird sometimes, but secularists don't have many of their own practices or even a real vocabulary for being dead, so"—Larisa shrugs—"I try to roll with it."

What I'm beginning to gather is that Larisa is a straight shooter, someone who does what's required while simultaneously seeing through the BS. I can respect that. In fact, I'm grateful for it—glad to know I'm not the only one who finds this place a bit odd.

Next Larisa shows me a series of self-expression studios and a small, sterile-looking chamber with complicated equipment where students go for "adjustments." (Also, thankfully, elective.) As I try to make sense of a wall of knobs and screens and what appears to be a medical gurney, Larisa pauses again. "Hey, Not-Funny Chick, you want to know how this place really works?"

I pull my attention away from a rack of disturbing-looking pincers.

"Um, yes, please. I'd obviously like to get out of here as fast as possible. Can you tell me how?"

"Not funny, but practical." Larisa's angled face is softened by an unexpected starburst of dimples. "Listen, kid, the real trick is there's no trick. It's all about the basics . . ."

We walk the length of one long corridor and double back the next while Larisa explains the settlement's point system in detail. The device on my wrist works like a karmic piggy bank, tracking points awarded for measurable efforts—classes attended, assignments completed, kind gestures—while deducting points for overt misbehavior. "Don't bother trying to cheat the system," Larisa warns. "It runs on AI—which isn't one hundred percent perfect; like, if I call you a shucking trashhole, it won't recognize those as curses—but it catches on to more than you'd think. I don't think you're a trashhole, by the way. That was just an example."

"Got it," I say. "Thanks."

Each day, Larisa explains, we're expected to practice positive actions and avoid harmful behavior in order to build our karmic earnings, which in turn fuel the whole grid. We need a minimum of a thousand points per day to cover food, rent, enrollment, and other basics. Surplus points can be spent on extras, like spa treatments to ease our vibes, or clothes that aren't pajamas. (Larisa raises a brow.)

"You get two hundred points per day just for showing up," she says. "Attending every class and completing assignments will get you more."

"It seems like you could hit a thousand pretty fast," I say.

"If you stay focused, sure. But you gotta watch out for the deductions. It's like that game Chutes and Ladders. Do good things, you climb the rungs. Do the stuff they don't like—as in, curse like the motherbreathing sailor you were born to be—and . . ." Larisa's hand slides down an imaginary chute. "Seriously, though, cursing's pretty minor," she says. "It's the other crap that'll nail you."

Laziness and mean-spirited behavior are the big no-nos—the ones the system is designed to catch—but Larisa lays out several additional ways people self-sabotage and get stuck: comparing yourself to others, getting caught up in negative feelings, blaming, doubting, undermining authority, worrying excessively, losing hope.

"You lose points for worrying?" I'm going to be in serious trouble if that's true.

"Well, technically, no. The tracker can't dock points for thoughts or feelings—I curse all the time in my head—but if you're constantly doubting and worrying, you're wasting energy better spent on the work. And all that anxiety will for sure drag down your vibes. That's the other thing the trackers measure."

She points to the red light on mine and the more pleasing limey-green on her own. Hers isn't fully emerald yet, but it's close. "Vibes are totally separate from points, unless earning points makes you feel happy inside, which is definitely true for me. The scale is based on some sort of algorithm that accounts for your breath, heart rate, aura, et cetera."

"Et cetera?"

"The science is squishy, but it's supposed to estimate your level of inner peace. Souls who've achieved a stable, pure green within ninety days are eligible to ascend."

I look at the red light on my wrist and feel my shoulders pinch.

"Hey, pal, no need for sadface. If you do the work and stick to the rules, your vibes will improve. Probably. It's worked so far for me."

My shoulders soften a touch. If there's one thing I'm good at, it's following rules.

"Look," Larisa says, "your best bet is to stay calm, do what they ask, even if it's goofy, and pray to the Powers that you're one of the lucky ones who make it."

The ones who don't, I've gathered, end up in that awful in-between zone. I almost ask Larisa what she knows about *that*, but we've come to a set of double doors and it's clear she's eager to move on. She places a hand on the door, then turns once again to look at me. "One more thing, Not-Funny Chick. You listening?"

"Mm-hmm." I pull out my mental checklist.

"Stay away from the virgins, the martyrs, and the wannabe prophets." She must see my confusion. "Just trust me on that one," she adds before bashing through the doors.

THE BRIGHT, HIGH-CEILINGED cafeteria buzzes with conversation. Larisa guides me along the side to the buffet, where she grabs a plate and begins heaping it with beige mush, wax-colored beans, and something called "tempeh tots."

"They're testing out a sugar-free, zero-chemical, all-vegan diet—cutting out stimulants and whatnot that might mess with your state of mind. And I guess eating simulated meat was too weird? I missed my hot wings and morning coffee at first, but this stuff grows on you too." She pops a tot in her mouth, concealing a tiny grimace. "Mostly."

As she reaches for the pot labeled KALE MOUSSE, I feel my virtual stomach tighten. "You realize it's nine a.m.?"

"And? Breakfast is for champions, my friend, the foundation of any reasonable self-care regime." Larisa slops a pile of vomit-colored mush onto her plate. "Best thing about this place is the flat-fee meal plan. All you can eat. You won't gain weight, lose weight, get sick. *Nothing* ever changes. Except the inner you. And my inner self likes to eat."

She licks a bit of slime from her finger, and I decide not to press.

I grab something that looks like a sandwich and follow Larisa out of the buffet area and into the lunchroom, which is remarkably busy considering the hour. ("Rotating schedule," Larisa explains. "Everyone gets two self-study blocks a day.")

Long modular tables radiate out from the center of the room, forming four quadrants. Students in business suits cluster in one area, the old-school cassocks in another. The far-left corner is for the quiet folks, Larisa explains. Literally. They've all taken vows of silence. The newcomers tend to gather near the front. Larisa guides me past my fellow pajama-sporting newbies to a center table with a prime view of everything.

As I slide into the bench seat, it hits me: This isn't that different from the first day in a new school, a realization that is simultaneously reassuring and depressing. After my first few moves with Faye, I learned how to read a room quickly, locate the safest group (student council nerds were a good bet), and settle along its edges. I never exactly fit in—never made actual friends or understood all the in-jokes—but my goal was far simpler: to avoid drama and scrutiny. I'd never have chosen someone like Larisa as a ballast back then, but I am grateful for her now.

The "virgins" hover around the vending machines, she tells me between spoonfuls of slime. She introduces them like that: with big air quotes and a wink. They may or may not be actual virgins—no one cares about that here—but the whole group, all female-identifying, is weirdly obsessed with proving their inner purity. In matching lycra pants and crisscross tanks ("They're really into Youga"), the virgins look like the afterworld's version of a shapewear commercial—different shades, different body types, yet somehow identical.

Larisa points: "That's Catherine of Newark in the pink, Catherine of Toronto in blue, and Milwaukee in lavender." She sees the question on my face. "Don't ask. I don't get it either."

"Cool," I say. Staying away from that group shouldn't be difficult.

The wannabe prophets are less noticeable at first. Larisa points out a few stray ones spread across the room, noting how they sit slightly apart from everyone else, holding their wrists aloft as they smile into the tiny screens on their trackers. "Documenting their path," she explains. "These dudes can't let a burp slide out without telling the rest of us how blessed they feel. I recommend getting familiar with your block button fast."

Larisa reaches for my wrist and shows me the string of videos and uplifting quotes that have jumped onto my screen since we sat down, pushed onto my feed by proximity. Two prophets have sent DMs, requesting a follow.

"They're trying to become spiritual influencers," Larisa explains.

"These guys aren't real prophets, though, just tryhards." A few clicks, and she's blocked them from my feed.

"Wow, thanks," I say. It would've taken me a least a week to figure this out on my own.

Larisa returns to her plate with gusto. "The martyrs are the worst," she says, pointing her fork toward a table of brown-robed souls seated by the garbage cans. "They're constantly doing hunger strikes and trying to be heroic. Last week, two of them tried to start a free shuttle service, carrying people to class on their *backs*." She shakes her head. "That BS doesn't even get you points. It's empty sacrifice."

I glance over at the martyrs, who are sighing miserably into empty plates. "If it doesn't count, why do they do it?"

Larisa slops another forkful in her mouth. "Guilt issues? Fear they're too messed up to make amends the regular way? Or maybe they just like attention. There's no knowing why some souls do what they do. I swear, dying sends some folks off the deep end."

"Yeah," I say quietly. That part I can comprehend. "So which ones are your friends?"

Larisa jabs her fork into another pile of mush, no longer meeting my gaze. "I'm not really a joiner. You know, a group person."

"Yeah. Me neither."

Larisa looks up.

"We moved a lot," I tell her. "After a while, it just seemed easier to do my own thing. I'm pretty independent, I guess."

Larisa nods slowly, like she gets it. "Same. Also, most people are trashholes, so."

We both smile.

"Who are *they*?" I point to a group at the far end of the room. They look fairly normal, mostly on the younger side like us, dressed in muted tones. They aren't doing anything strange that I can see. They just look . . . tired.

"Nope. Ignore."

"Why? Who are they?"

"Literal deadbeats. Total lost causes. Most of them will be kicked off the grid before you learn their names, so don't bother."

"Kicked off for what?"

"Bad vibes, poor participation, general noncompliance."

I find myself staring at one of them, a guy with pale skin and a swish of dark hair. He catches me looking, and an uncomfortable feeling slips up my spine.

"Bet you fifty points that one's a dangler."

"A *what*?" I pull my attention back to my companion.

"You know." Larisa mimes a crude noose, lets her head flop, one brow cocked.

"Wow. That's . . . dark."

Larisa shrugs, pops another veggie tot. "It's honest. And while we're on the subject, what's your damage?"

I blink.

"You know. What kind of trauma are you working with? You seem pretty unsettled. Do I sense some underlying shame? Are you a dangler too?"

"What? No, I'm not ashamed about anything or *traumatized*. I—"

My tracker lets out a beep.

"Discernible lie. Minus five points," Larisa says as I swat at my wrist. "Look, it's nothing to be embarrassed about. Depression's a monster. Suicide's a top cause for our age group, you know."

"Well, that's really fascinating, but I didn't—"

"Accidents are another big one. It was an SUV for me. Reckless driver, busted rotors, didn't see him coming until it was too late. Them's the brakes, as they say."

Larisa busts up at her own joke, and I begin to laugh too before remembering that dying at our age isn't funny. Not even a little.

"Look, if you don't mind, I'd rather not talk about it. My death. The past. All of that."

Chin up, eyes ahead. A solid motto, if you ask me.

"Hmph," Larisa says, stabbing at the last of her spongy tots. "Well, then good luck to you, kid. You're gonna have a rough time around here."

9 WAYS TO ELEVATE YOUR MINDSET

from your friends at Cloud 9

Grim thoughts are the worst, aren't they? We all have them: nasty recollections we can't seem to shake, could'ves and should'ves that make us wonder if we'll ever find meaning in this vast sea of—

Wait, where was I headed with this?

[consults notes]

Ah yes! Of course! We all have bleak days, friends. It's *normal*. But you can't—you mustn't!—let afterlife angst drag you down. There is light at the end of the tunnel! There is [consults notes] . . . a raison d'être! A reason to persist! Which is . . . hang on . . .

[riffles through pages once, twice]

[throws stack in the air]

Look. *Cloud 9* understands the tempting pull of the gloom spiral. That's why we're here for you, offering random tips and uplifting quotes that won't change your past but *might* change your mindset. So the next time you feel your soul sinking into the abyss, here's what we recommend:

1. Spend 9 minutes picturing yourself in the Ever After.
2. Select an upbeat mantra. Repeat it until the words lose all meaning.
3. Write down your darkest thoughts and then burn them.
4. Give a compliment to a stranger. Or better yet, someone you hate!

5. Reward yourself. Constantly.

6. Throw a goodbye party for your doubts and questions.

7. Select an outfit that says *Yes! I am dressed to be blessed!*

8. Adopt a soul model as your guide. (Check out our spring issue for the 50 Hottest Soul Models of All Time!)

9. When tempted by doomsy thoughts, illuminate your path with a limited-edition Scent of Paradise votive exclusively from *Cloud 9*! (Just 600 points for subscribers.)

All opinions expressed herein are intended solely as inspiration. Readers with serious existential concerns should consult a Certified Postmortuary Specialist.

AFTER

——

DAY 9 CONTINUED

WHEN I RETURN to the bungalow at the end of my first day, Faye is waiting for me at the door.

"So?" She hands me a cool glass as soon as I've kicked off my standard-issue sandals.

I take a sip. Ack . . . is that *celery* water? I set the drink down on a table beside her e-reader. *Forty-Nine Habits of Highly Evolved Souls*. I do not roll my eyes at the drink or the title. Can't afford the negative vibes.

"So?" she asks again. "How was it?"

I could ease Faye's anxiety by telling her my first day at the Center wasn't a total bust. I racked up 1,245 points for registering, attending classes with Larisa, and completing the assignments I was given. (Five bonus points for holding a door for folks during an extremely weird hallway processional involving tambourines.) All in all, I earned more than enough to cover the day's fees, and I feel good about that, enough that my vibes have improved a bit too. Larisa was right to warn me about the goofy assignments, though. Think: chanting circles, power poses, public displays of positive self-talk (an introvert's nightmare). I participated as much as I could while also figuring no one would judge the new girl for standing back a bit while the so-called virgins proclaimed themselves lovable, capable souls with compassionate hearts and whistle-clean chakras. ("Don't forget our hair!" one Catherine cried with a flick of her shiny ponytail.) It was . . . a lot. By the time the final class bell chimed, I was depleted, ready to curl into a dark hole and sleep. That's what I'm still gunning to do as soon as I can rid myself of Faye.

I hoist my new *Get Centered* tote onto my shoulder, eyeing my bedroom door. "It was all right, I guess."

"You liked it?"

Faye's eyes are playing tricks again, pulling me inward. Too much encouragement will bring on one of her blinding smiles. Something I definitely can't handle right now.

"It was all right," I repeat, and make my move for the bedroom.

"Mari? What does that mean? *All right.* Did you find some kindred spirits? Did you have any big revelations? Did you—"

I close the door with a snap and drop onto the bed. Faye's voice goes quiet on the other side. She's disappointed. Probably hurt. Maybe I ought to care about that, but I can't go there now. (*Anxiety is a vibes-killer,* Larisa warned.) By the end of the day, my tracker's red glare had faded noticeably, but after just two minutes in this house, it's already returned to deep crimson. Clearly I have work to do. I should pull out my books and get to it. Sort out my metaphorical baggage and rack up some more points to cover our shared rent before we both wind up evicted from this place and sent somewhere worse. But I need a minute. My head is too cluttered: images of nattering virgins, pushy prophets, and enthusiastic instructors urging us to *think positive* and *fix our gaze on hope*.

It turns out Larisa and I are in most of the same classes, along with several air-quote virgins and a couple of deadbeats. Teens take classes together because we're supposed to be less screwed up than adults. "Less time for mistakes, less damage to unpack," Larisa explained. Which . . . "Interesting theory," I said. "If you've never met any actual teens." She laughed at that.

Our first couple of classes were fine, all things considered. We worked on computers, charting out the daily actions to meet our point quota, and then an instructor led us through a deep-breathing exercise to take the edge off our inner turmoil. I could see my tracker's color improving after the first few breaths—a welcome surprise. In the next session, we spent ten minutes cultivating joy. ("First we plant the seeds. Then we watch them grow," crooned the teacher, introducing a shoebox-size contraption called a "joy garden.") That was less effective.

The other students seemed unfazed. They *leaned in* to self-love, kissing and complimenting their mirrored reflections, and sent their lemon-colored grief scarves sailing in a class called Expressive Arts. In Youga, I did my best to follow along, gripping my glutes in a self-empowered squat and standing on my head while an instructor urged us to let go of thoughts and *become your best YOU*. During a special group meditation ("Close your eyes and try to visualize yourself as a happy lotus bouncing on a lake of lime Jell-O . . ."), Larisa muttered something about her Buddhist ancestors rolling in their urns. But she pinched her eyes shut and exhaled as instructed, and I followed her lead because what choice did I have?

Don't be a sheep, baby.

That's what Faye used to tell me when I bent too quickly to authority. She hated being hemmed in by mandates, wanted our lives to be freer than her tightly scripted middle-class childhood. Faye believed most rules were meant as guidelines—*No one waits for the walk signal every time, baby!*—while in my view, they existed for a reason. (See as evidence: Faye's cause of death.) The way I look at it, if more people followed rules, there'd be less pain and chaos.

So, yeah, I guess I'm a sheep. Today I did everything the instructors asked: I painted a picture of inner peace, practiced loosening my vibes in a series of awkward pelvic exercises, and watched a ten-minute, extremely graphic illustration of something called a karmic colonic, which thankfully is an optional procedure because as far as I can tell, it's not much different from an ordinary colonic, and if you don't know what that is, consider yourself lucky. (No butt stuff for me, okay?)

As we traveled the halls between classes, I became aware of an anxious undercurrent, of students walking a little too quickly, pairs of guards standing at attention by the exits.

"What are they guarding?" I wondered aloud to Larisa. "There's nothing to steal, is there? We're already dead . . ."

"They're watching us," Larisa responded bluntly.

"Excuse me. *What?*"

"There've been a few incidents lately," she said obliquely. Then, to the bug-eyed look on my face: "Folks stirring up trouble, you know? Passing out contraband literature, spreading negativity, that sort of thing."

"You can get in trouble for handing out books?"

"It's considered a moral crime to interfere with or undermine another's progress. Which . . . yeah, policing that is all kinds of shady, but . . ." Larisa sighed. "I'm not going to fight the system when my own eternity's on the line, you know?"

"Yeah." I made a note to avoid any sketchy-seeming individuals carrying books.

The last class of the day was Advisory, led by a young teacher in a purple headwrap named Nasrim. ("Please call me Reenie.") Larisa explained that the instructors at the Center, along with the administrative staff, security guards, and secretaries, are part of a special class of souls who've elected to stay in the realm on an extended service mission. "They *chose* to stay here?" I asked. "Why?" Larisa had no good explanation; she thinks some of them struck deals to work off debt, while others seem to be in it for the love of the work.

"Reenie's the real deal," Larisa assured me. "She's everyone's favorite."

Reenie did make a good first impression, greeting me with a warm handclasp. "I'm so glad you're here, Mari," she said, and I could tell from her eyes that she meant it.

Within a few minutes, I knew this Advisory was very different from the one in my last high school. Picture it: fifteen dead teenagers huddled in a circle, racked by dry sobs, as they volunteer their most painful memories to an instructor who urges them to "let it all go."

They were responding to a prompt on the wall: **Tell us about a period in your life or an interaction that you look back on with regret.** After the first few students had spoken, I realized that my turn was next.

The girl next to me blubbered about having ditched her best friend for a group of more popular kids, who turned out to be intensely boring. "I didn't even give her a reason or apologize or anything. And then I died, and now she'll never know how much I missed her! Like, if I had known what was coming, do you really think I would have spent my last semester on earth listening to a bunch of idiots go on and on about eyebrows?"

Reenie encouraged the girl to apologize to her friend right here, with us as her witnesses, and after she had done that and her bawls quieted, I realized everyone was looking at me.

"Mari?" Reenie repeated my name. "Mari, is there a memory you'd like to share with the class? A moment you regret?"

I opened my mouth, let out a strange hum, then immediately snapped it shut. I felt the deadbeat guy from the cafeteria eyeing me, curious. The others were watching too, waiting for me to reveal some painful secret. What could I tell them? I pictured Faye's face the last time I saw her alive. Her final text: unanswered. I couldn't go there. Could I? My tracker turned a deeper shade of scarlet, and I felt my cheeks doing the same.

Larisa, glancing over, suggested Reenie give me a pass on my first day. She then jumped in herself, telling everyone how much she regretted all the times she mouthed off to her mother and also the one time she yelled at her hamster. ("Poor little guy. He bit me, but he didn't know better.") She didn't, however, regret the fistfight she initiated with her high school's student body president, who was "the biggest shuckturd anyone alive or dead has ever met." The Catherines gasped at Larisa's faux curse, and she replied with a lewd hand gesture that likely cost her a few points. If I hadn't still been so mortified by my own failure to speak, I'd have laughed.

By the time the Catherines got over their shock and our class's wannabe prophet had logged his disapproval on the feed, I'd been forgotten. I shot Larisa a grateful smile. She'd saved me. For the moment, anyway.

"So, we see," concluded Reenie, "the topic of regret brings up a lot of complicated feelings. Our job at this stage is to untangle ourselves from what came before as we write a new future-looking story. That which we cannot change, we must learn to forgive and, eventually, let go."

The class broke into murmurs. Only the deadbeat and I remained quiet as Reenie invited us to stand, acknowledge our past and our potential, and wait patiently as she ran a quick diagnostic on our trackers before releasing us for the day.

Let go. Reenie's words, equal parts saccharine and unsettling, followed me back to the bungalow and into my tiny bedroom, where now they sit like stones on my chest.

If only it were as easy as pointing to one incident—one bad decision, one hurt friend (or hamster)—and asking forgiveness. But what do you do when the whole of your past—the good, the bad, and the ugly—centers around a single person, arguably the most important relationship a human can have? What do you do if every aspect of that relationship feels impossible and the idea of apologizing—that *you* should own all of *that*—turns you spiky with anger?

What if I don't want to let it go?

In the other room, cabinets bang open and shut. Faye wants company, and it would be so easy to give her what she wants. Who knows, we might even have a nice moment, like we used to every now and then. But as the clatter grows louder—pots thumping, chairs scraping, Faye's need reaching through the cardboard-thin walls—it makes resentment harden around me, and I sink deeper into the bed.

I should pull out my notebook, dig into the list of assignments our instructors gave us, and focus on something productive. I will do that. Soon. I just need . . . what?

My tracker pings. Larisa has forwarded something, a video—one of those side-by-side reaction deals, where a girl watches as the karmic colonic cartoon plays on the other half of the screen. The girl's eyes widen and then flash horror as the cartoon figure fits the tube into his rectum. She locks eyes with the viewer, as though she's afraid to see what happens next. I find myself smiling with recognition. Her expressions—and timing—are genius.

When the procedure has concluded, the girl composes her features. "As we can see, Paradise Gate offers many very *creative* options for souls having trouble . . . err . . . letting ick go. Including that." Deadpan stare. "Like I always say, you gotta do what works for you. So you doo-doo you, friends, m'kay?"

Oh my god. I choke on a laugh. Who *was* that? I reply to Larisa with a laugh/cry emoji, and she responds with an upside-down poop.

I scroll back to other items Larisa's recently shared, all similarly silly. Several were made by the same girl, @RealRupiP. I click on Rupi's guide to thinking positive thoughts when your neighbor is breathing loudly, to doing Youga without splitting your pants. In one, she delivers a borderline pornographic speech about self-love in the voice of Lady Lu. That one got thousands of shares and many toothy-smile reactions.

@RealRupiP, I've gathered, is one of the big-time prophets.

Unlike my wannabe classmates, she has a legit following and official authorization from the PTB. Which is interesting because she's *definitely* trolling the Powers in some of these videos, isn't she? Maybe the humor—delivered slyly and largely through facial expressions—slips the AI's radar. Maybe it's the type of humor only decodable by teens. At the end of every video, Rupi offers a seemingly earnest pep talk, encouraging her followers to be their best selves, despite the inevitable mishaps, to make the improbable possible, and to always, always reach for the next rung. (Mimes a person falling from a ladder.) I honestly can't tell what's meant to be heartfelt and what's a joke. It's addictive, trying to figure her out. I click on another video and another.

Soon I've forgotten all about homework.

THE DAILY WITNESS

Paradise Gate's #1 source for trending news

FRENZY ON THE FEED

Has the afterworld's favorite it girl finally gone too far? On Thursday afternoon, Rupi Patel (aka @RealRupiP) shared her 3,468th post, an image of herself twerking during a handbell concert.

"Today's soul models aren't what they used to be," noted a viewer.

To which Patel replied: "YODO."

Afterlife administrators note that bawdy dance moves are not technically prohibited, but that has not stopped fingers wagging.

"It's about dignity," one critic intoned. "Soul models are meant uphold a certain standard."

"Why can't she spend more time with us?" asked @RealMaggieM, a prophet who rose to fame promoting a fifty-seven-step guide to breathing.

It's not the first time Ms. Patel has caused a stir. A native of Pasadena, California, the young tastemaker died while rescuing an injured rabbit from the road. According to friends and neighbors, Patel dedicated the better part of her adolescent years to comforting terminally ill kittens and victims of playground bullying. Upon her arrival in Paradise Gate five cycles ago, she quickly amassed a following after the PTB marked her "Sure to Ascend" based on early trends in her data. Her knack for crafting humorous advice videos has since earned the Real Rupi P stature among a new generation of dead.

She's gained official nods too. *Cloud 9* named Patel one of its 50 Hottest Soul Models. Chairman Ted and Lady Lu have praised Patel's ability to help younger souls connect with a mission of individual salvation. Based on her gift for inspiration, Patel was granted an extended stay in Paradise Gate, making it her mission to uplift souls online.

Some, though, struggle to understand the young prophet's appeal. "Is it a generational thing?" wondered one resident. "From what I see, this girl spends altogether too much time making videos. When does she find time for self-study?"

These days, Patel receives her education via remote tutors, partly due to her busy production schedule and also, she admits, to provide a buffer from her most enthusiastic fans. And detractors.

Criticism reached a fever peak two weeks ago when Patel virtually fist-bumped a former Center instructor who came out in favor of afterlife amnesty, a practice that would guarantee an unlimited stay at Paradise Gate for souls requiring more support.

"It's preposterous!" said a soul on track for a timely ascent.

"Insulting!" added another soul with excellent numbers.

"It's a true slap in the face," said a third. "If there are to be no limits on ascension, we might as well tear off our trackers and dive into the abyss! No good can come of this. No good at all."

AFTER

DAY 9 CONTINUED

DINNER IS AWKWARD. Faye asks repeatedly about my death, wondering again how I could have sustained such a serious blow to my skull.

"Maybe someone attacked you," she muses. "Did you notice anyone behaving strangely at school?"

"*No,*" I say firmly.

"Well, how about an ex-boyfriend? Girlfriend?"

I answer with a dark look.

Could it have been a deranged neighbor? A deranged teacher? My aunt Jenny? As she continues spinning out options, I feel the room go wobbly and I grab on to my head. "Could you. Just. STOP?"

I open my eyes, and the room settles back into focus. The small stove, bland vegetables, my mother's heart-shaped mouth pinched in hurt.

More softly, I say, "I told you to stop asking about it. I told you I don't *know*."

Small sniff, offended lift of the chin. "You don't have to snap."

"Yeah," I mutter. "Well."

I meant to ask her about clothes—specifically, where the nearest store is so I can go out and get some—but my daily quota for mother-daughter interaction has bottomed out and my tracker has turned an alarming shade of red. I decide to leave it till tomorrow.

Faye goes to the living room to watch a documentary about the founders while I work on reorganizing the cabinets.

Faye is my unfinished business, clearly. She is the thing I must reckon with if I want to have any hope of ascending. But how am I supposed to do that if every interaction feels like claws on my underbelly? It's what my AP English teacher would call a catch-22.

At ten o'clock on the dot, Faye rises from the couch, announcing her prescribed bedtime and offering one more sniff of hurt. I grunt an obligatory good night.

THE BUNGALOW IS quiet. I sit at my faux-wood desk, a small circle of light cast by a simple chrome lamp. By now I've read every meme and watched every ridiculous video. I've gone down a rabbit hole of ominous-yet-ambiguous references to "that other place," without learning exactly what or where it is. I've read through the Center's hundred-page guidebook twice.

With Faye tucked away and the kitchen tidy, there's nothing left to do but homework. I have three assignments tonight. The first is a basic worksheet and the second a simple breathing exercise.

I get those done quickly. The last, a journal prompt from Reenie, stares at me mockingly.

I'm not a procrastinator, not by nature. Avoiding homework feels like needing to pee and being told there's no rest stop for miles. And yet. I open my electronic tablet and squint.

Achieving full actualization requires dropping the baggage of our past so we can move on, burden free. What regrets can you release? Who can you decide to forgive? How can you begin to rebuild your narrative?

I picture Faye's pinched mouth at dinner. In the years we lived together, it's a look I grew to know well. She made the same face whenever I mentioned Nonnie. Or when I asked for something she couldn't give. Like money for field trips. Or a home where we could stay put. I learned to read my mother's expressions, to tiptoe around the pinched frowns, run for cover when her smile shone too bright. I learned the wounded limp that emerged when life became overwhelming and her nerves literally cramped. Her spine's sudden rigidity when she'd set her sights on a new plan.

I used to wonder if there was a name for what my mother was, or a cause. Had she experienced some terrible childhood trauma? (Not that I knew of. My grandparents were great, and Jenny came out fine.) Did she suffer from undiagnosed ADHD or some sort of mood disorder, or was it just your average, run-of-the-mill emotional immaturity? I once pulled a copy of the *Diagnostic and Statistical Manual of Mental Disorders* from the shelf in my high school's counseling office, spent an entire afternoon poring through its many categories of dysfunction. But while I found evidence of my mother on many pages, no single term encapsulated her exactly. I eventually set the book aside. Naming my mother's dysfunction wouldn't change her or make her easier to manage, I realized.

A hard-earned truth: My mother wasn't mine to fix.

Six months ago, when this wisdom crystallized, when my own spine finally stiffened and I told Faye my decision, I witnessed a new kind of reaction. I thought the wide-eyed shock of my choice would swallow her whole. Even tonight, I glimpsed the residual *how could you* in her eyes as she rose from the table.

She hasn't forgiven me, nor I her. There is no journal assignment or visualization exercise in the universe that could change this narrative. If forgiveness is a requisite for actualization, then the two of us are well and truly screwed.

Obviously, I can't say any of *that* in my first homework assignment. So I try for a gentler angle, figuring that some credit is better than none. I peck out a few sentences, delete them, try again. Delete.

I stare at the screen for an hour before flicking off the light, silencing my feed, and crawling into bed. I count down slowly to settle my mind's seething swirl—a trick Ms. Crawford once recommended—but I soon lose track of the numbers and tumble back into thought. Above me, the shadows deepen, then soften. Dawn creeps through the blinds, casting an uneasy gray light. I remain flat on my back, looking back on days I wish I could forget.

BEFORE

———

JANUARY (9 MONTHS EARLIER)

WE RETURNED TO Brookline in the middle of a winter freeze. The Green Line dropped us at Saint Paul Street, and from there we walked past the grand houses to a dingy corner of town on the edge of Boston, near the colleges. Neither of us had dressed warmly enough, and Faye was tired, still shaky after her most disastrous fall yet. This one had been bigger than a nasty breakup or workplace blowup. She'd been arrested for investment fraud, an accomplice to her sleazy, Ponzi-scheming boyfriend Chip, a guy I should have known was bad news the moment we met. (No decent person uses that much hair product.) Faye pled no contest to the charges and worked out a deal that involved a stiff fine, a probation officer, and a warning not to leave the state.

With no place to go and net zero in the bank, we spent a week with the sole friend Faye hadn't yet alienated, followed by a few nights in a shelter on the North Shore. Faye's sciatica went into overdrive then, producing a limp that added decades to her small frame. As the days slipped by, no solution or savior in sight, she grew jittery, clingy, only relaxing when my fingers drove through the knots at her hip. "Maybe I should call—"

"No." I jammed my thumb deeper. I knew where she was headed, and it wasn't an option. We weren't joining her former acupuncturist's weird hippie commune. Whenever things got bad, she always brought it up.

It was time for me to take charge. I began managing my mother's emails, getting up early to send inquiries from the shelter's one computer, leaving tabs open for Faye to find when she awoke, mostly job and apartment listings. I skipped the posh two-bedrooms and the tiny, overpriced studios. I gazed longingly at the single-family homes but nixed those too. Allston would've been cheaper, but I wanted Brookline. Needed Brookline. And there were affordable spots to be found if you knew how to look.

Eventually Faye got the hint and picked up the phone, reached out to a former boss with a piss-poor memory. He offered her a temp position in the real estate office she had managed back when I was in elementary school. He knew of a studio sublet that had just opened up—quirky, semi-illegal, dirt cheap—and that was all it took: The next day, we packed our one suitcase and headed home.

I was relieved to have space to ourselves again, even if it was just a single room owned by a batty old lady with an aggressively affectionate cat. I was cautiously hopeful about Faye's new commitment to the nine-to-five life too. She was getting up early, eating well, remembering to do laundry. She was trying.

Most of all, I was glad to be back in Brookline. The week we returned, I took a bus over to Nonnie and Pop-Pop's old place. I could almost see them in the doorway, waiting for me: Nonnie with her perm-tightened hair and weathered hands, ready to fuss over and caress me, Pop-Pop with a plate of fresh-baked scones and his tall-man's laugh. A new family lived there now, and Nonnie's once-beautiful garden had been covered in mulch. Still, seeing the old house with its neat porch and solid craftsman details—those wide columns and squared-off trim—had a calming effect, reminding me of how things had once been, and how they could be again: safe, secure, normal.

I enrolled as a sophomore at Brookline High School. On my first day, the registrar asked if I needed help finding my way around, but I told him I'd be fine. It was a big school but no more complicated than my last three.

One factor I forgot to consider: my cousin Izzy. Our hallway run-in came straight out of a bad sitcom. Jaws dropped, knocked heads, scattered pens. "Mari?" Izzy looked up at me, then around me, like I was a mountain she couldn't comprehend. I was a lot taller than the last time she'd seen me, it's true. Her changes were just as shocking: cropped platinum hair, nose ring, waifish limbs.

A pair of skinny, silver-studded girls broke the awkwardness, drawling, "Oh my god, Iz? Who *is* that?" Their voices pulled us back to the present. My cousin tilted her head at me, a mix of embarrassment and apology. But she didn't need to explain. I'd attended enough schools to understand where girls like me fell in the hierarchy. And anyway, this perpetual new girl had learned how to fend for herself.

Second period, I was back in the main office trying to explain that I'd taken Algebra already—twice—and Physics too. The registrar, overwhelmed, handed me off to a guidance counselor who looked like she'd just graduated from high school herself.

Ms. Crawford sat me down in her thoughtfully decorated office (plants, pillows, the whole nine) while she looked up my transcripts. With each click, her brow furrowed deeper.

"I know there are gaps," I said. "I missed some finals last time we moved, so my GPA's a mess. But I can catch up," I assured her. "I'll read the textbooks. I'm really good at math."

"I see that. Your MCAS scores are terrific." Ms. Crawford turned from the screen to me, and for the first time I noticed her eyes: warm, brown, kind. "You're a smart girl, aren't you?"

I shrugged. Caring adults weren't really my thing. It had been a long while since I'd spent enough time in one place for a teacher to turn gooey. I wasn't looking for that now.

"We're going to fix this," Ms. Crawford declared with a determined poke of her glasses. "First things first: We need to fill in those missing credits so there are no red flags on your applications. How are you with online learning?"

"Wait. Back up. Applications?"

"Yes. For college."

Oh boy. This lady needed to slow all the way down. It wasn't that I was *against* college. My grandparents had been big proponents. But a lot had changed since they were alive. "College is way too expensive," I said, pointing out the obvious.

"That's why they have financial aid," Ms. Crawford said. "And merit scholarships, which you could be eligible for if we play to your strengths."

"Okay, but . . ." I glanced politely toward to door, noting the uptick in hallway noise. "Don't I need to get to class?"

Ms. Crawford leaned in, speaking softly. "It's not that far off, you know. In another year, you could be setting your own agenda, creating the life you want."

I dodged her intense gaze. For such a green counselor, she was eerily good at reading her mark. What else had she seen in my file, I wondered.

I didn't yea or nay the college thing, but I agreed to see her again later in the week. And then again a few days after that. It turned out she had a small group of students who met with her regularly. It turned out she had a plan for each of us.

I began to dream of it: Four years in the same place, in a dorm room like everyone else. No more shelters, no more surprises. And after that? Predictable paychecks, a permanent home. Maybe I'd become like Pop-Pop, moaning about insurance and taxes. There was nothing I'd love more than to become an adult with no bigger worries than taxes.

I didn't tell Faye what I was up to. She had an aversion to college culture—for the same reason, I figured, that she hated anything requiring too much forward thinking. She believed in living in the moment, following her heart.

Lately, her heart had been blessedly quiet. There had been no major upsets at the real estate office. No new boyfriends or dippy activists trying to snag her up in their cult. She returned from work at six, watched me sling together dinner while she set up the pullout couch for our new evening ritual: binge-watching home-renovation shows. Perhaps a strange choice for two people whose last residence was a shelter, or maybe that was exactly the point. We loved the to-the-bones remodels best. We became connoisseurs of countertops, fireplace aficionados. We giggled over the botched balconies and carpeted bathrooms, and debated paint colors end-lessly. Faye stanned the bold boho interiors, while I leaned toward a softer cottage vibe. We were in alignment on beige: horrible, no healthy human would choose it, and were all over the place on architectural styles: Faye leaned historic and decorative; I preferred clean and simple but was susceptible to sprawling porches. And then once in a while, there'd be a house—a thoughtfully restored farmhouse or an enchanting seaside ranch—that managed to hit her notes and mine, captivating both of us.

"One day," she'd whisper, and for a moment, I'd let myself imagine.

A month went by, three. We made it through the first five sea-sons of our favorite reno show. I found a part-time job and passed seven of Ms. Crawford's online class modules. She turned her attention to scholarships; she felt we could bring in more money if I scored well on the SATs. Occasionally, the situation itched at my conscience. Was I being duplicitous? Pursuing one dream with Ms. Crawford—of independence, security, a life of my own making—while considering another, mostly fictitious future in the evenings with Faye?

I started to wonder if both dreams were possible: college and financial stability, plus a happy home with Faye. For once, the future felt open.

Hope was a spiky, unfamiliar thing. April arrived, and the sudden burst of springtime was almost unbearable. Green shoots everywhere, smell of soil, promise of sun. You could trick yourself into believing winter had never happened, would never return.

I walked the long way home sometimes, pausing at Nonnie and Pop-Pop's gate.

"I'm going to do this. I'm going to have the life you wanted," I promised them. The child playing in the driveway looked up, curious.

Spring infected everything, everyone. One night Faye came home from work, big smile, ran a long shower that used a full tank of hot water, and informed me she was going out. *What about season six?* I didn't say. I sat alone on the pullout, with a bowl of sad pasta, as I watched her sling on her open-toed heels and skip out the door.

Two things I knew: (1) Too much hope was dangerous. (2) When Faye was this happy, things never turned out well.

AFTER

—

DAY 10

AFTER CRAWLING OUT of bed Tuesday morning, I stare at the assignment for a while, willing it to shape-shift into a more normal task: **Solve for x if y is your total days remaining and z the patience you have left.** But it doesn't change, of course, and my tracker takes on a more stressed-out tinge the longer I stare at the prompt: **Who can you decide to forgive?**

I close the tablet and get ready for class, slipping out of the house before Faye's alarm sounds. I hurry across the bungalow's compact yard, feeling, illogically, as though I'm being watched. But the neighborhood is silent—no other soul afoot at this early hour. Not even the twitter of a bird to break the quiet.

Our new home is one of several dozen strung together into a sort of treeless complex known as Section #27C. The neighboring bungalows are all identical, differentiated only by numbered signs on their doors. It couldn't be more different from Brookline with its quirky homes and constant bustle. I have never, even in my bleakest days, felt so alone.

I want to believe what Faye said about my chances of ascending early, but my vibes tell another story, the constant red of my tracker making visible my unhappy internal state. I'm less worried about earning points. I did some quick math and figure if I can earn a 250-point surplus each day, I'll have my initial debt paid off in three weeks. That means hitting the mark on every assignment and picking up extra credit where I can. So far, Reenie's assignment is the only one that's stumped me.

At the complex's unmanned gate, I take a left out onto the street and continue past the small, hooded bus shelter. If I can find the afterlife version of a library or a quiet park, that will give me the space to think. I still have an hour, which should be plenty. I just need somewhere that isn't that bungalow with its paper-thin walls, where Faye's presence churns up unhelpful memories, magnifying my mistakes.

Mistake #1: Thinking I could stop worrying. Now that death's initial aftershock has faded, I feel the familiar worm of worry beneath my skin.

Was it silly to hope for something better?

Is inner peace possible?

What if I'm not built that way?

What if our damage is too great?

Faye has less than six weeks until her end-of-term assessment, and things don't look good for her. She's made little progress despite all the votive candles and celery water. My heart rate spikes just thinking of her mindfulness tips and strict sleep schedule. Faye, who never stuck to a schedule when *I* needed it. Faye, who—

I walk faster, past two more residential clusters and a row of neatly painted storefronts. SELF-CARE SPECIALISTS. FREE AURAL READINGS. INFUSIONS AND SUPPLEMENTS. Everything's closed at this hour, like an empty set waiting for the actors to arrive. There's no trash on the smooth sidewalk, no graffiti or cracked concrete, few cars aside from periodic buses and an occasional black van. There's something disturbing about a place that shows so little wear and tear. I find myself hunting for some little imperfection, some sign of life.

I come up on the settlement's central plaza—a perfect green rectangle threaded with symmetrical paths and neat rows of simulated trees. To my right, a gray building similar to the Center. A handful of souls in violet robes cluster at the base of the steps, staring silently up at the closed doors, a sign that reads HOUSE OF JUDGMENT. One is handing out flyers. Are they protesting something? Or engaged in some kind of spiritual exercise? I move to the opposite sidewalk to avoid finding out.

I'm about halfway across the park, in a thicket of manicured trees, when I check the time again. Thirty minutes until class. My tracker, sensing my panic, flares brighter.

I think of what Nonnie would say if she saw me in a state like this. *Deep breath, Bunny. Just find your first step.*

Maybe I'm making the assignment harder than it needs to be, cutting too deep too fast. Forgiveness is too big. What if I started with the other part of the prompt, regrets? I can surely come up with some ordinary, normal-size regrets.

For example:

1. I regret not being there when Nonnie died.
2. I regret never staying put long enough to make real friends...
3. ... or to become part of something, like a sports team.
4. I regret dying before I had the chance to fall in love.

Ding ding! There we go! That last one is promising. Just the right amount of normal teenage angst. It shouldn't be too hard processing something like that.

I find a bench and pull out my tablet. Three pages fill in a blink.

I'M FEELING PRETTY good when I arrive at the Center, the outsize glory of a girl with a completed to-do list. My tracker, noting the change, has taken on a distinctly orange tinge. Nowhere close to green yet, but moving in the right direction. Maybe I *can* do this, I think as I suck in a breath and push through the revolving door. Two hundred points ping onto my screen—just for showing up. YOU'VE GOT THIS! affirms a giant banner beside a smiling Lady Lu. I smile back. Maybe I *do*. Maybe if I steer clear of the bungalow as much as possible, focus on the most manageable next steps, maybe, just maybe—

Uff. I'm so focused on constructing my new plan that I don't see the trio of virgins until I've tripped on one of their glitter-thonged feet.

"Greetings!" the first Catherine chirps.

"Aren't you a sleepyhead!" says the next.

"We've been waiting for you since sunrise," adds a third, her smile faltering briefly as she takes in my stale-looking tunic.

"Um . . ." I glance behind me to find the person they must be addressing, but there's just the glass door, a pair of security guards standing motionless on the other side.

"You were waiting for *me*?"

"Yup!" The three Catherines beam in their pastel lycra getups, their headbands fitted so tight they must be painful. *Stay away from the virgins,* Larisa warned. Which hadn't seemed like it would be hard, but . . . I peer past the bubbling assemblage for some sign of my straight-talking ambassador. It looks like I'll have to navigate this alone.

Not wanting to be rude, I let the Catherines latch on to my arms and carry me toward class. Catherine of Schenectady asks what I think about charity versus chastity—does one virtue rank higher in my book? New Haven *must know* what type of diet I'm following. "Your vibes are *so unusual*. Are you all juice? Soy? Can I touch them?"

"Touch . . . my vibes?" I raise my hands as protective shields as she begins plucking the air around me.

"What about voices?" asks Catherine of Some Mid-Atlantic City I immediately forget.

"Voices?"

"Do you hear them?"

"Uhhh." I slip my hand from her grasp. "I hear *you*, right now."

"Ha ha, silly." She slaps my arm. "I mean the voices of our secular ancestors. Do you hear them sometimes? Talking to you and only you?"

She's all bright eyes and glossy lips, a giant GRATITUDE logo printed across her chest. On one shoulder, she carries a bejeweled tote bag that reads I ♥ RIGHT NOW.

I back away slowly. "The only dead voices I hear are the ones in front of me."

The Catherine's chin droops, and for a moment I worry I've shattered her vibes or something.

Her friends seem fine, though. Their chatter continues as they carry me down one corridor and into another, passing me off to a second set of Catherines like some sort of baton. As the first trio walks away, I notice the words ELEVATE YOUR MINDSET printed neatly across their three bums.

The second set of virgins is less interested in discussing disembodied voices than in whispering comments as other students pass.

"She's a deadbeat. He's a deadbeat. Total wannabe. Loser. Oh, yup, they're a loser too," Catherine of Milwaukee says, which sounds mean enough to merit a point deduction, but she explains that she's not *judging* the losers, not really. She just happens to know that they've literally lost more points this week than they've earned.

"A bad, bad trend," Catherine of El Paso notes.

"Once the spiral starts, it never stops," explains the third Catherine.

Catherine of Milwaukee, who has been at the Center longer than her peers, tells me that she's already seen at least five classmates follow this path. "One day they were here. The next: poof."

"Poof? What does that mean? They were axed from the grid? How does that work exactly?" I'm still a bit vague on the logistics.

The three Catherines circle me in an herbal-scented hug. "Oh,

Mari. *You* don't have to worry about that! Ha ha ha! You? Goodness, no!"

Milwaukee pats my arm. "You're one of us now, Mari. We've got your back."

"I am? You do?" I ask, but the second bell has chimed, and Catherine of Milwaukee passes me off to a third set of virgins who are eager to time the exact length of my exhalations.

This final group escorts me all the way to class.

When Larisa appears just before the final bell, she finds me wedged on a pillow between the Catherines of Montreal and Pittsburgh. Larisa takes a spot on the far side of the room, a distinct curl to her lips. I splay my hands feebly. Who knew that avoiding virgins would be this difficult?

THINGS REALLY TURN weird during the passing period before lunch. The virgins are still latched to me like glittering barnacles. Catherine of Someplace in Maine is going on about a new elective that sounds like the afterlife's answer to exotic dancing (did she call it *Soul*Dancing?), while another Catherine chimes in about an online mantra-writing intensive.

"What do you think of this mantra, Mari: *I am my best and only me.*"

She stares at me hopefully, and I honestly don't know what to say.

"That sounds . . . *true*?" I offer, not wanting to offend her.

I'm trying to find a way to ditch them politely and go in search of Larisa when a large figure leaps out from a doorway, flopping onto the floor with a groan.

I jump back as the Catherines let out a piercing shriek. A brown-robed martyr sprawls on the floor before us like a dead fish, eyes half closed as he pounds his forehead on the linoleum and whispers a jumble of *forgive mes* and *wash away my desires*. He extends a long tongue toward my feet, and oh, hell no—

My standard-issue sandals can't carry me away fast enough.

I skid through the halls, searching among the ponytails and headwraps for Larisa's jagged bob and finally find it—unsurprisingly—in the cafeteria. I wave her down from the end of the buffet line, spelling out three letters with my fingers: *WTF*.

Larisa continues piling on today's veggie surprise as if she hasn't seen me.

I dodge one incoming virgin by ducking behind a seltzer dispenser and deflect another by muttering something about a piece of cauliflower that looks just like Chairman Ted. "Oh my ancestors, it *does*!" That distracts her long enough for me to run in the opposite direction. "Sorry! Gotta meditate!" I shout as three more Catherines skitter toward me.

(White lies: minus five points.) (These: 100 percent worth it.)

I eventually locate Larisa at the same table we shared yesterday. The Catherines have fallen back to their own quadrant, as if fenced in by some invisible barrier. I drop onto the bench across from Larisa, keeping one eye on the virgins to be safe.

"Can you tell me what the eff is going on? A martyr just tried to lick me, and I swear that wannabe prophet over there got me to photobomb his selfie on purpose. What the actual fu—"

"Language," Larisa warns.

But a measly minus three points is hardly my biggest concern right now. "Are they hazing me? Have they lost their collective sanity?"

"Some people enjoy this kind of attention," Larisa says enigmatically as she smears something pea-colored onto something . . . also pea-colored.

I scrunch my nose.

"Which people? Is this more dead-people humor? 'Cause I don't get what's happening here. Not at all."

"Pfft," she says.

"Pfft?"

"Like you really don't know."

"Larisa! I swear on the Chairman and Lady Lu, I have no idea what's going on. That's why I'm asking. As my afterlife ambassador, it's your duty to explain things, isn't it?"

"Technically my duties ended after our tour."

I stare at Larisa until she places the pea-on-pea smear back on her plate.

"Can't you ask your new friends about this?" Larisa points to the table behind me, where the Catherines are staring at us from behind their invisible fence. One sees me looking and yelps.

"Those are *not* my friends. Do I look like I belong with them? Can you honestly see me in a headband?"

Larisa's frown relaxes another notch. "They seem to think you're friends."

"They're obviously *wrong*. I wouldn't choose the Catherines even if you hadn't warned me. They're . . . *terrifying*."

Larisa's mouth twitches. "It's true. They're like horror-movie scary."

"Like, now you're dead and you thought shizzle couldn't get any scarier—but whoops, here you go—scarier."

Larisa is full-on smiling now. "I forgot about *shizzle*. I should use that one more."

I wait.

Larisa hesitates, tapping her tofu kebab with a narrow fingertip. "You really don't know what's going on, do you?"

I raise my palms. "Honest to God. Or Ted, or whatever the correct secular phrase is."

"Okay. Got it. Hang on. Just . . . give me a minute." Larisa inhales her pile of green slop in what must be record time, then stands and shoves the tray to the table's center, not bothering to clear the remnants. "Gives the martyrs a little something to do," she says with a wink.

That seems . . . rude. But sure.

I follow Larisa out the back exit of the cafeteria and down a narrow hallway to an unmarked door. She checks over her shoulder before yanking me inside.

I steel myself for something terrifying—is this where the guards escort souls in need of "adjustments" or for reiki treatments? (I don't actually know what reiki is; it sounds potentially painful?) But when the door slams shut, all I see are books. Shelves and shelves full of books.

"Are we in . . . a library?"

"Yup. Where'd you think I was taking you, silly?"

I don't answer that.

Larisa drags me through the stacks to a computer terminal at the back. The Center's computers are glossy and sleek, way more advanced than any I've used before. Larisa opens a screen and types my name into the browser. A whole string of recent news items pops up.

"What the—"

"All of this should be on your feed," she says. "You must have muted your tags or something."

She grabs my wrist and presses a button on the upper right, and suddenly, my device explodes with buzzes and beeps.

"Holy hell. What is this?"

Larisa gives me a pitying look. "You need to start reading the feed before you leave the house, kid. Fewer surprises that way."

It takes me a second to understand what has happened. I silenced my socials before bed and must have forgotten to reactivate them this morning. I received dozens of notifications overnight, hundreds more this morning. Links, emojis, celebratory GIFs.

I turn to the computer, which seems a less-intimidating place to start. I click on the item at the top, and it opens to a full-page image of a sidewalk with a chalk-outlined body in the shape of a cross. *MARIANNA NOVAK AVERTS MASS MURDER, TELLS WOULD-BE KILLER "NOT TODAY!"*

"Uhhh . . ."

There are more headlines like it, more photos of the same scene—some include a city bus and a patch of green bike lane, the chalk outline broken by a smear of blood where my head hit the curb. I can't tell where it is exactly, this apparent scene of my death. It seems to be somewhere along Beacon Street, although the angles are ambiguous and nothing about the scene jogs my memory.

"This isn't *possible*." I hardly ever took the bus, even before Faye's accident.

The articles—if you can call them that—all seem to agree on a few details: An enraged shooter attempted to board a full public bus when I confronted him, shouting "not today" right before he shoved me and I fell to the ground, my head meeting an unforgiving sidewalk. I was declared dead moments later by a random medical student.

That last bit makes sense. Brookline was crawling with medical students.

The shooter, a white guy of disputed age and height, fled the scene before anyone could identify him with any certainty. His gun, meanwhile, got knocked away in the scuffle. It was a modified semiautomatic with enough ammo left over to wipe out a whole bus.

It's a lot of information to take in. I wasn't killed by a freak accident, as Faye conjectured, but by a deranged shooter? As for what they're saying about me . . .

I turn toward Larisa. "They're saying that I . . . ?"

She raises both brows. "That you . . ."

"Somehow—"

"Saved humanity, or a small slice of it anyway. Congratulations! *You* are the afterlife's newest hero! You're sure you don't remember anything?"

"No," I say. "I really don't."

Confronting a shooter? So boldly? It doesn't sound like me, not at all.

Something about this feels really off. Including the timing.

"Why now?" I ask Larisa. "Why are they reporting this ten days after it supposedly happened? And why does every single article sound like it was written by a drunk Hollywood reporter?"

"Because drunk tabloid writers are all we've got in this life. They work for the PTB, from what I can tell, and they don't seem to get much training. As for the timing"—Larisa chews her lip—"it's probably just the usual lag. It takes a while for news to trickle in. People gotta die, get their memories uploaded. Someone from your hometown probably saw your name on the news before they bit the dust. And now we're getting what they saw on TV. It can take a while for them to connect the dots."

"Them?"

"The drunk reporters. They aren't literally inebriated, in case that was unclear, just exceptionally bad at journalism."

"Yup. I got that part."

After ten minutes scanning through more clickbait headlines and reviewing all the shout-outs on my feed, I understand this isn't a joke. These folks really think I sacrificed everything for a busload of strangers.

"No wonder you acted all funny when I asked about your COD." Larisa pats my arm like she gets it now. Poor Mari, tragic hero. "You don't seem all that happy about this," she notes.

"Because it . . . makes no sense. Do you think everyone's seen this?" I think of the Catherines clinging to me all morning and that disgusting toe-licking martyr. The idea of everyone watching me, thinking they know things about my death that I can't remember myself . . . it's deeply uncomfortable.

"Being a hero is generally considered a good thing, you know.

Something like this could get you fast-tracked to the Ever After."

I picture curly-haired Nonnie and tall Pop-Pop waving to me from a heavenly front porch. Now, *that* wouldn't suck . . .

But no. I shake my head. "What if they're wrong? What if they look closer at my life and realize I wasn't anything special? Or, worse, what if they realize I had some fatal flaw—like, I wasn't kind enough or was deeply selfish or focused on all the wrong things—and now have zero hope of redemption?"

"Dang. You took that to a depressing place."

"I like to prepare for the worst."

In my experience, the worst often comes true.

Larisa suggests I take the rest of the day off. "I'll tell our instructors you needed a little time to meditate and whatnot. Don't worry. There'll still be time to earn points tomorrow," she says when I start to object. "You need to look after yourself right now, get those vibes under control." She points to my tracker, which has turned a shade of red I've never seen in nature.

"One thing at a time," Larisa says in the same tone my nonnie used when the world felt too big, too impossible. I give her a grateful half smile. The truth is, I do need space right now, somewhere to let this brain-vomit settle. It seems very unfair. Just when I felt like I was getting a handle on my new situation . . . this.

Larisa guides me to a side exit, one that leads directly to a quiet street behind the main square. I take the back roads home, tunic pulled up over my head. I don't let my shoulders relax until I arrive at the bungalow. Before I can reach for the doorknob, Faye flings the door open.

"Mari!" she cries, her face bursting with the news.

THIS WEEK IN BETWEEN

with your host, Jeremiah Waters

Greetings, seekers! It's been a busy few days in Paradise Gate. A surge of nearly one thousand new arrivals followed a week of natural disasters and man-made catastrophes back on earth. A flood, a tornado, a shooting, and a factory fire—each the worst in recent memory. (Though, according to our experts, no worse than the calamities of yore.) A fleet of counselors has been deployed to ease the transition of the most traumatized souls. Most are expected to begin classes next week.

On Thursday, Lady Lu and Chairman Ted celebrated the opening of a new Outlook Adjustment facility, which will provide spiritual recalibration services for noncompliant souls, a group of particular concern to the Chairman. At the ceremony, clients and clinicians honored the Powers' heroic leadership.

Speaking of heroes, by now you've surely seen today's big headline: *MARIANNA NOVAK AVERTS MASS MURDER, TELLS WOULD-BE KILLER "NOT TODAY!"* You've probably already ordered the T-shirt.

What you may not know is who Marianna Novak was before she became a total bada$$. Our initial research suggests Novak was a hard worker and an even-tempered youth, despite significant challenges throughout her upbringing.

"My daughter was practically a saint!" her predeceased mother exclaimed when we reached out for comment. "She was always so obedient, never made a fuss. I had to remind her it's okay to make waves sometimes, to stand up for what's right," the elder Novak continued before the phone abruptly hung up.

We expect more details to develop in the days ahead. We're hoping Miss Novak herself will break her silence and perhaps drop some wisdom on the feed. A message for her in the meantime: We applaud your heroic act and will attend to your every word and deed with utmost attention from this point forward. Wherever you go, expect us to follow.

AFTER

DAY 10 CONTINUED

ALL EVENING, MY tracker buzzes and the calls pour in—from reporters looking for the next scoop, well-wishers hoping for ascension tips, and a few absolute wackadoos. One new follower sends me so many praise-hand emojis that I begin to wonder if I'm being trolled. I block them after the fifteenth DM.

At first Faye is fizzy with the attention. To think of it! Her own little Mari, a true soul model! And she, the woman who shaped me! But the calls eventually wear on her too. One caller accuses me of lying and says Faye and I both deserve to spend eternity in the gray expanse. Another—Faye answered this one—says something I don't hear that makes her whole body quake. That's when I turn off the ringer and send Faye to bed. I tell her I'm going to sleep soon too so she won't think she's missing anything. (White lie: minus five points.)

The truth: There's no way I'll sleep tonight.

After Faye's room has gone quiet, I sit on the couch with the

TV turned low, monitoring both it and my feed. The halo-emoji reshares have slowed down a bit, giving me time to catch up on all the tagged items from earlier. Six thousand mentions since dinner.

Interest has turned quickly from the shooting itself to the details of my life. The PTB's media minions have somehow gotten hold of my state test scores and footage of me working as a food pantry volunteer. There's a still image of me, age nine or ten, kneeling in the garden beside Nonnie and a clip of Ms. Crawford, more recently, welcoming me into her office with a big smile and a sticker: "You made honor roll, Mari!" There's one of twelve-year-old me comforting my sobbing cousin Izzy, another of me up late studying, placing a meal in front of Faye.

They are my own memories, I realize in growing horror. The reporters have somehow accessed my consciousness—moments only I would recall—and fitted items to their narrative. There are no thoughts to provide context to any of it, though, just camera-like recordings of what I saw, said, and heard. All of it stripped of its original meaning. Somehow, these random clips are supposed to be proof of my virtue.

Seeing my own life displayed like this—outside my head, for others to interpret as they choose—feels like a profound violation. Even more infuriating: The stuff they've misunderstood or intentionally misconstrued. The food pantry was at the shelter where Faye and I once stayed and where everyone was expected to pitch in. And that GIF of me with my cousin Izzy? The reason she was crying was that I'd borrowed and ruined her favorite shirt.

They've left out my worst moments, and I guess I should be glad of that. But I can't help wondering if that was a decision or an oversight. It must be slow going sifting through almost seventeen years of memory. Is it just a matter of time before they strike on another version of my story?

They start pulling from Faye's memory bank around midnight. We see a montage of heated workplace arguments, terrible boyfriends, and unpaid bills. That time she was arrested for chaining herself to the State House gate. Again, no context. There's a clip of a jail cell, a judge slamming a gavel. In another, she stumbles as a dark-haired child guides her to bed.

"Clearly an alcoholic," one commenter says. "A woman in need of serious help," says another. It's the kindest comment on the thread.

Fact-check: Faye wasn't a drinker. She had a wonky hip.

But the commenters don't care about the facts. Nor do the reporters, or whoever is digging up this garbage. They're like a bunch of crows let loose on a pile of trash. They dip into one tangled memory here, another over there, plucking out stray bits and pieces and weaving them into a complicated nest.

I'm glad that Faye's asleep. I can only imagine how she'd react to all of this. I should turn off the news and go to bed too. But beneath my exhaustion runs a jittery undercurrent. What if I miss something important? I need to see all of it, need to know when they've hit on other parts of our past, more complicated ones that offer a less flattering truth.

I try not to let my mind root in that direction. I wish I could forget all of it—everything that happened in those final months. Too bad the mind doesn't work like that. The more I try to push them back, the more the memories rebound upward, like an irrepressible jack-in-the-box, demanding escape.

BEFORE

APRIL (6 MONTHS EARLIER)

SPRING. GREEN SHOOTS fanned into flowers, and Faye's smiles grew brighter, her wardrobe sleeker and outings more frequent. I waited for it, and then one evening, as the sun slid down behind a rim of still-bare trees, she let his name drop: Chip. He was back. Her criminal ex-boyfriend was free again, pending trial, and sorry for all the trouble he'd caused.

All the trouble. Did she tell him she got locked up for two nights, lost her job and our apartment, that we were *homeless*?

"He's a good person," she replied flimsily. "He just made a bad mistake."

She went on to suggest that it was his *boss* who was the actual bad guy. Chip hadn't come up with the scheme. He'd thought those investments he'd been selling to random vacationers were legit. A shady cover story that made me wonder, not for the first time, where and how Faye had acquired such terrible judgment.

"He bought a three-story colonial in New Hampshire!" she

announced a week later, as the trees burst out into canopies of pink and white.

"That's nice," I muttered. "Good for Chip."

I kept my focus on my task: ironing Faye's three work blouses and two skirts. She was required to look professional for her new office job, which she hated—said the skirts fit all wrong and her manager wouldn't stop ogling her rear.

"Baby, did you hear me? Don't you get it? The house is for all of us!"

I set down the iron slowly, dared to look up at her glowing face.

"It's got four bedrooms. On a cul-de-sac. A garage. A *pool*!"

Cul-de-sac? Pool? I heard the words but couldn't find their meaning. I looked around at our one-room studio, at my mother who hated all things bland and suburban, who had never learned how to drive. *Four bedrooms with a garage, in New Hampshire.* What was she even saying?

"You know you can't leave the state."

She let out a breathy laugh and swatted a hand, like criminal probation was a funny inconvenience, not something anyone would actually enforce.

Chip. *Goddamn.* I'd been bracing myself for turbulence, but I had not prepared for this blast from our far-too-recent past.

A little over a year before, Chip had appeared in Faye's life following the usual pattern—out of the blue, during one of her upswings—but right away, I could tell something was different. For starters, *he* was different. All starched shirts and well-oiled leather. Not Faye's type. At all. She'd always been into quirky artists, activists, *people who dare to live outside the lines*, she called them. (*Self-centered fruitloops,* according to Nonnie, with whom I mostly agreed.) Chip, though, he walked into her life like a graying Ken doll, office edition. I didn't get it, but I didn't hate it either. He seemed . . . stable.

Chip wore khakis, liked whiskey, and carried a well-stuffed money clip that he pulled on frequently to help with groceries and other bills. I definitely appreciated that. He told us, rather vaguely, that he worked in "finance." He kept odd hours, though, spent a lot of time reading newspapers, and rarely seemed to go to an office. He made Faye happy. She couldn't stop talking about the fun they had together. She cooed over the things he bought her—brand-name heels, posh dresses, and tiny little purses—the sort of items she'd never shown interest in before but now apparently adored. They went to jazz clubs and high-end restaurants, took several weekend trips up the coast.

Later, we'd learned that this was Chip's thing. He'd enlist women like my mother—pretty, innocent-seeming—and use them to lure in wealthy couples at a swanky bar or hotel. Preferably folks from out of town. While Faye put his marks at ease, giving him the appearance of a regular guy enjoying a nice night out with his gal, he'd pitch them on "amazing investment opportunities" that would triple their principal in a year or less. Some scams were shadier than others. The last one, a classic Ponzi setup, had bankrupted two dozen people and netted Chip a cool six million dollars.

Faye, following the arrest, had been given all this informa-tion. She knew who Chip was. And yet, here we were, a scant four months later. Had nothing sunk in?

"He says he loves me, baby, more than he's loved anyone in his whole life!" she exclaimed, her cheeks pinking prettily.

And that's when I understood: She wasn't kidding. Faye, the

romantic, had fallen right back into Chip's oily trap. And that left me where, exactly?

My thoughts shifted to Ms. Crawford saying, *You have options, Mari. You get to shape your own life.* All those months we'd worked—boosting my GPA, filling in the gaps, putting college into view—and here was Faye, ready to pull out the rug, drag me away from the place where I was thriving and up to . . . New Hampshire?

Unless . . .

I picked up the iron. "Nope. I'm not going. If you want to go, do it without me."

Her baby blues shot wide with shock. "What are you saying? Mari? I thought we were a team!"

"Hmph." I pressed the iron into a pleat. A team needs more than one player. I was so tired of this game.

Back in December, following Faye's arrest, our state-assigned caseworker had mentioned *emancipation* for the first time. I'd caught the word on my tongue, tried to imagine a life without Faye, every detail under my own control. In the next breath, the caseworker warned me not to get my hopes up. "Judges only consider it in extreme circumstances."

And now, here we were: Wasn't this extreme? If Faye's PO got wind of her plans . . . learned that she was back in touch with Chip . . . wouldn't that be considered an extreme circumstance?

Interesting fact: In Massachusetts, emancipated minors attend state college for free.

I held on to the thought for a moment, spun it around in my head before tossing it aside, unplugging the iron, and fitting the skirt onto the nearest hanger.

I couldn't get Faye into that kind of trouble, go behind her back and rat like that. Of course I wouldn't. She was my *mom*, for goodness' sake. She might be a mess sometimes, but she was *my* mess, my responsibility. Or so I still believed. No matter how bad things had gotten, I'd always chosen *us* over *me*. I just wished she'd make the same choice occasionally.

"Can't you and Chip wait?" I asked her, keeping my tone as calm as I possibly could. "I have a year left of high school. I can't switch schools right now."

Her whole face fell then, like I'd broken our pact. Me.

"But . . . baby. We can have the type of life you always wanted. Our very own *house*. Did I mention this place has quartz countertops? You should see the pictures. You'd absolutely think they were marble! Honey, I don't understand why you're making that face. You'd honestly rather stay *here*?" She looked around our tiny apartment, incredulous.

I followed her gaze to her unmade bed, the sag-backed sofa, the ceiling grown wavy with mold. The tiny slapdash kitchen area with its pathetically small (ugh, laminate!) countertop.

"Yes," I said. It might be ugly, but we'd come by it fairly. At this stage in our journey, it was home.

"But . . . you deserve so much more! I want to do better, Mari, for both of us! I know I've let you down before. I'm so bad with bills and things, and maybe I haven't always been the best mom, but—"

Something in my expression stopped her. Her throat worked as she gave me a moment to rearrange my face, to tell her, *No no no, you're a great mom, really.* I stayed quiet.

Her posture stiffened and her head lifted. "Well, if that's how you're going to be."

She turned to her purse, put on an extra slick of makeup—too harsh for her pale features—pulled on one of the frilly new blouses in our closet. The next second, she was out the door, tripping on kitten heels, headed to meet Chip. No jacket, though it was still early April, and it had just begun to rain.

She'd revealed her position and left the ball in my court. Who would I choose this time: Team Us or Team Me?

AFTER

DAY 11

FAYE'S ON THE couch, glued to the TV when I emerge the next morning. It's Wednesday, my third day of classes and eleventh as a dead person. Today's news is still all about me: "Novak was clearly an exceptional human," the reporter is saying, "developing into an ambitious and capable young woman despite so much adversity. By which we mean her mother."

Faye blinks hard at the screen.

"Turn it off," I say. "You shouldn't watch that."

But she leans in closer, hands clasped in a knot, as they share examples of her poor behavior—a moment in high school when she'd cussed out her principal, another as an adult when she cussed out a cop. A heated argument with Nonnie that resulted in a pile of clothes in the front yard, a slammed door, and a suggestion to never come back. Faye whimpers on that one, and my hand reaches toward the TV reflexively, though I have no idea how to interpret what I'm seeing. I never in my life saw my grandmother so angry.

Did she really toss her own daughter out of the house? What had Faye done?

It's a low blow, digging up moments like these, sharing them so publicly. Unfair to paint anyone—even Faye—with such a cruel brush.

"Don't listen to them," I tell her. "Everyone argues with their parents. And that cop was being a jerk, I remember. You were just speaking up for yourself. Yelling isn't a crime. Come on." I try to take the remote from her. "Let's turn it off." But her fingers clutch the thing, viselike.

"One second, honey. I just—"

The mug shots appear then—Faye and con man Chip. Real injuries. Certifiable crime. Two dozen people lost their life savings thanks to his scam. There's no way to dress up those facts even if I wanted to.

I sink onto the arm of the couch. "Can we please turn it off?"

Faye, ignoring me, continues watching as they run through ten different instances of Chip presenting innocent vacationers with fake documents, Faye posed brightly at his side.

When they're done smearing her, they return to the primary focus: me. There are clips of me at work, clips of me up late studying, ironing Faye's things, a moment when I gave up my seat on the train.

"I don't understand why they care about any of this," I mutter. "The old man had a cane. He needed to sit. What does getting employee of the month have to do with the state of my soul?"

"Three times, Mari. You earned employee of the month three times!" Faye's chest puffs, like the accomplishment reflects on both of us somehow. She looks at me. "Good people make the best souls, sweetie. That's what Lady Lu always says. You should be proud of who you were, proud of where you're headed. Positive examples help all of us."

"But . . ." How do I explain how wrong this feels? "Have they even looked at my tracker? Is this what a *positive example* is supposed to look like?" I point to the angry crimson light on my wrist.

Faye sighs. "The transition is rough for everyone, babe. They can't shame you for that. You'll start greening soon, I know it."

She said something similar when, as a flat-breasted thirteen-year-old, I asked when I'd finally sprout a chest. *Soon, baby. Give it another year or two, and you'll have a rack just like your mother.* I never did outgrow an A cup.

Faye slides closer to my end of the couch. "Look, sweetie, I know it's a lot, but you have to look at the big picture here. Think of your eternity, the boost you could get. A bigger following could earn you bonus points, and you can spend *that* on anything your soul craves. You could try some supplementals, maybe some energy work. Things that will calm your spirit. Once you start feeling better inside, your tracker will show it."

"You want me to turn our tragedy into *points*?"

"No, that's not what I'm saying. Just . . ." Her mouth twists, and she glances sideways at the TV before turning to me. "You were a good kid, Mari. Why not accept some credit for all your hard work?"

Faye's eyes are too blue, too open. I can't turn away, but I also can't look. How does she do this? Find a bright line of optimism in even the worst circumstances. Has she forgotten what they just said about her? Did she forget how things ended between her and me? It's like she really believes if she ignores the ugly, it won't exist.

I turn my gaze to my perfect, factory-model fingers.

"I wasn't always good, you know. And . . . I don't know what happened on that bus, but whatever it was, I can assure you, it's not what they think. I'm not that brave. I wasn't trying to be a hero."

"Oh, honey." She reaches for my knee. "Real heroes don't try. They just do."

I can see her considering whether to hug me, and part of me wishes she would. Part of me will always be a little kid who wants nothing more than that.

"There's no harm either in going along with things for now," she says, with a gentle knee pat. "Let them think what they want to think."

"You mean lie."

"No, I mean, just . . . let their imaginations wander, see where it goes. This could bump you onto the fast track if you let it." Her fingers drop from my knee to the edge of the couch, where she begins to pluck at the fabric. "You never know. It may help me too. Once they look at the whole picture, see all we went through together, the smart, resilient woman you became—they have to give me some credit for that, right?"

I check to see if she's kidding, but her eyes are unblinking.

"It's okay to want something better, honey. Everyone does."

"Yeah, well." I know all about wanting something better, about striving for it, over and over, and then—bam, suddenly it's ripped out from under you, again. "Weren't you supposed to get everything you hoped for in New Hampshire?" I say bitterly.

Faye blanches like I've hit her. I feel sorry, and not. It's too late to take the words back; the damage is done. So much damage—

years of it. The things we said, did, and did not say. I wouldn't know where to begin fixing things.

"Touché, baby," Faye says softly. "You really got me there."

AN HOUR LATER, I face off with a gaggle of paparazzi on the Center's front steps. A smaller clutch pounced on me outside the bungalow. "Can't talk now!" I told them brightly. "Gotta go get that karma!" Words which, apparently, delighted them. They began typing distractedly into their tablets, loosening their grip on the doorway and allowing me to pass.

But this second set—larger, more aggressive—is tougher to please. They chase me up the front steps, snapping and squawking like a flock of angry geese.

"Miss Novak! Miss Novak!"

"Tell us more about your painful childhood!"

"And your mother!"

"How many good deeds have you been keeping to yourself?"

"How many tragic obstacles did you overcome?"

"Don't be modest, Miss Novak! Tell us *everything*!"

I imagine the look on their faces if I did tell them all of it. But no—a quick duck and roll and I make it up the steps, within reach of the revolving door.

"Miss Novak, please! Your fans are—excuse the expression— simply dying to hear from y—"

Inside the Center's front lobby, there's quiet. The burble of a fountain, crispness of manufactured air. I exhale slowly and try to visualize a cloud.

Then: "Mari!!! Oh, Mariiiiiiii!!!" A deafening squeal sets me back on my heels.

May the Powers help me. The virgins are back.

I do a quick assessment of options. Before me: a rainbow of headbands and lycra. At my back: a knot of trench-coated reporters pressed against the glass. (No media allowed inside the Center. Even the PTB draw a line somewhere, and I guess I should be grateful for that.) *Go along with it,* Faye counseled me earlier. *Think of your eternity.* Shoddy advice, but what else can I do?

I take a deep breath, raise my chin, and let myself be carried away on a tide of sage-scented chatter. Catherines of Milwaukee and Pittsburgh each take an elbow, asking what I think about Soul-Strength versus SoulStretch, hot flow versus slow. "Is core strength a core virtue?" Pittsburgh wants to know.

For the record, I know nothing about hot-soul anything. Until very recently, the only thing I was concerned about heating was my poorly insulated apartment.

Luckily the Catherines don't really care what I have to say. They prattle on about hip openers and chakras while I make fake listening sounds.

"Yup. Mm-hmm. Arm binds are . . . awesome."

I'm trying to figure out how I'll make it through a whole day of this when the second bell chimes, offering a momentary reprieve. The first set of Catherines drops me at a split in the corridors, and I fake out the next group by briefly ducking inside an empty eternal rest room. I wait for my opening and then make a dash to class, arriving moments before the bell and snagging a seat beside Larisa. The remaining Catherines express their disappointment by bombing my feed with broken-heart emojis.

Larisa simply shakes her head.

Our first class of the day is a graphing exercise. We're learning how to glean lessons from the data our trackers collect. The instructor chooses a sample student, one of the quieter, less memorable Catherines (Phoenix, I think). She shifts awkwardly in her miracle-grip leggings as the instructor notes a dip in her vibes last Tuesday (Day 37 + 1300 hours) and an orangey uptick that seems to appear regularly around 3:00 a.m. She's been here five weeks, and the pattern hasn't changed. Recently, she's begun shedding points faster than she earns them.

"Insomnia is very common for new souls," the instructor says generously.

The other virgins shoot their friend skeptical looks. The ones sitting closest slide their chairs apart, giving the struggling Catherine a wider berth.

"Your task is to harness your energies to overcome this angst," the instructor continues. "You might try an herbal remedy or silent contemplation."

"A pre-bedtime massage always helps me!" Catherine of Bozeman offers kindly.

But the Catherine in question doesn't look assuaged.

I don't blame her. This is almost as bad, or perhaps even worse, than having your context-stripped memories aired on TV. I thought our data were our business. Luckily, Catherine of Phoenix is the only one up for public examination today. After a few more words, the instructor releases us to work independently.

My own data are mixed. I earned a solid number of points on Monday and Tuesday, more than enough to cover my daily expenses and a few minor deductions. If I keep going at this rate,

I'll be out of debt in ten more days, as I'd hoped. My vibes, though, remain an absolute mess. Seeing them displayed like this, a long red line that rises and falls and sometimes veers toward orange but never breaches yellow (forget about green)—it's even worse than I'd realized. The instructor asked us to look for patterns, and mine is obvious: Anytime I enter the bungalow, there's a steep scarlet slide. Hardly surprising, and yet.

I must let out a sigh of frustration. Larisa looks over, making a tiny *yikes* expression when she sees my screen. "You could try a self-massage," she offers.

"Ha. Gross. No thanks."

I click to a new screen and continue searching for patterns.

BY THE END of third period, my vibes have hit rock bottom. Again. (Faye isn't the only thing stressing me out, it seems.) It's been a long morning and I'm all out of deep breaths and power poses. If one more person tells me to stand in my light, I might punch out theirs.

Clearly, I'm a lost cause like that poor Catherine. Either that or I'm surrounded by nutjobs. Maybe it's a bit of both.

It's amazing to me that Larisa can tolerate any of it. Not just tolerate. She's *thriving*. At the end of first period, our instructor used her data as a best-case example—a soul on track for early ascension if she keeps it up. ("She could totally be a soul model," I heard someone whisper, "if she tried being friendly.") During lunch, while Larisa scarfs down a trayful of vegan horrors, her jagged bob moving in time with her chewing, I study her carefully, wondering how she's doing so well here. Honestly, *how*?

We have a silent contemplation scheduled after lunch, which I'm looking forward to—sounds off and zero conversation for twenty whole minutes. I settle onto the pillow beside Larisa's as a piped-in instructor guides us to close our eyes, turn our focus to the breath.

I drop my lids and push the pestering Catherines from my thoughts. I push out Faye, too, and all my questions and fears, hunting for the free space the instructor is urging us toward, a pocket of true quiet. After a second of total silence, I hear a jangle in my inner ear, see a trembling cup behind my lids. A voice whispers, pleading, and energy surges into my chest. I feel myself running, hear my heart thudding, my blood straining. Someone screams: "NOT TODAY!"

My eyes slam open.

Holy hell. What was *that*?

I suck in a long gulp of air and remain still for a moment, shaking, unsure what just happened. Was that me? Did I shout those words here, in this room? No. Around me, students sit calmly, eyes closed. Only Larisa, to my right, caught the gasp. One eye open, she gives me a *WTF?* eyebrow.

I don't know, I shrug back. I honestly don't know what that was. A tabloid-inspired nightmare? A splinter of memory?

Larisa's lid drops shut, and I watch her ribs expand and deflate.

The instructor, eyeing me, reminds us to keep our attention on the breath. So I close my eyes again, try to follow the directions, find the breath, all the while wondering what I just saw and heard. Is my amnesia lifting? I try to make sense of it: the cup, the words, the rush of feeling. But my thoughts spin face-first into a wall of blankness.

A chime sounds, and our trackers return to active mode. Mine pings with dozens of notifications: three hundred new followers since lunch. A pair of Catherines appears at my elbows, offering to put away my pillow, crowing about the bliss they just achieved. *Did my mind go empty? Wasn't it heavenly? Wasn't it—*

I can't. Can't do this anymore. I snatch back my arms and bolt toward the door, not even bothering to say goodbye to Larisa.

I head in the opposite direction from our next class, take a left followed by an immediate right and a— I lose track of the turns as the next bell chimes and a distant chatter fills the halls. I find an elevator and climb inside, jamming my thumb into the down button, aiming for the lobby level, for a quick escape. But when the doors open, I'm in a part of the building I don't recognize. The corridor is narrower, less brightly lit. It looks like the back passage where Larisa pulled me the other morning, but not exactly. I'm pretty sure I'm far from the Center's main library. A pair of voices approaches from the next bend, and I look for a spot to hide. Where can a dead girl find a little peace?

At the far end of the hall, there's a metal door marked NO EXIT.

I check over my shoulder, listening, then make a dash for it. When no alarm sounds, I push the door harder and it swings open, releasing me into . . . a great white blur. I can't tell if I'm inside or out. Alive or dead. I don't care. Everything is quiet here. Finally. I feel my body relax as I inhale slowly.

The next second, I double over in disgust. Gah! A foul taste fills my nostrils, coats my tongue. A taste like a bus station. Like dirty old men trading dirtier jokes. A taste like . . . cigarette smoke?

I cough harder.

"You need some medical attention over there?"

The question is followed by a soft chuckle.

I spin around, expecting—I don't know what, but the reply flies out of my head at the sight of sloping flannel limbs, a wash of dark hair. It's Deadbeat Guy, the one who Larisa pointed out the first day and who, I've since noticed, has a habit of sleeping through class. When he goes to class, that is. He's currently leaning against a sort of wall, a thin wisp of smoke curling from his wide, bow-shaped mouth. This space we're in is inexplicable. It's like an alley that someone began—chunk of wall on one side, narrow rim of asphalt—but forgot to complete. Beyond the asphalt, everything grows pixelated, blurry, white.

"Where are we?" I ask, adding another cough for emphasis. (Because really? Smoking in an alley? Could this guy be more clichéd?)

He shrugs. "Gap in the grid."

"Um." Another cough. "A what now?"

"They never finished coding past that doorway. Someone either forgot where it was supposed to go or got lazy. Anyway, it's the only quiet spot in this whole godforsaken place."

"Oh," I say. It *is* quiet. I'll give him that. (*God*forsaken. That's funny.) I take another step out from the door.

"Watch it." He points to my foot. "You gotta be careful not to get too close to the fuzz."

"Oh." I hop back, away from the pixelated edge. "Why is that again?"

"Could take off your foot or, worse, suck you right off the grid."

"Huh. That's . . . ." *Alarming.* I make a move back toward the door. This isn't the escape I was hoping for. "I think I'll, um . . . let you be."

"Nah. Don't go. I didn't mean to scare you. You're fine if you stick close to the building. Here." The deadbeat lifts off the wall carefully, unfolding to a surprising height. He extends an odd little stick at me. After a moment, I understand that this is the source of the smoke: a cigarette. Or some kind of crude replica. It looks like it was designed by someone with a very poor handle on afterlife technology.

"I know a guy," he says, as if that will explain it.

"Oh, yeah. No. That's . . ." I shake my head. "Cancer. No thanks."

The deadbeat laughs at that, or at least I think it's a laugh. It's a dry, scraping sound, like leaves crackling underfoot. My face fires with embarrassment.

"Cancer. That's a good one." He shakes back his hair, revealing a pair of soft brown eyes. "Too bad only karma can get us now. I hear she's a real bitch."

He meets my gaze, teasing, and I realize his eyes aren't so much brown as charcoal, like pebbles at the bottom of a mossy stream.

I feel a ripple and turn my attention to my foot. "I should really—"

"Stop saying that. Come on. *Here.*" Long arm stretching. Narrow fingers extending. The "cigarette" is sort of off-white with a plasticky sheen. "I promise it works better than *You*ga." He adds extra sarcasm to the *You*.

I'm tempted, inexplicably.

"But I don't—" My thought breaks. I don't what? Smoke? Cut class? Hang out with literal deadbeats in simulated alleys? The dos and don'ts of my old life seem very far away right now, and my chances of surviving this next life currently feel slim. "Aren't cigarettes illegal?" I say, trying to recall if they appeared in the guidebook.

"It's, ah, kind of a gray area. The AI can't detect things that aren't supposed to exist. Also"—the deadbeat's eyebrows tease upward—"we're in a blind spot."

I crane my neck in the direction he's indicated. No cameras wink from the building, no windows either. It's just a tall gray wall and then . . . nothing but white. I shiver.

"If they ask where you've been, tell them you needed a meditation break. We all do sometimes."

The cigarette's ashy tip is growing, threatening to drop. What the hell? It isn't on the no-no list, right? (Skipping class is another story, but that deed has already been done.) I reach out before the ash breaks. Flick of the wrist, and the tip crumbles, then immediately disappears.

Deadbeat Guy watches as I pull the terrible flavor into my mouth. It's a taste that matches how I've felt since I arrived. Foul and slightly desperate. My body exhales the smoke easily, like it's done it a thousand times.

I drop against the wall and stay there for several more drags, absorbing the silence.

"Not much of a talker, eh?" he says.

I check to see if he's making another joke, but his murky eyes are serious.

"Um, hello, kettle?"

At the squinch of his brow, I clarify: "We're in all the same classes, and this is the first time I've heard you speak."

I flush, realizing what that sounds like—like I've been watching him. Which, I haven't. Not really. Not more than I've been watching everyone and everything.

"That's fair." He takes the weird little cigarette from my hand

and brings it to his mouth, breathing a perfect ring up into the hazy white. He's not exactly handsome—not by conventional standards—but his eyes are intriguing and he has an excellent jawline. I'm glad for the several inches of wall between us.

While he studies the non-sky above, I examine the black seam of his jeans, the neat way it falls against an even blacker boot. I compare that to my own standard-issue sandals. I really need to go shopping.

"Want another drag?"

"Nah." I shake my head. I should go. This was a bad idea. Did I really think I could escape?

"You sure? No offense, but you seem a little stressed."

I feel my shoulders hitch. "I think I have a pretty good reason."

"Oh, yeah?" He exhales another ring. "And what's that?"

"Um . . ." Is he kidding? "Haven't you seen the news or heard the Catherines?"

"Those your friends with the headbands?"

"Not my friends," I say with a firm shake.

"That's good, 'cause I tuned them out a long time ago." He adjusts an invisible knob near his tracker, winks.

The wink sends a fresh ripple through me. A warning signal. I should go. One more minute and I will. But first . . . I place a hand on the wall. "You honestly don't know what they're saying about me?"

"Is it something sinful?" His brow lifts hopefully.

"No. What? I—" I shake my head, feel myself blushing again. Is this dead guy *flirting* with me? "I didn't do anything *bad*." Not the way he means.

"Well, that's too bad," he says, eyes sparking with amusement.

I turn to go.

"Wait. Don't go. Sorry. I'll stop being such a tool. Promise."

I face the door and pause—he *does* kind of seem like a tool, excellent jawline notwithstanding—but I also don't feel like going back inside, dealing with what awaits me there, not yet. I turn around again and accept his offer of the dwindling cigarette.

"Being dead really sucks," I mutter, and he watches as I take a slow drag.

"Yuuuup."

We don't say anything more, just lean side by side and pass the foul stick until it's barely more than a stub. I begin to relax and notice, with surprise, a slight improvement in my vibes. But then I catch the faint trill of a bell inside, and it sets off a flutter, another stab of crimson. I'll be in real trouble if I don't return to class soon.

I lift off the wall and stare out into the void. My panic from earlier has ebbed, but something still itches beneath: a wisp of memory, a half-remembered shout. Are they right about me? Am I a hero, or is there a side to the story that's better left alone?

I turn away from the alley's blurred edge, reach to hand him the cigarette. "I'm Mari, by the way."

"I know." Deadbeat Guy reaches for the stub, momentarily snagging my fingers. "I'm Jethro." A smile slides up his face, slicing it—and then me—in two.

He releases my fingers, and I step back. (Dang. What was *that*?) Suddenly, I'm in a hurry to get to class.

THE DAILY WITNESS

———

It's been just over thirty hours since Marianna Novak was declared the afterworld's newest soul model. How is our esteemed friend handling all the acclaim and adulation?

Not well, according to our sources.

While Marianna Novak has avoided direct contact with the press, we reached out to several classmates at the Center for Post-mortuary Progress, who requested anonymity to speak candidly about their newly anointed peer.

"I know she's like a hero or whatever, but she's kinda bad at meditation," one classmate alleged.

"Totally!" said another. "At one point, she was barely even *breathing*."

"We've tried to be welcoming, but she's super standoffish," said the first classmate.

"And she has no personal mantra!" added a third. "What's up with that?"

"What's up with her vibes?"

"And her clothes?"

"Hasn't she found time to go shopping?"

The conversation went off course at this point as the students hotly debated the merits of the realm's two leading Yougawear lines. (YouGoGear™ is a sponsor of *The Daily Witness*, so you know our opinion.) Eventually, the teens returned to our original topic:

"We really hope the best for Mari and whatnot. But soul models are supposed to be aspirational. If she wants to become the next Rupi P, we need more from her. We just do."

So what do you think, readers? Is Marianna Novak a soul model or no model at all?

AFTER

DAY 12

I CLICK THROUGH the latest items in my feed and groan. "Paradise Media Group is calling me the Worst Dressed of the Blessed. How is that a thing?"

"Told you not to read that crap," Larisa says, not bothering to look up from her screen.

But I can't stop. The images are . . . *harrowing*. I mean, I knew I wasn't making any leaps forward for afterlife fashion, but they've caught me in some truly unfortunate poses. Readers are going wild in the comments. Nothing overtly mean, of course. Instead, they dodge the AI's flags with comments that appear innocuous or silly on the surface. Peach emojis paired with cross-eyes; fancy-dress emojis magnified by monocles. Random smiling clowns. The derision is there between the lines, though. And the Catherines appear to be leading the tide change. (Yes, I saw right through that "anonymous" interview.) I'm not surprised that they turned out to be so fickle, but what does surprise me is how many others feel a need to join in.

I gasp at an especially awful shot that someone must have snapped in yesterday's Youga practice. "I was just following directions! Who looks good in happy clam position?"

Larisa rolls her eyes and continues typing.

We've found a quiet carrel at the back of the library, away from the hallway hubbub. "Self-study periods are for *working*," Larisa insisted when I suggested we go outside for a change. "Since when do you need air? News flash: You're dead."

I sighed but followed her to the library. The truth is I enjoy having someone else take charge for a change. No one has done that for me since Nonnie. Larisa reminds me of my grandma sometimes: bossy, direct, occasionally even harsh, but you know she has your best interests at heart. Like me, Larisa was raised by a single parent and had to figure out a lot on her own. I'm grateful to her for taking me under her wing. And yet as soon as we're seated in our carrels, faced with the prospect of more homework, my eyes drift toward the nearest exit, while my tongue searches my teeth for remnants of ash.

I haven't told Larisa about yesterday's rendezvous with Jethro, obviously. She'd really go all holier than thou if she knew about that. It was just one cigarette, I remind myself, one heart-slicing smile. It meant nothing, will never happen again. (I stayed up last night working on extra-credit assignments to make up for the missed points.) And yet, even now, the memory of our conversation—his long fingers gripping the cigarette, smoke curling—stirs up a thick swirl of feelings I can't quite explain.

My tracker buzzes. Another photo. Me ass-skyward, in another Youga pose. I can actually *feel* my vibes plummeting this time. "I don't get it. Why do they suddenly hate me?"

"You're famous," Larisa says. "This is how fame works. And why you need to *stop* looking."

Solid advice. And still . . . I flick through, like a masochistic rat.

"Seriously, kid. Turn it off." Larisa gives me an exasperated look.

I match it. "Could you please stop calling me *kid*? We're the same age."

"I've been dead a lot longer."

"A month longer. Hardly counts. Do you think my clothes are as bad as they're saying?"

Larisa scrapes back her chair with a sigh. "Are we really doing this? Fine, cool. Here goes." She gives me a thorough scan from head to toe, pausing on my half-hearted bun, unbuttoned tunic, hand-me-down tee, standard-issue flats. "You're perfect, Mari. Just as you are. A model for depressed self-help zealots everywhere."

"Hey. Ouch."

She shrugs. "You asked, I answered. Can we be done? Second period just posted a new assignment. These points ain't gonna earn themselves, you know."

I scowl at her briefly before flicking my tracker to vibrate and logging in to the student portal.

Task #1: Count your blessings. Literally. Make a tally of all the privileges, successes, advantages, and strokes of good luck you experienced in your life and afterlife.

Larisa ignores my groan. Whatever. She may be acting righteous, but I know she's not doing homework right now. Or that's not all she's doing. She's become obsessed with something called After-world Online, which as far as I can tell is a terrible version of the darknet. Like, if you took away everything useful and kept the conspiracy mongering and memes. She's found a chat room full of folks who think everything you need to know about the afterlife is secretly encoded in *Star Wars*, which—yeah, I don't get that either. Who wants to spend the afterlife dissecting old movies?

I finish making a (very short) list of blessings and then, needing a break, click over to the daily news page on my browser. Better than the feed, right? Barely. I'm featured in the top three headlines, with @RealRupiP's newest video, a semi-raunchy SoulDance spoof, right behind.

Farther down the page, I find something that makes me pause. They've released a list of this week's ascendants. I scan the list with interest.

Yesterday, we ended the day with an all-Center assembly. Students from every wing of the building gathered in the rooftop atrium to witness the latest cohort's ascension. There were celebratory speeches, a performance of flutes and stringed instruments, and *many* motivational one-liners. At the conclusion of Chairman Ted's on-screen convocation, the curtains parted to reveal seven multistory transparent tubes. Like glass elevators with no clear destination. We rose to welcome the ascendants, then watched as, in groups of seven, they filed into the elevators. Press of a button, and they shot upward to deafening applause.

Well, most of them shot upward. In the third group, one unlucky soul remained stranded at the base of his elevator until a guard escorted him offstage. The audience continued clapping, albeit more quietly.

I turned to Larisa, who shrugged. "Not everyone makes the cut. That's why we do our homework."

"Damn," I whispered. Booted just like that. In front of everyone. "What about the others? That's it?" I waved my hand upward. "Now we're supposed to think they're in the Ever After?"

"What do you mean? Where else would they go?" Larisa gave me a look like I'd lost it. "This is literally what the entire realm is built to achieve. You think they'd *lie* about that?"

"No." I shook my head. "It's just . . ." But I didn't know what was bothering me, exactly.

I stood quietly for the rest of the ceremony, clapping each time we were cued and watching as two more failed souls were escorted from the stage. We were meant to feel happy for the ascendants, to glimpse our own future in their success. And I'm not some conspiracy theorist. It's a future I want—*need*—to believe in too, but as we listened to a closing chant, something still didn't sit right. I figured it was my own self-doubt nagging. Now, in the library, I realize it's something else.

"Only two hundred thirty-seven souls ascended yesterday," I inform Larisa.

"So?"

"So there were more than a thousand new registrants this past week. Look." I point to my screen, where I've opened a second link to an article I saw yesterday. "If a thousand came in, how come only two hundred thirty-seven have left?"

"Well, this new cohort's really big. It says so, right there."

"Five times as big?"

Larisa chews her lip. "We know that not everyone makes it. Some drop off long before the ceremony."

"Okay. But how many?" During our intake orientation, Chairman Ted boasted about Paradise Gate's stellar ascension rates, but these numbers hardly seem worth crowing about. "And where do they drop off to? Could they really be axing hundreds of souls a week from the grid?"

Just yesterday, three martyrs were removed from the cafeteria after blockading the buffet in an effort to spread their hunger strike. (A questionable strategy in more ways than one.) I figured they'd been given a brief detention or talking-to for being disruptive. But what if their time-out was permanent? What if one misstep is enough to get you sent off into the abyss?

"What do you think it's really like out there? Off the grid, I mean."

The library is quiet. I feel Larisa looking at me, and I can't read the expression on her face. Is it pity? Or does she worry about it too?

"You better listen closely, kid, 'cause I'm only telling you this once."

"Uh-huh. Got it. Not a kid."

"They say it's the loneliest struggle you can imagine. Like a giant mental torture chamber, or a feed built for one, only you're your own worst troll. Just you stewing in your worst fears and doubts and regrets for all eternity. They say it's like three a.m. . . . forever."

"Dang. That's . . ." I meet her gaze.

"Exactly." Her dark eyes are serious. "Are you sufficiently frightened? Are you going to stick to the program and earn your spot in one of those snazzy elevators?"

"Yes. I mean, I'll try my best. Obviously."

"Good," Larisa says. "Let's not talk about this again, m'kay?

We don't have to worry about what's out there if we keep our focus here. Your number one job is *what*?" She raises a mock-teacher finger.

"Homework." I sigh.

"Do the work and the rest will follow." Larisa imitates the catchphrase our instructors love to repeat. And although her tone is at least partly ironic, I don't roll my eyes this time.

We both turn to our computers, close out the extra tabs, and get to work.

REENIE CATCHES ME at dismissal. She runs her little scanning wand over my wrist before tapping me gently.

"Mari, could you stay back a moment? I'd like to speak to you about something."

I, of course, immediately prepare for the worst. Reenie has seen the state of my vibes. Her role as adviser includes this daily diagnostic. Maybe she also knows about the class I ditched yesterday, that my "meditation break" excuse was utter crap. Will she report me? Should I prepare to be escorted into the eternal 3:00 a.m. directly from this class? Will anyone notify Faye, or will she sit at the bungalow, waiting?

Once my other classmates have gone, Reenie ushers me into a chair beside hers, and I wait for her to say it: *It's over, Mari. Stop pretending. You're no soul model. You're clearly beyond hope.*

Instead, she scooches forward so our knees are touching. "How are you holding up, Mari? These past two days have been a lot for you, haven't they?"

Caught off guard, I drop my gaze. "Yeah. It's . . . yeah, I guess. But I'm fine. I can handle it."

"Can you?"

I look up. What does she expect me to say? That panic floods me whenever I close my eyes? That every time I see my name on a screen, I feel like an animal caught in a scope, waiting for the shot that will destroy me?

"I don't know what I'm supposed to do," I admit. "My mom says I should just go along with it, accept the praise and hope for the best, but . . ."

Reenie nods. "You're being tested, that's for sure. Finding equanimity is tough for any soul, and you've been granted this extra hurdle."

"Didn't Chairman Ted say tests are a chance to show our strength? Should I be hashtag grateful?"

Reenie smiles. "There are no *shoulds* or *supposed tos*, Mari. You can feel however you feel."

"I'm pretty sure I'm not supposed to feel like this." I pull back my sleeve to remind her of my inner state.

Reenie doesn't flinch. "The only way past this pain is through it, I'm afraid."

"I know, I know. *Trust the process.*"

"The process isn't always easy. I'm here for one-on-one sessions anytime you need, you know. I can help you work through whatever's holding you back."

"Like, therapy?" I feel a small waft of terror just imagining what would happen if I told Reenie everything on my mind.

"Many souls benefit from the extra support," she says calmly. "If you don't mind my saying, Mari, your assignments have been on the skimpy side. I sense you're afraid to dive in. Perhaps I can help you get unstuck."

"No thanks." I shake my head firmly.

I'm not one of those people who goes around airing their problems. And I'm not sure I want to "dive in." Given the anxiety I'm feeling just talking about it (if this body could sweat, my pits would be gushing), I can only imagine what sort of flood would be unleashed if I talked to Reenie. No. I don't want to be one of those downward-spiral losers, axed from the grid, but I need to do this my way. Slowly. Working in from the edges, at my own pace.

I promise Reenie I'll give more attention to my assignments but decline her offer of support. If she's disappointed, she doesn't show it. "Of course, Mari. Whatever you need. Please find me if you change your mind."

"I will," I say, though there's very little chance of that.

BACK AT THE bungalow, I push silently past the clutch of reporters on the stoop, holding my breath until the door is locked tight behind me. I discard my sandals in the small foyer and drop my tote by the couch. Faye doesn't appear at the sound, which is unusual, so I crank my head toward her open bedroom door. Odd. She's usually home before me.

I place a teapot on the stove and flip on the TV, volume up, for company. Someone who calls himself the Soul Master is hosting a talk show / dance party.

All afternoon, since my conversation with Larisa, my thoughts kept slip-sliding off course, imagining what it must be like out there in the eternal 3:00 a.m. I want to do the right thing, thrive like Larisa, get "unstuck" like Reenie urged, but it's hard with reporters literally seated outside my door, watching my every move.

I sink onto the couch with a warm mug, tell myself I'll just watch for a little bit, until my vibes settle or Faye returns. Whichever comes first. Then I'll finish my homework.

An hour slips by. *The Soul Master* becomes *The Mourning Show* and *The Mourning Show* becomes a pre-dinner soap. When *The Dead and the Restless* reaches its usual cliff-hanger (will they or won't they resolve this latest obstacle in time to be redeemed?), I look at the clock. Did Faye have a meeting she forgot to mention?

I get up from the couch, peer through the narrow window at the front door. The reporters have mostly dispersed. It's the prescribed meal hour, and even though reporters aren't held to the same standards as the rest of us (I'm unclear what their deal is, honestly—are they public servants, like our teachers, or something else?), they must need a break too.

I consider starting dinner without Faye, searching my memory for something she might have said in one of her long bouts of nattering. Was there some sort of special lecture tonight? An extra prep session for the final assessment that she'll take in a few weeks? There's surely a simple explanation. Still, worry scratches beneath my skin. I wish I hadn't been so harsh the other morning, making that dig about New Hampshire. *Your mother never had the grit to stick things out like the rest of us,* Nonnie once told me. *Always chose flight over fight.*

But now that we're dead, where could she possibly run? I tell myself not to invent scenarios, not to fall back into the old pattern. All my life, I was trapped by that swirl—mayhem and stress spinning out from my mother's decisions like a terrible sort of hurricane. Me, the damage left in her wake. I can't afford to be sucked back in again. I cannot. But as six o'clock turns to seven and Faye's plate cools, the anxious thoughts take hold. Irrational, unbidden. History snags on its reels, like an old tape that refuses to stop playing, and I'm a child waiting for her mummy to come home.

BEFORE

THE FIRST TIME she left wasn't my fault. Nonnie and Pop-Pop were clear on that. I was six years old. Faye was the center of my life, her songs and abundant kisses a source of constant delight. The adventures too! Roadside picnics, theme parks, overnights on the beach. Not everything was rainbows and popsicles, though. There were nights in cars, forgotten meals, a rotating posse of quirky and off-kilter "friends." I needed school, stability, things my mother, for some reason, couldn't provide. That's what Nonnie and Pop-Pop explained when I asked why my mummy had left me with them.

My grandmother had a lot of harsh things to say about her elder daughter. But to Nonnie's great credit, she never directed that bitterness at me: "You're perfect, Bunny. You did nothing wrong. Pop-Pop and I just want you to have a good life."

And I did.

Over the next five years, nourished by Pop-Pop's gourmet cooking and Nonnie's firm routines, I lost my nervous edge, growing into a quiet but cheerful child. I became a straight-A student, an excellent sous-chef, and a reliable helper in Nonnie's prizeworthy garden. We weren't a typical family, but we were a happy one.

Still, I missed my beautiful mother. Of course I did. Her hugs especially. My skin ached for hers, especially at night. I squashed down my sadness to avoid upsetting my grandparents, but I still dreamed of her songs, her spark, her scent.

Listening in on Nonnie's phone calls, I learned that my mother was living somewhere on the North Shore with a bunch of lowlife, tax-evading hippies. (Nonnie's words.) I didn't know what hippies were exactly, but I imagined them—lounging, dirty, wasteful—with equal parts envy and hate. They had taken my mummy from me, or she had chosen them. I wasn't clear which. One thing I knew for sure: When I grew up, I'd pay my taxes.

THE NEXT TIME my mother left I was twelve. We'd been reunited for a year, following Pop-Pop's second heart attack. The big one.

Nonnie and I had managed at first, but Pop-Pop's death changed her. She grew soft-spoken and wispy where she'd once been so clear and sturdy. She forgot about dinner, lost track of time, and occasionally, when angered by a careless driver or late-arriving mail, flew off the handle with a ferocity that took my breath.

Aunt Jenny decided it was time for Faye to take me back. She'd left the commune by then and had found a steady job, a real apartment. One day, she showed up on Nonnie's stoop in a flowing maxi dress, her fair hair cut to her shoulders, and told me it was time.

Anguish laced with ecstasy. Here was the reunion I'd dreamed of, but what about Nonnie? Who would make sure she ate and showered? Who would pull the weeds from her garden come spring? And make sure she remembered to occasionally laugh?

Faye (I called her that now; *Mummy* sounded too childish) promised we'd stay in Brookline. I'd go to the same school I'd been in since first grade, and we'd see Nonnie often. We'd both help in the garden. She said a lot of things that turned out not to be true.

We moved five times that year: first out west, near Springfield, then down by Rhode Island, then we circled back north, closer to the city. The rare times we saw Nonnie, she seemed faded, her eyes gone watery and strong opinions grown thin. I'd make a pledge to call her, but more urgent concerns would crush in: Had Faye paid the gas bill? The electric? How long till our next move?

I worked hard to read my mother's moods, did what I could to fill in for her gaps. I learned to cook, to sign documents in her name, to keep nosy teachers and landlords at bay. I even attended the occasional protest to appease her, though I couldn't understand why she cared more about the wages of nameless workers than our own ability to pay the rent. Later I'd come to understand that the protests were a form of play for my mother, more a performance of goodness than a genuine commitment. For Faye, few things reached that level, including being a parent. So while she played at saving the world, I took over at home. Somehow or other we made it through spring, summer, fall.

Then came news of Nonnie's death.

Grief hit like a tsunami. Pinpricks of memory sent me spiraling into tears. Understandable, given everything. What made less sense was Faye. Faye, who'd always clashed with her mother, who called her an overbearing muggle, went dark. She slept through alarms, blew off her friends, missed two weeks of work. When I tried to remind her that we had bills to pay, she pulled the covers over her head. Late notices piled up. The landlord posted a warning. My lies no longer worked.

One evening, Faye pulled herself out of bed to go see Aunt Jenny. "We have a few details to discuss," Faye said.

While she and Jenny holed up in the dining room, I followed my cousin Izzy to her large third-floor bedroom. Izzy unspooled on her satin bedspread while I marveled at her packed closet and brimming bookshelves. (Proof of life's unfairness: Izzy hated reading, while I'd have killed for a single shelf of my own.) I don't know when Faye appeared in the doorway. I don't know if she'd begun crying before she mounted my aunt's well-polished stairs or after she caught me drooling over Izzy's unread novels.

Jenny appeared too. "You're going to stay awhile, okay, Mari?"

"Stay . . . *here*?" My gaze shot from the bookcase to my cousin, who didn't bother hiding her dismay.

The decision had been made.

Izzy's books were my respite in the coming months. Two things I discovered quickly: (1) My aunt's penchant for neatness bordered on mania. (2) Izzy had no qualms about pinning her messes on me. Luckily, or maybe unluckily, Jenny saw right through her daughter's lies, used them like a cudgel to batter her back into line. Which only deepened Izzy's resentment of me. On the rare nights my uncle came home, the shouting matches were epic.

We stuck it out through the winter. My thirteenth birthday came and went. Izzy stopped talking. The word *divorce* began to circulate, and I watched my aunt's anxiety reach a new fever pitch.

Then one day Faye appeared on the doorstep. Again. Had Jenny summoned her, or was it coincidence? No one ever told me. It seemed this was my plight now—to be tossed back and forth on the whims of adults, no explanation.

I moved back with Faye, but I was done being anyone's dependent. I decided to take control of my own fate. I lined up babysitting gigs, made a spreadsheet for expenses, took control of Faye's credit cards. I took charge of her too. Set alarms, prepared lunches, ironed her clothes.

I gave her pep talks too, many, many pep talks.

You can do this, I told her. *One more day until Friday.*

You said you liked spaghetti, I reminded her. *Fish is too expensive.*

Can't you date guys who are more stable? Or better yet, hold off on dating right now?

I pushed, I prodded. Sometimes it worked. Not always. We moved seven times in the two years that followed. Faye lost a total of nine jobs, more friends than I could track, finally hitting rock bottom on account of a con man named Chip.

Fast-forward four months, and she's talking about a house in New Hampshire, a garage, a pool. And the next night, a fresh bombshell: "Sweetie, Chip asked me to marry him! I said *yes!*"

As I stared at my doe-eyed mother, I realized with a thud that Nonnie was right. She'd never be the kind of mother I needed.

I said something harsh, something I prefer to forget but that was probably overdue, and then Faye was running out the door yet again, on her stupid kitten heels.

She left her silly, too-small purse behind, her cell phone too. And, of course, me.

AFTER

DAY 13

THE FRONT DOOR unlatches, and I bolt upright on the couch.

"Mari? Is that you? Did you sleep on the sofa?"

Faye stands in the center of the bungalow's living room in a gauzy purple muumuu, her gaze darting from the rumple of blankets to the stack of abandoned plates on the table.

"You're home," I note groggily.

My tracker tells me it's 5:03 a.m. I fell asleep, but not for very long.

"Oh, baby, you didn't wait up for me, did you?" Faye rounds the couch and lands lightly atop my feet. I extricate them carefully and shove aside the incriminating blankets.

"No." I'm ashamed of where worry took me last night. "No, course not." But when I see her in that silly purple outfit, shame hardens into something else. "Where were you? Why didn't you call? You can't jus—"

"Oof! I'm so sorry. Can you believe I fell asleep meditating? It's this new high-intensity method. I decided you were right; I can't expect to reach the Ever After if I don't buckle down, give it my all. But I guess I gave this one *too* much—I completely zonked out!" She laughs, reaching a hand toward my bare foot. "You must have been worried."

"No, no. It's fine . . . I just . . ." I scooch back my toes, rub my temple. "It's . . . fine."

It is *not* fine. Nothing about our situation has been fine for a very long time.

"Baby, I'm sorry. I'm trying. I'm really trying. Do you believe me?" Her hand stretches again, and I hold back the urge to kick it. To tell her not to call me that. "I'm honestly not sure how I slept for so long. All I can think is . . . my soul must have needed the rest."

She does look tired. And old. When did that happen? Her mouth sags, and her pale hair is more straw than gold. Faye hasn't *aged* since dying—that's impossible—but death has changed her, turned my once-fiery mother into someone more humble and sad.

She's looking at me too, studying my crumpled position and unflattering PJs, with something that resembles pity.

"Baby, how about we take the day off? I think it's time we went shopping."

WE SUBMIT OUR requests for a mental health day, and Faye talks me into taking the bus. "You and I don't have a great history with public transportation, do we?" she says jokingly, and I shudder. I still don't know what I was doing boarding a bus that fateful morning, and I don't like to think about the specifics of Faye's demise. But, she explains, a bus is the only way to reach Paradise Gate's main shopping area. If we want to find me better clothes, we have no choice.

We plan a ballsy escape from the front-stoop paparazzi using a back window and a pair of floppy hats. The ride over is surprisingly smooth. My tracker turns a warmish sienna tone as we sit silently together, watching the glide of clean streets or residential clusters blur past. I'll need to rack up extra credit to make up for today's classes, but this feels like a good decision. Maybe a change of look will unstick me from this low place I've been in and put me in the right mindset to succeed. *Dress to be blessed,* as they say.

I look over at Faye, who is smiling too. Yes. This feels like a step in the right direction.

The bus comes to its final stop, and I look out the window at a giant blue box with sliding glass doors. WELCOME TO PARADISE-MART exclaims a yellow-lettered sign. All at once, the passengers rise. Faye and I let the others go ahead, wait for their nattering to fade before loosening our hats and descending to the street.

ParadiseMart is several times bigger than any earthly department store and every bit as unsettling. The fluorescent lighting is scouring, bright enough to unpeel layers of dead skin. Instead of aisles, there are tall, rotating carousels stretching back for yards, possibly miles. There's one carousel for cooking supplies. Another for crystals and hypnotics. More for prayer beads and meditation cushions. Hopeful shoppers stare at the belts, patiently waiting for the items they seek to round the bend.

The whole setup is deeply depressing, and yet, as Faye and I push our carts past a carousel filled with candles and another dedicated entirely to self-reflection devices (aka "mirrors"), I thrum with the novelty of it: Here we are, a mother and daughter out shopping, as mothers and daughters do.

The plan is to get me something I can wear to the Center without fear of ridicule, plus some sort of face-concealing outer garments to help us both eschew the paparazzi. We find full-coverage robes fairly easily (think: Arctic explorer meets monk, in an unassuming gray). For my regular clothes, it's unclear where to begin. I steer Faye away from the genie pants. Yougawear is out of the question as well. And while Faye can somehow pull off a muumuu, that's not going to work for me. Which leaves us with . . . what exactly?

We find a carousel advertising "Aspirational Styles" and "Actualized Ease." Its wares seem innocuous from a distance. On closer inspection: not so much. The jeans turn out to be jeggings ("with 50% more aspirational stretch!"), and every T-shirt has been thwacked with a giant uplifting quote (LOVE THE YOU YOU'RE IN). Nope. Sorry. I'd rather die another traumatic death.

Faye and I begin playing a game. Who can uncover the most offensive item? She discovers a carousel full of crimson tunics that appear to have been designed for a cannibalistic cult. I find another full of gravity-defying togas. She: a shirt with built-in LED candles. Me: a dress made of thin, almost transparent scarves. For five thousand points?! Who in their right mind would spend a week's worth of points on *this*? What in the afterworld would you wear under it?

Faye's waving something in my direction. Are those *gaucho* shorts? They appear to have been patched together with peace flags. Before I can laugh outright and declare her the winner, I note the unironic curve of her lips. Oh no. I know that expression. It's the same one she made over every pink-painted Victorian on our favorite reno show. She . . . *likes* them.

"What do you think?" She twirls the shorts to reveal their many, many jewel tones. "They're just seven hundred fifty points! Can you believe it?"

I bite back a grimace. "Wow. No. I . . . can't."

How is it possible that we could be so aligned one minute, and the next so far apart?

I slip the scarf dress back on the rack and return to the cannibal tunics.

We spend the next twenty minutes sifting through increasingly terrible options. Faye's smile fades more with each of my adamant nos. I was naive to think this could work, that a day of mother-daughter shopping could fix whatever's broken between us. I'm on the verge of aborting the mission when I look up and see a poster advertising something called Sweatslacks. The name makes me twitch. (Ick. Really? They might as well be called Moist Pantaloons.) But the picture—of a girl sitting on a big bed in comfy-looking pants—is . . . intriguing.

I snatch a pair from the rack, test the plush cotton weave against my thumbs. ("Soft as Cloud 9!" the tag proclaims. Not a lie.) The pants have practical pockets, an adjustable waist, no quotes or gimmicks. And they're priced in a range I can afford. Ooh, is that a matching zip-up hoodie? I think I've found my fashion soulmate.

Faye tilts her head when I hold them up. She isn't smiling, but she isn't frowning either. Have we done it? Have we found something that appeals to both our tastes?

I'm ready to declare victory when a slight motion catches my peripherals. It's followed by an unmistakable burst of clicks. Oh, kill me now. A trench-coated reporter appears from behind the next carousel in comically large sunglasses. Then another appears, and two more. They rush through Ladies' Yougawear, cameras pointed.

"Nope. Uh-uh." I throw my new outfit over one shoulder and prepare to bolt.

Too late. "Marianna Novak? Can we ask you a few questions?"

I trip into a shelf full of scarves.

"Are you on a spiritual errand today, Miss Novak?"

"What's that you're purchasing?"

"Do you remember anything more about your death?"

"Was it painful? Was it thrilling? Would you do it all over again?"

Ugh. We should have kept our flimsy hats on or found a way to shop online. We should've known better than to think we could have a normal outing like normal dead people.

Using our cart as a shield, I grab Faye by the elbow and maneuver through Incense & Accessories.

"You're Miss Novak's mother?" The one with the sunglasses studies petite Faye, as if seeking some kind of resemblance. I motion at Faye to ignore him. But she takes the bait. She thrusts back her shoulders. "Of course I am! I couldn't be more proud of my girl."

That's all it takes.

"Is it true you were once affiliated with anarchists?"

"Did you really do time for fraud?"

"Were drugs a factor in your sudden death? Was it in fact a suicide?"

"Why were you estranged from your daughter?"

"Is that why Mari's college application form lists her as an independent minor?"

We're backed into a corner, wedged against a conveyor belt full of inspiration-quote socks. I squeeze Faye's arm in a vain attempt to hush her.

"What are you talking about? I never used drugs! Nothing stronger than weed! And if my daughter can forgive me, that's all that matters. Who are you to judge?"

I push Faye behind me, stepping between her and the reporters, who I give my most ferocious glare.

"Do you, Miss Novak? Forgive your mother?" they ask.

"No comment," I say.

They try again, skirting the nearest carousel to reach Faye from behind.

"You're approaching sixty days, Faye, is that right? How have you accrued so much karmic debt?"

"According to our records, you are at risk of default. Do you really think you have a chance of ascension?"

"Are you prepared for the alternative? Do you know what happens to souls like yours in the In Between?"

Faye whimpers, and a familiar instinct—ancient, protective—surges in me.

"Move the hell back!" I warn the nearest cameras. Raising my mama-bear paws, I punch through the first row of reporters. All questions stop. One reporter scribbles into a notebook, but I slap that to the floor, telling him to fuck off, extra loud, so there can be no confusion.

A camera clicks quietly, no flash.

The reporters part at this point, allowing our retreat, and I drag Faye toward the exit, cursing like a bandit the whole way.

ON THE BUS ride home, Faye is silent at first, shivering. Her whole body has gone cold, she whispers. But shock soon shifts to outage: "Who told them all of that? What right do they have?" Then swoops into despair: "They're right. I'm a lost cause. It's only a matter of time, Mari. You heard them. I'm at fifty-eight days, and I'm in worse shape than when I arrived. What's the use pretending?"

"Were they right?" I ask her. "What they said about you being at risk of default? Are you really that far in the hole?"

She shrugs helplessly.

"But *how*?" I ask. "You go to class every day. You're doing all that meditation. You even drink that awful celery water. If anyone should have a point surplus, it's you."

Faye bites her lip. "You know I've never been good with budgets."

"Okay . . . What does that mean? Where have you spent all those points?"

"Extra therapies. Sound baths. One of my instructors recommended breath lessons. Maybe I went a little too far. But, baby . . . what was that they said about a college application?"

"I don't know." I dismiss it. "They must be . . . confused."

I hadn't even started my applications before I died. Ms. Crawford and I were still figuring out how I'd afford it. Clearly, the reporters mixed up some details. But what's really messed up is

Faye's situation. "Are they really charging you for doing extra programs? Why did you keep spending if you knew you were in debt?"

"Because I'm hopeless," Faye mewls. "I screw up everything!"

"Stop. Those people don't know you. Don't let them get in your head."

Clearly, though, they do know a lot about her situation.

I grab her hands, urging her to hush. It's an old act, a mother-daughter reversal, one I thought I'd given up for good. But maybe some things never change. Maybe we just play out the same dramas, over and over, even in death.

I hold Faye's head and remind her to breathe (she paid for all those breath lessons, didn't she?). I remind myself to breathe too, but it's too late. A tingle of fear has spread to my belly. As Faye's whimpers pitch louder, I lose my calm, and fear erupts as anger.

"Oh, for fuck's sake," I say. "Would you please stop being so damn *dramatic*?"

AFTER

———

DAY 13 CONTINUED

THAT EVENING, THEY air the whole scene from Paradise-Mart on all four channels, along with a more detailed accounting of Faye's karmic debt. They elaborate on the odd detail about me too. Apparently, some reporter dipped into my archive and dragged up an image of the application I submitted for Boston University summer classes last spring. In the caregiver field, it clearly says *independent minor*.

Faye gasps when she sees it, and I feel my brow pinch. Did I really write that? The form was due right around the time of my big argument with Faye. The whole week was a blur.

"What does that mean, *independent minor*? Why would you write that? I was alive. You weren't independent."

Faye stares at me, her eyes accusing. And I can see her wheels churning, piecing together details from our final interactions, the gaps neither of us has dared broach.

The reporters have clips of my conversations with Ms. Crawford as we discussed my college strategy, including one rather blunt conversation where we mutually agreed that I should look at schools far from Boston, where I could build a life on my own terms.

"Is this true? Chicago? California? You were going to just leave? Did you plan to even tell your own mother?"

I open my mouth, then close it. What can I say? I knew how Faye felt about college generally. I knew she'd lose her mind if I even suggested a school that far away. Of course I didn't plan to tell her.

And there it is again. The same look she gave me last April. Just before she slammed the door and ran out into the rain.

Mari, he loves me.

Mari, this will be good for us.

Baby, we're a team!

Her eyes bright like shattered gems.

And I know this is worse somehow. A bigger betrayal. Not an argument but a cold-hearted calculation. I planned to leave her, my mother. I needed to, for my own survival.

Does she know what else I did? On that cold night in April? The phone call I made? If she's figured it out, she doesn't say it. She turns from me and hurries into her room. She doesn't come out again, not for dinner, not for breakfast. Not once all weekend long.

I feel terrible, of course I do. Guilty at first. Then, angry. I can't believe she doesn't realize how hard I tried to make our life work. How dare she put this on me?

When my alarm sounds on Monday morning, Faye's door remains closed. I don't bother knocking.

REAL TALK WITH RUPI

Episode #357

Hi, sprouts! It's your pal Rupi P coming to you with a quick chat about a serious subject. *Forgiveness.* Forgiveness is like so, so important, okay? This is our *last chance* to let go of anger and all of that ick. Plus, it's literally the only way to move on.

So first off, forgive yourself. You made some poor choices. We all did. For example: That time I tried bangs. Indefensible! But I'm dead now, and my hair is perfection, right? Gotta let those past mistakes goooooooooo.

Step two: Forgive your friends. I'm not talking about the toxic ones you so wisely kicked curbside on trash day. I'm talking about the ones who did medium-awful stuff, like good old Trisha, who told me I couldn't hold a tune. In front of the entire senior class. On my birthday. But, like, Trish loved me and thought she was helping by keeping me from the mic. So even if I don't understand her choices (or agree: that's the whole point of karaoke!), I can still FORGIVE.

The other ones we've got to forgive are our family. Family is everything. Unless your family sucks. In which case, blame them for everything and move on.

So in conclusion, forgiveness is the best thing unless it is impossible, in which case, do as Lady Lulu advises and release the shadows to become your own sun. Cool. Right. That makes sense . . . sort of?

Deep breaths, my little sprouts. You can do this!

Here's the best part of all: Forgiveness is free!

AFTER

—

DAY 16

"IT'S AN IMPROVEMENT," someone offers.

"At least they aren't pajamas," another says more quietly.

I step into the computer lab on Monday morning in my new Sweatslacks (shoplifted, oops, then paid for via the feed), feeling pretty upbeat. While the outing with Faye didn't go anywhere close to plan, I'm determined to make the best of its result. New look, new me, etc.

It can't hurt to at least try.

My vibes bottomed out again over the weekend, tanking further when I went to pay my share of our weekly rent and discovered a 30 percent upcharge for something called "karmic overhead." (Seriously? Add-on fees in the afterlife?) But today I'm not dwelling on the negative. I'm turning a new page. I've recalculated my daily minimum and am going to earn those additional points. I'm definitely *not* going to think about Faye still sulking in her bedroom. *Chin up, eyes ahead,* as a wise woman once said.

Buffeted by a soft cloud of jersey, I rise to my full five feet eight inches and cross the classroom toward the chair Larisa has saved for me. She stands, hands beating in silent applause. "Massive improvement. *Much* less clinically depressed."

I spin to show off the Sweatslacks' convenient pockets and ankle zips.

"Stylish *and* practical. Very nice." Larisa grins approval.

Catherine of New Haven is less certain. "I don't know, Mari. A cotton blend?"

Schenectady quivers in her miracle-fit leggings. "Are you sure sweatpants are aspirational enough?"

Larisa's eyes narrow. "Maybe you should mind your own as—"

Nope. I catch my friend by the shoulders and plunk her back in her seat. I appreciate the support, but I've had enough drama for one afterlife.

I smile at the two Catherines and compliment them on their new headbands. (Something else I don't need: classmates griping about me to the press.)

The Catherines whip their ponytails, pleased by the flattery. "What, *these*?"

"I can make you one!" New Haven offers brightly.

"Oh, wow. That's . . ." I force a gracious smile. "Thanks! I can't wait."

Today's resolution: Earn maximum points, acquire no unnecessary enemies.

"YOU TRYING TO win him over by hypnosis or something?"

"Hmm?"

Twenty minutes into class, Larisa pulls my attention back to our screens. We're taking practice quizzes today in preparation for our assessments, and my resolve is already fraying. Larisa recently passed her own midterm with flying colors, and I want to do well too—*need* to do well—but I can't seem to stay focused. The inanity of the quizzes isn't helping.

> **How Resilient Is Your Soul? Answer 10 Easy Questions to See!**
>
> **Discover Your Spirit Animal with Just Five Clicks!**

Larisa groaned when she saw the second one ("Indigenous appropriation much?"), but it didn't stop her from putting in an effort and urging me to do the same.

Now she points her chin in the direction I'd been staring. "Lust is wasted energy, you know. Gotta channel those vibes into *self*-love, kiddo, and I don't mean masturbation."

"Thanks." I feel my neck flush. "But I wasn't . . . *lusting*."

My gaze betrays me, though, boomeranging back to the corner of the classroom, to a familiar flannel hunch.

Okay, yes, maybe I *was* looking at Jethro. He arrived late today (typical), without even a flicker of acknowledgment. I'm starting to think I imagined the whole cigarette incident last Wednesday. Did he look me up on the feed after we parted? Did he see the awful pictures? I finger the zipper on my new hooded Slacket, wondering if he'll notice the change.

I know I should find Jethro's deadbeat energy repellent, and Larisa is correct: Postmortem crushes, romantic entanglements, etc. are a complete waste of energy, according to Chairman Ted. A distraction at best, and a dangerous detour for souls unable to invest in themselves, such as yours truly. And look, I'm not saying that's what this is—a crush. I don't understand why I keep looking at him, honestly. It's something about the way his shoulders curve, that strip of skin that peeks from his collar as he slumps over, asleep. Or maybe it's his utter disregard for schedules, points, and the rest. I guess I find Jethro's unmasked misery . . . refreshing.

"Have you finished undressing him yet? I know there's a lot of plaid."

I punch Larisa. "I wasn't—" Ugh. I feel my neck warming again. "I'm just curious," I say quietly. "You know, about what you told me my first day."

"You mean about what constitutes an air-quote virgin?"

"What? No. *God.* Larisa! I mean, do you think he really . . ." I mime a noose.

Larisa gives me a funny look. "It's a theory. And a bit creepy that you're so interested. Also weird of you to bring up God. You know we're all secular here, right?"

"Yes. I'm aware. Thanks for the chat."

"Anytime, pal. You know I got your back."

I square my shoulders toward my screen and plunk at the keys. Larisa didn't answer my question. While I appreciate her concern about my eternal future, she can be exasperating sometimes. I skim through the quiz, selecting a color that feels peaceful, an image that says *paradise*, the quote I find most inspiring, and something about baby goats. I'm starting to think that whoever made this quiz really lost the thread when—

Congratulations, Student 4,572!
Meet your spirit animal!

A turtle pops onto the screen.

You tend to keep to yourself, TURTLE, though you long for connection and will do anything to protect the lucky ones who get beneath your shell. Beware, TURTLE, for those who cling to privacy are often those most in need of light.

A glum-faced turtle stares at me, accusing. I hit return, delete, escape. But the little bastard won't go away.

"What'd you get?" Larisa rocks back in her chair to sneak a peek. "I'm a rhinoceros, in case you're curious. I don't take crap. Need to work on being more tolerant. Lol. Okay. Maybe when other people stop being such trashholes."

I bite down a smile. "A rhino?" Yeah, I can see that.

Larisa cranks her head, and I clamp one hand across my screen while with the other I hunt for the power button. Too late. "Okay, Turtle." She snorts. "Looks like they got your number, didn't they?"

I glare at my friend. If I had a shell, I would absolutely batter her with it.

Class is almost over, and one of the Center's tutors has popped in to say something about assessment prep. The Catherines are aflutter. *How many questions are there again? Does the tutor offer individual sessions? Should they message him privately?* Ick.

The bell chimes, and suddenly chairs are scraping and everyone's standing. Everyone except Larisa, who's typing away again. I'm debating whether to leave her—what type of force does it take to separate a rhino from its favorite toy?—when my tracker pings.

A cigarette emoji. The sender's identity has been masked. My chest stutters—is it . . . ? I dare another glance. This time Jethro meets it with a crooked smile. He raises two fingers toward his lips as he slouches toward the door. A question. An invitation. And I'm glad I'm dead because for the briefest of moments, I forget how to breathe.

JETHRO STRIKES A match, and we both settle back to watch it burn. It's a self-study period, so we're not doing anything overtly wrong. Nothing that will cost us any points anyway. Still, my toe moves toward the edge of the asphalt, teasing the blur.

It's quiet out here, peaceful. Between puffs I sneak a look at my companion, his folded shoulders, the sadness that envelops him like a thick smoke. I wonder if this is going to be our thing now, inhaling foul substances in a forgotten blip in the grid. I wonder, too, what type of animal he got on that quiz. A savanna dweller, maybe, all long lines and arced glances. Or perhaps something smaller, silkier. The type of creature that slips up a trunk and gets caught in your branches before you see where it came from or what it wants.

(Okay. It's possible Larisa had me on the lust thing.)

Jethro catches me looking and raises a brow. "Not worried about missing class again, are you?" He releases a neat curl of smoke with a mischievous glint.

A mink, I decide. Or maybe a fox.

"I'm good. I have a self-study now, same as you. And anyway, this is basically the same as Youga, isn't it?" I lift one foot into a joyful warrior pose. "Inhale, exhale."

Jethro hands over the cigarette with a small bow. "Well, in that case, namaste."

Uff. That smile again. He's *definitely* flirting.

I steady myself and take a slow drag, watch the smoke disappear up into the unformed white. It feels good. Being out here. Off the hamster wheel of points and obligation. No to-do lists or silly exercises. No Faye.

I tip my head back so it grazes the building's smooth surface and close my eyes. I have a sudden, strange longing for rain. For the feel of real breath in my lungs and cold, clear drops on my face. Even though being alive was hard, I really miss it.

"You okay over there?"

I mutter something unintelligible.

"Mrrphllmrrm?" Jethro repeats.

I press my skull harder against the rigid wall. "I wish I could turn it off sometimes. You know?"

Jethro doesn't answer. I pry open one eye, look over.

His throat is working. I've hit a nerve. "Yeah," he says. "I do."

Oh god. I realize my mistake. I wasn't talking about suicide, but that's what it sounded like, didn't it? "It's just . . . a lot in there,"

I clarify, nudging the building behind us. "The classes, the quizzes, the *feed*. How is anyone supposed to find inner peace with all of *that*?"

"I find the best thing to do is avoid."

"Avoid?"

I drop my foot and twist to face him more fully; he's closer than I realized, right at eye level thanks to that long, bendy slouch. Eyes like murky pools, a jawline that's practically edible. (Silly girl. Put that thought away.)

"Yeah, like . . . when they say *lean in*, I do the opposite. Ignore, block, delete. As far as I've seen, all that *inner you* mantra stuff only makes things worse anyway."

His bowed mouth flattens, like maybe he's said too much.

But I get it. I do. Stirring the pot of memory hasn't turned out well for me either. I *want* to do the work, *want* to keep my chin up, eyes on the prize, etc. But these days, wanting and doing are two different things. I worked so hard for so long—to get good grades, please teachers, keep our life on track. And now? I'm tired of the constant churn. Just when I think I've made progress, the rug slips out again. More stress, more arguments, more disappointment.

Still, I have to at least try, don't I? Avoidance doesn't really seem like a viable option.

I let out a lazy puff. "At least you get plenty of sleep," I say, changing the subject.

Jethro chuckles. "That's kind of my superpower. Too bad our instructors aren't into it." He gives me a closer look. "What about you? Not sleeping much?"

I shake my head, rub my eyes. (A reflex. They're dead; they don't hurt.) It's been days since I've closed them for more than a few minutes, and even though I don't technically *need* sleep, I'd like the chance to turn off my thoughts once in a while. But every time I lie down, the past rushes up, demanding review. I don't know what's worse: the parts I do remember or the bits I don't.

Jethro tugs the cigarette from my fingers, flicks a bit of ash. It arcs upward, past the alley's blurred-out edge, melting into the void. He takes a long drag, and I wonder, not for the first time, what his damage is. Whether it's worse than mine.

"You know," he says, after another thoughtful puff, "some folks think it's better to skip all of this. Face shit the old-fashioned way. Out there."

"Out where? In the abyss?" I laugh, figuring I've misunderstood him. This place might be absurd and frustrating, but face an eternal 3:00 a.m.? No thanks.

"It makes more sense in a way, don't you think? Like knowing my ghost animal is somehow going to fix me?"

"Your *spirit* animal," I correct, although honestly, Jethro's spin is probably less problematic.

He's said out loud exactly what I've been secretly thinking: Our classes are pointless. It's a relief to hear someone else say it, and also terrifying.

"What did you get anyway?" His foot nudges mine.

"My spirit animal?" I shake my head. No way I'm telling him that. "What did *you* get?"

Our eyes lock for a long second, a silent dare.

"Lynx," he whispers.

"Turtle," I breathe.

We both crack a grin.

"That's a big cat, right?"

Jethro bobs his head, clearly embarrassed. But I think it's perfect. Even the word—I whisper it: *lynx*—feels perfect on my tongue.

"So, what?" he says to me. "You've got a thick shell or something? Hide when you get nervous?"

I wriggle my nose, feel my shoulders twist. "Can we not talk about that?"

Jethro lets out a rusty laugh. "Okay, Turtle. I see you."

He nudges my shoulder with his, and I curl inward but also smile. I'm not used to being seen. I can't tell if I like it.

Thankfully, Jethro knows when to let a topic go. We pass the dwindling cigarette and remain quiet for a nice, peaceful stretch. I'm still mulling something he said a few minutes ago.

"You wouldn't do it, would you? Go off-grid? On purpose?"

He studies the cigarette's plasticky coating, removing a flake of ash. "Honestly? I might blow up the whole grid if I knew how to do that."

My brows shoot up. I should probably feel scared right now. *Loner Deadbeat Threatens Violent Act.* We've all seen that headline. But the way Jethro stands there, head bowed and lips twisting, I recognize a pain that makes my own dead heart squeeze in sympathy.

"Forget I said that," he mutters, tossing the last of the cigarette into the void.

"Consider it forgotten."

THE FINAL BELL chimes and Reenie calls out a reminder about homework. It's another doozy—*What internal walls do you have the power to bring down?*—and I do my best to appear cool, calm, and capable as she scans our trackers for dismissal. But then as she peels back the sleeve of my Slacket and we both take note of my device's unhappy red glow, I slump. Zero improvement, despite the new outfit, despite another day of work.

"Remember, I'm here for you," Reenie whispers with a gaze that digs a little too deep.

I pull my sleeve back into position. "Thanks. I'm good. I've got this."

Her smile twitches. "I'm so glad to hear it."

Larisa and I are quiet as we shuffle out toward the lobby. I hate lying to Reenie, even if it's the sort of vague statement that no one could fault me on. Who can prove that I don't have this? Not my tracker's AI, that's for sure. Only I know how far I am from feeling at peace with my circumstances, or the dread that enfolds me as I think about returning home to Faye, still enclosed in her bedroom. I consider what Jethro said about going out into the void—whether it's really a more viable alternative for some souls than this whole game of Chutes and Ladders. Would he really take that chance? Would I? I don't think I'd have the guts.

Larisa is unusually quiet. She marches along beside me, chin tucked tight. Has she guessed where I spent our afternoon self-study period? I'd told her I had an errand to do, and she didn't react at the time. No, I'm being paranoid. It's probably something else. Maybe something someone said in her chat room. I have enough to worry about. I decide not to poke.

We reach the Center's front doors, and Larisa heads outside first. I pull in a breath and follow close behind. We emerge onto the wide front steps and Larisa, acting fast, throws out a few elbows to knock back the paparazzi that lie in wait.

"Thanks. Owe you one," I say as we make our way to the curb.

"You owe me like a million," she says gruffly.

"Okay..."

She's not lying. But still. *What?*

I'm relieved when she peels off in the direction of her bus. I strap on my new full-coverage robe, and as Larisa turns left, I move right and melt into a cluster of brown-robed martyrs. I stick with them for two blocks east, checking behind every few yards to make sure no paparazzi have followed.

All clear.

I break from the group at the next intersection, taking a quick left into the square's central common and then doubling back along the edge of the manicured park, toward home.

A sort of encampment has sprung up under a sparse fringe of trees. A cluster of army-green tents surround a sort of makeshift living area strewn with abandoned folding chairs. It reminds me of a protest camp Faye once joined in downtown Boston.

I stick to the sidewalk, taking note as a man and woman emerge from a tent. They're dressed oddly, a mishmash of camo green and faded black. If we weren't dead, I'd guess they were war veterans down on their luck, but of course that doesn't make sense. One of them sees me looking and returns my gaze. I shift my focus to the ground before me and walk faster. I only make it a few hurried steps when a hand latches on to my biceps.

"GET FREE!"

The shout nearly capsizes me. My hands grab for my chest. What the—

"Who be the Powers That Be?" It's another man, dressed similarly to the other two but more ragged and grizzled. He has my arm in a viselike grip.

I yank back, but the man clutches tighter. He's wearing an odd little cap and a pair of dark sunglasses that stare directly at me. Into me. I'm glad most of my face is covered.

"Who be the Powers That Be?" the man repeats in a guttural rasp.

His gaze drops toward my bared tracker, and I pull hard against his grip.

"Resist despair," he murmurs. "Reject conformity. There are other ways if you look."

My arm flutters like a trapped wing. I glance back toward the tents, but the other two have disappeared. There's not another soul in sight.

The man's hand slides from my biceps to my fingers, and I wonder at the stillness in my legs. I should run. I should scream bloody murder. I should kick him in his dead balls and get as far from here as possible. But I'm paralyzed, staring, as he reaches into his satchel and places something in my palm.

"Get free!" he whispers once more before he releases me and stumbles into the street. I watch as he weaves up the block, just missing the path of an oncoming van.

Get free. The strange man has left a small sheet of paper in my hand. Chaotic type careens across a bright tangerine background.

Change The Channel
Look To The Next LEVEL
There's More Than One Route
    More Than One REALITY
SPEAK YOUR TRUTH
The Options
        Are
            Y(OURS)

There's a swirled infinity symbol stamped at the bottom, followed by a phone number.

The whole thing—the guy, his words, the flyer—is creepy as hell. And completely incomprehensible. This is why they installed guards at the Center, I realize, to keep out nutjobs like him.

Suddenly, I can't wait to get out of here, back to the safety of the bungalow. I shove the paper in my satchel (littering: minus five points; getting caught with contraband literature: unclear), wipe my hand on my hip, and hurry toward home.

BACK AT THE house, I make a beeline for the shower, ignoring Faye's closed bedroom door. Under the hot stream of water, I scrub at my dead skin until the feel of the man's fingers fades. Afterward, I put on my standard-issue PJs and set up my desk for a long night of homework.

The man's voice still echoes in my head: *GET FREE,* he rasped. Like he could see right into my skull, saw all my fear and doubts, and understood what I want more than anything.

BEFORE

FAYE WAS GONE. An accident, they said. After a period of shock, I picked myself up and life carried on. What other option did I have?

Six classes, afternoon shift at the store, four hours of homework, midnight pillow fight with a gnarly old cat. Rinse, repeat. After a month, I'd found a sort of rhythm. Was I exhausted? Sure. Was I taking care of basics like nutrition? Not remotely. But my chin was up, and a better future was within view.

By late September, Faye's presence—those trembly, unexpected apparitions in the corner of my eye—had become less constant. I began sleeping a little better. Then one afternoon at the outset of October, I came home to find old Mrs. MacAfee inside my studio. Oscar was there too. Dirty paws up on the counter, licking at crumbs, while the old lady rummaged beneath the sink. "A leak," she moaned. "There must be a leak."

I rushed toward the cabinet, slammed it sharply. Mrs. MacAfee teetered. One part of me wanted to leave her crouched on the floor, vanquished by arthritis. A better self intervened. *She's just an old woman. She doesn't know.* I offered her an arm. "Did you check the guy upstairs? He takes a lot of showers. Sometimes three a day."

"Is that right?" Behind her thick glasses, the old bat's eyes widened to moons.

I hated making an innocent neighbor the focus of our landlady's penny-squinching obsession, but this business about the water had gone far enough.

"Where's your mother?" Mrs. MacAfee asked as I guided her toward the door. "Vacation? Still?" She hadn't seen the box of ashes, then.

I made a noncommittal sound and nudged the old woman over the threshold, kicking the cat out with her. I waited in the doorway, listening as she tottered up the porch stairs and rapped on the window above. When the upstairs door opened, I closed mine and ran to the sink: My hidden stash—$284 and dropping—was intact. Faye's ashes were untouched too.

I needed a better hiding place and perhaps a better plan.

MS. CRAWFORD CAUGHT me at my locker the next morning. "Allergies," I said when she remarked on the shadows beneath my eyes. She had a new idea about scholarships; what did I think about one more go at the SATs? "Yes, of course," I said. Anything to bring hope closer to reality.

"There's a sixty-five-dollar fee," she explained, "but we can cover that through a school fund if you just have your mom call me to give her consent. One of these days, I'd really love to meet her."

My throat caught. "I have cash. I'll bring it tomorrow."

$284 − $65 − train fare − lunch money = . . . what was a few more skipped lunches?

"Don't worry about a waiver," I assured Ms. Crawford. "I've got it. It's fine."

In fact, I'd discovered some new tricks: If I stayed in the library through lunch, I barely missed eating. Gum kept my stomach from rumbling. SAT practice kept me occupied in the afternoon. The next test date was in less than two weeks. Ms. Crawford stopped in often to praise my focus, and to drop occasional granola bars on my desk.

Chin up, eyes ahead. A tight choreography of classes, work, study, sleep.

After another long day, I settled in for an evening cram session when, moments later, a sharp knock awoke me from an unplanned nap.

Mrs. MacAfee whined through the open window: "The electricity! What's going on with the electricity?"

Crazy old bat. Faye's voice crackled from the corner, amused.

"Leave me alone," I muttered at both of them.

"What's that? What did you say?" the old woman asked.

I shook my head, pointed to the unit upstairs, noting the space heater's near-constant hum. "It's not me," I said, before turning out the light and climbing into bed.

Over the next week, Faye returned again and again. I felt her in the early autumn breeze, found her in blurred-out reflections, smelled her on my pillow. She was there in the bus lanes I avoided, the walk signals I firmly pressed, old texts I didn't want to revisit but couldn't bring myself to delete. She was there at night, especially. Once, in the wee hours, her kitten-heeled steps startled me awake. I creaked open the outer door, peered out past the driveway to the shadowy walk.

What did I expect to find? It was no one. Nothing. I was alone.

My cash dwindled. Instant ramen became my go-to meal. For two nights in a row, I pulled all-nighters. On the Thursday before the test, I came home late to an empty apartment and promptly sat down to study. Less than thirty-six hours remained. I reached the final chapter in the prep book shortly after eleven, but before I could read more than a paragraph, the lights cut out and the space heater upstairs went silent.

Mrs. McAfee was screwing with us.

Well, I wouldn't give her the satisfaction. I flipped the page, studied by the light of the moon.

The next morning, I took a cold shower, slapped peanut butter on an untoasted slice of bread. Outside, there was no sign of Oscar. Had he given up on me? Moved on to a better source for food? I tossed a bit of bread to the ground anyway, listened as Faye laughed.

AT THE TRAIN stop, the girl with the cup looked up at me, her amber eyes questioning. "A dollar?" she asked without the usual singsong. Her eyes tracked me carefully as I reached in my pocket, pulled out a dollar, and stuffed it in her cup. It was the last time I did this, the last time I recall seeing her. It was twenty-four hours until I'd meet the blank wall of my own death.

The Green Line was delayed. I decided to walk.

THE PARADISE MEDIA GROUP

EVENING ROUNDUP

Today's top-trending word: Sweatslacks.

There's been a run on ParadiseMart's comfort fashion line following a recent purchase by Marianna Novak. While some argue that Sweatslacks' relaxed lines make them an underwhelming style choice for upwardly mobile souls, we're here for this mold-breaking look!

Something else we're here for: Fascinating new theories about young Novak's death. Deep in the feed, folks are beginning to ask questions. It's odd that Novak and her mother died just a few weeks apart, isn't it? And that both deaths involved public transportation? Could Novak's run-in with that rogue shooter have been more than chance? Was she, perhaps, a target?

Marianna's memory of her own demise remains unavailable. We've therefore turned a closer eye on her mother, whose archive suggests she was estranged from her daughter in her final days, though the nature of the dispute is unclear. Also unclear: What exactly caused Faye Novak's death? While her official COD has been deemed an accident, further analysis of her final moments give a distinct impression of unbalance. Was the elder Novak unwell? Was her death intentional? Was she being *chased*? By the same madman who attacked her daughter?

We'll keep you posted on every conjecture as we continue riffling through the Novaks' bewildering past.

When you want the dirt, PMG buries you in it. So to speak.

AFTER

DAYS 17–19

BY TUESDAY OF my second week at the Center, the questions about my death have become incessant. Online, total strangers conjure wacked-out theories about the probable identity of the shooter, his possible motives, his connection to me, to Faye. They've invented love triangles, monetary ambitions, a drug-trafficking angle, a sex-trafficking angle, fifty outlandish reasons why a mother would abandon her teenage daughter and why they'd both then suddenly die. It's a lot of high-drama, ripped-from-the-headlines BS. Nothing to do with me.

Still, some of the theories manage to rattle me. While the details are improbable (the maniac could not have been simultaneously shooting at strangers and driving the bus—pick one; Faye had zero connections to the Irish mob—hello, Boston stereotype!), their intensity shakes something loose in me, sending my thoughts spinning in uncomfortable new directions. Was I being stalked? Had I pissed off the wrong person? Had Faye played a role in my death somehow, reaching back from beyond the grave? My vibes churn and bubble, then finally boil over in the middle of a silent class meditation, causing my tracker to burst out in a series of embarrassing bleats.

When I open my eyes, my classmates are all staring. Larisa leans over, peering cautiously into my face, and then at my tracker, whose light has turned from red to an ominous black. Someone suggests calling postmortem services. I wave them off, insisting I'm fine.

"A glitch," I say. "It happens."

When the class ends a few minutes later, I run for the nearest exit. A few minutes after that, I'm in a blurred-out alley, sucking on a fake cigarette.

"HERE. LET ME."

Jethro reaches for my hand, and at first I don't know what he's doing (does he want to hold it?), but then he fixes his fingers on the hard band of my tracker, pressing down two tiny buttons at once.

"This will override your GPS for a bit. A little hack I learned. If you're going to keep coming out here, it's a good idea."

I'm not sure which part of this is more startling—the fact that trackers can be disabled (where did he learn this trick?), or that he expects our meetups to continue.

I focus on the part that's easier to digest: the GPS.

"Does it make me, like . . . disappear?"

"Nah, that'd be amazing, though, wouldn't it? No, this just freezes your status at your last check-in point." He looks at me warily, like he's doubting his decision to reveal the trick. "You don't want to do it for super-long stretches, all right? That might catch someone's attention. But . . ." He smiles crookedly. "Every now and again? No harm in that. Everyone needs a break sometimes, right?"

"Definitely." I pull from his gaze and lean back against the wall, feeling a small reservoir of stress drain out of me. "A break is exactly what I need."

He bumps my elbow and I smile.

It's not that I've done anything wrong out here in this alley, strictly speaking. (Aside from smoking the faux cigarette, which, well: consequences not entirely clear.) I still attend every class, do the assignments, earn the points I need to pay my way. I've only ever come out here during designated self-study blocks, but for some reason taking these little moments to step off the wheel, to stand in a blank spot in the grid, puffing on a fake cigarette with a checked-out boy who doesn't ask questions—it helps.

We don't talk much during these meetups. Mostly, we just lean against the wall, stare into the blur, and breathe. I don't understand any of it, including why Jethro seems to welcome my company. Is he bored? Lonely? (Does it matter?) Between puffs, I learn that Jethro is in Paradise Gate on his own, staying in a youth dorm like Larisa. He's well past midterm, just short of seventy days, with little sign of progress. He tells me he's more of a dog than a cat person (despite the lynx thing), believes forgiveness must be earned, and that random acts of gratitude (the topic of that morning's lecture) are bullshit.

"So is there anyone you wish would earn it? Your forgiveness?" I ask.

"Other than myself?"

He chuckles, and I laugh too because: Ouch. That's real.

"Nah, but like sometimes I wish I could get in touch with my uncle to, you know, explain a few things."

"Is he . . . ?"

"Here? No. He died a while back, a bunch of cycles before me."

"Oh."

I don't push any further. I don't ask how Jethro got the tattoo I've glimpsed on his wrist (three dots) either. Or how he died, or what type of inner work he's avoiding. Beneath his uneasy laughter, I sense some topics are off-limits. That's fine by me. He has the good grace not to probe my touchy subjects either.

"I'd love to see my grandma," I say simply. "She died a while back too."

FAYE HASN'T SPOKEN to me in four days. She's stopped going to classes, has barely emerged from her room since Friday's fiasco. I'm watching her self-implode again, and this time it feels like my fault.

What can I do about it? Nothing. I can't manage her emotions. I can barely manage my own.

I go out to the alley and I puff.

On Wednesday, Jethro shares something he saw on the feed. I lean over to read from his screen. It's a poem, or maybe a manifesto, by someone going by the moniker Freedome.

Who you are and what you know
No one else will ever fully understand

Your pain
      Your past
            Your truth
Cannot fit in another's mantra
Cannot be contained in one pose
      Or in a single breath
Your truth
Your self
Requires its own nurturing
Its own time
And recourse
To get free.

Get free. There are those words again, but this poem sounds nothing like that creepy man in the park. These words are crisp, ringing out with the distilled clarity of a bell. They capture something that feels true. Isn't it what everyone wants? To get free of stress, doubt, lingering questions, and, in my case, nosy classmates and pestering paparazzi? To be free to finally relax. Or, you know . . . rest in peace.

I look up Freedome on my own device, but the page that comes up is blank.

"You have to subscribe," Jethro says, "and read as soon as something drops. She takes them down after a few minutes. Too risky to leave something like that posted."

Jethro, it turns out, isn't just into risky poetry. He's also a bit of a philosopher, though his theories, like Freedome's, fall outside the edicts of the Powers That Be. He doesn't believe that anyone should be forced to practice Youga, for starters, or be told when and how to release their grief. "It might be good for some, but who says it's good for me?"

I try to picture Jethro in a self-empowered squat—I cannot. I can, however, see his point. It mirrors my own feelings when I try to do those exercises that make no sense.

Jethro's also interested in something called Universal Amnesty, a fringe theory that says all souls, no matter their flaws or misdeeds, are capable and worthy of a happy Ever After.

"Everyone?" I ask.

A laugh like sandpaper. "That's what they say, but they probably haven't met anyone as messed up as me."

It is a joke, but also not.

According to Jethro, the Universalists don't believe that redemption is a function of effort. They believe it's a matter of choice—in their version of an afterlife, when a person decides they're ready to ascend, they simply do. No quizzes or homework, no vibe-monitoring trackers, no final assessment.

"It's pretty out-there," Jethro admits. "Really more an idea than anything."

As someone who has always followed rules and believed in effort, I find the idea both uncomfortable and oddly compelling. Still, I play it safe. During class time, I do everything asked of me—the poses, the breaths, the quizzes. Earn every point I can. Ignore the speculation that continues to swell online. And during breaks, in these precious twenty-five-minute snatches, I allow myself to drift—not quite on the grid, not quite off—to a nonplace that exists somewhere in between the prescribed path and whatever lies beyond.

FAYE HAS RECEIVED a warning letter, the afterlife equivalent of an eviction notice. She tried to conceal it from me, but when she finally emerges from her room Wednesday night, I read trouble written all over her face. It's not the first time my mother has been threatened with eviction, but this time the stakes are different. She has one week to stop the spiral, get back to her routines, turn things around. Show *some* sign of improvement. (From the tone of the letter, it sounds like they'll accept almost any signal of progress.) If she doesn't comply? Bye-bye, this place. Hello, eternal void.

You'd think a threat like that would light a fire under her, but Faye's sunk to that place she goes sometimes, a place beyond my reach. I don't know what the right move is. Should I try to fix Faye's situation when I can barely get a grip on mine? What do I owe her, if anything?

Thursday morning, when she doesn't get up for breakfast, I stand outside her bedroom door for several minutes, considering. But there's nothing to consider, really. I grab my bag and head to class.

I SLIP UP, arriving late to third period. Twenty-point penalty.

Jethro slides in a few moments after, and Larisa shoots me a suspicious look.

I focus on the instructor, who is saying something about embodying the self we wish to become. She demonstrates: fists on hips, puffed chest of a lion, open-mouthed roar. From across the room, Jethro's eyes catch mine, and he swipes a faux paw. I squash down the smile that threatens to erupt.

BLANK SKY, WARM shoulder, smooth exhale. I meet Jethro again on Thursday afternoon. I set a timer to avoid a repeat of what happened this morning. We stand a little closer than last time, shoulders touching, and the moment he lights up, all the chaos that's been stirred in me settles like a sigh.

Ironically, I think these self-study periods with Jethro are helping me grasp the whole mindfulness thing. When I'm out here in the blur, a plasticky cigarette to my lips, I forget about Faye stuck in her bedroom; I forget about the paparazzi waiting for me out front and the wild theories about my cause of death; I stop trying to unfurl complex concepts like "loyalty," "love," and "responsibility." Instead, I notice how it feels to be present, right here, this strip of pavement, this feeling, this breath.

"Mari?"

"Mmm?"

My fingers fumble as I pass Jethro his strange little torch.

"Listen. Mari." He lifts, and something in his posture makes me straighten too. "Look, I don't know how to say this but"—flick of ash, chewed lip—"I don't think you should be out here so much. With me."

I blink hard. Is Jethro sick of me already? Did he read something embarrassing on my feed?

"If you want to be alone, I can—"

"It's not that I don't want to see you—"

"Wait."

"What?"

We both pause.

"You." I point. "You go first."

"Right. Okay." Jethro scruffs a hand through his hair, mouth twitching. "There's just some stuff . . . and I don't want . . ." Another push through his hair. "Look, I *like* you. It's not that. It's . . ."

"Wait. You *do*?" He *likes* me? As in, *likes* me likes me, or . . .

Jethro's lashes lift, murky eyes catching mine just as a smile bursts unbidden across my face.

"Sure. I mean . . ." Bashful bob. "Mari, the truth is you're the first person I've really talked to in . . . well"—he swallows—"a long time."

"Okay . . . So, then . . ." What's the catch here? If he likes me and enjoys talking to me, why does he want me to leave?

Jethro doesn't get to explain this gap in logic. Before he can say another word, the metal door swings open, crashing against the outer wall.

We both turn to find Larisa, hands on her hips, looking absolutely furious.

"**WHAT. THE. ACTUAL.** Fuck."

Larisa waits until we're tucked inside one of the Center's several dozen eternal rest rooms—quickly checking that all the power-nap stalls are vacant—before tearing into me.

"*That's* where you've been? All these weird little errands and appointments suddenly filling your free blocks. *That's* what you've been doing? Seriously? *That* guy?"

I draw back toward the row of wash stations behind me. "What do you mean? He's not . . . I haven't . . . God, Larisa. What's your problem?"

The way she stomped out there and ripped me away from Jethro, mid-conversation—it was humiliating. Not to mention rude.

"My problem isn't with anyone's deity, that's for sure. My issue is with you, kid. Were you two smoking? Couldn't you come up with something more original?"

I narrow my eyes. "I asked you to stop calling me kid. Also . . . how did you know where I was?"

"I followed you. *Duh.*" Larisa rolls her eyes, like this is a totally normal friendship behavior. Which, honestly, what do I know? Maybe it is. "I was worried about you, Mari. Showing up late to class, running out for breaks like the building's on fire."

"I wasn't . . . running." (Minus five for detectable lie.)

It's hard to think straight with Larisa glaring like that, her entire body twitching like a broken fuse.

"We were just having a conversation," I say in the calmest voice I can muster. "He's actually a cool guy."

Larisa snorts and grabs a wad of hand towels. "Yeah, okay, keep telling yourself that. Now come on." She lunges for me, waving the towels roughly at my chin.

"What are you doing?!"

"Cleaning up your mistakes," she says, making a swipe for my mouth.

I push her back. "Cigarettes aren't *prohibited*, Larisa. It's not even tobacco. What are you so stressed about?"

"Um, well, let's see, I'm no expert on dudes, but I do know a train wreck when I see one. Have you learned nothing from the movies? You ever see the one where the smart girl gets together with the derelict? Spoiler: It doesn't turn out good."

She comes for me again, this time with a bottle of patchouli-scented spray.

"He's not a—" I push her back, harder this time. "Would you cut that out? I don't need you to *clean* me. I'm not *dirty.*"

Beneath my cuff, my tracker flares angrily. (Peaceful alley vibe? Long gone.)

"Jethro isn't a bad person, Larisa. He's just, I don't know . . . *sad.*"

"Okay. Excellent. So you're casting away your last chance at eternal happiness for a sad sack."

"I'm not—" Ugh. How do I explain this? "I'm not you, Larisa. I've tried keeping my eyes on the prize and whatnot, but it's exhausting. The media stuff doesn't help. I just need a break sometimes, and Jethro's a good listener. He feels the same way I do about a lot of things, and he . . . *likes* me." I flush, hearing how stupid that last part sounds.

Larisa snorts. "News flash: Someone who *likes* you wouldn't risk your eternity just to get in your pants."

I shrink back. "We haven't . . . There've been no *pants.*" My cheeks flame hotter. "That's not— You know what I'm saying. Everyone's still wearing pants!"

Our eyes meet for a second, and we both snort. We can't help it.

"Tell you what." Larisa turns to the nearest wash station and scrubs her own hands beneath the faucet. "The way I see it, you've got two choices. Pull it together before this loser gets you in serious trouble, or keep this crap up and get yourself on the express bus to—"

The rest room door creaks open, and Larisa bites off the rest of her warning.

A pair of sparkly blue sandals appears, above them, an expression of pure misery. It's one of the Catherines—a blond one whose origin city I can never remember. Something with a *P.* Phoenix, maybe, or Portland. She's the same Catherine whose tortured vibes we analyzed in class last week, a girl with features so perfectly apportioned, so symmetrical, that you could blink and forget her face completely. She looks from me to Larisa, back to me, like she wants to say something, but Larisa raises a hand to stop her.

"Uh, we're having a conversation?"

The virgin's symmetrical features twist sideways, and with a sound like a cow giving birth, she bolts for the nearest napping stall.

"Why are you such a bitch?" I whisper when the stall's door has clicked.

"Why are you such a sucker?" Larisa retorts.

She glowers at me, and it occurs to me that she's too mad for this to be only about Jethro. "You're acting like I broke an actual law. I was just finding my own way to relax, during my *free time*. Not everyone can be a model student like you. News flash: Homework doesn't fix everything!"

"Oh, and smoking does?"

"I mean . . ." It's hard to explain. How smoking a foul little cigarette at least feels honest.

"This is brilliant, Mari. Tell me more about *finding your own way*, please. I want to hear all about these alternate paths you're discovering."

"Wait. What? I didn't say anything about—" I put my fists to my forehead, feeling like I've entered some other dimension. "Can you tell me what this is actually about?"

Larisa thrusts a hand in her bag, produces a slip of paper in bright tangerine. Exactly like the one I got from that creepy camo dude in the park. Did he give her one too, or—

"Have you been going through my things?" I leap forward to snatch it, but Larisa lifts her fist out of reach. Impressive for someone so short.

"'Course not." She glares. "But maybe I should. One of the martyrs knocked it from your bag when you were busy mooning over Emo Loser. Thank the Powers I saw it before someone else did."

"Give it back." I reach again for her hand, but she jumps.

"Do you even know what this is? Do you have any idea what would happen if you were caught with something like this?" She lowers her voice, glancing at the stall where the Catherine remains hidden. "More than one path? Speak your *truth*? These guys are total wing nuts, PTB's Most Wanted. You get caught spreading their philosophies—even associating with these dudes—and you could get sent away for eternity."

So, I was right about that guy in the street . . . But if he's so dangerous, why hasn't PTB security gone after him? He was hardly hiding.

I try once more to grab at the flyer, so I can destroy it properly. Again, I'm too slow. Larisa makes a show of crumpling the page in her fist.

"What's that loser been telling you, Mari?"

"What? Jethro didn't . . . He's not a . . ." I look at her. "I didn't get it from him."

Is that what this is all about? Larisa thinks Jethro is some kind of recruiter for a rebel cult?

"You have him so wrong, Larisa. And anyway, I can't believe you think I'd—"

A tortured wail interrupts us.

Larisa and I turn to the stall now occupied by a weeping Catherine. The wail is followed by something more guttural. Larisa mutters something, and I swat at her to hush.

"Hey, you okay in there?" I step closer, tapping gently on the door. I have no interest in getting wrapped up in some random virgin's drama, but she clearly needs assistance. "Did something happen? Are you . . . hurt?"

Catherine of Someplace with a *P* responds with a jagged yowl.

I place a tentative hand on the door handle and turn to Larisa, who mouths something that will cost her at least twenty points.

The door swings open, revealing Catherine curled upright on a narrow bunk bed. Her perfect face has been contorted by tearless sobs, her mouth pulled into an agonized maw. She looks . . . awful.

"Can we get you someone?" I suggest gently. "One of your friends maybe?"

"Agh!!! No!"

I edge back. "Okay, no friends, then." I start to draw the door shut. Honestly, I have enough on my plate without taking on this.

"I'm a phony," Catherine mewls to the closing door. "A total worthless fake."

Larisa chuckles. "Well, I coulda told you—"

I glare at her to be quiet.

To the Catherine I say, "I'm sure that's not true. No one is worthless." She may not be our responsibility, but we can at least be polite.

From her position on the bed, Catherine blinks her hazel eyes at me, her lashes two identical fans. "I'm a fraud," she moans. "Just look at my tracker. No matter what I do, it stays ORANGE." She flashes her wrist. Indeed, it is an unfortunate shade. Not as bad as mine, but still.

"Maybe you just need more time to settle in. If you do the work, your vibes will surely follow, right?"

"No." She shakes her head violently. "I had my midterm this morning, and I bombed it. My tracker *knows* what I am. I'm a bad, bad person. I'll never sort things out in ninety days. I've done terrible, *unforgivable* things."

I step inside the stall, closing the door behind me to block Larisa's muttering.

"You had your assessment today?" I ask softly.

She nods miserably. "They had all my data. They could see I've been doing everything, trying everything. But nothing I've done makes a difference. I'm . . . *stuck*!"

"Well, I'm sure you're not the only one who's struggling. Lots of folks have stuff to work through, messy pasts and stuff they're ashamed of."

"You're just saying that to be nice."

"No. I—" I hesitate, then: "Look." I pull back my sleeve to show her my tracker's telltale hue.

The Catherine's lashes fan wide with horror. "Oh my! That's bad! That's very, *very* bad! How many days till your midterm? What will you do? How will you make things right?"

I let my sleeve drop, reconsidering my decision to share. "I'm . . . working on it. I hit midterm in three weeks. I'll . . . figure things out. One way or another." Even as I say it, though, I feel a fresh stab of anxiety.

"You'll find your own path, you mean?"

Holy—*what*? I squinch my eyes shut, pressing fingers into sockets. She overheard my argument with Larisa. Of course she did. Suddenly this is all a bit much. Wing nut deviants handing out batshit flyers. Faye, stuck in her bedroom, spiraling. This Catherine, staring up at me like I'm an actual soul model with answers to anything. Larisa, out there preparing to murder us both.

I open my eyes and take a deep breath. "Just . . . try to think positive. Okay? It was only the midterm. You still have time. Focus on what's in front of you, one step at a time, and, you know. I'm sure it will all work out."

"You really think so?" Catherine smiles like I've said something prophetic. Her trust is so genuine that for a second, I almost believe it could be so simple.

OUT IN THE hallway, Larisa snorts. "Is it all sad sacks that have this effect on you?"

I blink. "We couldn't just *leave* her."

"Uh. Yeah we could."

"There's this thing called compassion," I say, making a face. "You should look it up."

"Oh yeah? Did all that compassion make a difference with your mom?"

I stop in my tracks. "What did you say?"

"I've seen the stories on the feed, Mari, what you did for her. Paying bills, basically being her parent. You probably thought you were helping, but it wasn't your job. And look where it got you. Pointless sacrifice, just like those martyrs. Another self-serving trap."

"I didn't— Self-serving? She was my *mother*." I stare at Larisa, disbelieving.

Her rhino face softens slightly. "Look, I'm not trying to be a dick, Mari, I promise. What you did in the past is in the past. Things are different now. You can't waste your time here trying to save folks who are past fixing."

I blink at her (the irony!), before slowly shaking my head. "Maybe you should take your own advice, yeah?"

I march ahead, leaving Larisa behind. Because, eff that. She doesn't know me, or Faye. She doesn't know where we've been or what I need. I haven't always gone running to save my mother, not this morning, and not last summer. Not that last time. Not when she texted me, desperate, and I—

I make it halfway to class when I remember: the flyer. I spin around, discover Larisa a few paces behind, looking contrite. "Where'd you put it?"

Her brow creases. "Put what?"

"The flyer. You know." I step closer, lower my voice. "*More than one path*, et cetera?"

Her shoulder twitches. "Oh, that? I put it in the trash. Where it belongs."

"Larisa! What if someone else finds it? What if they trace it to me? What if—"

I don't have time to figure out all the what-ifs. I push past her and run all the way back, ignoring the bell for class. But the rest room is empty, the faucets still, the garbage can filled with nothing but balled-up towels.

I kick over the can, furious. I can't believe Larisa would say those things about my mother, accuse *me* of being a martyr. She has no idea what really happened between me and Faye. None.

BEFORE

——

APRIL (6 MONTHS EARLIER)

SPRINGTIME RETURNED WITH its green shoots and flow-ers. I awoke to an early alarm. Faye came home sometime in the night. I watched as she slept, her soft hair nestled on the pillow, no sign of last night's hysteria or the gape of betrayal when I refused her ridiculous plan to move to New Hampshire and she tripped out into the rain. I know I didn't dream it, though. She'd chosen Chip. She'd chosen his big house and shady promises over the life we'd built together, leaving me (and her extremely impractical purse) behind.

And so, after she left, I—well, I'd picked up the purse and done what had to be done: I called Faye's probation officer, explained exactly what my mother had been up to.

In the pale morning light, I gathered my blankets from the couch, pulled on a fresh set of clothes. No goodbye. At school, I set my phone to silent and my mind to Calculus, *not* to the events unfolding back at the apartment, *not* to the seventeen messages blinking on my phone.

At the end of the day, I took the long way, pausing at Nonnie and Pop-Pop's old place and imagining my grandmother telling me *You're a good girl, Bunny. You make us proud.* Praying it was still true.

Back at the little apartment, I took my time jiggling the key in the lock. The studio was quiet. Sheets ripped from the bed. Spill of clothes from the closet where she'd dressed in a panic. Under the sink, my stash of cash was untouched.

"I'll be fine," I whispered to myself. "It will all be fine."

A RAP SOUNDED at the door just after dusk. A new family case-worker, this one more on the ball than the last. She informed me of my mother's arrest, and I told her she didn't have to worry about me—I had a job, was sixteen, ready to be emancipated.

Her smile thinned. "Let's not get too far ahead, okay? Tonight we need you in state care. There's a spot waiting. Up in Lynn."

Here was the part I hadn't anticipated.

"What about school? How will I get to school tomorrow?"

"They have schools in Lynn," she replied calmly.

We stared at each other for a long, slow minute.

No way was I letting her ruin everything I'd planned with Ms. Crawford, letting another school slash holes through my transcript. No way would I spend one more night in a group home. "I have family," I said, placing a big bet. "An aunt here in Brookline. Can we talk to her first?"

Twenty minutes later we pulled into my aunt Jenny's driveway. Izzy came to the door on the fifth ring, headphones dangling, gaze skewering. "Mari, what the fuck."

"Hey. Nice to see you too."

Jenny was only a shade more welcoming when she returned home a short while later, appearing frazzled. When she heard the news, my aunt, to her credit, focused her anger on her ne'er-do-well sister, not me.

The caseworker explained, "If a family member is able to step in as guardian, that's certainly preferable. Otherwise, we're talking about a DCF facility."

I made eyes at my aunt.

Jenny, murmuring something about tea, gestured at me to follow her to the kitchen.

Safe from view, she pulled me gently by the elbow. "Mari, I can't take you right now. I would, but . . ." She closed her eyes, pinched the bridge of her nose. "A few days ago, I finally did it: I filed for divorce. Your uncle won't move out, says the house is his. He's taken over the guest room and put a boot on my car. I had to take an Uber to and from work today! I don't know what I'm going to do, if we can even stay here much longer. Things are really . . . hard."

It was a little TMI, but I felt for my aunt (this explained Izzy's stink face too). Still, I needed her to listen. "I'm not asking to stay here. I just need it to *look* like I'm living with you."

I explained my plan. The guardianship thing would be temporary. I'd seek emancipation and stay in Brookline, in Mrs. MacAfee's studio, until graduation. My expenses weren't enormous. Between my job and whatever the state gives, we'd be more than covered. In less than a year, I'd be headed to college, on full scholarship if all went according to plan. I'd turn eighteen soon after that and then, well, I'd really be free.

Jenny seemed torn.

"Can we try it for a few weeks? I'll check in as often as you need."

After a bit more negotiating, Jenny relented, and we sent the caseworker packing. We sorted out the rest by phone. Emancipation—according to Jenny's lawyer—would be slow, complicated. We decided it would be easier if she stepped in formally as my guardian, on paper. She'd receive a small stipend, which she'd cash and then pass along to me to cover rent. I had my job to cover the rest.

It wasn't ideal, but I insisted I'd be fine.

And I was. I found a new rhythm. Long days at school, extra shifts at work, late nights in the silent apartment cramming for tests. I still slept on the couch, avoiding the bed that smelled of Faye's soft perfume. I didn't sleep much anyway, my dreams interrupted by Oscar's midnight escapades and visions of Faye, alone, fending for herself. Second-guessing what I'd done.

Mornings were rough. I acquired a taste for coffee.

On the one hand, I was grateful for the quiet, the chance to shape my own schedule. But there were days when I'd come home to the darkened studio and picture something different: lights, love, a warm meal in a tastefully restored country cottage. I'd fix myself boxed mac and cheese, turn on a home-reno show for company, and remind myself that I was lucky for the roof I had, this freedom.

I ignored Faye's messages and texts. The first ones came from an unrecognized number.

> Mari I need to see you
> why aren't you answering???
> did they tell you what happened?
> did you know I was arrested???
> baby, it's a big mess
> baby, let me explain
> baby, PLEASE

Through the caseworker, I knew Faye was staying at some sort of transitional facility down in Foxborough and that she was barred from returning to Brookline or seeing Chip or me according to the terms of her release. It was clear that she still had no idea what I'd done, or she wouldn't be texting me. She said she needed me, things were bad, real bad, could I come to her, she was sorry, **so sorry, please forgive me, baby???**

Sometimes, late at night, I was tempted to text back, to ask how she'd been sleeping, did her hip hurt, was she taking her meds. I made more tea instead.

School let out for summer, which simplified my schedule. I spent mornings at Boston University, taking college credits through a program Ms. Crawford had discovered. The rest of my time, I worked at the store, saving. *Chin up, eyes ahead.* I was close. So close.

Jenny called on a Tuesday morning near the end of August. "There's been an accident," she said. Faye had been struck by a bus.

Later, we'd get a few more details. A witness would attest that Faye had walked out, right into the bus's path. It was an accident, they insisted. But of course, late at night, I saw things differently. I suppose some part of me will always wonder if she did it on purpose, did it because of me.

AFTER

DAY 20

ON FRIDAY, THE day after our rest room dustup, Larisa crashes her lunch tray down across from mine and starts crunching away like nothing's happened. And like reconstituted-potato kebabs are a good idea.

It's not that I'm still *mad* about what she said about my mother—not exactly. I know Larisa was just trying to help, in her own way. Faye, meanwhile, got dressed this morning and went to class for the first time all week. She has a deep hole to climb out from, but it's a step, and it's relieved some of the tightness in my chest.

The memories Larisa stirred up haven't been pleasant. Nor has the worry she planted about that stupid flyer. I've been keeping an eye out for the mewling Catherine all morning, hoping to get the contraband back before it winds up in the wrong hands. (I can just imagine how the media would spin that one. *Hero Turned Rebel: Has Marianna Novak Gone Off the Deep End and Joined a Most Wanted Cult?*) Catherine must have snatched the flyer from the trash after we left. That's my best theory. Although I can't work out why, or what her plan was next.

"You don't think she'd join them, do you?" I ask Larisa while keeping one eye on the guards flanking the cafeteria's main exit.

"Did who join what now?"

I turn to face Larisa, who is working something green from her teeth.

"The Catherine we talked to yesterday. You don't think she'd call the number on that flyer, would she? Go join the . . . you know . . ." I lower my voice. "The Most Wanted wing nuts?"

"Nah." Larisa bats a hand. "Her? She wouldn't have the ovaries." She picks up the kebab skewer, pokes it into her teeth.

"Okay, but . . ." Something nags at me. The look in Catherine's eyes as she talked about the *terrible things* she'd done. "What if she was really in trouble? Is this how it happens when they axe someone? One day they're here, the next . . . nothing? What if I was the last person to talk to her before she—"

"Stop!" Larisa pauses her teeth-prodding. "She's a whiny twit who mucked up her afterlife. Boo-hoo. Take a number. Honestly, Mari, some folks deserve the fate they get."

"Wow. That's . . . harsh."

Larisa sets down her skewer. "No. It's real."

I'm quiet for a minute. "Is that what you'll say about me? If things go bad, and I end up . . . you know, *out there* . . . will you say I deserved my fate?"

"If you keep talking like this, I might."

A beat passes before Larisa's brow relaxes and she chucks a carrot my way.

"I'm *kidding*. Wow. You've got to learn how a joke works, Mari.

We're *friends*. Friends joke around and even argue sometimes. Then they get over it. Haven't you ever had a friend?"

I glance at my hands, which I guess is the wrong move because when I look back up, Larisa's whole face has split open with incredulity.

"I've told you, we moved a lot," I say to make it sound less pathetic.

Larisa shakes her head. "Geez, kid. No wonder you're so into sad sacks. You're the biggest one!"

I don't wait for the woof of laughter that confirms that this is, indeed, another joke. I snatch a carrot from her tray, lob it at her head.

LARISA WANTS TO use the rest of lunch period for homework, so I tell her to go on without me, that I have a quick errand to do first. Her brow quirks. ("Not Jethro," I clarify. "That's not some gross euphemism. Stop looking at me like that.") The truth is, I haven't spoken to Jethro since Larisa dragged me out of the alley yesterday. He wasn't in class this morning, and I didn't seek him out during our morning break. I'm embarrassed about what went down with Larisa and still unclear why he asked me to stay away.

After Larisa takes off toward the library, I approach one of the lunch tables by the vending machines. Hesitantly.

"Mari!!! Ooh, look, girls! Look who's finally joining us!"

The Catherines rearrange themselves to make a space for me at the center of their large table.

"Can I get you a carob smoothie?" Catherine of Milwaukee asks.

"Or how about a kale dog?" says Catherine of El Paso.

"Oh, no, thanks. I already ate . . . I was actually looking for one of you. She . . ." I scan the assortment of hair colors and headbands. "She's blond?" I say. "Or maybe you'd call it sandy?"

A blonde at the far end of the table perks up, but her face is too round, smile asymmetrical. No, she's not the same virgin.

I turn to Catherine of Milwaukee, who generally seems to be in charge. "I talked to one of you yesterday. She'd just come from her midterm and was really upset."

Milwaukee stares at me blankly. "I'm not sure who you could mean. We've all done exceptionally well on our evaluations, haven't we, girls?"

Ponytails bob vigorously.

"All right . . ." I say, now feeling uneasy. "But I definitely talked to a Catherine—from Portland, maybe? or Providence?—and she was definitely upset. I just . . . I wanted to make sure she's okay."

"Hmm," muses Catherine of Milwaukee. "Are you sure she wasn't a Caitlyn or a Christine?"

"Perhaps a Katherine with a *K*?" suggests Catherine of Pasadena.

"Or a Katie?" says Jersey City. "Ick. Katies are always so *emotional*!"

The others nod and huff, agreeing that Katies are, indeed, the worst.

My eyes narrow. Are these quote-unquote virgins gaslighting me? "She was definitely one of you. She had the headband and everything."

The Catherines shrug as a single, blank-eyed unit.

"Sorry, Mari. We don't know who you could possibly mean,"

says Catherine of Milwaukee. Beside her, a dark-haired Catherine casts a glance at Milwaukee's bleating wrist. She's totally lying! But why?

I back away from the table. I don't know what's going on here, but I'm obviously not going to get anything helpful from this bunch. So I exit the cafeteria and trace my way to the rest room we were in yesterday, unsure what I'm looking for exactly. I need a minute to think.

As soon as I get inside the stall and sit atop the mattress, an idea occurs to me. Our locations are recorded each time we enter a room at the Center, right? It's how we receive credit for attendance, and as soon as you enter a room, everyone else in proximity shows up on your feed, like a feature on a nightmarish dating app. Or maybe an extremely useful feature for moments like this. If I examine my own record, and click through to yesterday, during the afternoon break . . . Yes! There it is. Three avatars appear in this location. Larisa's, my own, and one called Annabelle Schreiber.

I click. The face that pops up is definitely her. In the space below the photo, it reads: **Catherine of Phoenix. Headstand enthusiast. #TheresAlwaysAnUpside #YougatItGirl.**

The items Annabelle/Catherine posted over the past few days—mostly inspirational memes and pictures of upside-down animals—have received zero likes. When I look back farther, I find that while she shared many of her peers' posts, they almost never reposted hers.

Her last message—a picture of an inverted otter—was posted yesterday morning during first period. She hasn't checked into any location since lunchtime yesterday.

When I toggle over her face, it says: **Current location unknown.**

AFTER

DAY 20 CONTINUED

I SPEND MY afternoon self-study period in the library's basement with Larisa. Jethro remains MIA.

Beside me, Larisa slams busily at the keys, talking to her online pals again, probably. I log in to the machine beside hers and launch a video tutorial on positive reframing. *Orphaned or abused? Betrayed by the ones you loved? How can you reframe these losses as opportunities?*

Beside me, Larisa woofs at something on her screen.

"Wild times on the board? Serious question, though: Is a chat room basically the nerd equivalent of a party?"

Larisa shoots me an irritated look. "There's a lot more to it than you think. FYI."

"More than dead teens debating plot twists from old movies with no relevance to our current situation?"

The truth is, I'm a tiny bit jealous. Larisa has all of these other friends online, and I just have her.

Larisa hits a few more keys, ignoring me. Then, as if changing her mind, she stands and twists her screen toward me. The interface seems raw, old-fashioned compared to the apps we use for class. It's basically just long strings of dense green text. "Is this supposed to be proof of how it's not boring?"

"Look closer." She points to a lengthy—no paragraph breaks— spiel by a user called TruthOrDie, who evidently has a lot to say about transcendental philosophy.

"Oh, yeah. Changed my mind. That sounds *super* interesting."

"You have to look beyond the code, dodo. They're talking about transcending the baseline curriculum, finding your truth."

"Uhhh. Similar to those wing nuts you told me about? The ones you were shouting about yesterday?"

"Nah. These folks aren't causing anarchy. They're like low-key philosophers. They ask some interesting questions about this place too. Like, whatever happened to the third guy who supposedly helped found Paradise Gate? And what happens to unaffiliated souls that don't get scooped up by the PTB? Where are they? Have any of them created their own settlements?"

"They think there might be other afterlives?"

Larisa lifts both palms. "It makes more sense than thinking this is the only one, doesn't it? Or that the PTB were the only ones to figure it out. But . . . listen." Larisa glances behind us. "That's not why I'm on here. These guys talk about practical stuff too."

"Stuff like what?"

Larisa bites her lip. Then: "Okay, look. Right here." She points to a thread in which a commenter called ForceBU has asked some very detailed questions about the father-son relationship in *Star Wars*. "ForceBU is me."

"You're looking for Darth Vader? I knew you were pretty geeky, but . . ."

"Ugh." Larisa huffs, then hesitates. She turns to face me, as if trying to decide something. "I can trust you, yeah? We're really friends?"

"Of course. Yes." I smile a bit bashfully. "Yes, we're really friends."

"Okay. Well, then." She points at the screen. "I've been trying to find out what happened to my dad. You know, I'm Luke and he's—"

"Hang on. You have a dad?"

Larisa pops her eyes like I'm an idiot. "Yeah? He died when I was little?"

Right. Okay. I thought she was like me, with a single parent from the get-go. But this backstory makes sense too.

"So, then, you think he's here?"

"Unclear. When I first got here, I searched for him on the ascension list, obviously, but he grew up Christian and still was sort of spiritual, so I figured he'd gone . . . wherever semi-Christians go. But then a couple of weeks ago, I was looking up my mentions on the feed and it pulled up an old post of his. Franklin Liu. It was totally him! His face, his twisted sense of humor. He was here, taking classes, poking fun at the breath exercises, and then . . . he wasn't."

"What does that mean? He just disappeared?"

"Are you even listening? That's what I'm trying to find out! When you mentioned the ascension numbers last week, it got me wondering too. And then when I saw that flyer—you know, *Speak Your Truth*, *Look to the Next Level*, et cetera . . . it hit me: My dad was totally *that* guy. All about sticking it to the man. My mom said that's what got him in so much trouble. She worried I'd turn out like him. Which—sidebar—maybe I have in some ways. Point is, I'm thinking maybe my pops got caught up with these folks somehow, that he took things too far. Again."

Larisa's dad sounds a bit like Faye. That's the first piece of the story that sinks in. Then, "So *you* took the flyer." That's the next part that lands.

"Oh. Yeah. Sorry about that. I didn't want to worry you. I needed to figure this out on my own."

"And?"

"And what?"

"Have you found him?"

She shakes her head. I look closer at the screen. ForceBU has made what looks like dozens of posts in the past twenty-four hours. Most got few if any responses.

"You must be really worried," I say, suddenly understanding Larisa's recent edginess. Her rudeness that day as we left the Center, our spat in the rest room. It really wasn't all about me.

"Sure . . . I guess." She lifts a shoulder.

"Larisa, this is your *dad* we're talking about."

"Yeah." She shrugs again, but her eyes, stuck on the screen, have a faraway look. "None of this is really a surprise, though, or it shouldn't be. He was a big mess. It's just . . ." Her lips twist. "The way I remember it, he wasn't a bad guy, like, not on purpose. He made a lot of mistakes, took things too far, sure. But deep down, he had a giant heart. He just *cared* too much, maybe. He didn't deserve . . ." Her voice trails off.

"Eternal three a.m."

"Exactly." Larisa's chin has lost its rhino edge. She seems smaller somehow, less together. I want to say something comforting, but what? If Larisa's father has been pushed off the grid—if he's out there now, lost in eternal self-torture—nothing I can say will change it.

"You can't mention this to anyone, okay?" Larisa says.

" 'Course not." I know what it's like to wrestle with a parent's messy legacy. I wouldn't add to her stress.

"I'm serious. You rat and you're dead to me." She mimes a knife across her throat.

"Are you really making a death threat right now?"

"It's metaphorical. You should be terrified."

We both crack smiles. Dead-people humor. It's . . . a lot.

I'm honored that Larisa would trust me with this secret, and a little relieved (selfishly) to know her past has tangled bits too. It makes me want to share something knotty of my own.

"You know what you said yesterday about my mother?"

"Oof." Larisa grimaces. "Sorry. I took that too far. Always do. Got that from my pops, I guess." Her grimace becomes an apologetic grin.

"It's fine. I mean, I was pissed when you said it. You weren't completely wrong. But you weren't right either. It's . . ." I take a deep breath, check to confirm we're alone. "I didn't always go running to help my mom," I tell her. "I did for a long time, but . . ."

I tell her about Chip, their arrest, and everything that came after—the shelter, our return to Brookline, our slow recovery—then the blowup when she announced, out of nowhere, that they were back together and she was going to marry him.

It takes a few hesitating breaths before I can say the next part.

"I turned her in."

It's a thing I haven't told anyone. After I called the probation officer, reported that Faye was violating two major terms of her probation—consorting with her criminal accomplice and planning to leave the state—they came for her. A day later, child welfare came for me.

"Daaayum." Larisa sits all the way back in her chair. I try to read her expression. She must think I'm a monster. What kind of person turns her own mother in to the cops?

"What happened then? Did she wind up in prison?"

"For a few days. Yeah." I'm too ashamed to tell Larisa the rest—the texts I ignored after her release, Faye's desperate pleas for forgiveness. The news that came shortly after: She'd walked out in front of a bus. How I knew that her death was in some part my fault.

"Hang on." Larisa's brow furrows. "What happened to that Chip dude? Did he know what you did? Was he pissed? Mari"—Larisa grabs my arm—"*was he the shooter?*"

I unwind my arm from Larisa's grip. "That's—I think you've watched too many movies—that's not at all what I'm saying."

"Okay. So what *are* you saying?" Larisa eyes me carefully, gently. "Mari, I'm real sorry you were put in that position, but your mom made her own mess. What happened obviously wasn't your—"

"Yes, it—"

"Shhh." She clamps a hand on my mouth (rude!), then rises slowly from her chair, peering over the carrel.

Ugh. The last thing I need is some gossipy Catherine knowing about this. I stand too, but the opposite carrel is empty. And so, it seems, is the rest of the room.

Larisa puts a finger to her lips, and I follow her gaze to the bookshelves near the stairs. There's a gap among the spines, a swatch of flannel peeking through. Is it—

"Jethro?"

"Mari?"

He emerges, looking as startled to see me as I am him. He places a book back on the shelf and begins to cross the room.

"What are you doing here?" we both say at the same time.

"Stalker much," Larisa mutters. I wave at her to hush.

"We were just . . . catching up on work," I lie, as Larisa smoothly shuts down her computer.

Jethro doesn't explain his own presence. Was he looking for a book, or for me? Where was he all morning?

"Sorry, I didn't mean to interrupt . . ." Eyeing Larisa, he starts to backtrack toward the stairs. Something in his slouch draws me forward.

"No, it's . . . fine. We're basically done here anyway, right?" I nudge Larisa. "We were just doing some, uh, extra credit."

"You're extra *something*," Larisa mutters, reaching for her bag.

I feel Jethro watching, his eyes shifting between us, and I don't know what to do. I don't want Larisa to be mad, but I don't want Jethro to think I don't want to hang out with him either, especially after that weird confrontation in the alley. I've never been in a situation like this before—with multiple people vying for my attention.

Jethro retreats another step, chin tipped in invitation. My pulse quickens. I glance back at Larisa. Does she want me to stay? Is she going to be mad about this? But she waves me off with an expression I can't quite read.

Okay . . . I guess I choose Jethro.

JETHRO AND I have made it up the stairs and partway across the library's main floor, me with a pit in my gut, wondering if I made the wrong call, when something pulls me from my thoughts. The silence. It's way too quiet. The library's main floor usually hums with activity, but the students appear frozen. A few exchange whispers, while others glance down at their feeds, then up at me.

Stomach sinking, I double-click on my muted tracker. My feed explodes to life.

I scroll quickly, discover a sea of applause and halo emojis, GIFs of superheroes with my face cropped in, and a small, grainy image of a girl boarding a bus, captioned *"NOT TODAY!"*

"What the—"

On a large flat screen above the circulation desk, a video is playing of a crowded sidewalk, a bus waiting at the curb. Then a body lying still on the ground. Someone in the video screams for an ambulance.

The camera zooms in on the body's face—*my* face—and I see myself take one last shuddery breath.

My current self lurches forward, and Jethro's hand finds my back, steadying me.

"What . . . is this?"

Jethro scrolls on his own device. He's trying to make sense of it too.

The large screen is now playing an interview with . . . who *is* that? I draw closer.

"Our young witness, recently arrived in Paradise Gate after twenty days in a medically induced coma, says she knew Marianna Novak, that they'd interacted on numerous occasions. She is the second victim of the same gunman responsible for Novak's death, and she asked that we call her Z."

The screen cuts to a woman in bone-white newbie pajamas. Her face is turned from the camera, shielded by a curtain of sand-colored hair. "Sorry," she murmurs. "I'm sorry. Could you ask the question again?" She speaks in a soft singsong, like she's afraid to be heard. The reporter repeats a question about how she knew me, and realization slams into me like a fast-charging train.

Sorry, I'm so sorry. Can you spare some change?

"Z" is the girl who camped out at the T stop near my apartment, the one whose requests tugged at me even when I didn't have much to give.

"She stopped almost every day to give me a dollar or two," a faceless Z tells the reporter. "Some mornings, she was the only one who'd stop."

"Can you tell us about the day of the incident?" the reporter asks.

Z nods, squares her shoulders. "Let's see. It was a rough morning. Lot of noise. They had shuttles running 'cause of construction on the tracks. Normally Saturdays are quiet, but everything was backed up and people were upset. I saw Mari coming and asked if she could spare anything. She gave me a dollar. I could tell she was in a rush."

"Please tell our viewers what happened next."

Z winds her fingers through a long, sandy lock. "Well . . . I didn't see all of it. My memory is still fuzzy . . ."

"Just share what you can recall."

A quick, wavery exhale. "So there was a crowd, right? A shuttle bus had just pulled up, like the ones they use when the trains aren't running? And the people were all angry and stuff, down by the curb. I was in my usual spot, minding my business. And then some lady screams and people start running—like, *away* from the bus. That's when I saw her."

"Miss Novak?"

"Yeah. She was at the back door of the bus, already halfway on the steps, and there was a sound, a shot. She turned around quick— to see or whatever—and that's when she—"

"That's when she shouted?" the reporter offers.

"—that's when she punched him."

"She *what*?" The reporter gasps, delighted by this twist.

Z nods nervously, and the reporter makes her repeat the statement two more times. "She punched the guy, the shooter, right to the ground."

The storyline falls apart at this point. They cut to jumbled footage of people running, while Z explains that she didn't exactly *see* my fist connect, but I looked super mad, and no, she didn't hear what I'd shouted. Everyone else was yelling too. And that's the last thing she recalls.

"Because that gunshot you'd heard seconds earlier—it had struck you."

The girl nods.

"Did you see who it was? The person who killed you?"

Z twitches, fingers still twining, and shakes her head.

The reporter makes a dramatic spin to the audience. "Here we have it, an eyewitness who attests to Marianna Novak's generous spirit and knockout courage. Although this new angle certainly raises questions, it offers further evidence that we have a true soul model among us. Catch more analysis at five o'clock!"

Everyone in the library turns from the screen to me. One by one, they begin to clap. I'm frozen, still staring as the program shifts to a PSA about emotional self-harm. I'm trying to make sense of what we've just heard. "Z." The shuttle, all those people rushing. I can almost see the scene as it was that morning—as it must have occurred—but—

"Mari?"

"Why would she lie?" I turn to Jethro.

"What do you mean?"

"I didn't give her a dollar that day. I had lots of other times, but I know for sure that I didn't that day. *Why did she lie?*"

Jethro's eyes flicker. He glances behind me, and I become aware of the small crowd of students who've gathered. A trio of Catherines, cheering. "Mari! Ooh, Mari! You *attacked* that guy! We *knew* you were a shero. We totally totally *believed*!"

My head suddenly feels all wrong—glitchy, swimmy, tight.

"Come on." Jethro pulls me away out into the hallway, where there's more room to breathe. He waits as I press my forehead, trying to piece together what we just heard.

Train construction explains why I'd be on a bus. It was the morning of the SATs. I would have been headed to the high school. I'd woken up . . . late. Bits come into view: the surge of adrenaline when I realized what time it was. I scrambled to dress—no shower, no breakfast—and hurried to the T only to learn it wasn't running. I'd never make it. I was going to miss my test, the test I'd been cramming for all spring. Someone was trying to get my attention—that girl with the whiny lilt, always looking for help and always knowing I'd give it because I was such a sucker. "Sorry," she whined, more insistently than usual. "Sorry, could you—" and I pushed past her, barked: "No. Can't."

Running, pushing, my feet grab the step just in time, a tug on my arm, and I spin. That pushy little bitch, always there, always pleading, didn't she understand the word *no*? I turned to face her, opened my mouth to shout—

I wobble as I realize.

"Mari?" Jethro has me by the arm. "What is it?"

Students have begun to swirl around, and he places himself between them and me, his gaze like cool stones in a river of froth.

"Is it coming back? Your memory?"

A thousand question-worries splinter outward as I realize: It was Z I shouted at, not the shooter. To her I cried: *Not today.* Was the shooter there the whole time, waiting? I try to picture the moment, the one where I turned, said those words, but it's still a big bright blank.

"Mari, we need to get out of here." Jethro uses his shoulder as a shield against the curious onlookers, but they only press in closer.

Z lied about at least one crucial detail, likely more, and now those vultures will be searching. They'll be pecking through my archive and hers, trying to make sense of it. They'll soon realize it's not how it seems. I didn't shout down—or punch—a shooter. I shouted at a girl who had nothing because I was tired and stressed out and alone. I'd chosen speed over kindness. Just as, a few weeks earlier, I'd chosen ambition over my own mother.

I drop my head onto my fists, pounding my temples. If they judged my fashion so meanly, I can only imagine what they'll make of this.

Jethro pulls my hands from my face. "Stop, Mari. Don't do that. Just—what do you need? Do you want to go home?"

"I *want* them to stay out of my effing business!"

Not an achievable goal, obviously. But Jethro pauses, looks at me strangely.

"I know this place. It's . . ." He glances behind him at all the students swarming, then back to me. "You can look things up, from your past, and put a cap on anything you want kept private."

My mouth hinges open.

"Yeah. It's not exactly . . . legal or whatever." Doubt skitters across his face. "Is that what you want, though? What are you thinking? Mari? Say something."

"I'm thinking, why are we still standing here? Fuck it, let's go!"

I throw out both elbows and blast through the gathered students. Jethro follows close behind.

WE'RE QUIET AS the bus pulls out of Paradise Gate's busy center and toward the eastern settlements.

Jethro uses his trick to disable the GPS on our trackers. He sits quietly, watching as I tremble against the glass, fighting back a fresh wave of memory.

BEFORE

"SORRY, PLEASE. CAN you help me?"

She shakes her cup, reaches a skinny arm as if to a stranger. But can you be a stranger to someone you see every day? To someone who's seen you at your absolute worst?

In January, soon after we'd arrived back in Brookline, there was an incident. Faye hated her new job. It was mind-numbing, she said. Meaningless. She wanted to go north to see her friends, the ones with the commune. I listened silently, filled her up with caffeine, and insisted she take the early train with me. Left to her own devices, I knew she'd go back to bed.

"It's too hard," she whined when we reached the outbound platform. "I'm not made for this life."

"What are you talking about?"

"This." She pointed to her close-fitted skirt, the platform full of commuters, and in what may have been an unintentional flourish, or an accidental slip of truth, her finger circled me.

I fought to check my anger, held it in until the inbound train arrived, until the people piled on and the train disappeared with a deafening clatter. When the noise faded, I was screaming.

"You're not made for this? You're not made for being my mother? You're not made for being a goddamn adult?! Well, maybe you should just . . . go away then! Leave! I'd be better off without you!"

I recognized, too late, that we weren't alone. Our audience had shrunk to one. An amber-eyed girl hunched by the poster-size station map, a cup at her feet.

Faye was crying, then sobbing, begging me to understand. Her coat came unbuttoned. She dropped her silly purse. I cussed at her. "You're right," Faye moaned wetly. "I'm no good."

The girl pretended to look away, but who was she kidding?

I didn't wait for our train to arrive. I walked to school alone.

AFTER THAT, I'D see the girl Z every day. A golden-eyed reminder of my screaming ugliness, holding out her cup like a nun exacting penance. She was there on the platform the morning after Faye was arrested, and again on the morning after Faye died.

She was there the day I died too.

"Not today!" I shouted as I ran toward the bus, sensing her behind me, pleading, demanding . . .

The pieces shuffle into a new order, a different meaning. My single-minded focus on college. Those final frenzied days—*chin up, eyes ahead.* The sense that everywhere I went, Faye followed, nipping at my heels.

Back in early January at the shelter, Faye had put her mistakes in the rearview. *Let's go back to Brookline,* I insisted, but Faye offered up a million excuses. *Rent in Brookline is sky-high. I haven't talked to my sister in years. I prefer to move forward, not back.* I held strong and won. I was looking out for us, returning to the one place I knew to be stable. That's what I told her and myself.

And everything *was* better for a while.

Until it really wasn't.

The day before the SATs, I arrived at school out of sorts. Out of cash, low on food and sleep, the future so close I could taste it. Faye's death hung from my shoulders like a massive boulder.

Ms. Crawford guided me into her office after the last bell. "I was checking over your FAFSA." She closed the door, caught my panicked look. "You did everything fine. I was rechecking the guardianship rules and needed to confirm a few things with your aunt."

Zing of panic. "You called Jenny?"

"Mari, why didn't you tell me? About your mother. She . . . you didn't tell me she . . ." Ms. Crawford's eyes filled. "Your mother *died*?"

I needed her to stop.

"Jenny is my legal guardian. That hasn't changed. I don't see what this has to do with financial aid."

"Well." Ms. Crawford touched her temple. "Your aunt informed me that your mother had some accounts, some investments."

"She what?" Jenny had called a few times this past week, but I was so busy studying that I hadn't found the time to call her back. "Scam accounts, you mean?"

Did Chip screw over my mother too? Was I on his hook? I felt faint from lack of sleep, felt it all spiraling.

"It wasn't a scam, Mari. Your mother, when she passed, was actually quite wealthy."

"What? But that's not—"

Chip, with his big house and wedding ring. Chip, promising the impossible. Faye, walking out into the path of a bus. I began shaking so hard I couldn't stand, though I wanted more than anything to run, to leave before Ms. Crawford could say anything more.

"Your aunt believes Mr. Randall set up the accounts for his own benefit, as a sort of shelter scheme. One investment did especially well. There was a prenup outlining Mr. Randall as the beneficiary, but then when she didn't . . . when they didn't . . ." Again Ms. Crawford's eyes fill. "Because they never married, the money goes to you."

It sounds crass, but I have to ask: "Is it enough for college?"

"Mari, it's over a million dollars."

MAYBE I PASSED out. I don't know. The next thing I knew, we were sitting in chairs, and Ms. Crawford was filling me in on the rest. All of this had come out when my aunt Jenny hired a lawyer to handle Faye's affairs. Things immediately turned complicated. Chip was arguing they had a civil union, that the money was his. Everything was jammed up among lawyers and likely would be for some time. In other words, I was rich on paper, and only that. Barred from most financial aid while also penniless.

Ms. Crawford sighed. "It's extremely unfair."

Everything I'd worked for. All those hours studying, all the ways I'd pinched and scrambled just so I could have a real shot. The terrible decision I'd made to turn in Faye. It was all pointless.

Maybe the money would come to me someday. Maybe it wouldn't. It didn't matter. There was no way the lawyers would have this sorted out in time for me to finish my aid application, and there was no way I could pay for school next fall without a federal grant.

"There are still merit scholarships," Ms. Crawford said. "Those aren't based on income. You have excellent grades and a sympathetic story. With a knockout SAT score . . ." Her voice trailed off. We both knew scholarships, on their own, weren't enough.

"Thank you for telling me. Thank you for everything."

I lifted my chin, let it pull me to my feet. What else could I do?

Back at home, I broke open the SAT books and stared at them until night fell. In the margin beside the test problems, I scratched out some math—the money I'd need to pay for college outright (impossible), the cost of staying in Brookline on my own (also impossible).

Was this it? Was this the point where I gave up and accepted a life of never having enough, of bouncing from bad situation to bad situation like Faye had her entire adult life? Was our past to be my destiny?

I stayed up all night, plotting, cramming, too stubborn to give in . . . yet.

The next thing I knew, the sun was shining on the table where I'd fallen asleep. I jumped up, snatched my dead phone from a dead socket—the electricity cut again—and found Faye's watch beside her bed.

I was late for the test. Very, very late.

It was a long shot, chance of success barely more than zero, but I had already lost so much. Long shots were all I had left. Still in yesterday's clothes, I flew toward the train, running, reaching.

AFTER

DAY 20 CONTINUED

THE BUS GLIDES away, leaving me and Jethro in front of a wasteland of trash heaps and pitted pavement. Last stop, end of the line. To the right, there's a wall marking the edge of a gated community—the last of the settlement—and farther beyond, a smooth road leads back to safety. To the left, the landscape changes. A long chain-link fence blocks off what appears to be an enormous lot filled with grit and rust. It's hard to tell what's back there because the whole scene has an uneven texture, blurred with patches and dark spots, like the whole thing's been filtered through a pair of dirty glasses . . . or like this entire reality has gone on the fritz. I try to pull the scene into focus, to pick out the soupy lines of concrete hollows where structures once stood, of giant piles of rubble and blackened metal shards. A few hazy buildings are scattered along the periphery, a testament to whatever stood there before. The rest has crumbled back into pixels.

Jethro watches me take it all in. "The next bus will be here in twenty minutes. You can still change your mind."

And let the media continue harvesting my memories without my consent? Go an eternity without knowing who killed me?

"Nope. I'm doing this. Let's go."

On the way over, Jethro explained a bit about where we're headed—a place where folks have hacked into the archive, accessing all the camera-like memories that were uploaded when each of us was hooked onto the grid. (A onetime upload, unaffected by everything that's happened since.) I can lock down any memory I want to keep to myself, but Jethro explained that I'll need to be careful. Too many blocks will raise flags and can have nasty side effects. My plan, then, is to go in, find out what really happened on my final morning, block off the bits I want kept private, and leave the rest be.

Jethro reaches for a section of the fence that's been slit, lifts its ragged flap, and waits as I scuttle through.

Inside, the scene is even more striking. All jagged lines and crumbled structures. Like refuse from a war zone or the ruins of a past civilization.

Jethro, as if reading my mind, explains: "This is what's left of the previous settlement. Before Paradise Gate."

"Right," I say, as if it had occurred to me that the afterlife might have its own *before*.

"How did you find this place?" I ask him.

"It's kind of a long story. I'll tell you when we're someplace safe. We should hurry now in case someone spots us."

We pick our way past the mounds of dirt, sticking close to the chain-link perimeter and skirting the soupy patches. I remember what Jethro warned me in the alley: Touch a gap that's big enough, and it could suck you right off the grid.

I keep my eyes focused in front of my feet, shove back the junk in my head that wants to surface—that girl Z, my panic, Faye's texts, her face streaming tears, eyes wide with shock—

"Watch it." Jethro grabs my elbow, pulling me away from a body-size gap. I look up at him, grateful. He's standing taller than usual, appears more confident, purposeful. We still haven't talked about what he said to me yesterday—his suggestion that we stop hanging out. At this point, all that seems irrelevant. I have bigger concerns now.

We reach the center of the lot, a hulking shell of brick that appears to be an old warehouse of sorts. Jethro guides me to the back entrance, where two hollowed-out trucks flank a metal door stamped with a crude swirl. An infinity symbol. Like the one on that contraband flyer.

Was Larisa right? Is Jethro involved with those afterworld wing nuts?

I consider my options. If I go back to the settlement now, I may never know the whole truth of how I died. I'll be forced to sit helpless as a bunch of incompetent reporters try to make sense of it on their own. Or I can take this calculated risk: one time, one visit, put my past into the rearview, under my own control, and finally move on.

Jethro motions for me to hide, so I crouch behind the nearest metal carcass while he approaches the warehouse. I listen for his knock, the brief silence that follows, then the groan of hinges, a murmured exchange. The door closes and moments later creaks open again. This time, a different voice, followed by a sharp hiss. "Come on!" Jethro's hand beckons.

I emerge slowly from my rusted hiding place, then pause.

I'm not sure who I expected to see. A burly bouncer? Wizened mobster? In the open doorway stands a girl not much older than us. Chestnut skin, tight dreadlocks tipped in crimson, ears studded in silver. I touch my own naked lobes instinctively, but my piercings disappeared with my scars and chewed nails.

"You sure about this?" the girl says to Jethro, giving me a doubtful once-over. She's dressed in dark colors, like Jethro, but her combat-cut pants and asymmetrical top have more style, more edge. It's unclear whether she recognizes me from all the tabloids or just doesn't like my look.

"She's cool," Jethro tells her. "I told you, Havel cleared this."

The girl hesitates, and I glance at Jethro. *Who's Havel?*

Jethro misreads my question, points his chin back in the direction we came, asking, do I want to go back? I shake my head. No, I have to do this.

I swallow any remaining doubts and follow the girl inside.

She guides us down a narrow hallway and into a large, echoing hangar. I crane to get a glimpse of a—spaceship? submarine? The vessel in question is unlike anything I've seen before, its armor-gray sides pocked with long arms like caterpillars, the front end banged up like it's been through more than one war.

The girl makes a clicking sound and Jethro nudges me forward.

We descend a clanging set of metal stairs to a large basement room filled with a subterranean light. One wall is filled with maps hashed with black markings and dashes of chalk. Long tables slice through the open room, hosting a few dozen computers unlike any I've seen anywhere. Old, boxy monitors have been patched to a tangle of metal plates and copper wires. Each one is stamped with what's becoming a familiar infinity symbol.

The girl points us toward one of the Frankenstein computers. There are fifteen or twenty other people seated at monitors, all dressed in dark colors and camouflage, like members of some kind of punk rock army. No one acknowledges our presence.

"Who are all these people?" I whisper after our guide has disappeared.

Jethro places a finger to his lips and presses a button. "You don't see them, they don't see you."

The computer groans to life. The screen that comes up looks even more outdated than Larisa's chat room.

"It's pretty old-school," Jethro says. "They built all of this themselves."

"But what *is* it?"

"It's basically a port into the main server, a way to access all of the data saved on the grid."

Jethro types quickly, and I wonder how many times he's been here before. He mentioned a dead uncle, unanswered questions. Maybe he came here on a quest of his own.

"Here. I've got it," he says after a moment.

He plays the same clip they had on the news, only this one is longer, more complete, filling in everything from when Z first saw me arrive at the T stop until the ambulance drove away.

"We can look inside other people's archives too?"

"Yup. Anyone who's passed through the settlement. Everything that was in their brain when they died—all the physical memories anyway; thoughts are more complicated—now lives on the server."

I take in all the snaking wires and patched-up computers, trying to wrap my head around it: the idea that so many thousands of histories, existences, could be coded and uploaded and held as bits of data.

It's tedious work, I soon realize, scrolling through all that footage, trying to interpret so many disembodied sounds and images. No wonder the PTB's reporters miss so much. We comb through Z's final moments several times but don't find a direct view of the shooter or of my alleged punch.

"Check it out." Jethro clicks, and dotted lines sprout from the image, threading together other perspectives on the same moment. Most of the threads end in black dots: inaccessible. (Folks who are still alive, presumably.) Only one other dot is active. Jethro clicks and suddenly we're seeing the same scene from my point of view. We rewind to the moment I arrived at the T stop. Jethro hits the play button again, and I'm running toward the bus. *Sorry, sorry. Help me, please help me.* A low whine cuts beneath the chatter, the hum of cars whizzing up the street. I press pause to view each face more closely but recognize no one. Live Mari scrambles onto the bus, squeezing into the last spot on the steps. There's a sound, a blast. She/I turn. She/I bellow: "NOT TODAY!"

There's still no view of the shooter. Instead the screen seems to tumble as live Mari falls, slamming hard to the ground. The sound of feet shuffling. A scream. Then darkness.

I stare into the blank screen, feeling the scream's residue reverberate in my head.

After a moment, Jethro clears his throat. "It must be tough, not knowing. Who did it, I mean."

"Yeah." I swallow. Until a little while ago, I never thought I'd know the story of my death. Now, crucial pieces have been filled in, everything except the who and the why. Maybe there is no why. I guess the only good news is that if I don't know, the PTB's minions will never know either.

"Block it," I say.

"Really?" Jethro looks at me. "Why?"

"Because I look like a monster, screaming at some girl who asked for help."

"No one's going to blame you for being in a rush, Mari."

"Have you ever been on the feed? They judge everything. Block it, please. Or cap it, whatever the word is. Just make it go away." I watch Jethro make the fix and then say, "I need to look for some other things too. Can you walk me through the steps and then, like, go away? Sorry."

But I'm not. Sorry. Now that I've seen how easy it is to clean up the past, I have a few other things to take care of, and I can't do it with Jethro watching. I need to do this myself.

"Uh, sure." Jethro hesitates before showing me how to search by date and key word. My own archive is littered with the bread-crumbs of other people's searches. Some memories (the ones I've seen on TV) have been flagged or downloaded multiple times, while others appear untouched.

Jethro warns me not to block long stretches. "Anything more than a few minutes will draw attention, and if the Powers discover that you've been manipulating your memories . . ." He makes a slic-ing motion.

"Yup. Understood."

Jethro migrates to another computer, and I quickly locate the day I made the call to Faye's probation officer: block. (That was less than one minute.) Then I look for Faye's last few texts. It takes a while to find all of them, and only when I'm done do I remember I need to lock down her perspective too. She sent the first two from a friend's apartment. Block. The third comes from a park bench, and the fourth from what appears to be the inside of an old factory. She's huddled on the concrete floor. I recognize the suitcase beside her, the heel of her extremely impractical shoe. The next text comes from the same location. There's a low murmur, and I pick out the silhouettes of two more people. I rewind to a moment where Faye checks herself in a smeary mirror, her hair dull, face pale. She places a hand on her hip, wincing. I watch as she walks along streets I don't know, her step uneven, as she pauses to send another text.

I fast-forward, find a spot where the footage gets wobbly. She's running. Toward what? Or from whom?

"Whose archive is that?" Jethro reappears behind my chair.

"My mom's," I murmur, still mesmerized by what I've seen. Was Faye living on the street? Hiding? Why wasn't she in the transitional shelter? Who or what made her run?

"Nope. Bad idea." He reaches over, lands a few keystrokes, and the scene disappears.

"But—"

"No. Trust me. You don't want to mess with other folks' archives. You can view but don't touch."

He continues typing something, leaning close enough that I can feel his soft flannel against my neck.

"What are you doing?"

"Covering your tracks."

I don't want to make a scene or draw attention to my presence, so I let Jethro finish, and when he suggests we leave, I follow quietly.

If I need to come back here, I'll have to finagle a way in on my own.

AFTER

DAY 20 CONTINUED

DINNER IS TENSE. I can feel Faye waiting for me to say something, perhaps praise her. She made it through a full day of classes, her first since the ParadiseMart fiasco. They've assigned an afterlife mentor who's supposed to help her get back on track. I still sense the blame in her eyes.

I've been watching the feed nervously for more revelations about my final weeks, for some gossip-hungry reporter to stumble on the memories I put a block on earlier today. So far they haven't. It seems the trick Jethro showed me may have actually worked.

I watch Faye take bird bites of her meal and wonder if she's been doing her own recollecting. Did she recognize Z in the interview? Has she been thinking about all those unanswered texts? Whatever's on Faye's mind, she doesn't say it. Her gaze keeps traveling toward my face, though, like she's searching for something.

"What?" I finally ask, exasperated.

"Nothing, honey." She pulls an innocent frown. "I just wondered if you might like to watch some TV."

"Huh? Yeah. Okay. That's ..."

I reach for the remote and slide my chair around to face the living room. I spin through the dial, skipping past two "news" channels for something that will be safe for both of us. I land on a new episode of *The Dead and the Restless*. (Spoiler: They're still dead.) It's perfect.

The TV's chatter relieves some of the tension, but it doesn't do anything to ease the noise in my head. So many unfinished thoughts and questions have piled up since my chat with Larisa in the library. She seemed to think that my call to Faye's PO wasn't that bad (which I doubt Faye would agree with), and then there was the stuff I saw in Faye's archive this afternoon. I picture her couched alone in that warehouse, wobbling out into the street with a desperate, hunted expression. After I'd ignored her cries for help.

"Baby?" Faye's looking at me funny, hand outstretched. It takes me a moment to realize that the show has cut to commercial. She's reaching for my plate.

"Did you do it on purpose?" I blurt.

Her hand drops back to her side and she stares at me, feigning incomprehension, but she must know what I'm asking. It's the question that's been on my mind since that muggy August morning when I learned she'd died.

"Did you commit suicide? Did you do it because of me?"

"*What?* Oh, baby." Faye falls into her chair, her eyes disbelieving. "Is that what you've been thinking this whole time?"

I glance at my fingers and shrug.

"Oh, baby. No. No, no, *no*. With a bus? What a way to go!

Who would choose that? No, baby, it was an accident. You know me, such a flake, never looking where I'm going. It was bad timing, terrible, terrible luck. I didn't . . . I wouldn't . . . Why would you think . . . ?"

She appears genuinely confused.

"Because I moved on. I was making a life without you. Because I . . ." I still can't say it, the part about the phone call. "Because I didn't answer a single one of your texts."

Her expression turns sad.

"Was Chip threatening you? About those accounts? Is that why you needed my help?"

"Chip?" Her face shifts back to incredulity. "Why on earth . . . ? No, baby, he was living on some island near the Bahamas last I heard. Probably still is."

There's a pause as I take this in.

"Yup. Turns out it's a great place to sell fake vacation shares, or yachts, or whatever it is he's doing now."

"So you never heard from him after the arrest?"

"Aside from one email instructing me to send back the engagement ring? Nada." She drops her ringless hands onto the table and sighs. "For the best, I suppose. You were right about Chip, honey. He was *not* a good man."

At least we can finally agree on that.

She still hasn't responded to what I said about my moving on without her, how that affected her in her final days, but that feels like a much bigger conversation.

"Sweetie, what was that you said about accounts?" Faye's brow furrows again.

"Nothing." I shake my head. "It's . . . really, nothing." If Faye doesn't know Chip's marriage proposal was another get-rich scheme, I don't need to add to her shame.

The commercial break has ended, and we return to tracking the ins and outs of a plot far more improbable than our own. (The protagonist has fallen for a neighbor who she has yet to discover is a dangerous rebel in disguise. The rebel, meanwhile, can't seem to keep his snarling backstory straight, and neither of them are getting any closer to actualization.) At one point, Faye twitches in my direction, like she wants to ask something else but then reconsiders. I want to ask her things too—like, why were her final text messages so frantic? Where was that place she was staying near the end? But I'm not supposed to have seen all of that, and I'm not sure I want to know either. So we sit side by side, holding our tongues, as between us the ledger of unspoken items grows.

The episode comes to its usual cliff-hanger: Will they correct course in time or lose their one shot at redemption? Does anyone really care? I exhale and check my wrist.

"I should get going on homework, I guess."

"Right. That's my girl. Always so focused."

Faye doesn't say anything about her own homework, just watches as I gather our dishes and stack them in the sink.

FREEDOME RELEASES A new poem minutes before midnight. I'm awake, of course. (I'm always awake.) This one is shorter than the last, words landing like strong beats of a drum.

The problem isn't you
You are everything you need
The question isn't how
The tools you choose are irrelevant
The question is when
When will you finally face your truth?

Freedome's settings don't allow screenshots, so I read it over and over until, after a few minutes, the poem disappears, and I make another attempt at sleep.

AFTER

DAY 23

I ARRIVE AT the Center early on Monday, exhausted by two days of nonstop scrolling and thoughts. Although I have plenty of questions about this whole PTB setup (see: the fee surcharges, murky ascension rates, and relentless positivity), a part of me is looking forward to the regulated schedule, a more containable task.

The tide of online gossip shifted this morning, and my feed has gone mercifully quiet. Maybe this week will be the one, I think, the restart I need, a chance to rack up points, chill my vibes, and get on the right track. Or maybe it's pathological: this belief, however tenuous, that my efforts matter, that success is still possible.

Chin up, Bunny. Don't think like that.

As soon as I enter the Center's front lobby, I discover the cause of the online shift. One of my classmates has gone missing.

"Her details aren't public yet," Catherine of Milwaukee tells me as she links an arm with mine, "but my breath worker talks to this other breath guy who chants with *her* energy specialist sometimes, so . . ." Pointed eyebrow. Milwaukee's got the inside scoop.

Catherine of Albuquerque has been analyzing the missing girl's feed, which has some seriously weird posts. ("Like, why so many headstand pics? Why otters?") No one, they realize, has seen her since Thursday. Her tracker's GPS has gone totally silent.

I pause the procession. "Hang on. Are you talking about Catherine of *Phoenix*? The blonde I was asking you about last week?"

"Her name is Annabelle," Catherine of Milwaukee corrects. "She's not one of us. I mean, she sort of used to be, but she never exactly *fit*, you know?"

Still, the description matches. This is definitely the same air-quote virgin who confessed her failings to me in the rest room last week. And who I thought stole the rebel propaganda, but then that turned out to be Larisa . . . so . . .

"She really just vanished? She didn't tell any of you where she was going?"

The other Catherines hadn't spoken to her for several days, they inform me. They'd placed her under social quarantine for acting "icky," Catherine of New Haven tells me.

"Yeah," says Schenectady. "She went back on soy and kept doing this weird crying thing for no reason."

I picture the big-eyed Catherine who pled her case from atop a napping station. Was I the last person to speak with her? Has she been cut from the grid?

The other Catherines don't think so. "She just had her midterm," Catherine of Milwaukee explains. "The losers usually stick around a little longer. You see them start to drop off near the end of their term. This is . . . something different."

"What do you think happened?"

The Catherines have theories: One thinks Annabelle joined a weird headstand cult. Another believes she's hiding nearby with an illicit lover. But why wouldn't her tracker give away her location, someone asks. Another Catherine thinks she went fully off-grid with a band of dangerous rebels. The rest say that's a stupid idea. Annabelle wouldn't have the guts to pull off something like that. Not unlike what Larisa argued last week. I, too, have a hard time picturing doe-eyed Catherine of Phoenix among those pierced and tattooed rebels I saw out at the warehouse. No, there must be another explanation.

First period—an unsupervised drumming circle—deteriorates almost immediately. Annabelle had an accomplice, my peers decide. There's no way she could have pulled off this disappearance all on her own. Catherine of Toronto notes that, in hindsight, they might have seen this coming: "I mean, she meditated with her *eyes open*. Only psychopaths do that." The others nod, shuddering. One recalls the time Annabelle wore that weird shawl thing, another remembers the time her arms gave out in bird pose—proof of a shaky character? They refer to her exclusively as "Annabelle," like she was never a member of their group.

I cast an eye in Larisa's direction. She's really going at it, banging away on her bongo like her afterlife depends on it, and I wonder if she's thinking the same thing as me: Did Annabelle/Catherine of Phoenix in fact have the ovaries to do something risky? *Could we have stopped her?*

I set aside my instrument and open my tracker's feed,

clicking back to the avatar I found the other day—Annabelle Schreiber, headstand enthusiast. Are the headstand pics some sort of code, or did Annabelle/Catherine just have a thing for acrobatic animals?

Before I can find a moment to confer with Larisa, a pair of guards enter the room, demanding silence. Larisa gives her bongo one more *ba-ba-bump* and the room falls eerily quiet.

The taller guard presses a button on the wall and a screen drops down, revealing a squirrel-faced man in a tweedy suit, one of the Center's vice-vice administrators.

"How many of you were familiar with Annabelle Schreiber?" the man asks.

The room is silent for a long moment until, one by one, everyone raises a hand.

"Sir, we all know her. She was in this class," offers one of the meekest martyrs.

"Right, yes." Squirrel Man looks down at his papers, then barks something unintelligible to someone off-screen. "And who among you was a close companion of Miss Schreiber's? A confidant, as it were?"

No hands go up this time. The vice-vice administrator narrows his gaze, speaks again to someone we can't see. Then: "For everyone's safety, the rest of today's classes will be suspended as we implement an enhanced screening protocol."

A tambourine crashes, and one of the Catherines lets out a squeak.

"Our guards will escort you downstairs, where your trackers will be evaluated for any relevant insights," says the administrator. "As you might infer, participation is mandatory."

WE SPEND THE next three hours in a colorless waiting room in the basement. Apparently, the Center only owns one deep-screening machine. We sit clustered at tables, staring at our fingers, as our classmates are called in one by one. A recorded voice suggests breathing exercises to keep us occupied while we wait.

Beside me, Larisa huffs, wheezes, and finally gives up on the exercise, slumping into a half-hearted nap. At a table in the corner, Jethro dozes too. I wish I could do the same. I can't stop picturing Annabelle, sobbing in that rest room stall. What had she said? *I'm a phony. A total worthless fake. . . . My tracker* knows *what I really am.* I glance at my own tracker, still an unhappy red, and feel a familiar clutch of self-doubt.

So much for my Monday restart.

The interrogations move slowly, and after two hours, they send us upstairs for lunch. I can't eat. Larisa is going on about the opportunity cost of all this wasted time ("Three missed classes is three hundred points lost!") as she crams her mouth with mush. She seems completely unperturbed by Annabelle's disappearance, and I don't have it in me to pick another fight. The truth is, I'm more worried about my own situation—what the Powers might discover if they dig into my data and uncover the blocks I've placed on my past.

My attention shifts toward a table toward the front of the room where the newbies gather. One sits slightly apart from the others in standard-issue PJs with a long braid of sand-colored hair. My breath catches. It's her. Z.

I excuse myself from Larisa and make my way across the room. Z's tawny eyes flare as I settle into a seat beside her.

"Can we talk?"

She shifts, and I consider the best way to start. Lunch ends soon, so I don't have a lot of time to ease into things.

"I'm sorry for yelling at you that day. I'm not sure why you made me seem so much nicer than I am. Are you—what I really need to know is—are you *completely* sure you didn't see him? The shooter?"

She shakes her head without meeting my gaze.

"I just wish I could remember *something*," I continue. "Like, if I could picture the guy's face, or any detail really, then maybe I could know why he did it and put it behind me. Did he *say* anything? Why did I—"

"I'm sorry," Z interrupts me. "I don't know any of that. Sometimes these things just happen, right? Death doesn't have to make sense, does it?"

Z looks utterly depleted. I remember how I felt when I first arrived and feel another wave of guilt for shouting at her on that fateful morning. The bell is ringing—we're due back downstairs— and I still want to know: How did a bullet find her, all the way back on the platform? Why would she make me out to be a hero when she must have seen so clearly that I was not? I can't help feeling like she's holding something back.

"Doesn't it bother you? Not knowing why you died?"

"Not really." Z stands abruptly. "I prefer to leave the past where it belongs: in the past."

"Well, then you're really gonna hate it around here," I say, echoing what Larisa told me on my first day. The past, I've by now realized, is inescapable.

AFTER LUNCH, LARISA is one of the first students called in for screening. She's in the room for a long time, almost an hour. I double-check my tracker to make sure I've read it correctly. When she finally emerges, her face is a blank. She ignores me when I mouth, *What happened?*

An attendant appears a few moments later with a frown. "Our system is down, folks. We'll pick up tomorrow. Please head to your last-period class."

We let out uneasy sighs—relief, but not quite.

Reenie greets us upstairs in Advisory and asks how we're feeling. The Catherines immediately rip into Annabelle, her questionable spiritual hygiene, the way her transgression has inconvenienced all of us. Reenie reroutes the conversation, asking what Annabelle's absence provokes on a more personal level. "It would be normal if this type of thing made you nervous," she tells us. "Even a bit scared."

My classmates are silent. Reenie's eye catches mine, holding it for a prolonged beat.

"Uncertainty feeds our worst fears and instincts," she tells us, "but it's important for us to remember that even in our most anxious moments, there is always room for hope. I'd like us to take a moment of silence for Annabelle. Let's wish her a safe journey, wherever she is and whatever she seeks. Let's wish the same for ourselves too."

We gather in a quiet circle and wish Annabelle/Catherine our best.

AFTER

———

DAY 23 CONTINUED

AT THE SOUND of the dismissal chime, I scramble toward the lobby, slowing to a more calculated pace when I reach the cluster of guards on the Center's front steps. I take my time descending the stairs and walk an extra block east, in case anyone's watching. Then, hood on and GPS disabled, I grab the next bus to the edge of the grid.

I wasn't going to do this. I was going to get myself together and be a model student this week—eyes on my own page and all that—but the Annabelle situation has triggered a fresh slug of anxiety. My run-in with Z didn't help.

As I pick my way through the dust heaps surrounding the warehouse, Jethro's warning echoes: He told me not to block long stretches of memory. *Anything more than a few minutes will draw attention,* he said, and I intend to follow that advice. I don't like it—coming back here—and I'm not even sure they'll let me in without Jethro, but there are a few things I need to check on before it's my turn with that squirrel-faced administrator. I'll be in and out. Then I'll never return again.

The girl with the scarlet-tipped locs greets me at the back door. No, *greets* isn't the right word. She stares at me coolly, like I'm an insect she can't be bothered to shoo.

I've prepared a whole little spiel about why she should trust me, but she hushes me with a raised fist. Uh . . . I step back, then watch as her knuckles meet the door in four hollow raps: Quick-quick-slow-slow. A code.

"You got that?" she says. "For next time."

I swallow. "Got it."

I don't understand how I've made the cut, but it looks like I'm in with the rebels now. I'm not sure what to feel about that.

As we make our way down the long interior corridor, the girl says I can call her Simone. "We gotta be careful who we let in," she says. "The PTB have spies everywhere. We ran a little background on you, though, and . . ." She glances at my tracker, like *'nuff said*.

There are more people in the basement than last time—more tattoos, more piercings, more combat gear. They're too focused on their screens to register my arrival, thankfully, and Simone leaves me to do my thing.

I find a computer off in a corner and open the archive. First stop: Annabelle. When Jethro showed me around last week, I realized the archive was more than a peephole into the past. In addition to the lifetime of memories uploaded upon my arrival, my account also holds a record of everything the PTB have collected since—points earned and deducted, fees paid and bills outstanding, GPS locations, my consistently miserable vibes. I should be able to find similar data on Annabelle—maybe find a clue about where she went, and for sure hide our little interaction in the rest room—but when I enter her name, nothing comes up. It's like she's been scrubbed from the system, or never existed.

I sit back to collect my thoughts, and as I do, I glance around the room at all of the tatted and camouflaged hackers staring into screens. I feel nervous asking any of them for help; I don't want to draw any more attention to myself than needed. I clear my search and open a fresh tab.

I enter my own archive this time and scroll back to my final day. The section I blocked appears seamless. You can't tell I manipulated it at all. I'm tempted to lift the cap and watch again, but Z is probably right: I'm not going to find meaning in the act of a random shooter, so instead I check on the other firewalls I placed to make sure they're well concealed. Then, I can't help it, I search for another moment that's been haunting me—an argument Faye and I had more than a year ago. She was collapsed in bed in a different apartment, a different city. I stood over her and yanked back the blankets. "You're pathetic," I spit. "Why do you let them do this to us? Why do you fall for such scumbags? Can't you find someone normal?"

Exactly one week later, Chip showed up with his money clip and khakis, like Google had searched for *normal* and found him.

I know it's not my fault. Not exactly. Neither of us could have known what Chip would turn out to be. I had reason to be angry too. Faye had let me down again—let a broken heart interfere with the basics of mothering. But when I called Faye *pathetic*, there was true rage in my voice. Real cruelty. I can't let a moment like that go viral. I place a block on that argument and, to be safe, I do a quick search of Faye's archive for memories involving me that her brain coded as *angry*, *stressful*, or *sad*.

Dozens of clips appear. Hundreds. Jesus. The list goes back several years.

I steel myself, then click on one of the older clips.

Me: twelve years old. Her: digging in her purse. It's late at night. We're at a subway turnstile, somewhere far from home. We both look tired. "How could you lose your wallet?" I shout. "Did you lose your brain too?"

The next clip: Faye forgets a rent check, I deliver a rebuke.

And next: She pleads, and I slam a door in her face.

Now here we are at the shelter, me nudging, pushing, berating.

Click, click, click. More harsh words. More tears. Some are small moments, things I'd forgotten, but in her archive, they remain coded with hurt. I block one moment, then another. Jethro's warning rings in my ear ("If the Powers discover that you've been manipulating your memories . . ." *Slice*), and I do it anyway, select a whole string, hit the *block* key and wait.

The screen churns, flickers, churns some more.

A message pops up: **Command denied.**

I try swiping again, again. I slam my thumb into the return key, the exit key, alt + command + escape.

"Hey now." A voice behind me. "Don't take it out on the equipment."

I turn to find Simone looking at me quizzically.

"This is bullshit," I say, thumping the keyboard in front of me.

"No. That's a computer," she says calmly.

I crack a smile. I can't help it. I'd probably laugh if I weren't so close to screaming. I don't know what to do. I can't fix my past. I can't escape it. If I have to sit through one more lecture on the proper way to breathe, I might tear off my simulated skin.

Something like recognition appears in Simone's eyes.

"It's not you," she says simply.

"What isn't?"

"Any of that." She points to my screen. "How far did you go back? A few months? Few years? You're not the same person you were then. You have different tools than that girl did."

"But . . ." What is she talking about? Tools? She doesn't know anything about me or my past.

Simone's face, cool, almost expressionless, doesn't budge. "Trust me. Every single person in this room has sat right where you are. I'm saving you time. You won't find answers there."

"But . . ." I point again to the screen, which is still frozen. I press the escape key again, and once more for good luck.

Simone sighs, reaches around, and yanks a cord. The whole rigged-up system goes still. She's annoyed, and now I am too.

"Come on." She waves at me to stand. "I think you need a break."

I'm too surprised to object, so I push back my chair and follow Simone from the room. Who *is* this chick? I make a mental note to ask Jethro next time we're in the alley.

Simone guides me toward a back hallway. Others are turning off their screens and pushing in chairs too. I follow Simone up a winding set of steps to another long hallway with doors on both sides. At a dead end, Simone raps softly against the smooth wall, her bare brown wrist gleaming in the gloom. I blink, taking in a detail I'd missed until now. Simone isn't wearing a tracker. Like, at all.

A hidden door creaks open, revealing a large man sporting an extremely small beret.

"Almost ready?" Simone asks. "I've got a guest."

The others who've gathered behind us slide through the narrow doorway, and I consider making my exit while I still can. Is this some kind of rebel meeting? Nope. Not what I signed on for. But the beret guy grabs my hand before I can make a decision. He snaps my tracker from my wrist and drops it in a basket. "Insurance," he says. My eyes widen and my hand clamps on to my naked wrist.

Simone nudges me forward. "Come on, you'll thank me later."

We've entered a large room with plain white walls and a musky odor I can't place. There are no computers, just a semicircle of metal chairs like you'd find in a church basement. But the people milling around are no choir members. With their combat boots, metal-laced jackets, and military caps, they look like they're part of a guerrilla-themed costume party. A look that says *eff the system* in an *I have way too much time on my hands* sort of way. I recognize a couple of faces from downstairs. I get strange glances from a few others. They likely recognize me from TV. Two of the hackers have wonky cigarettes like Jethro's tucked behind their ears.

I take an empty chair near the back and squeeze my hands between my knees to hide my nerves. I've lost track of Simone. It's too late to turn and walk out. Besides, that beret guy has my tracker. I can't exactly wander around the realm with bare wrists. I'm pretty sure I'd get in serious trouble for that.

I sink in the chair and wait as the seats around me fill.

A guy wearing far too many zippers is the first to stand and speak. "They're controlling our minds! Lulling us to sleep with their lies." He speaks fast, spit flying. Something about wounds that don't heal. Pain that festers. A long rant about the commodification of good deeds. His words swirl loose and chaotic, like a bunch of unrelated thoughts that got caught in a high-voltage blender. "We deserve truth!" he concludes with a spittle-y roar.

The others snap. A few stomp. One whistles.

The girl beside me leans over and smiles. "They aren't all this nuts, I promise."

I smile back at her, uneasy. I wish I knew where Simone went. Why did I let them take my tracker? I sit quietly as several others move to the front to speak. They introduce themselves with weighty-sounding names—Bolívar, Toussaint, Indira, O'Connell. A short woman calling herself Bella talks about throwing off the bonds of mass-market spiritualism. Another speaker wants to escape the anesthetized prison of self-help drivel to commune with their raw inner self.

It's . . . a lot.

The more these folks talk, the more uneasy I become. There's something about their energy that has a distinct whiff of desperation. That's when I recognize it: That musky odor. Sweat. But . . . how? I scan the circle, note moisture on one guy's lip, beads on a fast-talker's brow. One woman has a jagged scar running from eye to lip. An older man has a cane looped on his chair. These things, like the tattoos and piercings, should be impossible. These bodies are replicas, with none of the wear and tear of life. They definitely don't emit sweat . . . and yet. Here's a whole group of people oozing imperfection.

Simone reappears, and I sit up to watch as she glides to center stage. The room goes hushed, expectant. She's twisted her locs high onto her head and holds out her hands like a preacher.

"The Powers That Be have set up a system of points and ranking to control our souls," she says, wasting no time in finding her point. "But while they claim the noblest of intentions—and promise eternal reward—they feed us nothing but platitudes."

A few listeners break into snaps.

"How did they gain such authority? Not from me, not from you. They've achieved their power to guide and judge us through self-appointment and obfuscation."

She stares into the gathered group, and we stare back.

"Is there danger in speaking these facts aloud? Out there: of course. Here, among friends, we can—and must—say what we know to be true. In here, we can admit we are sick of their flavorless mantras and crackpot spiritualism. Admit that the same tired recipes cannot feed every soul. That there exists no monopoly on righteousness."

The snaps grow louder as she talks about honoring our own histories, our traumas and triumphs and unique needs. "Youga ain't it," she declares, and several listeners shout their assent. Apparently Simone despises self-empowered warrior poses even more than I do. Despises posing in general. I find myself wanting to snap as Simone talks about how alien these practices felt when she first arrived, how out of sync she felt, and self-doubting. Until she met someone who encouraged her to look deeper. She talks about the myth of the individual, the power of the collective, the danger of chaining ourselves to a binary system of good/bad, yes/no, points/deductions. Some of it, I follow. Other parts wash over me, inaccessible.

"It is time for all souls to demand honesty," she tells us. "Authenticity. Like these bodies we've coded to reflect our truest selves."

"Yes," the group murmurs, touching their tattoos and scars. I watch them, and something clicks. These folks have hacked their own bodies, reconstructing lifelike quirks and imperfections.

Simone gazes on the group almost lovingly. "Conformity and obedience are a trap. Why should we live within the lines drawn by someone else? Follow *their* rules? Deem ourselves failures when we don't measure up? Who says their measures are the right ones in the first place? Who gave them the authority to decide what we should let go and whom we should forgive?"

She punches the air, her words growing louder, landing with the cadence of a drum.

"The problem isn't you, my friends. And the question isn't how. It is when. It is time to rise together, to cast off the Powers That Steal, and demand our truth!"

She drops her arms then, and the whole room jumps to its feet, buzzing, clapping. I stand, frozen, understanding with a jolt why Simone's message seems so familiar. *The problem isn't you. The question isn't how.* Simone is Freedome, the poet with the disappearing posts. She's even more electric in person.

"Take back the truth," the others are shouting. "All souls rise and report."

A jolt of fear shoots through me. What does that mean? Report what? I turn to the girl beside me, the one who reassured me they weren't all nuts, but she's busy clapping. Suddenly, her hand thrusts into the air. Others follow. "Rise and report," they shout, fists pumping. As their words coalesce, they sound less like random wing nuts and more like revolutionaries.

THE CHAIRS SCRAPE apart, and folks scatter into fast-talking clusters. The room feels too small to contain their energy. One factor may be coffee. *Coffee.* Oh. I haven't had a cup since the morning before I died. It's strictly forbidden at the Center, along with other stimulants. Someone passes me a piping cup, along with something that looks like . . . a doughnut? I take a sip and the heat zings straight into my veins.

"Jesus, this is good," I mutter, going for the doughnut next. "Or, you know . . ." but I don't know which secular entity to thank for the gift of sugar.

The girl who'd smiled at me earlier has sidled up and is chin deep in a jelly-filled danish. She looks pretty ordinary compared to the others. Simple scoop-neck jersey, jeans with no rips or zippers, curly hair pulled back in a low ponytail. I'm guessing she's new to this place too. Between bites we commiserate about the terrible food at the Center, the tragedy of being dead and having to eat whole grains. "The only whole grain I want is my abuela's homemade tortillas!" she says.

"Eva" (most folks adopt a code name, for safety, she explains) tells me she followed the PTB's program for a while, attended all the classes and did all the work, but it never felt right. Last week she dropped out officially, and moved out here.

"Wait. You *live* here?"

"Yup." She smiles. They've turned a set of old barracks into dormitories, Eva explains. More than two hundred souls have relocated here, including many who outstayed their ninety-day terms and needed a place to hide.

I slurp my coffee as I listen, letting its bitter energy slip into my skin. The pastries come around again, and we each take another. "I have no issue with salad," Eva says. "But kale mousse should not be a thing!"

I agree wholeheartedly. "Have you ever tried celery water?" I ask. Eva gags.

We offer up more revolting examples from the Center's buffet. ("Tempeh? What *is* that?" "Soy mayo? Come on!") Soon we're sugar-tripping so hard I almost miss the sound of a familiar, scraping laugh.

I do a double take, but there's no mistaking those long flannel limbs or that signature slouch. The energy of the past few minutes goes cool in my veins. Did Jethro *follow* me here? He stands with his back to me and says something to the person beside him—Simone—who is smiling broadly. It's clear they know each other better than he'd let on. Something about this doesn't feel right.

Simone nudges Jethro and he turns my way, a crooked smile slicing up his face. I feel myself soften slightly. A moment later he's at my side. "I wish you'd told me you wanted to come back," he says in my ear. "You shouldn't be here on your own. You shouldn't be here *at all*."

Eva, after a quick glance at Jethro, has drifted away to chat with others. I wish she'd come back. Jethro's unexpected presence, and concern, is confusing.

"You're here too," I point out.

"Only because Mo paged me."

Mo? Jethro makes a motion (and, okay, Mo = Simone, yup, got it). They're on a nickname basis and apparently monitoring my movements. That's . . . a lot to process.

"How well do you know these people?" I ask, mostly meaning Simone. "You never told me how you found this place."

Jethro snags the doughnut stub from my fingers. "Long story," he says, chewing. "For another time." He glances over his shoulder, and my gaze lingers for a moment on his sugar-dipped mouth. He catches me looking.

"Do you want to get out of here?" he says, and I do. It's suddenly too much. All of this. The caffeine is making me shaky, and the musky odor has grown too intense. I have a hundred questions that I can't ask him here.

We start to slide away and are stopped by a pointed cough.

A man in dark glasses gestures toward Jethro. He's traded his camouflage for a bomber jacket, but I recognize him immediately. It's the guy who accosted me on the sidewalk that day, who gave me the flyer that caused so much trouble with Larisa.

"Havel. Hey. Didn't expect to . . . This is . . . uh . . ." Jethro fumbles, looking at me.

"Margaret?" I say, reaching for a quick alias and landing on my nonnie's name. They likely all know who I am, and yet . . . if everyone else is going by code names, I figure I should too.

"Margaret." The man stretches a hand. "I believe we've met once before."

His dark glasses point past my shoulder, reflecting the empty space behind. For a moment it occurs to me that he could be blind. But if he remembers our previous encounter, that means he knows my face. No, the dark glasses are clearly a fashion choice, or maybe a power move. Either way, the effect is unsettling.

"It's always good to bring fresh energy into the room," Havel says, his glasses now trained on my face. "Perhaps soon, you'll be ready to join us on a mission."

Jethro's fingers find my wrist, and he stares hard at the older man. "I don't think so," he says quickly. "Mar—Margaret's just here for research. But she's done with all that now, right?"

I meet Jethro's worried eye, remembering my actual reason for coming here today. Not coffee. Not speeches. Not conversations with camo-clad wing nuts. "Yeah, that's right. I found what I needed."

"We were just leaving, actually." Jethro tightens his hold on my wrist, and I'm suddenly glad he showed up. This Havel guy makes me extremely uneasy. It's not just the glasses. It's his whole vibe.

Jethro sets down my coffee cup and nudges me toward the door. Eva offers a friendly wave as we snatch our trackers from the basket. Then we're back in the dim-lit hallway. I hurry behind Jethro toward the stairs, our steps uncertain in the gloom.

Once we're safely outside, among the dust heaps and daylight, I sputter. "Who is that guy? What was going on in there? Is this some sort of cult? What are they up to exactly? *A mission?* Rising up? Against who, the PT—"

Jethro places one hand softly on my mouth and waits for me to quiet, to settle to the ashy earth. His eyes glimmer with something like fear. There's still a spot of sugar on his lip.

"Mari, promise me you won't come back here."

"But . . ." I rise onto my toes. "But what if I have a question, what if—" I recall the long string of arguments I unearthed in Faye's archive. So many layers of hurt.

"Promise me." Jethro squeezes my shoulders, bringing my gaze from the warehouse to him. As if reading my mind, he says, "You can't fix the past, Mari."

I pull away from his grip.

"I know that." To his doubting expression, I say, "I do. I know."

His concern is sweet. I should be grateful he's looking out for me. That he showed up when he did.

"You need to be careful who you trust around here."

"Do you mean that creep with the dark glasses? Believe me, I don't trust him. What's his deal anyway? Who wears sunglasses indoors?"

"Not just Havel. All of them. You need to be careful around all of them."

"A bit hypocritical, don't you think? It's clear you've spent a lot of time with *Mo*."

Something flickers in his face. "Mari . . ."

I wave a hand, deflating. "Don't worry. I get it. I don't plan to come back."

It's true. While Simone's speech was intriguing, even inspiring—and while I'd kill for another cup of that coffee—this place has trouble written all over it. I don't need any more trouble than I've got.

Relief spreads across Jethro's face, loosening its tense angles, that lovely chin. Was he really that worried about me?

"Here. You have . . ." I point. "Sugar."

I dare to reach out a finger, brush the sugary crumbs from his lip. As I do, a sharp sound startles us both. I crane my head past his shoulder to see what it was, but Jethro's palms are on my face, holding me still. I giggle. I'm not sure why. Maybe it's the caffeine, or the dust, or the sudden nearness of his face. "Shhh," he says, his eyes fully serious. The next thing I know, Jethro is kissing me, and then the thing I notice after that: I'm kissing him back.

WE PART WAYS at the eastern bus terminal. We kept some distance on the ride home, a narrow rib of space neither of us dared cross. Did it really happen? Did Jethro *kiss* me? My entire body zips with the memory of it, pulling and pointing in his direction like a ship controlled by an external radar. I've never kissed another person before, not like that. I thought I never would. I certainly never imagined I'd kiss a dead boy in a forlorn lot at the edge of the afterlife grid. Or that it would be so . . . sweet. I don't trust myself to speak.

As we turn to say goodbye, Jethro's mouth opens like he wants to say something. He opts for an awkward wave instead.

I walk the rest of the way to the bungalow, my mind filled with kissing.

I cook dinner for Faye, not hearing anything she's saying. She's working hard to meet the new terms set by her adviser and is feeling anxious. Anxiety makes her talkative. I nod at the right moments, fill her glass when it empties, think my own thoughts, and don't snap when she calls me baby.

For a moment, I picture it: the two of us, a unit again. Then I remember where we are and how we got here. After I've cleared the dishes, we return to our designated corners: me to my bedroom, her to the living room couch.

Behind the safety of a closed door, my thoughts return to a boy with a laugh like sandpaper and lips dipped in sugar.

THE DAILY WITNESS

CHAIRMAN ADDRESSES RUMORS

———

Chairman Ted spoke to an adoring crowd from atop his favorite pedestal earlier this evening. He recalled the presettlement days, a time when souls wandered the vast expanse and philosophical disagreements frequently erupted into war. "I knew we could do better," he mused, "with a clear vision and best-in-class leadership—"

Our founder was jolted out of this familiar retelling by a shout.

"Mr. Chairman!" An unfamiliar reporter waved his arms from the center of the crowd. "Mr. Chairman, sir. There are reports of several souls who've gone missing recently. There are no records of their ascension or detention for any known crime. Do you know where they've gone?"

The Chairman tapped his earphone, murmuring something to his attendants offstage.

The questioner persisted. "We're hearing rumors that some souls may be attempting alternate paths to the Ever After. Is this true? Could there be paths to actualization that the Powers have overlooked?"

The speakers crackled loudly then, and the Chairman squinted into the crowd. "Must I remind you that Paradise Gate's Official Guidelines are the product of *extensive* research and have been thoroughly vetted by our esteemed committee? Eternal redemption is *not* a subject for hobbyists or neophytes."

"So that's a no?"

The Chairman turned his attention to the adoring fans gathered at his feet. "Friends, be wary. There are no quick fixes in the afterlife. Anyone who promises otherwise is no more than a swindler and a thief. I might add that such miscreants, upon apprehension, are eligible for immediate disconnection. Have I made the stakes clear?"

His acolytes nodded, wide-eyed, and the Chairman smiled. "Well, then." With that, he spun from the crowd, dismounting the pedestal with an elegant, if top-heavy, leap.

Seconds later, guards appeared, searching for the questioner, but he was nowhere to be found.

AFTER

DAY 24

ON TUESDAY, THE security screenings have been abandoned, no explanation. We're told to resume our regular schedule. There's been no further news about Annabelle/Catherine of Phoenix, but that hasn't slowed the conjecturing. One classmate suspects she's been kidnapped by radical deviants. A few others wonder if she's attempted one of the "alternate paths" Chairman Ted is suddenly so riled up about. A funnier take: She took a wrong turn and fell off the grid.

I half listen to the chatter in the computer lab, considering how unlikely it is that any of my gossiping classmates have met any actual afterlife radicals or know anything about "alternate paths." Honestly, I don't know exactly what these paths are either, but I feel pretty sure the radicals I've recently met would have no use for an emotionally volatile virgin in their ranks.

I want to ask Larisa what happened in the screening room yesterday—what did they ask her that took an entire hour?—but she seems extra spiky this morning, so I decide it can wait.

Jethro drifts in just after the bell. He hasn't messaged me since we parted at the bus terminal yesterday, and I've started to worry that I made it all up—the kiss. I resolve to play it cool, but at the last second, I can't help it, my gaze pops up. His mouth crooks, and there it is: that smile, splitting me down the center. A smoke emoji appears on my wrist. I reply with a heart, but then catch myself and swap for a more measured thumbs-up.

For the next forty-two minutes, I follow my computer's instructions and make a list of mindful intentions, while keeping a close eye on the clock.

Five minutes before the bell, a voice crackles through the classroom's speaker. "Marianna Novak? You're needed in Administration. Immediately."

For a moment, I don't move. The Catherines murmur, big-eyed, and Larisa grunts something unintelligible at her screen. I don't dare look at Jethro, or anyone, as I hurry from the room.

This can't be good.

Dora, the front office secretary, waves me past her desk to a private office in the back. Maybe it's just my paranoia, but her lipsticked smile looks decidedly grim.

There are two men waiting for me inside the office. The first I recognize as the same squirrel-faced administrator who called us to the screening room yesterday. (If he said his name, I missed it.) The other man is taller and wears a dark, collarless suit. I take a seat and watch as the Suit paces the small office before finally perching, fingers steepled, atop the desk.

"Some troubling information has been brought to our attention, Miss Novak."

"Really? About me?" My hands feel slick suddenly, though I know that's impossible. I inch my fingers beneath my thighs as the administrator opens a drawer and pulls out some sort of plastic sheath containing a bright tangerine square of paper.

"Do you recognize this, Miss Novak?"

"Umm . . . I'm not sure. Maybe?"

I can't believe Larisa didn't trash that stupid flyer as soon as she was done with it. I can't believe I didn't throw it away myself.

"Can you tell us anything about this?" The administrator points a wand toward a large screen behind him. Grainy security footage appears from what appears to be one of the Center's rest rooms. Oh geez. Two figures enter. One wearing smart-but-casual sweats, and the other looking like she just stepped off a goth chain gang. My heart pounds as Larisa waves around the flyer. The administrator fast-forwards to me standing in a rest room stall with Annabelle. There's no sound, but it's clear we're having an intense conversation.

I press my legs against the chair to keep my hands from trembling. If they've got this, I can only guess what else they know.

"Yesterday, we asked Miss Schreiber's classmates to share pertinent information about her recent activities. You didn't think to come forward with this?"

"I barely knew her," I say truthfully. "We just spoke that one time. I didn't think it was . . . important."

"And this?" The administrator waves the flyer.

"Some guy on the street gave me that. I didn't *want* it. And I definitely didn't contact the number or anything. Sorry, what does this have to do with Annabelle?"

"We discovered this contraband among Miss Schreiber's belongings," the Suit says.

"You did? But that's . . ." *Impossible,* I think.

Something is happening here that I don't follow. Larisa took the flyer. I *saw* her with it; she explained why she needed it. This doesn't make any sense.

The Suit leans down from his perch. "Let's go back, shall we? Where did you obtain this material, Miss Novak?"

"I told you the truth! It was some guy, a—a stranger." I picture Havel with his dark sunglasses and creepy intensity. I didn't know his name the first time he spoke to me in the street. "He just *grabbed* me. Near the park. I was minding my business, headed home."

"And you didn't see him again?"

I shake my head, taking a chance. My GPS wasn't active the next time I saw Havel.

"We don't expect you to understand the danger of such propaganda, Miss Novak. We do, however, expect all souls to report suspicious activity. We wouldn't want you to be charged with collusion or sedition, both serious moral crimes."

"Yes," I say. "Of course. I'm sorry. I don't want that either."

The Suit adjusts a button at his throat. "You're not a typical soul, Miss Novak. We want to give you the benefit of the doubt, but if an incident such as this became public, there would be consequences."

If? I dare to raise my gaze an inch.

"We intend to keep this between us for now. No need to draw more attention to these fear-mongering radicals than necessary."

"Right," I say, catching on now. Sort of. "Right. Of course."

"We're aware that there are, ahem, events from your past you wish to keep concealed, Miss Novak, including a particularly fraught decision regarding your mother."

My hands quake beneath my thighs. He knows about my call to Faye's PO? But I blocked that memory. Jethro said there'd be no way anyone could access it.

It occurs to me that the PTB could have accessed the memory before I placed the block, but that doesn't make sense either. If they had something this juicy, why hasn't it shown up on TV? They've depicted Faye in the worst light possible; why not go in for the kill with the moment her own daughter turned her in to the police? And anyway, the memory hadn't been flagged or downloaded before I got there. The PTB's minions left their marks all over my archive, but this memory had been untouched.

No, they must have found out another way.

The Suit stares into me like he can see right through my skin. "We can appreciate your desire for privacy, Miss Novak. We will respect your wishes if you respect ours."

As if reading my question, Squirrel Man clarifies, "We expect you to come forward with any further contact you have with suspect individuals. In particular, we expect an immediate update should you hear from this man"—he waves the flyer—"again."

"Yes, yes. Of course." Is that it? All they want? "I promise. I'll tell you everything."

I DON'T BOTHER waiting for an official break. As soon as the administrator dismisses me, I head to the alley. Jethro is already there, waiting.

"What happened? What did they want? Are you okay?" His eyes are swampy with concern.

I point to his hip, and he pauses before realizing I want a cigarette.

"Right. Okay. First things first."

A click of the lighter, and I fall against the wall.

Blank sky, warm shoulder, smooth exhale. I take several slow drags. It's not enough, though. My hand is shaking and my vibes remain a deeply disturbed red, even for me.

The Suit's words ricochet through my head. *Events from your past. Decision regarding your mother. Your desire for privacy. We will respect your wishes if you respect ours.*

Beside me, Jethro scuffs at the ground nervously. It takes a few more puffs before I'm ready to speak.

"What's the deal with Havel?"

Jethro's foot scritches to a stop. "Havel?"

"Yeah. Who is he? Why was he so eager to talk to me yesterday? How afraid should I be?"

"Mari. Forget him. Forget all of them. You promised you wouldn't go back."

His gaze jerks from my face to the building behind us and then back again. I've never seen him this jumpy.

"Tell me about Havel," I repeat.

More shifting. "Right. Well, let's see. I don't know much. I used to go to those meetings my first month here, and . . . I got the sense he was kind of a loose cannon. Why, did he say something to you? Something you didn't tell me?"

I don't bother answering. "And Simone? What about her?"

Jethro's shoulders relax a little. "She's cool. You've got nothing to worry about with her. But like I said, you shouldn't—"

I fling the cigarette onto the pavement. "Did they take Annabelle?"

Jethro blinks. It's clear that this wasn't the conversation he was expecting. Maybe he wasn't expecting much conversation at all. Last time I saw him, we kissed, and until a little while ago, that was the main topic on my mind. But lip-locking with Jethro has fallen way down my list of priorities.

"Annabelle? You mean that girl who went missing?" Jethro has regained some of his composure. "No. They didn't . . . That's not how it works. They don't *take* people."

"They recruit them, though, right? They were trying to recruit me. How did they pull you in?"

Jethro pushes off the wall, putting some distance between us. "I told you. It was a while ago. I'm not involved anymore. It was a mistake."

"Mmm. Well, they lied to you about some stuff. 'Cause their firewall's crap. Yup, that's right," I say to the quirk in Jethro's brow. "Those administrators went through my archive. The blocks didn't work."

"No." Jethro shakes his head. "That's impossible. If you did it the way I showed you, no one can access that memory now but you. They can't see what's in your mind."

"And yet somehow they knew."

"Maybe they got in before you added the block?"

I shake my head. "That part of my archive was quiet. It didn't have all of the flags and downloads like the other memories they'd grabbed."

"Well then"—Jethro looks at me—"maybe someone else knew."

"This was a *secret*. No one knew."

Jethro gives me an odd look. "What about that friend of yours? The funny one who's always online? You tell her a lot of stuff, don't you?"

"Larisa?" It's true. I did tell her the gist of what went down with Faye and that phone call, but . . . "No. She wouldn't rat."

Jethro makes a noncommittal sound.

"I'm telling you. She wouldn't."

Larisa is loyal. We've only known each other a couple of weeks, but I feel quite certain of this. And yet . . . I picture her yesterday as she left the interview room, her face oddly blank. She still hasn't told me what went on in there.

My thoughts spin onto a disturbing new track. What about that orange flyer? How did the flyer that Larisa snatched from me end up in Annabelle's things? None of this makes sense.

"People do crazy stuff when they're desperate," Jethro offers quietly. "Or in trouble."

"But Larisa's not in trouble. She's a perfect student."

"Maybe someone she cares about is?"

I go back to what she shared with me in the library—her dad, the eternal rebel, mysteriously vanished from the grid. How desperate she's been to find him. Did that administrator know something about Larisa's dad and use it to turn her against me? It sounds like something out of a spy movie.

Jethro is quiet as I take in the possibility—immediately reject it—then consider it again.

"What else did they say? Do they want to see you again?"

"No. They just . . . told me to report back if I see anything weird or talk to anyone. Anyone strange."

Jethro lets out a deep breath. "Good. That's good. That means they don't have much. If you stay away from the warehouse, you're fine."

He leans back against the wall and closes his eyes. He looks . . . tired.

"Here." I reach down for the abandoned cigarette. "You look like you need it."

He opens his eyes as our fingers catch, and maybe it's the rush of fear I've just weathered that makes my skin so alert, or maybe it's something I read in Jethro's eyes. Suddenly I'm not thinking of traitorous friends or frowning administrators. I'm thinking of something much more immediate. Jethro pulls me toward him, completing the thought.

AFTER

DAY 24 CONTINUED

JETHRO DROPS ME off outside our next class. He has something to take care of, he says. Quick squeeze of my hand, and he leans in to whisper, "Later?"

While he retreats down the hall with that long slinking step, I replay our most recent kiss, allowing myself a mini-preview of what *later* will bring.

"Thirsty much?" Larisa appears at my elbow, giving Jethro a distinctly disdainful look.

I prickle. I'm in no mood for her judgment right now. I'm not really in the right headspace to talk to her at all, in fact. Jethro's suggestion left a tangle of questions I still need to process. I enter the Youga studio without saying anything.

A minute later, she slaps a mat down beside mine.

"New spot?" She scans the corner I've chosen. Our nearest neighbors are a dingy-gowned martyr and a couple of cast-off virgins. The other Catherines aren't taking any more chances after Annabelle.

Poor Annabelle. Could Larisa have planted the flyer in her things? Why? Why does she hate the Catherines so much anyway?

Larisa drops cross-legged onto her mat. "I like to change things up sometimes myself. They say it's good for the spirit." She twists her back and wiggles her toes.

I stare at the pale green wall before us, trying to call up a more peaceful feeling. The happy glow of Jethro's kiss is fading fast.

"Um, hello? What crawled up your chakra?" Larisa peers more closely at me.

I bite my cheek. *What's wrong is I trusted you. I shared my biggest secret, promised I wouldn't rat about yours, and then you, you—*

"Betrayal creates really bad karma, you know."

"Uhhh . . . Remind me what we're talking about?"

I throw back my shoulders, like a character in one of my afterlife soap operas. "I can't believe I trusted you. I should've known you were full of crap with your constant advice and all your . . . vegetables. Nobody eats that much kale on purpose."

Yeah . . . that one didn't quite hit the mark.

Larisa looks mystified. "You're mad at kale?"

"No, of course not. It's . . . ugh." I drop my head into my palm. I'm no good at this.

"You're gonna have to give me more to go on, kid."

"I told you to stop calling me *kid*!"

The room goes hushed. The instructor has arrived and urges us into a welcoming warrior position. I copy as best I can, feet splayed and arms forming an upward W. Standing like this is supposed to open the doors to our inner power or something. So far it hasn't worked.

"They brought me down for questions," I tell Larisa, out of the side of my mouth. "They knew stuff about me and my mom, about *a certain decision*. The only way they could have found out was—" I spin my warrior sideways to face Larisa.

Her arms drop to her sides. "Hold up. They know you called your mom's PO? Couldn't they have pulled that from your archive?"

The nearest Catherine gives a warning tut. My arms windmill down to a plank.

("Planks build *persistence*!" cries the instructor. "*You* have what it takes!")

"No," I grunt. "Don't ask how. But they couldn't. And you're the only other person who . . . who . . ." My arms start to buckle.

"You think I told?" Larisa drops flat on her belly, not even pretending to plank. "Okay, assuming for a second that any part of what you just said made sense . . . which, hi, nope . . . why would I tell anyone *your* business?"

"I don't know." I fall to my stomach too. That's the part I want her to explain. "Maybe it's some deal you worked out for your dad?"

Larisa lifts a finger. "I told you—"

"Don't worry, I didn't say anything. *I'm* not the rat here."

Larisa pushes into a tabletop. "Well, then I don't know what you're going on about. You've really lost me, kid."

"I asked you to stop calling me—" I catch myself. Not the point right now. "What about the flyer?" I pull up onto all fours. How is she going to explain away that?

"The flyer?" She arcs into radiant rainbow position, then peers under one armpit, confused.

"They found it, right where you left it: with Annabelle's things!"

"Whoa." Larisa's rainbow arch flattens. "You've gone fully off the rails, you know that? Why would I do that? What would— It was a *flyer*, Mari. As in, a thing with many copies. Couldn't she have got one from the same dude who handed one to you?"

"But . . ." I deflate. It's a good point. Still, Larisa's know-it-all attitude isn't helping. "I don't think you know as much about how this place works as you think."

"Oh yeah? And who's teaching you how it works, your little emo boyfriend?"

My hands clench. "He's not . . . emo." (Or my boyfriend, exactly.) "For your information, Jethro looks out for me. He . . ." *Cares about me,* I almost say, but I realize how sappy it sounds.

Larisa snorts, pulling into an upside-down V. "Don't fool yourself, kid. He's using you. It's what dudes like him do."

I lift my head. "Using me? For what? I told you—*he hasn't been in my pants!*"

I shout-hiss the last part, and one of the off-brand Catherines tumbles in shock.

The instructor gives me a stern look. Cheeks hot, I flatten my palms and pull back my hips as we've been taught.

Larisa clucks something about dudes all being the same, and I'm about to jab her with an elbow when it hits me—a thought so obvious I can't believe it hadn't occurred to me sooner. Both knees buckle to the ground. "Are you *jealous*?"

"Ha. What? Jealous that you caught a deadbeat boyfriend?"

"No, jealous of him. Jealous that he"—wrong word, wrong thought—"caught *me*."

Larisa drops to her knees, jaw working. "Don't take this the wrong way, Mari, but you're not exactly my type. I prefer girls with a bit more . . . What's the word? . . . Spine."

My entire back stiffens. I don't know whether to be more offended or embarrassed. (What a stupid thing to say to her. Why did I say it?) More than anything, though, I'm confused.

"Then why does it bug you so much that I hang out with him?"

Larisa sits back on her heels, no longer pretending to follow the flow. "You really don't listen, do you? Because I'm your *friend*. And friends look out for each other. But you know what? Forget I ever bothered."

The yogic breathing around us has gone quiet. The martyrs stare at each other wide-eyed. I know I'm supposed to say something, but I don't know what.

Larisa slides back into satisfied snail position with an irritated grunt.

"There's more than one way to screw a girl, Mari. You ask me, this dude's screwing you good."

I GO BACK to the warehouse that afternoon to double-check on the firewall I created. When I run a search for the incident (key words: *probation officer, phone call, April 25*), nothing comes up. It's like the whole thing never happened. Obviously, the trick Jethro showed me worked, so either those two administrator dudes got to that memory by some technique I can't fathom, or *someone* told them about it. And the only someone who knew was Larisa. Unless . . . is it possible the Suit was referring to something else? Some other *particularly fraught decision* regarding my mother?

I don't want to be here, don't want to be doing this again. I enter a few more search terms into the Frankenstein computer, ignoring Eva's friendly wave. No doughnuts for me today. I'm going to finish this search and get out fast.

A search for *decisions* leads to *arguments*. Fear and curiosity get the better of me. Soon I'm in Faye's archive again, watching the worst of our fights from her perspective and my own. My biting words, her crumpled lips.

She's the mother. Her failures are obviously the most egregious. But I don't look so good from this vantage point either. I look like a bully. A monster. The more I watch, the more I'm convinced of something I'd already intuited: We are unfixable, both. Our damage too deep to repair.

I place a firm cap on the worst bits because, while I may not be able to save two irredeemable souls, here's another truth: What went down between my mother and me is nobody's business but our own.

BEFORE

FAYE HAS A new plan. She's tired of shuffling papers. Sitting all day is wrecking her back. Her job is a bore, and her boss doesn't appreciate anything she does anyway. She hears all the artists are moving to Lowell.

"You're not an artist," I remind her.

"So? I love artists! Baby, I don't think you're hearing my point."

"You were fired again, weren't you?" My mouth is too hard for my young face.

The memory's perspective shifts. Faye nods, head bowed. "But that's not the reason, baby. I swear, that's not the point."

"Please," a younger me spits. "Since when do you have a point?"

HER HAIR IS longer. It's winter. The whole world shivers. We argue about the heat.

"It's not magic, Faye. When you pay bills, things work. When you don't, we—"

SUMMER TURNS TO fall. I'm thirteen years old, headed to ninth grade. Faye wants to rejoin her old co-op. She ran into a former housemate at the library. A quick chat turned into a mug of tea, and now it's all she can talk about. "They share all the work, you know? *And* the bills! They take turns cooking. On Fridays, we get together and sing."

"*We?*"

My voice rises by a decibel, but she doesn't notice. I haven't seen her this excited about anything in a long, long time. It's been a hard year, more moves than usual. More ill-fitting jobs. A smooth-talking boyfriend with a rough undercoat we'd both prefer to forget.

I agree to meet the housemates. Just once. She corners me into it. But also? The truth? I'm curious about these people, these hippies she fled to the first time she left me. Their siren call has caught her attention more than once in recent years. Armed with more info, I figure I can put this business to rest once and for all.

We go over on a Friday around supper. A rambly, saggy, peeling Victorian surrounded by a clusterbomb of overgrown plants. (Our favorite home-reno pros would declare this one a gut job.) Inside, someone is playing a banjo while a free-balling toddler slams a pan with a stick. A woman who calls herself Liberty throws her arms around me before I can object. Liberty is not acquainted with deodorant. Or bras, it seems. She swoops through the living room, her magnificent breasts swinging, while the toddler directs a yellow stream into a potted fern.

"Isn't this wonderful?" Faye says, starry-eyed. "Don't you feel right at home?"

I try to picture living here. I imagine what Nonnie would say (*They're crackpots, Bunny. Steer clear. Run fast!*), try to imagine bringing a friend to a place like this, if I had friends, if . . . well, there are a lot of *ifs* in this scenario, aren't there?

Liberty hands me a bowl of undercooked lentils, asks, "So, what do you think?"

I avert my gaze from her nipples and murmur something vague but polite.

Back at home, my answer is more direct: "No. Absolutely not."

ANOTHER DAY, ANOTHER apartment. Another bill marked with a red *X*.

Faye's crying. I'm angry. Words the shape and size of bricks: "You're pitiful! Lazy! I hate you!"

Faye's face goes blotchy and the image scrambles.

Her memories, my memories, swirl, stutter, skip. Chip appears, gray-haired and frowning, Faye on his arm like a gift.

I'll have my own room, she says, a good school. "What is it you want, Mari? What?" She's pleading, she's sobbing, she's hoping. I stare back at her, granite-faced.

One memory blinks into another. The years flip, roles reverse. Parent, child, dreamers both. Me, envisioning stability. Faye, imagining freedom. The two of us face off at an ironing board, in a homeless shelter, beside the whoosh of a train. I grab at the tendrils of memory, trying to make sense of us, how we got to such a place, but the more I watch, the more all of it—past, present, future, what was and could have been—mashes and bleeds and finally blurs into smoke.

AFTER

———

DAYS 25-27

MY MEMORIES HAVE begun to glitch. Jethro warned this might happen. Too many blocks, he said, would have nasty side effects. Specifically, problems with recall and general functioning. Whoops.

I've developed a sort of patchy double view. Entire years have grown blurry, and Faye's perspective splices into mine, scrambling basic facts. Recent events seem so distant that I begin to wonder if they were real or my imagination.

Faye's acting strange, too. Arriving home late three days in a row, no explanation. Waking up early, barely touching her dinner. Yesterday (or was it Monday?), she got up in the middle of her favorite program, walked to the kitchen, then stopped, staring into space, like she'd forgotten where she was.

I begin to avoid the bungalow. Lady Lu says it's unhealthy to dwell on negative thoughts, better to lean into hope. I decide to lean into kissing. Kissing, I've discovered, is a very effective vibe-chilling tool. Far better than meditating or smoking. When Jethro's hands find my waist, it's like a cool stream slips over. Every thought, fear, memory—disappears.

Sometimes, after a really good stretch, I'll come up to the surface and notice my tracker glowing a soft golden green. I glimpse Jethro's wrist and notice it's helping his vibes too. See: Kissing works!

Too bad it doesn't last.

Kisses are a temporary Teflon. After a class or two—after another self-talk experiment or messy meditation—the seal melts away, doubts burst through, and my vibes slide back to vibrant red.

Larisa hasn't spoken to me since our blowup. She brushes past me in the halls, and in our classes she scowls silently into her screen. I want to ask her if she's heard more about her father. If she still believes doing homework can help.

I'm nearing my one-month milestone, almost thirty days as a dead girl, and nothing has made a difference. When I close my eyes: nightmares. When I strike a power pose, I feel anything but. The more I try to follow the PTB's formula, the further I get from inner peace.

I start skipping classes, spend longer stretches with Jethro. Sometimes he leaves and it's just me in the alley, staring out into endless white.

One afternoon I head home late, after the other students have gone. I watch from the sidewalk as the Center's large windows turn dark. There are protests happening in the park across the way, a group gathered in the dusk, linking arms, chanting. "Freedom!" they shout. "Freedom now!"

I'm starting to think Simone and her rebel tribe are right.

About all of it. This place is a sham—whether it's a full-on evil conspiracy or just a fundamentally flawed experiment, I'm not sure. I don't know if it matters.

I return to the warehouse several more times. With each visit, I burrow deeper into the past. Here is Faye pregnant. Here she is in college with a messy boyfriend who looks an awful lot like me. Here she is in high school, making honor roll, skipping classes, holding picket signs, starring in a play. Is she a good girl? A bad girl? Maverick or maladapted? Impossible to tell. Here is Nonnie, shouting, tearing at her temples, equally confused.

I see the woman who loved me, raised me, and the one who was supposed to do both things but somehow couldn't. I watch these two women break each other's hearts.

I don't attend any more meetings. I avoid Simone's impenetrable glances and Eva's cheery attempts at hello. The rebels may be right, we may need a revolution, but I don't want to get involved. Are they an army? A cult? The afterlife's answer to Faye's hippie commune, only bigger and badder and slightly better groomed?

Or, what if . . .

What if it's not the rebels who're off their rocker but everyone else? All of us brainwashed? *Chin up, follow the rules, pay the bills, stay out of trouble. Get the grades, go to college, stay inside the lines. Do the next thing and the next and it will all turn out fine.* Until it doesn't. Until it all falls apart and you're dead and the rules aren't working and you've tried . . . everything. You thought you were a decent person, a good person, but you clearly aren't.

You were duped, by all of it. You're a hopeless mess.

I've begun shedding points, spending more than I take in. I'll never have enough to pay this week's rent. Jethro is worried.

Between kisses, I feel his concern billow around me. Sweet Jethro, always attentive. Less lynx, more Labrador, I'm beginning to think.

One afternoon—a Thursday, I think, or maybe a Tuesday—we've been at it for a while, built up some real kissing stamina, when my tracker lets out a series of bleats. "Mari, is that—?" I grab for Jethro's collar, but the insistent beeping pulls him back.

Warning: Unauthorized absences. Check-in required.

"No big deal," I say. "Come on." I nudge toward Jethro's lips.

"What? No." He pulls back more firmly. "Mari, is that the first time that's happened? How many classes have you missed?"

"Unclear." I shrug.

I should be more concerned, but instead it's Jethro who seems agitated. Jethro, who, I mean, look at his wrist, he really shouldn't be talking.

I fall back to my heels and assure him I've got things under control. (Minus five for detectable lie.) He really does look more torn up than usual, his muddy eyes full of things I can't name. I want to lift his shoulder blades, tell him it will all be okay. (Will it?) One of these days I'll find the courage to ask him how it happened, what kind of choice he made at the end of his life. For now, I extend to my tiptoes and place my mouth against his throat.

What I can't say with words, I say with a kiss.

THE PARADISE MEDIA GROUP

EVENING ROUNDUP

As she cruises toward the 30-day mark with her vibes on the fritz and karmic earnings veering into a deficit, we must ask: *What in the afterworld is happening to Marianna Novak?*

"She's gone off the rails," said an anonymous classmate.

"She's almost never in class," affirmed another.

"She's really bad at Youga too," reported a third.

PTB archivists, meanwhile, inform us that the young soul's memory bank has come to resemble a block of Swiss cheese. It's a rare and mysterious condition, only reported once or twice in the past. We wonder: Is Miss Novak self-destructing before our very eyes?

Just weeks ago, we were convinced that Miss Novak would become the latest in a line of venerable soul models, but it's becoming increasingly clear that this prediction was premature. By contrast, at 30 days, Rupi Patel (aka @RealRupiP) had already amassed a following of many thousands and a spotless spiritual record. We asked Ms. Patel for her take on Novak's situation. She replied rather cryptically: NOMB/NOYB.[1]

Miss Novak, meanwhile, has ignored all requests for comment.

---

1. Huh? Does anyone know what this means?

AFTER

DAY 30

THIRTY DAYS. MY notifications churn. The Catherines stare as I scurry past. *An archive like Swiss cheese,* they whisper. Surely the Powers know what that means? Will their guards come to collect me? I can't just show up to my class like nothing's happened. I don't have it in me to face a bunch of lycra-loving gossips. Or Larisa.

The alley beckons, but I can't face Jethro right now either.

I pull up my hood, scoot out a side door to the street. Faye won't be home until evening. I need time to think.

BACK AT THE bungalow, a surprise: I open the door to find the TV on full blast, the front entryway clogged with piles of bags and boxes. I step back, thinking I've entered the wrong house, but nope: Quick check finds the usual group of reporters camped on the stoop. The one with the oversize sunglasses points her camera with a decidedly judgmental click.

I shut the door and kick back several boxes before pausing. The area between the couch and television is flooded with smashed-in bottles, balled-up papers, and . . . trash. My mother's pale form floats in the middle, like a ship lost on a sea of junk.

"Faye? What happened? Did someone . . ." I hunt for a logical explanation—trash bombing? reverse robbery?—but come up short.

"It was Chloe," Faye says miserably.

Chloe is Faye's new mentor, the one who's supposed to help her get back on track. "Chloe trashed our house?"

"What? No, sweetie. Ha ha. Chloe suggested I do a cleanse, and this one sounded"—Faye casts her gaze about the room—"promising."

"So you did this on purpose." Faye has imported a bunch of literal garbage into our living room intentionally.

"You're supposed to sort everything out, like a metaphor for the past, or . . . you know." Faye bites her lip. "It made more sense the way Chloe explained it."

"Yeah. I bet."

I push a raft of discarded foam cups off the sofa and take a careful seat. I don't ask where she even got this stuff (a sketchy refuse exchange out on the edge of the grid, she'll confess later, which charged an obscene fee). I don't have the heart to tell her that it sounds futile. I've looked through her archive—there's no way sorting a few bags of garbage could bring order to her past.

A beep from my tracker. This week's rent fee is officially over-due. I silence it for now.

On TV, they're interviewing the mother of another missing soul. There are a surprising number of families in the afterlife—victims of house fires and accidents, mostly—and apparently a few moms have formed a support group in the wake of Annabelle Schreiber's highly publicized disappearance. This one is crying. "My boy was having a tough time. His final test was coming up. Then one day, he left for classes and just . . . never came back."

Faye makes an odd sound.

"Have you been watching this all day?" I ask gently.

Faye has just ten days left before her final test, and while she's pulled herself out of the recent spiral, she still has a *lot* to prove in a very short time. In her final week, they'll run Faye through a bat-tery of tests—there's an online exam, a physical, and several inter-views. Faye's especially worried about the vibes portion. Despite all the meditation, hers remain erratic, and her anxiety only seems to intensify as the big day approaches.

The TV host probes her sobbing guest for details—"Was the son lax in his daily intentions? Did he consort with the wrong kind of souls?"—but the woman only cries harder. I can't take it. I hit the mute button.

Faye, wringing her hands, looks up at me. "Baby, I'm so wor-ried. Is it true what they're saying? About you skipping classes? This is so unlike you. How worried do I need to be?"

I look at our topsy-turvy living room, then back at agitated Faye. "Hang on. It's *me* you're worried about?" This is a switch.

Her hands twist harder. "It's my fault, isn't it? I know it's never been easy, being my kid. I put you in some impossible situations, didn't I? You were right to want to leave. You were right about everything."

Eyes like small oceans. Something in me pulls.

"I wasn't, though. I wasn't right every time."

I think back on all the moments I've uncovered in our past, all my prodding and angry words. It was never enough. Sometimes it made things worse.

"You were happier in that commune, weren't you?"

Faye's hands pause their wringing. "You mean the co-op?"

"Yeah. I didn't want you to go back there. I thought we'd be better off on our own. But it was too hard, just the two of us. You were happier with them, weren't you?"

Faye blinks, like something has clicked. "Oh, honey. Liberty and the others helped me get on my feet at a time when I needed it. But I wasn't *happy* when I was with them. Couldn't be. I didn't have you."

Suddenly I'm six years old again, left with my grandparents, no explanation, wondering why my mummy chose those hippies over me. Words jam in my throat.

"Listen, baby, I've been trying to sort it out, why I never got things right, with men, with you, my own mother. I've been trying to rebuild my narrative, like they tell us. Why did I fail at all of it? But the more I think things over . . ." Faye touches her temple, wincing. "The more I try to make sense of all of it, the more mixed up it gets."

"You're forgetting things?" I say softly.

"Oh, baby. No, the opposite! I'm remembering too much! Things from way back. Did you know I was voted 'Most Likely to

Shine' in eighth grade? Everyone back then thought I had so much potential. Joke's on them, huh?" She laughs bitterly.

"What happened to you?" It comes across harsher than I intend, but Faye just laughs at that too.

"You really want to know?"

I nod. "Yeah. I really do."

"Okay, here." She pats the floor beside her, and I hesitate only briefly before sliding down to meet her.

She tells me about the fights she had with Nonnie and Pop-Pop. They'd started in high school; she can't recall exactly why. "Maybe it was just the age, hormones, growing up," she muses. "Probably I would've been okay if it hadn't been for the people I was drawn to. All those radicals and misfits. Did you know at one point I dropped out of high school to explore acting? Your nonnie flipped, threw me out of the house when she heard about that."

I think of the scene I uncovered of Nonnie screaming, tossing Faye's clothes into the yard. And another memory, a bit later, of Faye in college, with an older man, heavy-boned like me. "Was my father a misfit too?"

"Oh no. The opposite. Your father was one of my attempts at normal. He was a grad student, in architecture. Smart, driven. *Handsome.* Girls flocked, but he only had eyes for me."

"So what happened?"

Faye sighs. "I was young. We got pregnant. Things got messy. He was a good man in many ways, but he had a mean streak too."

I swallow. "Like me."

Faye crooks her head, studying me. "I suppose he was a bit like you. You're smart like him, disciplined. Not mean, thank goodness. You get frustrated sometimes, but I'm pretty sure most teenage girls get like that with their moms, Mar. I've certainly given you enough reasons."

As I meet my mother's eyes, I think of all the awful spats I've revisited, all the times I chastised her for not being the sort of mother I wanted her to be. I'm angry at her still. I'm disappointed in myself, too. I don't know where to begin to fix this.

Faye grabs for my hands. "Don't you dare blame yourself, baby."

"But I—"

"It wasn't your—"

"I made it worse, though."

"No, it was—"

"But that's not—"

"Yes, it—"

"What?"

Our voices break and we both begin to laugh. An uncomfortable laughter that sounds closer to tears. There's still so much I don't understand, so much we haven't said. I don't know how to say it all.

Faye is looking at me. "Sometimes I wonder how things would have been different if I'd stuck it out, you know? If I'd never sent you to live with your grandparents, if—" She casts about, then suddenly picks up a can and hurls it. "Would you look at this mess I've made!"

She means the room. The past. All of it.

But is it all her fault, really? Once upon a time, I might have said yes, but now I'm not so sure. My mother might be a mess, but at least she tries. I think of Simone's speech to the rebels. What if it's not my mother who's broken, unable to fit inside the lines, but the lines themselves making everything harder than it needs to be?

Where were Faye's friends and teachers when she needed them? Why couldn't Nonnie support Faye's dreams the way she believed in mine?

Questions I'll likely never be able to fully answer.

Faye surveys the garbage heap. "Maybe this wasn't such a good idea."

"No. Probably not." I smile. I can't help it. It was a terrible idea. Chloe was a fool for suggesting it.

Faye sinks at my smile. "I'm hopeless, aren't I? I can't do anything right, even death!" She pulls at her fingers, violently.

"Stop. Don't . . ." I quiet her hands with mine. "Here. Look, we can handle this." I grab a couple of boxes. "Bottles here. Paper there. Yeah?"

Faye watches as I toss one item, then another, into its corresponding box.

Maybe I should leave her to handle it on her own. A few days ago, I would have. But something in me has shifted. All those hours in the alley. Simone's electric words. It doesn't seem right that any of us has to do this alone.

Faye catches on quickly, placing a can here, a bottle there. I begin to move faster, flinging things into boxes. I'm angry suddenly. At every adult who ever misunderstood her, at the Powers That Be for making us both feel so desperate. If a wide-eyed, celery-water-drinking optimist like Faye can't redeem herself, can't earn a place in the Ever After, then what's the point of any of this?

It takes several hours before the mess is gone. When it's done, we make a deal. We're not giving up. Time is tight, especially for Faye, but we can't let desperation get the better of us. We're going to focus on the stuff that actually helps us. After all, it's *our* eternity on the line, and we're not letting anyone tell us we don't deserve a chance at peace.

"If you need anything, I'm here, baby. You know that, right? You can trust me."

Although I wouldn't trust my mother with a can opener, I know she means it, with her whole heart. She is here for me, as long as she's allowed.

Faye unmutes the TV as we gather up our neatly sorted containers and drag them across the carpet. We're stacking the boxes in the foyer when a frantic voice cuts in with breaking news: There's been another one. Another soul who lost contact with the grid. This time the name knocks me sideways.

It's Larisa Liu.

THE DAILY WITNESS

BREAKING: SECOND TEEN DISAPPEARS

———

New intelligence confirms: Larisa Liu of Section #64F has vanished under mysterious circumstances. The teen missed her dormitory's curfew yesterday, and there have been no pings from her tracker in more than twelve hours.

Originally hailing from West Haven, Connecticut, Liu passed into the realm fifty-one days ago. Liu's instructors describe her as an exceptionally strong student on track for an on-time ascension, which makes her disappearance all the more peculiar.

Chairman Ted warned residents that the afterlife's radical network may be more dangerous than previously understood. "This is a malignant cancer that wishes to attack every cell," he informed a sparsely attended rally. "Be watchful, friends, wary. Refuse the company of any who stray, and maintain your spiritual hygiene at all costs!"

Following the rally, the Powers That Be issued a joint decree: All Paradise Gate residents must remain alert. Any resident who fails to report suspicious activity or disclose information regarding Liu's whereabouts will be deemed an accomplice and penalized accordingly.

AFTER

—

DAY 31

UNIFORMED GUARDS BLOCK the Center's front entrance, muttering into walkie-talkies as they inspect students' belongings for contraband literature and other signs of misdeeds. The lobby's usual chanting and nattering has been replaced by an uneasy hush.

Larisa is missing. Fear flits across my peers' faces. *Was she taken?* they whisper. *Did she flee? Where? Why?*

Their most pressing question: *Who will disappear next?*

I picture Larisa frowning in the registration office on my first day, introducing the air-quote virgins with a snort. Larisa shoveling kale mush while explaining the trouble with martyrs. Larisa failing at Youga, telling me about her missing dad. I try to recall specific conversations—clues I might have missed—but the more I try to remember, the murkier it gets.

A booming announcement directs all students to the auditorium at the start of first period. We leave our meditation cushions behind and form a line in the corridor. For once, the Catherines are quiet. Reenie appears outside the instructors' lounge and pulls me toward her.

"Have you talked to her?"

"Larisa?" I shake my head, unsure what information I'd share with Reenie even if I had. Doesn't she work for the Powers?

Reenie nods, as if understanding. "If you do hear anything, tell her to be careful. You be careful, too, okay?"

She says it like she knows what I'm about to do, then slips back through the wall of students, leaving me to be carried on their tide.

I'm not going through another interrogation, that's for sure. I can't risk it, not in the state I'm in. I break away from the procession at the library, half expecting to find Larisa at her usual computer, scowling into the screen. But the basement room is quiet, her chair empty and screen dark.

I log on the way she showed me and maneuver through the discussion tiers. The transcendentalism thread has been active, lots of posts by ForceBU (Larisa's handle) earlier this week, and several more by TruthOrDie. It's all space talk, outposts and transponders and words I can't decipher. Another user, Eternal_Taco, pops in briefly with what looks like a math problem: **50 + 1500**.

ForceBU's last message was posted yesterday: **Coordinates received, takeoff confirmed. If signal lost, discontinue communication.**

I may not know much about space movies, but I know this sounds like trouble.

I scan through the other messages, trying to make sense of what they're saying. My gaze sticks on the equation: **50 + 1500**.

It takes a moment for me to recognize the format: It's a time code. Day fifty, fifteen hundred hours. Same format we've seen in class when we analyze our tracker data.

We want you to come forward with any suspicious activity, the Suit commanded me.

Anyone with information about Ms. Liu's whereabouts must report it, decreed the Powers.

I picture Larisa stuck somewhere, having trusted the wrong information, the wrong people. I know what I have to do.

I'M ON THE next eastbound bus, GPS disabled, face pressed against the smear-proof glass.

I wasn't going to go back to the warehouse. I've done enough digging through the past. After yesterday's talk with Faye, that pull has diminished. But Larisa's disappearance doesn't make sense, and as her former friend, I feel a responsibility to find out what I can.

ForceBU's final message made sense once I broke the code: Larisa disappeared on her fiftieth day, and when I went back through the chat room thread, sure enough, she'd made a plan with Eternal_Taco to "storm the fort" shortly after fifteen hundred hours. I don't know what fort she planned to storm—and there was a whole back-and-forth about *Star Wars: Episode II* that went over my head completely—but I'm hoping she left some digital crumbs that will point me in the right direction. I'm hoping I'll get there before they scrub her from the system.

I arrive at the warehouse without a hitch. The computers are sparsely populated today, just a small handful of rebels hunched over screens. At least one looks like he's been there for days. Not for the first time I wonder what they're all doing here, who or what they're searching for exactly.

I settle in at my usual station and do a simple search for *Larisa Liu*. I'm too late. Her account has already been scrubbed, just like they did to Annabelle.

Deep breath. I knew this might happen. There's clearly something about the two disappearances that's related, something the Powers don't want anyone else to know.

It occurs to me that I'm sitting in a room full of experienced hackers. Might they have a workaround for a problem like this? I scan the stations near me. I recognize one of the fast-talking guys from the meeting I attended and then, a couple rows over, hunched low over a keyboard, a crown of scarlet-tipped locs.

I hesitate before rising from my chair. Simone's wearing large sound-blocking headphones. I take a breath and tap her shoulder.

Her eyebrows jump, then settle when she sees who it is.

"Can I help you?" she says in a way that suggests she'd really rather not.

I want to walk away, but I have to do this. Larisa's in trouble, her eternity on the line. "I was wondering . . . is there a way to locate a hidden account, break past a firewall or whatever?"

"Depends who built the wall."

"Pretty sure it was the PTB?"

Simone stares at me a moment. "Well, in that case, yeah. Their tech is terrible. Who're you trying to find?"

I tell her quickly that I have a friend who's gone missing. I whisper Larisa's name but don't say much more—Larisa's in enough trouble as it is—and Simone's posture immediately changes, like she's reassessed her opinion of me. She nods toward the chair beside her. She punches a few keys, moving through one screen into something that looks like an admin backend.

"The PTB's code is a mess," she says while she works. "The third founder left them with all kinds of problems they haven't been able to fix. We think it was his way of saying FU to Ted and Lady Woo before popping off the grid for good. It's been a gift to us, though."

"You know him?" I ask. "The third founder?"

Simone shakes her head. "But I've spent enough time in his system that I sure feel like I do. Here." She jabs through the menu, types Larisa's name, and an error message appears: **Account Not Found.**

"Dang. They deleted the backup too. What exactly did your friend do?" Simone sounds impressed.

"I have no clue," I admit. "She was into chat rooms and stuff, but I didn't think it was anything serious."

"Do you know which rooms she was in?" I share Larisa's handle and the name of the chat room I've seen.

Simone clicks around a bit more, makes a face.

"What? What is it?"

"Your friend had some interesting connections, that's for sure. But the good news, it looks like she took precautions. She planned to capture her mission on a livestream using a duplicate account."

"Mission? Duplicate? How did you figure that out? What does that even mean?"

"That's what they're talking about here: *Episode II: Attack of the Clones*. The code's pretty see-through for those who know."

Simone types something else, then opens what she tells me is a cloned version of Larisa's feed. I never in a million eternities would have figured this out on my own.

"You ready?" Simone says, before clicking on a video posted yesterday.

The footage opens on Larisa's face, talking fast and low into her tracker's tiny camera. Behind Larisa, a public bus retreats from view.

"Some quick background for anyone who finds this," she's saying. "I just arrived at the outpost. From here, I'm going to take you on a walk, due east, toward the edge of the settlement." The camera begins to bounce, catching more of Larisa's chin than her face, as she moves in the opposite direction of the bus. "I've received information about the last-known location of my father, Franklin Liu, who arrived in Paradise Gate two years ago, March, and was gone by early May, an entire month before his term was up. I believe he was deliberately disconnected from the grid, punished for challenging the system. Which would make sense if you knew my dad. He was . . ." Larisa checks over her shoulder and lets out a small huff. "The point is, I've been sent the address of his last-known location, a highly secret PTB facility."

Larisa's throat pulses visibly, and I feel myself clutching the table, barely believing she's doing this, that she'd be so brave. Or foolish?

"There's a chance I'll find my dad today. It's not a great one. More likely, he's long gone, disappeared into the fuzz. But if I can find proof of what they did to him, that will be something. And if I don't make it back from this errand, I hope one of you watching this—Taco, you got me?—will pass along the truth."

Larisa stops talking and points the camera at the scene before her: a sprawling white building with large metal doors. Its sloped roof is translucent, like a giant greenhouse, and its corrugated walls seem to stretch forever. Larisa looks down at her wrist, as if confirming the address, then approaches the front door. She presses a buzzer and waits. A moment later a guard appears, his uniform a similar style but darker shade than the guards' uniforms at the Center.

"I'm here with a records request," Larisa says.

The guard peers past her, puzzled. He begins to close the door, but Larisa juts out a hand. "I have questions about someone who was taken into custo—"

She's snatched through the door and it shuts with a bang.

There's a sort of scuffle, the outline of a desk, a chair, of Larisa's flailing foot.

"Where are you taking me?" Larisa grunts as the guard drags her down what appears to be a narrow corridor. "I haven't done anything wrong! I just want information!"

The guard, ignoring her complaints, yanks open another door, and everything goes sideways. Larisa murmurs something, a muscled arm reaches, there's a clicking sound, and the screen turns to black.

The video ends, and the window shrinks back to a thumbnail.

I stare, mouth agape, trying to make sense of what we've just witnessed. Did the guard turn off Larisa's camera? Or disconnect her completely? Is that how the cut to 3:00 a.m. works? What was that place anyway?

Beside me, Simone clears her throat.

"Your friend is pretty bold."

"Yeah." I swallow. "Or stupid . . . Can we watch it again?"

We start again at the beginning, pausing at key points to zoom in on pertinent information—the number of the bus, a small sign by the front door, which we missed on first viewing, that reads REALM SECURITY with the seal of the Powers That Be.

It's so much darker than I imagined. Larisa isn't missing. The PTB know exactly where she is, and their reporters likely do too. That news alert last night was a total fabrication. Simone appears less shocked. As we rewatch the last sequence, the wild tumble of the screen as the guard throws Larisa around like a doll, I feel my stomach rise into my throat.

"Did you—? But. Why would—? Holy shit, is this real?" I'm rocking on my chair, chewing my thumb, unable to contain the anger and shock.

A squeeze on my shoulder brings me back into the present.

"You. Need to chill."

Simone.

"But—" I glance at the screen, then at Simone, whose brown eyes wait patiently as I stutter for an explanation.

"I need to help her," I say hoarsely. "I need to find my friend."

"C'mon." She waves me up from the computer and toward the back hallway. I follow this time without hesitation. Is she going to show me how to find Larisa? Maybe I can take the same bus to its final destination, or we can locate the building's coordinates from her video. Maybe we can use her GPS to track her location right now. I pause my own train of thought. And then what? What happens then? Do I follow Larisa like some kind of loose-cannon detective? Knock on the same door? Will she even be—*alive*'s not the word—*intact*?

"There's nothing I can do, is there?" I say to Simone's back.

Simone turns to me, head shaking. I expect her to repeat some version of what our instructors are always saying: *Eyes on your own path.* Or worse, text Jethro to come fetch me. Instead she surprises me. "This helpless act really ain't cute. Haven't you been listening? There are options, always. Especially for a fighter like you."

Excuse me? Did she call me a . . . *fighter*?

Simone sighs like she can't believe how dense I am. Then, expression turning to pity, she drags me through a doorway into a small, cluttered office. Books are everywhere, the walls plastered with notes, maps, and fluttering flyers in bright tangerine.

"Gotta be careful what I say out there. Pretty sure we've got spies inside the operation now."

"Spies?" I feel my eyes widen.

"You bet. The PTB are dying to take us down. You don't need to worry about that, though. Here." With the door firmly shut, Simone says, "Let me spell some things out for you."

AFTER

——

DAY 32

ANOTHER BUS PULLS away—the third one to come and go since I arrived. Dozens of passengers have filtered through, most headed to the outer sectors after another long day of classes. Only one person has stayed put. It's a face I've grown accustomed to seeing, partly hidden behind large statement sunglasses, often just a few paces behind. She's currently perched on the far end of the bench, reading a newspaper through her dark glasses, though there's zero percent chance of sun breaking through the colorless sky.

A fresh group of passengers will arrive soon. I only have a small window to do this.

I slide onto the bench.

"I have a proposal," I say calmly to the reporter's startled face.

"Um." She adjusts her sunglasses, eyes darting behind the tinted glass. "I'm sorry. Have we met?"

"Stop. You know who I am. I know *what* you are." I point to the small microphone—barely concealed—beneath her lapel. "And I've got a proposal that I think you'll like."

She slides the glasses onto her head.

"I have some footage I need you to release. About Larisa Liu."

The reporter pulls back, lips parted. "Oh no. I'm afraid I don't— You must be confused. There's no way *I* could do that."

"Please. Let's cut the crap. We both know how it works."

Simone helped connect several missing dots—things I might have picked up on if I'd been paying closer attention or knew how to look. Those sleazy reporters with their rag-bag memory dumps and uncanny questions about Faye's and my past? Reporters, Simone explained, are failed souls who've become indentured servants to the Powers That Be, working in exchange for an extended stay in the realm, one more shot at redemption. Not everyone gets an extra chance, Simone told me, and not everyone would want one on these terms. The folks chosen for media gigs have an especially bendable moral code. There are strict guidelines for the type of stories they're allowed to tell. Their job is to share news that regular people will like, full of intrigue and uplift, while always painting the PTB in a positive light. Occasionally, though, if the incentives are right, reporters (see: flexible morals) will take a freelance gig, releasing snippets through back channels. It's risky business for the leakers, but the payoff can be big if it helps them land an even bigger story.

Simone explained that there's a network of loved ones and activists who've been trying to share information about what's really happening to so-called missing souls, but none of them have the leverage I do. Simone walked me through the steps I'd need to take.

None of us are in this alone, she told me. *That's the first lie they feed us.*

"So, you'll do it?" I say to the reporter.

She twists uncomfortably in her seat. "Look, I'm just a beat reporter, trying to avoid the abyss same as you. I don't have that type of clearance."

"Bullshit," I say. I feel almost bad for her. Living a constant lie, doing the PTB's dirty work. Did she realize how it would be when she signed on?

"You must be confused," she insists. "Someone's given you bad information."

"Bullshit," I say again.

Her face changes then, from nervous to irritated. "What do you want? Why pick me?"

"Because you're here. You're always freaking here every time I turn around. All I'm asking for is a trade. You do a favor for me—share a twenty-second clip, during prime time if you can—and I'll give you what you want."

She cocks her head.

"An exclusive interview. My first. Pitch it however you want. *Hero Gone off the Rails. True Confessions of a Former Soul Model.* I don't care. Folks love that crap, right? You'll suddenly be everyone's favorite reporter. I bet the bosses will love it too."

I can see her mind calculating. *Ratings are a reporter's best friend,* Simone explained. *It's how they get bonus points. Give them what they want. Be their Britney, their Whitney. Folks love nothing more than to see someone who was riding high fall from grace.*

"I'll tell you whatever you want to know. About the shooter I definitely didn't punch, my terrible vibes, my overdue rent, why I hate meditating. You can ask me anything."

The reporter is now sitting all the way forward. "You have this clip with you now?"

THE DAILY WITNESS

BREAKING:
FIRST-EVER INTERVIEW WITH MARIANNA
NOVAK, A PMG EXCLUSIVE

———

This Friday, Marianna Novak will speak live on the 24-hour PMG Network. In a no-holds-barred interview, PMG's own Juniah Harper will speak with Novak about her life, death, and what's happened since. We'll learn more about Novak's recent misdeeds and failures, getting to the bottom of whether she is a victim, a hero, or just another soul who can't hack the work.

Set your clocks for Friday, 8:00 p.m. This show's guaranteed to be revealing.

AFTER

DAY 32 CONTINUED

THEY AIR LARISA'S video exactly once. Shortly after dinner, a reporter breaks into one of Faye's evening shows with an announcement. Faye calls me from my room.

I'm there in time to see Larisa yanked inside the building by the guard. We watch as they travel the corridor and he shoves her into some sort of room. The final tussle has been cut, but it's plenty to spark a fresh wave of chatter on the feed. Everyone has seen where Larisa went. Someone even got a screenshot of the building. Within minutes, the image goes viral.

Was that really a PTB facility? they all want to know. How did Larisa find it? Some muse that she must be caught up with dangerous rebels. Others surmise that she's a victim, duped or entrapped.

The PTB step in quickly to manage the spin, as Simone warned they would. There's a press conference at 9:00 p.m. The man at the microphone is someone I recognize—the same suited man who interviewed me about Annabelle/Catherine of Phoenix. Turns out he's not just another Center administrator; he's head of PTB security.

"This latest information is a surprise to all of us," he tells the cameras. "We're not sure where the clip came from—who leaked it or how—but the facility you saw is not ours. We believe this video to be a fake." He pauses to hold the gaze of those watching. "Miss Liu's whereabouts are under investigation. We promise that updates will come as soon as we have them. In the meantime, we ask residents to refrain from idle speculation."

Faye watches me as I watch the screen.

The camera cuts back to a newsroom, where a cheery reporter smiles broadly. "Don't forget to join us Friday for an exclusive interview with Marianna Novak! What would you ask the settlement's most underperforming soul model if you had her trapped in our studio for thirty minutes? We're taking questions right now on the feed!"

Faye reaches for my hand and squeezes it gently. If she has an inkling of what I did, she doesn't say it.

I'M A MESS as I get ready for class Thursday morning. My vibes are spiking and nerves jangling as I wait for more news of Larisa . . . or for someone to tie the leak to me.

Simone advised me against chasing after Larisa myself. "One more missing soul helps no one," she said. Instead, she urged me to use my position to put the PTB on notice, help wake up the settlement to what's really going on. Folks who don't fit the program—those who fail to hit their final benchmarks or who challenge the regime directly—are being disappeared, detained by the PTB's security forces, and taken who knows where.

It remains unclear how much impact the video clip really had, though. The screenshot of the PTB facility vanished from the feed almost as soon as it went viral. Other chatter about Larisa quieted overnight, or maybe just went underground into less public and more carefully coded chat rooms.

Around 2:00 a.m. I received a private message that made me sit up in bed. I'd been DMed by the one and only @RealRupiP.

Her message: **You got this one, sis. Your fan, Rupi.**

Did she mean the upcoming interview? Or did she somehow know I was behind the leak? Either way, there was no sleeping after that.

I arrive at the Center fuzzy headed and wondering if I've shorted my own system with too much worrying. A second rent warning arrived this morning, more ominous than the first. With no way to pay it, I had no choice but to hit "ignore."

I stop by the library on the way to class. There've been no new posts from Larisa, but Eternal_Taco has left a reply to her most recent post: **Hello?**

I can't tell if the message is for Larisa or me.

The avatar is active. Whoever it is, they're online now. **What happens now?** I type.

We wait, they write. **We let the dust settle.**

"MARI?"

Jethro steps out into the alley minutes after me. Usually I wait for an official break to slip away, but this time I just walked out of class.

"Are you gonna explain why you ditched Youga in tomorrow's prime-time interview?"

I can tell from his chuckle that he has no idea about the trade I made. Simone must have kept our plan secret.

When he passes me the cigarette, I reach for his whole hand, pulling him toward me.

"Namaste," he says as our foreheads touch.

We're still for a long moment, not talking, not kissing, just looking into each other's faces. I feel my jittering vibes begin to steady for the first time in twenty-four hours and understand something: Larisa was wrong. This isn't your usual good-girl-meets-deadbeat story. It's something else. Something I don't yet know how to name.

REENIE PULLS ME aside at the end of the day. I prepare for a scolding. I have not gotten on track, despite multiple promises. My vibes are a mess, classwork unpredictable, point balance in the crapper. If I don't pay my rent soon, I'm pretty sure I'll be among the next to be disappeared. Still, the depth of her frown surprises me.

"Mari, I'm worried about you."

"I'm so sorry. I totally forgot about last night's homework. It won't happen again."

I put on my most convincing honor-roll smile, the one that's worked on so many teachers in the past, but Reenie's frown doesn't budge.

"You've said that before, Mari. At some point, one has to question your sincerity."

I drop my gaze. She isn't wrong. My teacher's-pet act has grown pretty shabby. (At what point does a former good girl become something else entirely?)

"Mari, your eternity is in serious jeopardy. Is it true you've fallen behind on your fees? You know you'll only get three warnings. What do you need? What can we do to get you back on the path?"

"We?"

Reenie is being far too kind. Why? I'm not her problem to fix. And anyway, I don't know what I need. I think of the pledge Faye and I made earlier this week. We both promised to get back to work, to not let desperation get the better of us. Secretly, I'd added an additional pledge: to stay away from that warehouse. And I'd meant it at the time. I don't need a *revolution*. I just need for things to not be so messy. I need Larisa to be safe, Faye to be happy, the afterworld to stop calling me a soul model when it's clear that I'm not. I'd like to know a secure, peaceful future is possible, that I won't always feel so helpless and alone. More than anything, I need space to breathe.

"I just have to focus, do the work. I promise, I will."

Reenie squints at me doubtfully. "Are you sure you want to do a TV interview when you're still so early in your process? They'll aim to catch you off guard, you know. You won't be able to put them off with half-baked stories about wishing you'd played sports."

I squirm. I guess my journal entries haven't been very convincing. And Reenie's right. I haven't prepared for this or even considered the questions they'll ask. If they're even half as difficult as the ones Reenie assigns us, I'll be screwed.

"I can't back out of the interview. It's . . . complicated."

Reenie nods in a way that makes me wonder if she knows the type of commitment I made. "How about you let me help? I can prep you for the toughest questions."

"You'd do that?"

"Sure. Here, let's play this out." She smooths her hair and leans in, like a coach in a huddle. "They'll begin with a story in mind. Their questions will be designed to have you tell it their way. They'll make it hard for you to remember the truth you want to tell . . ."

REENIE AND I stay in her room past dinnertime. Her questions are brutal.

What's going on with your vibes?

Where do you go when you miss class?

What are you still avoiding, Mari?

What really happened on the day you died?

Why are you still so angry at your mother?

I pause. "You really think they'll ask about that?"

"I don't know. But it's all on the table, Mari. They're looking for your weak spots, and excuse me for saying this, you aren't very good at hiding them." Reenie's brown eyes twinkle, causing me to cringe.

"That's fair."

We start with the mom question. I tell Reenie all of it, beginning with Faye's arrest and death, and then looping back to the many moves, lost jobs, and bitter fights. How I grew to resent Faye and blame her for everything. How more recently I've come to see that she was hurting too.

Reenie listens quietly, betraying no shock when I mention, in a roundabout way, my deep dives into memory. I tell her how the deeper I dug, the more conflicted and ashamed I'd felt. And exhausted. Is there a way to reframe my narrative? If there is, I don't yet see it, and doing a bunch of power poses hasn't helped. So many years of following rules, and it never made an ounce of difference. I've given up. On points, on classes, on trying.

"On yourself too, it sounds like," Reenie said.

Dang. I guess Reenie really has found her vocation.

"It sounds to me like you've been afraid of failure for a long time, Mari. Not just your mother's but your own. That's not so unusual for young people who've been forced to self-parent. Perhaps you believed if you didn't handle everything perfectly, it would make you less worthy of love. And when your best efforts were upended—due to no fault of your own, I must say—you took it as proof of your own lack."

I blink hard. I'm way out of my depth here.

"Mari, is it possible this isn't really about your mother? That the one you've been too hard on is you?"

I open my mouth, but all that comes out is air. My mind paddles, seeking something to anchor on to, words that will bring me back to shore.

Sensing my discomfort, Reenie sits back in her chair. "Let's try something different, shall we? Why don't you tell me about a happy memory?"

"Happy?" I croak.

"Yes, there must have been good times, positive memories from your past."

"I was happy when I lived with my grandparents . . ."

"Do you remember anything before that? From your early life with your mother?"

"Well . . ." I have to stretch, push through swaths of blanked-out history to what lies beneath. "I remember her hair—it was so long and shiny—and the way she laughed. With every inch of her body . . ."

Something twitches under loose bits of memory. No, it's not quite a memory. More like an image. I'm seated on a white bed stacked high with pillows. Faye's laughter fills the whole room. She's jumping, shimmying. There's music. We grab each other's hands, and she lifts me up up up over the blankets, over her head, till we're a whirl of sheets and hair and light.

It's a tiny thing, barely a moment, but in telling it, a dam breaks loose.

"I missed her," I tell Reenie. "When she left the first time and the times after that, I missed her. A lot. And I think . . ." Is it possible? A bed piled high with pillows. Warmth, rest, safety. "I'm pretty sure that ever since, I've been trying to get that moment back."

My own Ever After.

I don't cry, don't break, but in saying those words, I feel myself let go of something, not everything, but something that leaves me feeling lighter.

"This is good," Reenie says, hands clasped. "I think we've got to the heart of the matter. Now let's talk about which parts you should say on camera."

AFTER

—

DAY 34

FRIDAY, 7:55 P.M. The TV studio is simply decorated: two chairs on a spotlit stage. Offstage, the camera crew bustles, adjusting angles and testing microphones, while I sit tall in my chair, waiting.

I feel better than I have in a while. Braver. After my conversation with Reenie, it's like someone took a shovel and scraped all the sediment from my head. What I found underneath was messier than I expected, more wormy and raw. But not quite as scary as I'd imagined. Reenie says a lot of souls arrive with baggage related to their families; the sad truth is not every kid gets parents who are well equipped for the job. She said it's normal to feel angry about that. It's also possible to find the parent I need in other places— in friends, grandparents, mentors. And, on the best days, within myself.

When I got up this morning, the strange, glitchy feeling of the past few days had subsided, and my vibes had turned a yolky sort of orange. I felt awake for the first time in ages, like I'd discovered a hidden pocket of energy.

I knocked through three mini-assignments and immediately applied the points to our overdue rent. It wasn't the full payment but enough to show good faith. (Reenie's suggestion.) My vibes softened further as soon as I sent it, to a yellow more like the sun.

This morning's news gave me more fuel. The Powers That Be announced that they've located more than a dozen souls who'd been reported missing. They offered no names or specifics but said the individuals are undergoing a security assessment and will be released in the next two to three days.

Is Larisa among them? Will the Powers honor their promise of release? I've seen enough by now to be skeptical. Still, there's not much I can do except wait, and hope. And survive this dang interview.

The reporter—"Please, call me Juniah"—looks a lot younger without her sunglasses. Maybe it's all the makeup she's wearing; the faux lashes make her look like a frightened baby deer. I don't think she's covered such a big story before.

The camera guy gives us the okay, and Juniah turns stiffly to me. The first question, predictably, is about my alleged savior moment. I tell her what I told Reenie: It was all a misunderstanding, a mistake.

"So you didn't stand up to the shooter?"

"Not on purpose. Honestly, I doubt I even saw him. I was yelling at that panhandler, the witness who calls herself Z, telling her *not today*. I was in a rush."

"It sounds like you were having a rough day," Juniah says.

"Try a rough decade."

Juniah asks me to tell her more, so I share a truncated version of what I told Reenie: the financial troubles, my dwindling scholarship options, my mother's death. I go light on the details about Faye, who I know is glued to the screen, watching this.

Juniah presses on the Faye parts, but I hold firm. She shifts to asking about my archive. "It appears to have been damaged somehow. Do you know how that happened?"

I lift my head. "*My* memories are *my* business."

There's a stir in the studio.

Juniah glances over her shoulder at whoever sits behind the glass. Did they catch that?

"Are you suggesting that you mutilated your own memory bank?"

"I'm saying what is or isn't in my archive is none of your concern, or anyone's but mine. Why should my life be your entertainment?"

She stares at me a long moment before flipping to another cue card.

"Rumor has it you knew Larisa Liu?"

"We were classmates," I say carefully. I let her get to me with the last question. *Keep it calm and simple,* Reenie advised.

"I see," Juniah says. "And do you know what led her to take on such a risky errand? Some are suggesting she may have been recruited into an elaborate plot to break up the settlement."

I snort. "Sounds like some folks wouldn't know a fact if it bit them on the ass."

My tracker pings at the curse word, and I smile blandly. If Juniah thinks I'm throwing Larisa under the bus, she's got another think coming.

"You seem a bit angry, Miss Novak. Why is that?"

"Oh, I don't know. Maybe because I've had my privacy repeatedly violated by a bunch of incompetents? Don't you think we'd all have a better shot at redemption if all of you so-called reporters dialed down the drama and let us sort out our lives in peace?"

Juniah goes baby-deer-in-the-headlights, and I decide to back off. I'm not here to create more trouble. We made a simple deal: a thirty-minute interview about my life and death. According to the clock over her shoulder, there are only three minutes left.

I relax into my chair, answering the next round of questions crisply. Juniah tosses a few softballs about my hopes for eternity and favorite mantras. Reenie helped me choose a few I could live with if this question came up. (My selections: *One step at a time. Forget perfection. I am enough.*)

But then, as the clock hits the hour, Juniah throws a curveball. "What about romance, Miss Novak? Do you have any wisdom to share on that topic?"

I frown. "Romance?"

"Yes, don't be shy. Tell us. Has there been anyone . . . *special?*" Juniah reveals a straight line of pretty teeth.

"Oh." I tuck my chin. "No. I . . ."

I think of Jethro's soft touch and crooked smile. She couldn't mean . . . could she?

"My life was messy, like I said. I didn't have time for any of that."

"How about now?"

I go still. Reenie and I didn't cover this topic. What do I say? If I lie, my tracker will ping, giving me away. And if I tell the truth . . . on live TV . . . for the entire realm to see? Juniah crooks her head, watching me fumble, reading my face like a book.

"That's um . . . an . . . uh . . . interesting question," I say, stretching my syllables to buy time. I glance at the clock as the second hand rounds the bend. Juniah sees it too. There's a stir in the back of the studio.

Juniah turns to the cameras with a slow, floppy-lashed wink. "What do you say, folks? Shall we let Marianna Novak keep one secret?"

I smile at her in relief.

I OPEN THE front door to gurgling music and a burning odor. "Faye?"

A bare foot juts out from behind the couch. I race over, panicking briefly at the sight of my sprawled mother, before remembering, for the umpteenth time, that we're already dead.

Faye's eyes flutter open as I plunk onto the sofa. "Mari? What time is—" She reads her tracker. "Oof. Did I fall asleep?"

"Trying to meditate again?" I ask gently.

Faye nods. "I can't seem to get it right. No matter how hard I try. Baby, I'm *trying*."

"I know. I've seen you. You have to just . . . keep at it. You'll get there."

I try to sound convincing, but Faye has only six days until her final assessment period begins. She'll take the computerized portion on day eighty-five, followed by the interviews and the rest; on day ninety, she'll appear before the Center's board for her final ruling. There is very little to suggest Faye will "get there" in time.

Unless something changes dramatically, my mother is just eleven days away from being axed from the grid, a true and final separation, and there's nothing I can do.

Faye pulls herself up onto the couch. "You really killed it with that interview, baby."

"You watched all of it?"

"Of course! I was so proud of you! I got a little worried when you cussed and told off that reporter, but I practiced my deep breathing and it looks like you did too. Did you see that the Real Rupi P gave your interview *three* sets of praise hands?"

"She did?"

I unmute my tracker, then immediately regret it. I have more notifications than I've ever seen—more new followers, more reactions and shares and frowny faces and praise hands and . . . ugh, yup, there's a thinly veiled death threat in there too. Which I guess is meant ironically, but still.

"Everyone's saying it's the most honest interview they've seen in ages," Faye says. "Look here. I bet they're airing clips." She flicks on the TV before I can object.

They're replaying that final curveball, my pathetic fumble as Juniah asked me about romance. A panel of commentators offer sly-eyed conjectures of who my mystery lover could be. *Lover.* That's the word they choose. I cover my face, praying that Jethro hasn't seen it.

"So . . ." Faye says, pulling a foot up beneath her. "Are you going to tell me about this mystery guy? Or girl? Has my baby fallen in love?"

"Ugh. What?" I shake my head firmly. "They're exaggerating.

Like they always do. And you know romance is frowned upon."

"The best stuff always is," Faye says with a sigh. "But my spiritual adviser says there's no guide more important than your own heart."

"Please tell Chloe I said thanks."

Faye misses the sarcasm.

"Chloe also says it can help to confide in others when we're feeling muddled." She pushes a curl from my forehead, pats the spot beside her on the couch, urging me closer. I make the mistake of looking directly into her eyes—so open, so ready. Faye isn't the mother I need—she likely never will be—but there's real love waiting there. I've told no one about Jethro, except Larisa, and that was more confrontation than confession. I'm bursting with questions, and feelings I can't explain, even to myself. Like, the way he looks at me sometimes, how I've begun to wonder if this is more than an afterworld distraction. Maybe I am starting to feel actual feelings. Not quite love. Not yet. But something close.

"His name is Jethro," I tell Faye. "He has an adorable smile, and he's a good listener."

Faye claps. "I knew it! How did it happen? When did you meet? Tell me everything."

It's the type of mother-daughter moment I've always wanted, the type I didn't use to believe could be real. And although I know it's only that—a moment—I give in and tell her all of it.

AFTER

DAYS 34-37

THE FEED WEIGHS in Friday evening. It's even worse than I'd imagined: my possible, probable (*didn't her silence say it all?*) love life the topic of nearly every thread. The bit about my mutilated archive seems to have gone over everyone's heads. I half expect stiff-backed security to come banging at the door to ask what I meant when I said *My memories are my business*, but the weekend slips by. #MarisMysteryLover continues trending, I continue doomscrolling. No word of Larisa.

On Monday morning, Faye makes a sympathetic murmur when I appear in the kitchen and offers to brew me a spirit-centering tea. "You can do this, baby. I believe in you."

With the bulk of our rent bill still outstanding, what choice do I have?

At the Center, I stop by the library first, but there are no updates on the message boards. It's been seven days since Larisa disappeared. My big media risk has produced nothing.

Reenie catches me as I head up to class. "You did good," she whispers with a quick press of the hand. "Really held your own."

I make a skeptical face.

"Ignore the chatter. This may work in your favor, as distractions often do."

Easy for her to say. It's not her romantic life being scrutinized.

The hallways are all bold stares and whispers. A few people whisper Jethro's name—they've noticed us together—but others dismiss the idea as ridiculous. I'm glad he's MIA today because one glance between us, and they'd know for sure.

"Is it a student?" Catherine of Pasadena asks in the lunch line. "Or an instructor? Or . . . a *guru*?" She almost loses her tray at the thought.

Another asks, "Was it a spiritual connection at first but then, slowly, things started to blossom and—"

"Did it happen during a reiki treatment?" interrupts a third. "As the pressure grew stronger, did you feel all of that energy coursing straight to your—"

She gets a sharp elbow.

"Sorry, I don't have a thing for any gurus," I tell them, "and I've never tried reiki. Not sure I will now?"

With no Larisa to buffer me, I steer my tray to the far end of the cafeteria, toward the group who've taken an oath of silence. I settle in and stare at my 100 percent plant-based sandwich. Just as I'm thinking that the eternal abyss would be preferable to my current situation, everyone's tracker pings.

Breaking news. Dozens of mouths pull into simultaneous horrified Os.

"Him?" Catherine of Pasadena shrieks.

"HIM?!" Milwaukee echoes.

I almost can't do it. I hold my breath as I flick open my feed. The image that appears is grainy. Two figures, hip to hip. Baby-blue Sweatslacks, dark gray flannel. His face is concealed by a wash of dark hair, mine bared to the camera. In the distance: tall mounds of dust.

It's our first kiss behind the warehouse.

But how? Had a reporter followed me there? Or—hang on, check out the angle—was this taken by someone *inside* the warehouse?

The cafeteria is mayhem. These folks don't need to see a face to know exactly who it is. They see that flannel slouch every day.

"Seriously?"

"A deadbeat?"

"Mari, what were you thinking?!"

He's actually very sweet! He looks out for me! I want to shout back at them. *Unlike you assholes.* But one glance at the accompanying article, and I'm running.

It's my turn to look out for Jethro.

HE'S IN THE alley when I find him. I don't have to ask if he's seen the news because his broken posture makes clear he has.

I skimmed the article on my way down the stairs. They revealed Jethro's identity, along with numerous details from his life. Addict mom, no-show dad, six rounds of foster care. Then, in a hopeful twist, a loving uncle swooped in, only to get killed in a house fire alongside his loyal retriever. Cause of the fire:

a carelessly disposed cigarette. Prime suspect: You guessed it.

Jethro died by suicide a few weeks later. "I deserved to die, not him," he told his afterlife intake interviewer. "I'd do it again."

They included that. In the "article." Not sparing a single cruel detail.

My sweet, sunken-shouldered boy.

"Beyond hope!" they've declared him after reviewing his data. "Star-crossed or slumming?" they asked about me.

I slide along the Center's outer wall until our arms are almost touching. The reporters never would have dug all of this up if it weren't for that stupid interview. Why didn't I just keep my cool and say *no comment*?

Jethro takes a long drag from the cigarette, releasing the smoke in a lopsided ring.

"It's fine, Mari. Really. Nothing I didn't know. I'm a lost cause, it's no secret."

"No. Don't . . . say that." I touch his arm. "Tune it out, remember? Delete that noise. They're vultures. They don't know you."

I tug at his shirt gently, but he remains glued to the wall, staring straight ahead.

When he turns to me, his muddy eyes have turned completely opaque. "You gotta be more careful, Mari. I've been telling you, you can't been seen with—"

"Nope. Stop. They don't get to tell me who to hang out with, or who to—" I catch myself. *Love*. Is that the right word? Probably not. It's hard to tell when his eyes are like this—not letting me in.

"Except they *do* get to tell you. That's exactly how this place works."

"But . . ." A trickle of air escapes my chest. I feel it coming, the thing he's going to say next.

"A lot of people are watching you right now. I don't want to be the one who— If I was the reason—"

I put a hand up. I can't. "Are you seriously *breaking up* with me? Over this?"

As if the revelation wasn't embarrassing enough, now Jethro's giving up? Ditching me? Just like Faye did every time things got difficult.

He drops the unfinished cigarette, crushes it with his heel. "I wouldn't put it like that."

"How would you put it?"

The stub splays on the ground, leafy bits scattered like the remnants of a small explosion. Jethro stands over it, hard-faced and quiet.

"How would you put it, Jethro?" My voice ratchets up, angry.

He lifts a shoulder. "Don't look at me like that, Mari. It's not like we . . ."

"Like we what?"

"Were really together."

Slam of air. Silly girl, didn't you know? This wasn't the real thing. It was all temporary. He didn't care about you. Not really.

I don't say anything else. Jethro doesn't either. I stare at the smooth asphalt, watching as that stupid splintered cigarette fades into nothing.

Eventually, he shoves off from the brick, black boots pausing briefly in the space between us. He changes his mind, resumes his shuffle. I only raise my head at the sound of the door slamming shut.

AFTER

———

DAYS 37-40

THERE'S A REBEL meeting underway when I arrive. A guy in zipped-up pleather unleashes his outrage to the group. As I slide into a chair beside Eva, a few folks look over and nod. One pumps a fist.

"They've seen your interview," Eva whispers, smiling. "They were impressed. We all were."

Her kind eyes glow with admiration. I wonder if this makes me a real rebel now.

I don't know why I'm here exactly. I guess I've run out of places to go. I can't deal with the Center right now or face Faye. I'm too ashamed to tell her that Jethro and I split up, too raw to hide it. Most of all, I'm mad. At Jethro. For giving up just when, in my view, we should have sheltered together to ride out the storm. At the first sign of bad weather, he was gone.

The guy at the front of the room is picking up steam, talking—

ranting, really—about some sort of PTB embezzlement scheme. He's accusing the Powers That Be of siphoning our karmic earnings for their own use, which . . . huh? If the Powers run the system, why would they need to steal points from us? According to this guy, points work like crypto. They can only be created through a specific set of value-add activities built into the original code. Even the PTB can't invent points out of nothing, and without their original partner, they don't have the skills to override the system. So, they've added massive surcharges to our rent and tuition bills, using the excess collected to construct their own little paradise on the grid, complete with a full-time breath coach for Lady Lu and a gold-encrusted podium for the Chairman.

"Don't you get it?" the man bellows. "They're building their own Ever After off our spiritual sweat!"

I sit taller. I do. I get it. Could he be right? I think of those surcharges that came as such a surprise in my first weeks. Are the PTB really using those extra points for their own benefit? If what this guy's saying is true, that would be an unbelievable violation of our trust.

I listen more closely to the next speaker, a young woman with thick platform boots and honey-gold skin who begins with a metaphor about baggage. "We're lying if we claim we're all carrying the same weight," she says. "So, why pretend that the same methods will work for everyone? What if, instead of penalizing those who can't keep up with the program, we pitched in together until all our suitcases were safely stowed?"

I find myself nodding, considering. Thinking of Faye, whose final day is drawing near. When the audience snaps, I snap softly too.

Simone steps forward next, and the room falls quiet as she pulls back her shoulders and rises into her full height. "Are you all ready for some *truth*?"

"HELL YEAH!" someone shouts over a chorus of claps and whistles.

The outburst sends a smile across Simone's typically serious face. She waits for the noise to settle. Then: "We've all seen the numbers," she says somberly. "By our calculations, fewer than thirty percent of those who begin their time in Paradise Gate make it to the Ever After."

I stop breathing. This. This is exactly what I'd tried to say to Larisa, back when I first took note of the ascension lists. But Simone's numbers are even worse than I'd imagined. *Thirty* percent?

"What happens to the other seventy? That's what we all want to know. That's what many of us have dedicated a small eternity to figuring out. We've come to suspect that some are being held in hidden PTB detention facilities, somewhere offshore of our grid. A few lucky ones may have escaped, found their way to other settlements. The rest have been discarded completely."

Simone's gaze moves across the gathered rebels, and I feel a collective intake of breath, the anticipation of what she'll say next.

"The question I bring to you, comrades, is what we ought to do with this knowledge. Should we all head back to the Center and play it safe? Ignore our doubts, ignore the silent cries of so many missing friends, and hope we have what it takes to join the lucky few?"

"Nah!" someone growls.

"One for all or all for none!" shouts someone else.

Simone nods, a smile flickering. "That's right. There's no *me* in *us*. We're all in this together."

She makes a shift then to something more personal. She'd been one of the lucky few in her hometown, she tells us, plucked from her middle school and sent to an elite secondary program. "I thought I had earned it, thought I was special. A *leader*, they said. Some folks argued that these programs for the so-called gifted were sapping our community of talent, creating divisions we couldn't afford. I figured they were jealous. It took dying for me to see their point: What good did my fancy school do me in the end? It didn't protect me from teachers who confused my ambition for aggression, or from the vigilante *citizen* who saw me—walking home, minding my business—and decided I was a threat she needed to quell with her gun."

For once, the rebels are quiet.

"It's easy to fall for the success narrative, to believe our individual talents are what we need to lift ourselves up, that if we put in a good effort and stick to the program, we'll be buffered against failure and suffering. And look. I get it. That old story is familiar, comforting. But real heart, true courage requires bigger thinking. We need to look beyond our small hopes and individual fears to envision something greater for all of us. Imagine something better than we've ever dared imagine on our own."

Rumbles roll through the room and Simone seems to feed on the energy, rising to her toes as she cries: "Can you see it, comrades? Can you see the future coming?"

A switch flips then. Hope and anger crackle through the gathered bodies, like a storm about to burst. In one motion, the whole room roars to its feet, clapping, stomping, words like a hard pelting rain: "THE FUTURE IS US. ALL SOULS RISE AND REPORT."

I SLIP OUT at the end of the meeting, turning down Eva's friendly offer of coffee and pastries. But then the next day, I come back. And again the day after.

During the rebels' meetings, I sit mostly hidden in the middle row, next to the plainly dressed Eva. I listen. To the personal stories and the meandering rants. To the common threads of anger and betrayal weaving through everything.

I listen especially closely to Simone. It's shocking what she reveals, but also not. She is saying out loud things that feel true: This world isn't fair or right. The Chairman and Lady Lu are selling snake oil. The system they've created does little to repair the harm and injustices inflicted on us in our lifetimes. If anything, their system of chutes and ladders only makes things worse.

Before the meetings, I join Eva on the computers. I no longer feel pulled to look at the past. Instead I work with Eva. She's part of a team that's investigating the discrepancy in ascension numbers. They've accessed intake lists, mapped them against ascensions, and are trying to track down all the individuals who disappeared in the gap between, to document their moves right up until their disappearance. Some made it to their final assessment, received notice of their failure, and were escorted away. Others disappeared prior to the end of their term, with no notice or explanation. Most, unlike the young and relatively hopeful

Annabelle Schreiber and Larisa, never made the news.

It's painstaking work. And gut-wrenching.

Eva reveals her own motivation: "My girlfriend is one of the missing." They met during their first week at the Center, formed an immediate bond, followed by a rapid tumble into love. By mid-term, they'd developed some suspicions about the Center's services. Neither was making the promised progress. Eva's girlfriend began corresponding with people online. She missed a few classes, showed up one day looking harried . . . "And the next thing I knew, she was gone," Eva says.

It's almost exactly what happened to Larisa. There are thousands with similar stories, Eva tells me.

Other teams are working on related investigations, trying to make contact with other settlements they believe may be nearer than we think. And even bigger than that, they're seeking to learn the full truth about the Powers That Be. Is the whole realm an embezzlement scheme, or a well-intentioned effort that has gone off the rails? Are the Chairman and Lady Lu altruistic leaders who've been corrupted by pride, or something more nefarious? What happened to the third founder anyway? Did he grow disillusioned and split off to found his own settlement like some people say? According to Eva, these are all open questions.

"We are all here with one goal," Simone tells the group one afternoon during my sixth week in the afterlife. "We're here to find the truth. If we can tell the story of our missing comrades, and reveal the true nature of this regime, we will break the spell and breathe new hope into a broken realm."

Simone, aka Freedome, has a vision of something better. For true liberation.

AFTER THE MEETING I wait for Simone's groupies to offer their fist bumps and words of solidarity before approaching. She spots me and waves me over. "Still no word from your friend?"

I shake my head. It's been over a week since Larisa's video clip went public. There have been no new messages. On TV and the feed, it's like she never existed.

"Maybe I should've done more, demanded they air it more than once or posted it on my own feed."

"Nah. You got all you could hope for from that action. And if what they aired wasn't proof, I don't know what is. You did right by your friend."

Simone frowns at me sympathetically, and I realize she isn't as cold as I'd once assumed. Just serious, thoughtful. A shy girl who comes alive before a crowd.

"You're right," I tell her. "Everything you've been saying. The way they separate some of us as soul models, or gifted, or whatever—it doesn't help anyone except the ones in power. It makes it seem like our success is all our own doing—"

"And, by extension, our failures," Simone says.

"Exactly. Yes."

The truth of it has landed fully: All these caricatures they paint in the tabloids, heroes on one side, losers and anarchists on the other. They elevate examples like mine, place us on a pedestal, whether we ask for it or not. But it's a dangerous, two-faced devotion. They'll pretend to be your biggest fan, then tear you to pieces when you fail to live up to their impossible ideal.

"The media makes it all worse," I muse. "I guess we had the

same thing back on earth, but at least there, you had an option to turn the channel."

I'm pissed, I realize. At the Powers and all of them, for using me this way. For turning their backs on Larisa, Annabelle, and all the others. For making Faye feel so hopeless.

"It can be a lot when you finally catch on to the bigger picture," Simone says, reading my anger. "Everyone in this room has gone through some version of what you're feeling now."

I meet her steady eye, wishing I had her kind of courage. She's right. It *is* a lot.

"Listen." Simone tips her head. "We have an action coming up. If you feel ready, you should join us. In fact, hey, hang on—" She waves a hand, and suddenly creepy Havel is headed our way. "Havel, what do you think about including Margaret in this week's action? Wouldn't she be perfect?"

Havel instantly agrees, and Simone explains the idea to me: "Every month, the PTB gather to review the Chairman and Lady Lu's newest initiatives—curriculum add-ons, intervention programs, that sort of thing. The meetings are televised and open for public comment. We always send a contingent, but they're choosy about who they allow to speak. We almost never get anyone through. But you . . ."

"You want me to . . . ?"

"Disrupt the whole enterprise," Havel says with a burst of phlegm.

I begin to laugh until I realize he's serious.

"Wait. What would I say? What makes you think they'd let me in?"

Simone gives me a patient look. "What were we just talking about? You're their favorite little soul model—"

"*Was,*" I correct her. "*Was* their favorite. They aren't so sure anymore."

"Doesn't matter," Simone says. "The settlement has its eyes on you. They ate up that interview. You've slipped in stature, maybe, but they all want you to succeed. Need it, really. Why else would they let you keep running around with an archive that looks like Swiss cheese? If anyone else did that, they'd be long gone, zero questions. But folks got attached to you. They *need* you to bounce back. Not to mention, you're great for ratings."

I stiffen. A minute ago I thought Simone understood my situation, how it felt to be used by the Powers, but now she wants to use me too.

She must see what I'm thinking. "Listen. This is your chance to have your say—to show everyone exactly what you see."

"She's right." Eva has appeared at my shoulder, listening. "You're the perfect soul for the job."

"Perfect," Havel agrees, his dark glasses glinting.

I . . . don't know. It's one thing to push back in an interview, or to attend a few meetings, to listen and consider. But I'm not a rebel, a troublemaker. I spent my whole life following rules, pleasing authority figures. Not that it made any difference, in the end.

"Just hypothetically, if I did agree, how would it work, what would I say?"

"Well, you'd arrive on your own, put your name on the list, and wait your turn," Simone says. "Then you tell them what you said to me a few minutes ago—the thing about being used by the media was perfect. You won't get a lot of time, but you don't have to say too much. It will be enough for folks at home to hear you question the PTB's motives."

"Won't they arrest me?"

"Not on live TV. Not you. They can't risk those optics. But"—Simone's voice grows more serious—"you only get to pull a trick like this once. Once they realize you're not on their side, you'll be like us. An outlaw. You won't be able to go back to the Center, be part of their program. You'd be giving up all of it. Including your little pedestal."

"I hate the pedestal," I say.

Simone smiles. "I know."

Though I haven't agreed to anything, Havel is shaking my hand like a deal has been struck. "The meeting is on Sunday, four p.m. You'll see some of our folks there, dressed for the action. We'll have a contingent ready to help if you need a distraction." He reaches into his poncho and pulls out a small silver button. "If anything goes wrong, press this and we'll come straight to you, wherever you are."

"It's just a precaution," Simone assures me. "You probably won't need it this time."

So many alarm bells are ringing (*probably* won't?) (*this* time?), but the one thing I'm stuck on is that Simone—brilliant, electric, truth-telling Simone—wants me on her team.

For once, I tune out the risks.

AFTER

—

DAY 40 CONTINUED

I RETURN TO the bungalow late and find Faye already in bed, curled against the wall, wailing.

"Faye? Are you hurt? What happened?" Last time I saw her, she was chugging celery water and manifesting her bliss. Getting herself in the right frame of mind, she said, for her final assessment. She was scheduled to take the computerized portion this morning, her eighty-fifth day, and judging by her current position, it didn't go well.

I lower myself onto the bed. "It was that bad, huh?"

Her head flops back pitifully. "I tried everything, baby! I fasted, I visualized, I meditated. Nothing I do is ever enough!"

I place a soothing hand on Faye's shoulder. Because I understand something now: My mother may be flawed (and melodramatic), but she has a good heart. She tries.

It takes some effort to get the details: Faye bombed the test. Froze up completely. No one has ever recovered from a score as low as hers, she claims. She has interviews and physical tests scheduled tomorrow and Monday, and a final appearance before the board on Tuesday (day ninety), but her adviser suggested none of it would be enough to make up for today's score.

"What happens now? What are you supposed to do until Tuesday?"

She lifts a limp shoulder. "Wait."

Wait. Wait to be told she's a failure, wait to be tossed out into the ether like a piece of afterlife trash. Although I'd anticipated the possibility that this day would arrive, it doesn't make it any easier to accept.

They're going to take my mother from me. After everything we've been through, all the work she's put in, it's been confirmed: We won't get an Ever After.

"Fuck it," I say. Faye's eyes pop open, and she glances at my tracker in alarm.

"Fuck it and *them*. Fuck the Powers That Be and their whole system," I say, enunciating so my tracker's AI can catch every word. "They don't know you, Mom. They don't know what you've been through. You've done everything they asked. *More.* If that's not enough, then what's the point of any of this?"

How can anyone believe in a system that offers no way forward for someone who tries her best, applies her whole heart to everything she does? Faye repeated their mantras, did all their exercises, truly believed that if she worked hard enough, she'd be able to earn her spot in the Ever After. Some part of me managed to believe it too, that somehow we'd arrive there together and find the happiness we missed the first time around.

"Did you just call me Mom?" Faye asks.

I've begun to shake, tearlessly, and Faye reaches out a hand. "Oh, baby, I've let you down. Again!"

"No. I promise, it wasn't you that let me down. Not this time."

Unconvinced, Faye rolls back toward the wall, her spine a fragile curve. There's nothing I can say that will soothe her, nothing I can do to fix it. No authority to plead to, no points I can earn on her behalf. We're long past the time when I believed I could protect my hapless mother, that her problems could be mine to bear, and yet . . . what else is there to do? I lay my head down beside hers, round my body to fit.

"Try to get some sleep, Mom. We'll figure this out."

She holds on to my hand, on to that *Mom*, and I hold her back fiercely.

THE PHONE RINGS sometime after midnight. I've retreated to my own bedroom, where I rewind the events of this impossible week, one that began with me getting dumped by a deadbeat and ended with my heart getting smashed by my own stupid hope, a stubborn belief that if we just did the work, it would somehow turn out okay. I think of Simone's invitation.

Could I be a person who speaks up like that? Do I have that kind of courage?

After several loud peals, the phone goes quiet. I close my eyes, make a fresh attempt at sleep.

The phone starts up again. Three, four, five rings. Whoever's calling isn't giving up. I check the time on my tracker (3:17), and groan as I drag myself out to the kitchen. Whoever decided to put landlines in the afterlife should be murdered.

"Hello?"

No response.

"Hello?" I repeat.

There's a faint rustling on the wire. I start to hang up when, "Hello?" a garbled voice replies.

I bring the receiver back to my ear. "Who is this?"

"Hey," a familiar voice says, but it's muffled and strange. I hit the volume button. "MARI?" A blast to my eardrum, followed by a sludge of background noise: the rumble of an engine, a series of harsh scratches and clicks.

I pump the volume back to normal. "What's going on? Who is this?"

"Mari?" the caller asks at a more normal volume, laying the *a* flat on his tongue. There's only one person who says my name like that. One person whose voice could make my heart hammer and my stomach tank at the same time.

"Don't hang up, please," he begs.

I resist the urge to crash the phone back into its cradle. I *should* do it. I still think Jethro's a coward or worse for giving up so easily. For acting like what we had was nothing. But he's never called me at my house before. How did he get this number? Curiosity beats out pride. Hope lands a jab too. Has he changed his mind? Has Jethro realized he needs me too?

"It's late. What is it? What do you want?" I say, keeping both the hope and hurt out of my voice.

The line is quiet.

"I miss you, Mari."

And there it is. The thing I wanted to hear, with all the appropriate jaggedness. And yet . . .

"You can't miss me, idiot. *You* broke up with *me*."

"Where have you been? You weren't in class this week. Mari, you haven't gone back to the warehouse, have you?"

"Can't you page 'Mo' and ask?" I sound petty, but the connection between Jethro and Simone still doesn't sit right.

"It's not like that, Mari. I swear. It's—"

There's a clatter in the background, a rumble, another voice. The phone goes still.

"Hello? Jethro? What the hell?"

I shake the phone and Jethro returns with a cough. "I gotta go. Just be careful, Mari. You don't want this kind of trouble. Promise me you'll be careful?"

"The only thing I'll promise is that you—you can just—"

But I don't get to tell him where he can shove his concern. The phone is dead.

It's my first time being dumped, but I'm pretty sure you don't get to exact promises from the one you left behind.

I set the phone in its cradle, feeling a sudden sense of clarity. I've made my decision.

AFTER

DAY 43

THE SIDEWALK IN front of Civility Hall is packed with protesters when I arrive on Sunday afternoon. Parents and grandparents and young people toting neatly printed signs. ALL SOULS DESERVE PARADISE. 90 DAYS IS NOT ENOUGH.

I recognize a few faces from the warehouse, but they've traded their usual garb for long ash-colored robes. Eva flicks back her hood to reveal her familiar brown curls, giving me a thumbs-up from across the crowded square. On her bared wrist I notice a tracker. Everyone's wearing one today.

The protesters begin to chant, and the robed rebels form a protective outer ring, standing silently with raised fists. "Freedom," the folks in the center shout, like the protesters I heard in the park a couple of weeks back.

No, I listen more closely: It's free *them*. "Release our soulmates," they're saying. "Free them now."

A new group has solidified seemingly overnight, led by the

mothers who began meeting after Annabelle disappeared. They call themselves the Soulmates of the Missing. They're demanding the immediate release of their disappeared children, loved ones, and friends. And amnesty for all. It's got to be a PR nightmare for the Powers That Be. Hearing all these brave voices only heightens my resolve to speak up too.

Someone passes me a booklet filled with faces, names, and dates of arrival and disappearance. I recognize a bunch from the list Eva has been researching and find Larisa on page 7. It's her intake photo, with the same blue background as everyone else, same standard-issue tunic. Someone must have urged her to smile, but the result was a painful grimace. I'd laugh if . . . well, if not for everything.

"Where did you take him? What did my baby do?" To my left, I spot a mother I've seen on the news. As her cries pitch higher, two fellow protesters loop their elbows through hers, but they don't try to hush her. Instead, they match her wails with calls of their own: for their own kids, their partners, old friends and new. I can't help staring. The curtains have parted, revealing so much more hurt than I'd imagined.

I clutch the little booklet tighter and press through the crowd to the steps. A line of guards stands at the top of the front stairs. They're scanning trackers, letting in a few and sending the majority back to the street. I reach into my pocket to check for Havel's panic button. Still there.

The three souls in front of me are denied entry. The last, a woman about Faye's age, descends the steps, her sign drooping. SHE WAS MY ETERNITY, it reads, with a picture of a young woman's face.

I step forward, holding out my wrist to the guard. A moment later, I'm whisked inside. Simone was right.

There are no protesters inside the bustling lobby, just a lot of attendant types and no-collar bureaucrats. Nerves take over as I feel the weight of my situation, of all the people who won't get to tell their stories. I spent all day yesterday and most of this morning trying to write down my thoughts. Should I start with the data I've been investigating with Eva? Or begin with what I've witnessed personally with Larisa and Faye? Should I talk about my own vibes, which remain stuck in an angry state of crimson? Do I try to speak for the grief-stricken folks outside? It's all connected, I know: the way some are lifted up while others are shuffled out of sight; how they make it seem like we deserve the fate we get, each of us some-how accountable for both the outcome and the cards we were dealt.

I don't yet understand how all the pieces fit exactly, but I'm starting to grasp the outlines. I just wish I had Simone's magnetic eloquence. Because I'll only get one chance.

The meeting chamber is hushed, the front rows filled with reporters, administrators, and other importants. The rows toward the back—reserved for the public—are more sparse. I find a seat behind a trio of ladies dressed like New Age nuns.

The session comes to order with the chime of a metal bowl. Chairman Ted enters in an extravagantly embroidered suit, Lady Lu in extra-billowy genie pants. They're joined by five other com-mittee members in equally absurd getups. The Chairman gives a long-winded opening, which is followed by a tedious PowerPoint. Something about sub-sub-amendments and returns on karmic investment. The audience shifts with impatience.

Finally, after what seems like multiple eternities, the bowl chimes again and it's time for public commentary. I stand, following the New Age ladies into the aisle.

The first three commenters shower the Chairman and Lady Lu with praise and thanks. *We're so grateful for your wise and magnanimous leadership, blah blah.* The line inches forward, and I eye the guards at the back, the news cameras up front. If Simone was right, they'll take care with me on-air. My challenge will be to say just enough before they shut down the cameras.

The New Age ladies reach the podium. The shortest among them, a deep-voiced woman with smooth almond skin, throws back her veil as her sisters fan out on either side. "We have come to speak about the Powers' abuse of ancient traditions and their regime of coordinated deception."

There's a rolling gasp from the audience. These are not harmless Lady Lu groupies but rebels in another guise. The first woman continues, her voice ringing out boldly, while up at the dais, the Chairman rings his little bowl in panic.

The guards, catching on, make their move. There's a crash of chairs, a scramble for the door. The Chairman's metal bowl clangs, and I stand frozen.

The meeting is over before I have a chance to speak.

IT'S CHAOS IN the lobby, bureaucrats and attendees stumbling around, asking questions: *Who were those women? What just happened?* My body thrums with a mix of alarm, disappointment, and relief. Also worry (always, worry). Outside, the front sidewalk has been cordoned off, the protesters moved to the park across the street. They lift their signs and chant louder as we exit the building.

"Hey. You okay?" An arm slips through mine. Eva. She guides me toward the crowd's periphery, to an area that's less packed, out of view of the menacing guards and fast-clicking cameras. "What happened?" She peers at me from beneath her hood, her friendly face lit with concern and excitement.

I relay what happened with the veiled ladies, and ask Eva who they were, if they're affiliated with Simone and the others, but Eva seems as surprised as me.

"Had you seen any of them before? You said the first one had a yellow veil? Would you recognize her again?"

"No, I don't think so. I only saw her from the side . . ."

An anxious jitter has infected the crowd, drowning out our conversation. Grief-stricken friends and family mingle with robed rebels, heartache and rage swirling in a heady mix. My own nerves are still cranked, primed for a fight that had no release.

Suddenly the crowd bursts into a riotous shout. The main doors have been thrown open. Helmeted guards stare into the crowd, mouths pressed to walkie-talkies, while around me folks link arms and stare back. A person to my left begins hissing; someone else lets out a long, low boo. Chairman Ted has emerged, squinting into the gray light. He starts to say something, then reconsiders, making a rush for the waiting vehicles.

"Free our loved ones. Free our souls!" a woman screams.

"Down with the Powers! Free us from your lies!"

The chants pick up energy. Toward the front, a woman facing the guards rips off her tracker, hurls it to the ground. The protesters around her pause for a moment, then, one by one, follow her example. Trackers snapping, flapping, cracking to the ground.

I look at Eva. She reaches for her wrist at the same moment I reach for mine. Our trackers fall away with a snap.

A wild rush of freedom spikes and swirls through the crowd, lifting us all to our full height. As one, we raise our arms in a naked-fisted shout.

THE LAST CAR in the cavalcade pulls away, and the guards move in. Protesters disperse quickly, leaving dozens of trackers scattered on the ground. A few pause at the last second to scoop up their devices. I leave mine and don't look back.

As I walk toward the bungalow, I feel weightless. My tracker was small, but I realize now what a burden it was to be monitored and measured at every step. It's thrilling—also, terrifying—to consider what comes next. An eternity without a rule book to follow? What does that even look like? Will I be punished? Captured? Can I convince Faye to come with me, to hide out at the warehouse and figure out what comes next, before we're each, for different reasons, sent into the oblivion?

At the turnoff to the bungalow, I slow my pace. A pair of unmarked cars and a van sprawl across the narrow drive. I consider running, but then I hear Faye's cry.

She's seated on the sofa, surrounded by officers. At the sound of my entry, she looks up, eyes wretched, and I don't know what to say. I pull my naked wrist into my sleeve and give Faye a look that says *hush*.

"Please, leave her be," I tell the officers. "She doesn't have to be part of this." I focus on the officer who seems to be in charge, a short, stocky guy exuding a sort of bulky, hyper-masculine authority. How will I explain my missing tracker? What do I tell Faye? I had no idea they'd come for me so quickly. I consider options for buying time.

The officer cuts off that whole train of thought. "Ready, ma'am?" he says to Faye, who replies with a strangled yelp.

"Wait. You're here for *her*? But I thought—"

I thought we had another two days at least. I thought on her final day—*Tuesday*; it's still only Sunday—there'd be some sort of formal procedure, paperwork, an opportunity to make a final appeal and say goodbye. Unless she decided to skip all of that and escape with me first.

It's only day eighty-eight. I didn't get a chance to make my case. We haven't said goodbye.

The officer speaks to a trembling Faye. "Faye Novak, you have been summoned by the Powers based on suspicion of seditious activity. All rights have been forfeited and—"

"Stop. No. *What?* Seditious activity? What are you saying?" This is not an end-of-term removal. This is something else. "You have the wrong person! I'm the seditious one, not her!"

They shove me back and grab Faye's arms, lifting her from the couch.

"I'm afraid our facts are correct, miss. Your mother's been spending extended hours at a meditation center where rebels are known to recruit. During her end-of-term assessment, we uncovered evidence of significant archival manipulation."

"But that's not—" I catch myself. *I'm* the one who messed with Faye's archive.

She gives me a warning glance. Does she know?

I focus on the officer. "Look. She was prescribed extra meditation. Her spiritual mentor suggested that place! My mother has followed every recommendation!"

They elbow me back, blocking Faye's face from my view. Her legs go limp as they lift her from the couch.

"You can't just do this! Doesn't she get to tell her side? This isn't right!"

I follow the guards as they carry Faye out into the yard, trying to catch up to them, to touch her hand, find her gaze, tell her I'm sorry, but the guards are much bigger than me, faster. One steps in my way as the van's doors fly open. They toss her in like a rag doll, then leap in behind.

"Faye? Can you still hear me? Say something! They can't do this! I'm going to get help!"

Except I know that they *can* do this, that there is no help. Faye must know it too because as the doors of the van slam shut, my beautiful mess of a mother doesn't cry out once.

AFTER

DAY 43 CONTINUED

THE SECURITY VAN peels through the section's front gates, its smooth lines swallowed in the distance. There's a sound like a broken, gurgling drain. It takes a full minute before I realize it's me, retching.

They took her because of me. Because of what I did to her archive. When I blocked those old memories, I must have marked Faye as a dangerous radical. It should be me in that van. I can handle the repercussions. I deserve them—not Faye.

I peer back at the empty bungalow, down at my naked wrist.

Hang on. I fumble, finding the panic button in my pocket. *Press this and we'll come straight to you,* Havel said. I press several times. It doesn't make a sound, so I can't tell if it worked.

I don't have to wait long before a dark van pulls up. I squint into the tinted windows, unsure if I made the right call. Three figures hop out, all dressed in black. The first is slighter than the others. A wisp of a curl escapes from a cap. I let out a breath. It's Eva. Thank god.

She gestures toward the bungalow, then murmurs something to the driver.

"What happened? Are you okay?" Eva places a steadying hand on my shoulder and urges me inside.

Simone and Havel were caught up with other urgent business, she tells me. That's why they're not here themselves. "But we've got this. Tell us what happened. Why the nine-one-one?"

The three rebels are quiet as I tell them what happened to Faye. "They didn't even give me a chance to explain."

The taller guy grumbles something I don't catch, and Eva shoots him a silencing look. She seems older suddenly. Maybe it's the black outfit. A few more words are muttered, and the two guys finally give up and stomp back outside. Apparently, Faye's arrest doesn't register to them as an emergency.

"Ignore them," Eva says. She pours me a glass of non-celery water and sits at the table as I explain the situation with Faye's archive, my role in the mess.

"She's not a bad soul. She's just . . . different. The PTB program wasn't a fit for her. Motherhood wasn't either. Faye didn't do the stuff they accused her of, the sedition and whatnot. She got discouraged sometimes, sure, but she did everything they recommended. *More.* She really tried her best."

Eva's brow lowers in sympathy. "I hear you. I do. Unfortunately, there's no way to undo what's been done. That is, unless . . ."

"Unless what?"

She lifts her thick lashes, holds my gaze. "There's been a lot of buzz on the feed from a group that calls themselves the Transcendentalists."

My water glass slips in my fingers, clunking onto the table.

"I take it you've heard of them."

I nod. That day in the library, Larisa told me her online friends were harmless philosophers, but Eva tells a different story now, says they're a splinter group of the resistance who operate on the far edge of the grid. Not at the warehouse, farther out. Much farther. On the edge of where the grid fully ends and the eternal 3:00 a.m. begins.

"They've been trying to disrupt the transports for a while now," Eva tells me. "They think the PTB are sending their discards—the troublemakers and failures—out into the fuzz on special vessels every night. They've figured out that there's a giant detention facility out there, on a little digital island just offshore. That's where they're all being kept."

"All of them? But I thought . . ." I make a slicing motion.

"Yeah, we all thought that. Another lie. Apparently the PTB aren't that cruel, or maybe they just haven't figured out how to discard folks entirely. So they're keeping them hidden, out of the way. I don't know about you, but eternal prison doesn't sound a whole lot better than an eternal three a.m."

"No." I picture Faye, whose last experience with arrest just about broke her.

"Anyway, last night they finally traced the transport's path. They're going to try to stop the next one, tonight."

My eyes widen. "You think Faye will be on it?"

"If not this one, she'll be scheduled for the next. They'll want her gone before the feed wakes up and realizes where she went. But here's the good news: All we have to do is stop one transport for the whole process to fall apart. Once the whole realm sees what they're doing, it's over. So"—she looks at me—"are you in?"

Everything in me somersaults. They're going out there tonight—out into the fuzz—and Eva wants me to go too.

"Is it safe?" Stupid question. Of course it isn't safe.

"Do you feel safe right now?" Eva asks. "With guards busting into your house, taking your mother?"

Touché.

"I can't promise we'll find your mom or my girlfriend, but as far as I can see, it's our only shot."

"What about Simone? Is she going too?"

Eva pauses. "Simone and the Transcendentalists don't really vibe. It's a beef that goes a ways back. And look..." Her face softens a bit. "Simone's great. I appreciate all she's done, but between you and me, Simone and Havel and the rest spend too much time talking and not enough *doing*. Maybe because they haven't lost someone like we have."

I slide my glass closer, keeping one finger on the base. I want to help, *need* to do something. Just the thought of Faye out there—trapped on some kind of vessel—makes my whole head explode. But I don't know anything about sabotaging transports. What can *I* do?

As if guessing my question, Eva says, "They have a plan worked out, leaders to guide the mission. They just need bodies, folks who can show up and follow orders."

"I have a body," I say, lifting slightly. "Or, you know... whatever this is."

Eva chuckles.

Dead-people humor. It's catching.

"Don't tell those guys, okay?" Eva indicates the front door, beyond which her two companions wait. "Best if we keep all this between you and me."

I AGREE TO meet Eva just after midnight. She's secured a map, a couple of off-road bikes, and a black hoodie for me. I zip it up, and we're gone, racing down unlit streets, away from the Center, away from the warehouse, to the opposite edge of the grid.

The road grows rough as we reach the border, fading from smooth concrete to a narrow, pitted path. The air seems crumbly too, hazy even in darkness. We dismount carefully and conceal the bikes between two dunelike heaps. We scramble up the steep slope, using each other's weight for balance. At the top, the ground falls away completely.

There's a sort of narrow lip below, connecting the ledge we stand on and the murky, impenetrable expanse beyond. I can just make out the outline of a handful of tents on the strip beneath us.

We're silent as we descend a narrow path chipped into the cliff, concentrating on finding our footing. At the bottom, our feet sink into what feels like heavy sand. A low buzz of activity drifts from the camp several yards away. Several dark silhouettes skirt around the tents, headed toward a group of odd-looking vessels, like over-size fully encased canoes, planted farther up the beach.

The coastline (is that what you would call this place?) is dark, silent, the sky a pure black. To the right: nothing. It's impossible to see how far the darkness stretches or what, if anything, lies on the other side.

Eva pulls me toward the largest tent, and we both duck through the unzipped door.

It's larger inside than I expect. A circle of electronic torches splash yellow light across the tent's canvas periphery, while giant shadows dance above. Three black-clad figures cluster around a table, tracing something with a flashlight. One guy's grown agitated. "Not a chance!" he tells the one holding the light.

At the sound of Eva's cough, they look up.

"Who's this?" A woman points to me, though I can tell she knows exactly who I am.

"They sure don't make soul models like they used to," her companion says with an amused woof.

I'm considering possible retorts when the third figure spins around and all thoughts punch out. He's dressed like the others— dark military gear, tight cap—his lovely jawline etched sharp by the gloom. It notches open when he sees me.

"What are they doing in here?" he says gruffly.

"I imagine they want to help," says his female companion, who appears to be the leader. "You'll have to ignore my partner here," she tells me and Eva. "It's been a long night already. But we've got our sights, and we're eager to keep moving while we have this chance. And we'll need every body we can get to pull this off. Isn't that right, Taco?"

The woman catches the question on my face. "A bit lazy with his alias, right? But this guy's a whiz with intel. His latest find could change everything."

Taco? my brain repeats. *As in Eternal_Taco?*

The truth lands with a crash. Jethro was the one corresponding with Larisa. Jethro is one of them, a Transcendentalist. Jethro has been lying to me this entire time.

He's making a face I can't read, mouthing something, but Eva latches on to my elbow, blocking him from view. "Did you hear that?" she whispers. "They've located it. The transport. Your mom."

The commander woman is still speaking. "After we board, we'll let the vessel guide us to the place just offshore where we believe thousands of souls are being detained. If all goes to plan, we'll overrun the island's digital barrier and free them before daybreak."

Eva squeezes my arm tighter. Her girlfriend. My mother. Larisa. *Thousands.* In less than a few hours, all will be reunited, and the Powers will finally be exposed.

The commander claps her hands. "Ready to get to work?"

I nod eagerly, ignoring Jethro's grumble.

"Okay, then, first things first. Let's see how good you are at reading maps . . ."

WE SPEND THE next hour poring over old-fashioned paper maps in one of the smaller tents. We study the arc of the grid's blurry border, and the route the transport will take to the island detention facility, the roles we'll each perform, every possible approach. The maps are hand drawn and at least partly based on conjecture, a mix of online intel gathered by Jethro and others, plus a bit of rumor and guesswork. So we have to be ready.

The Transcendentalists have been studying the outer realm for a while, we learn. They believe there are at least a dozen other settlements out there—a few built on remnants of an older grid, others built of newer, different stuff—each floating like its own island in the vast gray expanse. They've been hunting for every type of signal they can think of—Wi-Fi, radio, sonar—and finally located one, very close to home, just north of our settlement's upper quadrant. At first, they thought it was a small settlement, but they've since realized it's a satellite grid operated by the PTB for a single purpose: detaining "inconvenient" souls.

We'll depart from the encampment in less than an hour, using the special encased vessels to move directly into the fuzz, heading east to where the expanse narrows. From there, following Jethro/Taco's map, we should cross paths with the PTB's prison transport before daylight. The plan is to follow it discreetly until its destination is within view, and then board, take control of the ship, and catch those on the receiving end by surprise.

While we're being assigned tasks, Jethro tries to get my attention, but I'm not interested. I manage to avoid his pointed glances until Eva and the others are pulled away to prep the boats and we're left alone in the tent.

Jethro edges closer, but I put up a hand. "*Taco?* What the fuck?"

He lifts a shoulder. "*Eternal_Freedom* was taken. It was that or *sandwich*."

I glare at him. That is *not* what I meant.

"You're the one who set Larisa up? Who even are you? Was anything you said to me real?"

Jethro blinks. "Of course it was real. Mari, you and me, that was—"

"Stop." I raise my hand again. It's too much, too many layers to unpack. (Why did he bring me to the warehouse? Why try to stop me from testifying? Where do Simone and the others fit in all of this?) "I can't. Not right now. Just stop, please?"

Jethro glances toward the tent's opening, hitching his voice lower. "Mari. You shouldn't be here. Go now, while you can, and just . . . run. It's not—they're not—this isn't safe."

There's genuine worry in his voice. For a second I falter. But then I remember who I'm talking to and why I'm here.

"I'll make my own decisions from here on out, yeah?"

"But—"

"It's kinda creepy, don't you think? All this concern for my safety? Where was that chivalry when we were skipping classes together? Or when you introduced me to an underground rebel enclave? Excuse me if I'm having trouble trusting your motives here, *Taco*."

The jab lands. "Mari—you know I—"

"Everything okay in here?" The tent door lifts, and Eva pokes her curly head inside, looking from me to Jethro. "We're almost ready."

Jethro starts to say something else—another warning? Another weak apology? Would either make a difference? I'm so mad at him right now; I feel so betrayed and . . . *confused*. But there's no time to unpack it. More urgent matters are at stake. Before Jethro can spit out any more BS, I follow Eva from the tent.

It's almost 3:00 a.m. now, the realm's darkest hour. Black-clad rebels emerge from the tents and move toward the waiting vessels. They're enclosed on all sides with large, fortified hulls meant to slice through the soup-like ether and protect us from debris. Along the sides, fingered oars splinter outward to help propel us toward our destination.

They divvy us into groups: Eva goes with four other rowers and a navigator, and Jethro and I are assigned to another boat. I can't think of a subtle, non-petty way to request a swap, so I go where I'm told, avoiding Jethro's gaze.

Eva offers me a parting fist bump of solidarity as I clamber aboard, taking my place on the middle bench as other volunteers fill in behind. Jethro, our navigator, takes the seat beside mine. "Mari, I'm sorry," he whispers, but the oars have already begun to rotate. Someone barks an order, and we fall into silence as our boat slips off the shore and into the blurry expanse. Soon the whole cabin echoes with slurps and sloshing, rowers grunting to keep their oars moving in the heavy liquid that surrounds us.

We travel for what feels like an eternity but is probably no more than fifteen minutes according to the map I'm holding. Small portholes allow us to see in every direction. The shoreline disappeared as soon as we left it. Ahead of us, there's nothing, no sign of life or death.

A finger of doubt creeps in. Was I stupid to agree to this? Stupid to take such a risk?

Did I really have a choice? I picture Faye, thrown into a van like a broken toy. All those grieving protesters in the park. Simone called on us to have courage, to think bigger than ourselves, to look beyond fear toward something greater. I wonder if this is what she meant. Does courage look like jumping into the void with a bunch of determined rebels and a boy of questionable intent?

In my head, I practice a tune, one I haven't thought about in years. Faye sang it to me when I was small and frightened. Nonnie taught it to her long before that. Now its simple notes soothe my mind, holding it still.

We reach the place where the expanse narrows, according to my map. Up ahead, and to the left, soft lines blur in the distance. If I squint, I can make out the edge of a hard cliff or fortresslike wall.

Jethro shifts on the bench next to me, and the rowers behind us change positions, bringing both oars to one side. Slowly, the vessel turns left.

I flick on my penlight to peek at the map. If what I'm reading is correct, we're approaching a checkpoint. Just behind that wall sits the PTB's giant detention complex, aka Limbo. Beyond that: more of the unknown.

There's a shout up ahead, and a sharp grating noise as the oars grab in the opposite direction. Jethro curses. With a few hard strokes, the rowers pull us away from the approaching cliff and back out into the shadowy breach.

"What is it? What happened?"

The rower behind me hisses to hush.

There are more shouts, followed by the rumble of an engine and a sudden flash of light. I duck, cover my eyes with my arms, try to make out what's happening through the slits between my fingers. A sleek motorized vessel about three times our size roars into view, kicking up a massive wake. Spotlights scan, revealing the other four boats in our party. Our rowers drop their oars and open the hatch, and just before the light sweeps back our way, I hear them splash overboard.

"PTB security," Jethro whispers. He grabs my arm as our vessel rocks up over a burst of motion and noise, spins in the darkness, then catches on something and jerks to a stop.

"Come on." Jethro clutches my hand, and I don't have time to think or be mad at him. Together we leap out onto a hard-pebbled beach. Is this Limbo? I can't tell. We scramble up a steep incline. The sky is inky and still, the ground craggy.

We hurry, ducking among rocklike outcroppings, climbing up up up . . . toward what?

Behind us, there's a strangled shout, a loud zip, and a blast. Jethro speaks in a breathy rasp, telling me to keep moving, to stick with him, and though just a little while ago I told him to leave me alone, in this moment I have no choice but to follow. I latch on to the nearest ledge and haul myself up behind him. Two more hoists, and my foot catches, jams in a crack. I'm stuck.

More shouts from behind. Lights bounce across the rock. Jethro slips down and works at my foot, releases it from its catch, and then pushes me up to the next plateau. I can hear the grunts of guards scrambling up behind us, getting closer.

"Here." Jethro pulls me behind a ledge big enough to conceal us both.

We crouch, knees pressed together and foreheads almost grazing.

The grunts of the guards are almost drowned out by the pulse in my ears. I'm aware of Jethro's shadow shifting. I feel him watching me, eyes tracing my lines. *You seem a little stressed,* he said the first time we met, and the memory provokes a wild urge to giggle. My hand claps over my mouth.

What? he mouths.

I shake my head, choke it down. "Wouldn't say no to a smoke right now," I whisper.

Jethro smiles in the darkness. He pulls me closer, leans his forehead briefly against mine. "After we get out of here, I'm going to explain, okay?"

"Mmm," I murmur, understanding that it's pure fantasy—the idea that we'll get out of here, the idea of another *after*—but in this moment, it doesn't matter. I let my forehead lean into his, let my breath drop to match his rhythm, feel his hand at my hip, holding off whatever's coming.

Another string of shouts, more harsh zips and thumps. A radio belches somewhere close, and my blood leaps.

"Mari." Jethro's voice is no louder than a breath. "Mari, stay here. Quiet. Don't let them see you."

"What?" I reach for his belt loops, feel his leg muscles tighten. "No, Jethro. Don't—"

But he's already standing. He's jumped out in front of the ledge that conceals us, shouting something at the oncoming guards. A bright light crashes in, cascading over the rocks.

I watch as they take Jethro to the ground, a whir of khaki and muscle. Someone curses, limbs press, his arm bends unnaturally. I can't do it anymore. Suddenly, I'm standing too, leaping down the incline, screaming.

AFTER

—

DAY 44, EARLY

MY ARMS ARE jammed to my sides, powerless. So I use my feet and teeth instead. Someone pulls a shroud over my head, and I snap through the cloth, kick my feet up and out blindly, connecting with large bricks of flesh. But my limbs are outnumbered by a steel-armed octopus. Everything is dark.

Jethro is talking to someone, saying something too low to parse. I feel my body pull toward him, toward his warmth. He tried to save me, threw himself into danger in a wild bid to protect me. And then I, even more brazenly, tried to save him.

I'd do it again.

There's no more playing it safe, I realize, if that ever was a viable strategy. Whatever happens next—wherever they take me—I have no regrets about coming on this mission. We may have failed to free the afterlife, but I don't regret trying.

Head still shrouded, I'm scooped up and carried back down the rocky ledge, thrown hard onto the floor of a different kind of vessel. Around me, voices murmur. A door slams and the air grows dense, crackling. The ship rumbles to life. I try to isolate Jethro's voice among the others, but I can't locate his familiar scraping tone. I whisper his name, then Eva's. No response.

The engine roars louder, and we pick up speed. I picture the guard leaning in, menacing, over Larisa. I picture Faye alone, weeping in a cell. I see an endless gray nothing, a lonely eternity to consider everything I never had the courage to do or say. I shut down the images as fast as they come, try not to think about what will happen next.

After a mini-eternity, the ship goes quiet, bumps against another shoreline. We're hustled off, marched across rough ground and into another sort of land vehicle. I hunch in the darkness, listening as it jerks to life.

As the truck hums along, rocking, I begin to doze.

I AWAKE TO pricks of light shining through my hood. Again, arms grip me, and I'm ushered from the vehicle to a hard, uneven surface. My foot catches, and I tip forward, dangling. A pair of steel arms yanks me to standing, shoves me forward.

When the hood finally comes off, I'm indoors. A large room. Concrete, cool. I'm shoved forward, and the door clanks shut. My eyes adjust, making out the shadowed shapes of others hunched along the room's edges. I don't recognize anyone.

The lock scrapes, keys jangle, and we're left to ourselves.

I stand awkwardly as my cellmates avoid my gaze. They stare at their hands, their feet, the smooth dull floor. One woman finally slides to her left, making a space for me. I sit, grateful.

Time passes and I become aware of murmurs, voices so low they could be a breeze or the gurgle of water in pipes. Other sounds drip through occasionally. Low chatter and louder calls. Once, laughter. Later, a scream.

I test the air in my throat.

"What is this place?" I whisper to the woman beside me.

She turns her head toward me but doesn't answer.

I don't know how long we sit, waiting. That's the thing about being dead. Without hunger pangs or other signals, one minute, one hour, is indistinguishable from the next. My thoughts lock into a loop: What did Jethro hope to explain to me? Did they get Eva too? Where is Faye right now? And Larisa? Was I foolish to think I could help?

No, I still don't regret trying. Not yet anyway. But I do finally understand why the PTB are so into schedules. Without the routine of meals and sleep, all that's left is thinking, its own kind of hell.

A guard arrives with keys, calls a name. A woman clings to the wall, trembling. They drag her from the cell. It happens twice more. Another woman, younger. Then a man with the dry, slanted lines of advanced age. We wait to see whom the guard will call next.

A DAY PASSES, maybe. There's no simulated sunlight or sunset in our cell, so all sense of time has evaporated. Half a dozen inmates have been taken away. Gone where? We don't know. The guards return, and the remaining prisoners tremble. This time they order us all to our feet. We shuffle single file down a long corridor, large cells on either side, some filled with crouching bodies. Others empty. A door creaks wide, and we're pushed out onto a flat patch of dirt. I blink up at the sky. Not blue, not gray. A brutal, glaring white.

The yard is studded with prisoners, several cells' worth it looks like. I recognize a few from the rebel camp, though their black clothes have been swapped for loose pajamas. Jethro and Eva are nowhere. I wonder where they're keeping him. I wish we'd had longer to talk, smoke another simulated cigarette, explain everything. I hold on to our last moment on the beach and wonder what it meant.

The prisoners cluster by the doors, like cattle afraid to roam. Several stare at me, recognizing me from TV, and I want to tell them to save their shock. Everyone's got a story; most are messier than you'd think.

I don't recognize her immediately. She's dressed like everyone else, swimming in a drab-colored tunic, but the sharp-eyed squint is unmistakable. "Larisa?"

She looks up, then turns away. I deserve that.

Later, she approaches as I pace along the yard's outer wall.

"Hey, kid."

We can't risk being overheard, she warns, so we speak in brief snatches as we trace separate circles around the yard, coming together and then apart in a careful dance. She confirms that this is the place they call Limbo—an island outpost where the PTB stash souls who've become inconvenient. She's met some folks who've been here for years. She isn't sure why we haven't been booted from the grid completely, but she doesn't think it's the PTB's last act of mercy. Based on what she learned in those chat rooms and conversations with other prisoners, she suspects the PTB simply don't know how. Without their tech-savvy co-founder, they're lost.

"Have you heard anything more about your dad?"

Larisa shakes her head. No one here has met her father. From what she's gathered, this facility is enormous—a sprawling campus. Her dad could be in another cellblock like this one, or he could have found a way out—to another kind of afterlife—beyond the confines of the grid.

"There's no way I'll find him now." She sounds defeated, not the Larisa I know.

We're shuffled inside before I remember to tell her I'm sorry. For doubting her loyalty. I know she didn't share my business with the Powers. I'm still not sure what they knew, or how they knew it, but I'm sure Larisa is a friend.

AFTER

DAY UNKNOWN

I AWAKEN WITH someone's head on my shoulder, a wheeze escaping her lips. Sleeping helps the hours pass.

I've learned a fair bit about my cellmates. The pair of women in the corner are moms who got caught up in the recent protest in the park. An older man was in Paradise Gate for just a few weeks before security whisked him away. He thinks it has something to do with questions he posed about the PTB's methods. (He has a background in behavioral therapy and is not the only former psychologist to be locked up.) A few folks are quiet, but I gather from glimpses of poorly etched tattoos that they belonged to rebel factions, possibly Simone's. The rest were arrested for more ordinary offenses: timed out, fell into insurmountable debt, failed to comply with the program. Some aren't sure what they did wrong exactly.

One of our cellmates has become a sort of unorthodox preacher. "Paradise is what we choose it to be," he says when the guards have locked us in for the night. "No form of contentment is better than another. The Ever After is right here." He points to his skull. "Ascension: an internal state. It's up to us to transcend our captivity and rejoice."

Some of the prisoners close their eyes as he instructs, willing themselves to a better place. But the woman beside me, the shoulder-sleeper, turns her back whenever he speaks.

"When someone comes up with an actual escape plan, wake me," she says.

LARISA AND I meet whenever we can. Our yard breaks are unpredictable—some days there are two, some days none. We never know who else will be there. There's been a steady trickle of new arrivals, conspicuous in their nervous confusion.

Larisa waves off my attempt at an apology, tells me she understands my paranoia. The squirrelly administrator used similar scare tactics on her. (No, she did not tell him about my call to Faye's parole officer.) They set us up to doubt one another, she says, to create fear and ensure obedience.

Still, I'm sorry I got her so wrong.

Larisa's mood fluctuates. Some days, she proposes escape—wild, impossible schemes she's spent hours concocting in her cell. Moments later, she'll scoff at her own plans, saying there's no point. More often, she's quiet, sad, the opposite of the brash, no-nonsense girl I met on my first day at the Center.

To pass the time, we guess at the fates of the souls who've been escorted from our cells. "Maybe they got another chance?" I say hopefully.

"Maybe," Larisa says, "or maybe they went someplace worse."

Before we can agree which is more likely, the guards come for me.

THERE'S NO SHROUD this time, no truck. They usher me down a long hallway, out a door, and across a narrow portico to another building. I glimpse more buildings—long and low—on either side.

My new cell is smaller, built for one. The walls are a blinding white.

The next person I see isn't a guard. She's a middle-aged woman in a tan suit and low heels who tells me, frowning: "You're being transported. You'll be housed in a different facility while they'll weigh the evidence in a public proceeding."

"Proceeding?" It takes some work to get the gist of what she's telling me. "I'm being put on trial?"

"Something like that" is all she says.

THE DAILY WITNESS

NOVAK CHARGED WITH COLLUSION

———

In a shocking turn, former soul model Marianna Novak finds herself in her deepest hole yet. The young soul has been arrested and charged with collusion with rebel agents and participation in a seditious plot to undermine and overthrow the Powers That Be.

The gravity of the accusations has caught the whole realm by surprise.

> "Busted or Wrongfully Accused?"
> Follow us on the feed for more fan reactions.

Novak's trial will be televised beginning this Thursday. Stick with us as we cover every uncomfortable detail.

AFTER

——

DAY ?

CROWDS GREET ME as I descend from the van flanked by
two muscled guards. We're no longer in Limbo but on a busy sidewalk somewhere not far from the Center. Shouts roll around me
in waves, and the voices rise to a crescendo as another car arrives
just behind. Sleek, gray. A carpet is unfurled, and the shouts grow
more aggressive as the Chairman and Lady Lu make their way to
the steps.

They're whisked inside, while my escorts pause for the cameras
to flash.

I worm my face inside my collar, away from the steady rain of
clicks, but it's no use. The circus has begun, and I am the main act.

We've arrived at the House of Judgment, a large gray building
in Paradise Gate's main square that I must have walked past dozens
of times. Trials are rare in the afterlife, I've learned, and public trials even rarer. Few moral crimes rise to the level of sedition and
conspiracy.

My defense scholar wasn't much help in clarifying the details of the charges against me. He stuttered through a list of pretrial questions, while I did my best to answer: No, I did not conspire to incite a revolution. No, I have never met or spoken with anyone named Alisha Lanford. No, I did not engage in a campaign to recruit and convert frustrated souls to a more radical ideology. No, I did not recruit my own goddamned mother.

"Language," he warned.

From his questions, I gather that my case is about more than the failed expedition into the expanse. They clearly know about the meetings I've attended at the warehouse, the larger community of rebels I've met. Someone has been tracking my movements and feeding them tips.

My defense scholar greets me in the courthouse foyer moments before the trial is set to begin, wearing a robe that resembles an old lady's housecoat. We're shepherded into a large courtroom. It's your basic legal-drama setup: two long tables before a high wooden bench, witness stand to the right, stenographer to the left. Multiple cameras fill a media bank. No jury box. This case won't be decided by my peers.

I crane my neck up at the gallery, looking for anyone I may know—even one of the Catherines would be a comfort right now—but all I find are strangers' eyes, glassy with excitement. The Chairman and Lady Lu are nowhere in sight.

We take our seats, and my disheveled defender leans in to ask: "Have we filed any final motions?"

"Wait. What? Shouldn't *you* know that?"

There's no time to discuss. The judge, a tall, bespectacled woman in cinnamon-hued robes, appears. We stand, the gavel sounds, and we sit.

The prosecutor—pinstripes, creases, appropriate lawyerly air—makes the opening remarks: "Good morning, Your Honor, members of the court, gathered guests. Today, I present the case against Marianna Elena Novak, who is charged with eight counts of radical interference in—"

I don't hear anything else because my leg has gone spastic. I press both hands onto my knee to keep it from jackhammering up against the table. My defense scholar glances over but says nothing.

"Does the defense have a statement?"

"Pass," my defender tells the judge.

Pass? I gape at him in his old-lady robe. Is that even court terminology? His finger taps the edge of a suspiciously thin folder.

I get it then: No one in this room, not even my so-called defender, is on my side.

The prosecution brings its first witness: Juniah Harper. My TV interviewer preens before the courtroom in a plum-colored suit, winking toward the cameras. She clearly expects a lot of viewers.

She tells them about the deal we made—I'd do an exclusive interview in exchange for a headline-grabbing leak for which she's received immunity. Honestly, I miss most of what she says because I caught sight of someone a couple rows back. Eva, her curls smoothed into a tight bun. She's dressed primly in a button-down shirt and blazer. They must have released her for the trial too. Have they coerced her into testifying about our fateful outing? I try to catch her eye, but she trains her gaze ahead, where Miss Harper is telling everyone that I pressured her into breaking the journalistic code.

I narrow my eyes as Juniah descends from the stand, mugging for the cameras.

Eva is brought up next, only they call her by a different name: Valeria Doyle. Her face is grim as she takes her seat, the lines around her mouth adding at least a decade to her face. I imagine she's been slapped with serious charges too. Likely worse than mine.

The prosecutor approaches: "Can you tell us, Officer, how you first met the defendant?"

I choke.

"I've been inside the Left Hand for a full cycle now," Eva/Valeria tells the prosecutor, referring to Simone's crew by their official name. "My job has been to monitor activities, building a case against key targets while our other agents gathered intelligence from their most skilled coders. It's a high-priority surveillance effort. Recently I was assigned a new target." Her gaze turns to me.

Sweet kingdom come. How many ways have I been screwed?

"And what did you discover?" the prosecutor asks her.

"Things were slow initially. There's generally more talk than action among most of the insurgents. They have big ideas but most lack the courage to execute. Marianna Novak, on the other hand..."

My hands slip their grip and my knee slams up, causing my defender to jump.

"It was her idea to seek out that reporter," Eva continues. "She was angry about how the tabloids treated her and wanted revenge. She sought advice from other Left Hand operatives but was motivated by her own grievances. She'd cooked up another plot too, prior to the expedition—she had a plan to challenge the Powers during a telecast hearing. In my opinion, Novak is an embittered soul of the most dangerous sort—it's her ambition to overthrow our system and leave her fellow souls stranded, no matter the cost."

The gallery goes wild. *Did she just say—? Does that mean what I—?* My whole body has gone still from the shock.

Eva—or Valeria; whatever her name is—twisted the whole thing around. I wasn't the one who came up with these plots. Simone proposed the first one, and the final adventure was 100 percent Eva's idea. Why pin it all on me?

The judge bangs her gavel, and the gallery quiets.

My defense scholar stands for the cross-examination. He has only one question: "Did you say my client was observed eating *pastries*? With *sugar*?"

More fluttering from the gallery.

"Simulated sugar, obviously, but yes," says Eva/Valeria. "She enjoyed the coffee as well, which I believe speaks to her weakness of character. She confessed to me that she'd rather die another violent death than eat another leaf of kale."

A snigger of sympathy and someone hisses *hush*.

Is that it? All my defender is going to ask? I stare at him as Eva/Valeria is guided down from the stand.

The next witness is less of a surprise: Havel. Identified to the court as Officer Stephen Mowry. I knew something wasn't right with him. Sunglasses off, his hawk-like gaze scuds across the room before locking on me.

"When did you begin monitoring Marianna Novak?" asks the prosecutor.

"Approximately eleven days after her arrival in Paradise Gate, we became aware of a so-called heroic act that, if made public, would likely elevate her status among the public. We immediately began a background check to see if her character held up under scrutiny."

"A background check? Tell us, what does that entail?"

"The usual. Data monitoring, some basic fact verification, a preliminary archival review. At that point, we did not encounter anything to merit concern, but we learned that one of our agents had established a rapport with the subject and he was assigned for further discovery."

"This was an agent working undercover at the Center for Postmortuary Progress?"

"Yes, a student on special assignment. Goes by the name Jethro Bernal."

MY BLOOD BEATS so hard I don't hear anything more.

Jethro Bernal. Assigned to me.

Not a badass rebel, but a double agent. In the PTB's pocket this whole time.

Pieces of the truth rush in, locking into place: Our first trip to the warehouse and my introduction to Simone. The way he suddenly showed up at my first rebel meeting. The failed expedition.

But then there are pieces that don't fit: him begging me not to go back to the warehouse, his late-night call of warning, then later, in the tent, urging me to run.

How does it all fit together? And what about that last moment on the beach—his forehead against mine, his promise (an explanation: soon), the moment he stood and—

The gavel bangs, announcing a recess, and it's just in time. My insides are ready to combust.

AFTER A BREAK, Jethro takes the stand. I keep my gaze on my lap as he edges up the aisle, only daring to look once he's safely enclosed in the high wooden box.

He hunches, quiet, as the prosecutor asks his first questions, then mumbles something about taking the Fifth, which the judge tells him doesn't exist in afterlife proceedings. "Failure to answer will count as contempt and result in immediate arrest," she adds.

Jethro's gaze skids toward me, pleading.

I look away. I cannot.

He begins with the first time we met in the alley—"Totally unplanned," he says, as was our second meeting—but as word spread about my possibly heroic death, his probation monitor saw an opportunity.

The PTB wanted to keep an eye on me, make sure I was thoroughly vetted to avoid some of the embarrassment they'd experienced with the often-controversial Rupi Patel, whose rogue activities had caused many a headache for the Powers. Jethro seemed perfect for the job; he already had my attention and the PTB had him by the throat after discovering that he'd hidden large chunks of his own archive.

Jethro tells the prosecutor that, at one point, he stopped cooperating—I was making too many visits to the warehouse; his handler was demanding detailed reports; he didn't like where things were going—but then they brought his uncle into the mix.

"They had footage of him in detention," Jethro tells the prosecutor, his face buckling. "I owed that man . . . everything. I had to do it."

Jethro tells the court he stepped into line after that, agreed to record our interactions, track my movements as much as he could. When he wasn't able to follow me himself—I'd become sneaky—he got reports from informants. I only slipped his radar once.

"But then"—Jethro scratches his head—"then she told me she didn't want to see me anymore—said it was too complicated and she had to focus on her eternity. I lost access to her comings and goings after that."

I squint. Why is he lying? I didn't say any of that. *He* was the one who broke up with *me*.

"Mari wasn't really one of them," Jethro tells the court. "She just wanted to sort out her past and help her mother, and things got out of her control. I honestly believe she didn't know what she was getting into, that we were the ones who led her astray."

What's Jethro doing? If he was working for the PTB all along, why try to cover for me now? Why put his uncle at risk?

The prosecutor seems baffled too, and the gallery is alight with chatter. This hasn't gone how anyone expected. Jethro hasn't toed the line like Eva and Havel. Which somehow guts me more than if he'd just played his part.

My useless defender declines to cross-examine. As the guards escort Jethro back to his seat, I feel him look in my direction, trying to communicate something.

But I can't do it. I can't look.

THE NEXT MORNING, the defense calls its witnesses. I'm surprised my scholar has even bothered. I guess we're still pretending this is a fair trial.

First up: Catherine of Milwaukee, aka Bethany Meunch, tells the court she never stopped believing in me and is sorry for telling the press otherwise. "Maybe my friends and I were a bit envious," she admits, "and confused. I mean, we all worked so hard and here she was, dressing so *casually* and cavorting with deadbeats. Who turned out to be undercover agents! Honestly, do you think *I'd* say no to a sexy double agent spy if I thought that was on offer? Do you think any of us *want* to do that much Youga?"

From the gallery: several chuckles and understanding nods.

Reenie takes the stand next. The audience is quiet as she describes the breakthrough she witnessed during our interview prep session. "I believe Mari is well on the way to finding her truth." She gives me a long look, mouths, *You've got this.*

Faye, who has been pulled from detention to testify, melts down the minute her butt hits the chair. She sobs to the judge about everything she's done wrong since I arrived. Plus, a lifetime of poor decisions and disastrous outcomes she's only just begun to own.

"Ma'am, is any of this relevant to the current trial?"

"Relevant? Of course it is! Don't you see? I'm her mother. If she doesn't know right and wrong, it's because I didn't teach her!"

They let her ramble for a bit longer before guiding her down from the stand.

I want to ask how she's managing. If detention has been stressful for me, I can only imagine how it's affecting Faye. Instead I sit at my table, watching in silence as the guards escort her from the room.

Larisa is the surprise witness. Fresh from lockup, she rolls her eyes and scowls at the judge before promising to tell the one and only truth.

"First off, my girl isn't half as smart as you all seem to think."

All whispering stops, and Larisa's scowl melts into a grin. She's clearly pleased by her impact.

"For real. You should hear the questions she had: *What is my tracker tracking? How does a buffet work? Why are martyrs so problematic?* I had to explain literally everything. She barely had a grip on the basics when the media got her in their scope, and then you all send some emo spy to creep around and make her afterlife even more complicated? Come on. This kid didn't stand a chance. If you think Mari was capable of cooking up a massive afterworld coup with all of *that* going on, you're even more clueless than her."

The gallery explodes in surprise and delight. Larisa raises a cool brow, and when they're finally quiet, she adds, "It's all a sham, by the way."

Wide eyes and silence as the whole room leans in.

"Ahem." My defender, perhaps remembering his role, steps forward: "Wha—what's a sham now?"

"All of it." Larisa waves a hand at the courtroom, the judge, the prosecutor. "This 'trial,' for starters." She uses air quotes with the same level of derision she once applied to "virgins."

Around me, bodies shift.

Larisa nods sagely. "I've had a lot of time to ponder since they locked me up. I've been talking to folks these past few days—innocent folks like me—who agree this whole case feels a little too made-for-TV, you know? Like *The Dead and the Restless*. Anyone here watch that?"

Dozens of hands go up, including a few of the guards'. The judge appears flummoxed, unclear where Larisa's headed with this. I'm unclear too.

"You think the heroine—what's her name, Fatima?—would really give up her last bit of karma to fend off that weirdly sexy but obviously sketchy rebel soldier? It's your basic prime-time mind trap. There are no deceptively attractive infidels seeking to ruin your afterlife. The rebels aren't trying to disrupt your inner peace or destroy the grid. They're brave and decent folks who're trying to figure out what else is out there, discover new possib—"

The guards have latched on to Larisa, who keeps talking until a hand clamps over her mouth.

"What the— Your Honor! This girl just bit me!" the guard yelps, and the judge bangs her gavel. The courtroom breaks into chaos. Whispers about Fatima and that *extremely* hot soldier. Shouts of conspiracy. Weeping, as someone wonders aloud whether everything she saw on *Soul Survivor* was a lie too. The judge bangs harder from her bench, declaring a recess.

WHEN WE RETURN from the break, it's my turn to take the stand.

AFTERLIFE PROCEEDINGS
FIRST SETTLEMENT / HOUSE OF JUDGMENT

Powers That Be v. Marianna Elena Novak
Honorable Maria Diego, presiding

PROSECUTOR: How did you first learn about the
    so-called Left Hand? [Refers to aforemen-
    tioned extremist group.]
DEFENDANT: It was that guy. [Defendant indi-
    cates Officer Mowry.] He approached me on
    a sidewalk with a flyer. It sounded really
    creepy to be honest. I mean, it is creepy,
    right? A PTB spy out on a sidewalk trying
    to recruit random souls to join an outlaw
    group? What's that about?
PROSECUTOR [coughing]: I see, and did his tac-
    tic work? Is that what drew you to the Left
    Hand's headquarters?
DEFENDANT: Nope. Though interesting you ask.
    Another one of your spies brought me there.
    [Points to the prosecution's third witness,
    Mr. Bernal.]
PROSECUTOR: Let the court note that the defen-
    dant refers to a PTB informant who does not,
    ahem, work for me. [Turns to defendant.] So
    you take no personal responsibility for
    what followed?
DEFENDANT: I made my own choices, sure, but I

never would've known where to go or how to
go about it if it weren't for your agents.

PROSECUTOR: Let the court note that the defendant suggests an unsubstantiated theory of
entrapment.

DEFENDANT: Um. Your spies literally just said
they entrapped me.

PROSECUTOR [to court]: Not my spies.

PROSECUTOR [to defendant]: Would you explain
how the media interference scheme came
about, then?

DEFENDANT: Sure. I . . . [Defendant explains
steps in excruciating detail.]

[Aside: Court stenos really aren't paid enough
for this.]

DEFENDANT: Blah blah blah, video archive something something . . .

PROSECUTOR: Interesting. Let the court note
the absence of regret.

DEFENDANT: I regret a lot of things, actually, but not trying to share the truth. I
died so suddenly and I've realized all these
things, all the ways I could have lived more
bravely. Obviously, there are no do-overs.
But I do get to choose how to lead my eternity, and if I have to break a few rules to
protect the people I love, I'm going to take
that risk. You can understand that, right?

[Dozens of nods across the gallery.]

PROSECUTOR [frowning]: Does the defendant wish to share further details regarding her interactions with fringe factions?

DEFENDANT: Only that they aren't all bad people. I mean, aside from your spies, who clearly are awful but aren't actually rebels, you know?

Audience shakes their heads, then nods, then shakes again, revealing lingering confusion about who's bad and who's good.

DEFENDANT [cont.]: My friend Larisa was right. There's a lot of talk about "deviant souls" and "dangerous radicals," but really, all of these folks are just trying to sort things out in their own way. They even make some smart points, if you stop to listen. Like, they have this theory about universal redemption—

· END TELEVISED PORTION ·

AFTER

———

DAY ?

I LOOK OUT at my captive audience, a bevy of Catherines gaping wide-eyed down from the gallery, and realize: This is my moment. This is my chance to tell my truth.

And the words—a personal philosophy that has been shifting and unwinding as I've looked back on my past, listened to others, and stared eternity in the face—finally tumble out.

"I'm not the girl who stopped a shooter. I'm just a messy human like the rest of you. A human who tried her best and got some crappy cards dealt and made some big mistakes. Living is hard, okay. But dying is harder. I won't apologize for trying to do what I believed was right and for getting it wrong sometimes. Today, all of you sit in judgment of me, but I'd ask you to consider: What if our worth has nothing to do with the state of our vibes, or how many points we earn? What if, deep down, every one of us has what it takes to become whole? On our own terms.

"Yes. That's what I've learned from those rebels who frighten you so much. That maybe if we lightened up with all the judgment for a second, all the pressure, the standards and the competition— maybe if we stopped making things so freaking complicated—we'd realize that every single one of us is worthy of happiness."

As I step down from the stand, my audience is on its feet, cheering.

THE DAILY WITNESS

RUPI PATEL SOUNDS OFF, PROTESTS ERUPT

"I think Mari Novak is brave," the erstwhile prophet told an agitated audience. "I think all of you are brave, too, because you're out here, asking for something different, ready to take charge of your own fates."

On cue, the assembled crowd broke out in chants of: "Take back our truth."

The protest grew louder and stronger until a fleet of vans arrived carrying a crew of security forces who made a number of arrests and quickly restored order.

But the melee at the courthouse wasn't the only sign of unrest. Leaked videos of Novak's full testimony took over the feed shortly after her highly publicized trial concluded. Few could have predicted what followed. First, a group of young women asking *not* to be called Catherine took to the streets with stolen drums and a giant banner reading FREE MARI! FREE US ALL. Headbands were tossed, lycra shredded beyond recognition.

The not-Catherines were soon joined by a band of individuals who rode in on gutted Jeeps. Though we couldn't make sense of this group's fashion choices (why can't rebels be pretty?), we were struck by the energy of a young leader who identified herself as Simone. (Keep an eye on this one, readers! We predict big things!)

By the dinner hour, hundreds lined the sidewalks, including many who say they've never engaged in existential debate before.

"We're sick of meaningless mantras!" many chanted.

"And Youga!" cried others.

One protester told us that she wants the freedom to select her own self-actualization practices. Another admitted he had no opinion on the self-determination question; he came out mainly for the T-shirts and atmosphere. "Seemed better than another online quiz, you know?"

Protesters have raised big questions about the legitimacy and protracted reign of the Powers That Be. "What makes them qualified to decide what our souls need?" one protester asked.

We paused, unsure how to answer.

When the protesters' questions turned toward the afterlife media—"Why do you make everything into us vs. them, good guys vs. bad guys? What's *your* role in this mess?"—we responded with a shaky "Don't blame the messenger!"

The crowd did not like that, and following a brief scuffle with a few of the angriest activists, we relocated to the sidelines to consider our afterlife choices.

In short, the current scene in Paradise Gate is confusing right now, and as afternoon turns to evening, many are on edge, awaiting tomorrow's verdict.

Readers, tell us what you think: Should Marianna Novak be found guilty of seditious conspiracy? Or has she helped incite the revolution we all need?

AFTER

DAY ?

I WAIT IN my lonely cell. For the first time, I miss the noise of the feed. There's no way of knowing what anyone's saying, or what the judge had to say about my testimony.

I'd trade half of my remaining points for a chance to touch base with Larisa. I'm grateful to her for standing up for me like that, for speaking so boldly. But I'm frightened for her too. What happens now? Will they declare me guilty and send me and everyone who spoke for me into the void?

I'm frightened for every single one of us.

My testimony comes back to me in anxious snatches—all the things I left out and could have said better. Worry settles in like a familiar refrain: Did I do enough? Am I enough? Does any of it matter? Will anyone listen?

The silence of my cell expands, contracts.

I'd trade the other half of my points for my old tracker or a clock, for some way of knowing how much longer it is until morning.

THIS WEEK IN BETWEEN

Protests Swell as the PTB Struggle to Maintain Peace

Jeremiah: Hello, folks. It's Jeremiah Waters and Billy Shrub, coming to you live from downtown Paradise Gate, where thousands are gathered outside the Hall of Judgment, demanding Marianna Novak's release.

Billy: I miss the days when we could talk about fun things, like attitude cleanses and the latest in ascension-wear.

Jeremiah: Yes, well. Times are changing, and our own roles are being called into question.

Billy: Are you saying the media should unionize?

Jeremiah: What? No. Or rather, maybe? Billy, please, focus . . . Hey, look! Here she comes. [Waves to elegant young woman with crimson-tipped hair.]

Billy [eyes enlarging]: We're talking with her?

Jeremiah: Simone! I mean, Alisha! Alisha Lanford? Hello, we're so glad we caught you!

Simone/Alisha: [Chilly silence.]

Jeremiah: Right. Ahem. Can you tell us how you developed what I must say is a truly unique fashion sense?

Simone/Alisha: [Chill deepens.]

Billy [whispering]: Why isn't she saying anything?

Jeremiah: Let's try another tack. You've taken a rather controversial stance on our benefactors, Ms. Lanford, haven't you? When did you choose to become an outspoken traitor?

Simone/Alisha: Let's see. Probably around the time I realized Chairman Ted and Madame Eat-Pray-Woo are karma-skimming frauds, which I guess would've been the first time I heard them speak.

Billy: But . . . but they saved us! From an eternity of angst!

Simone/Alisha: So they say. Look, they may have had good intentions in the beginning—if that matters—but they've abused their power for years now, bent the entire afterlife media complex to feed their own egos and ambitions.

Jeremiah: You're *really* mad at the media, aren't you?

Simone/Alisha [calmly]: I'm outraged. Yes.

Jeremiah: What if I told you we're just regular folks like you, doing our best to avoid the abyss?

Simone/Alisha: With a karmic kickback? That's how it works, right? You were promised an extended term and bonus bennies in the meantime in return for spreading the PTB's messages?

Jeremiah [coughing]:

Billy [squirming]:

Simone/Alisha: Ironic, isn't it? A man who insists everyone stick to his special program gives free passes to those willing to carry out his dirty work. If you ask me, he has you right where—

Jeremiah [flinching]: Hang on. Is that—

Simone/Alisha [also flinching]: What the—

A large object hurtles toward the camera, followed by a beige blur, the color of a security force uniform.

Billy screams.

The image cracks, tumbles, capturing a quick scuffle followed by darkness.

· PROGRAM TERMINATED ·

· ETERNALLY ·

· THIS IS NOT A TEST ·

BREAKING:
NOVAK VERDICT ANNOUNCED

———

Hello and welcome to the first airing of the *Completely and Eternally Free Press*. No jingles, no mottoes. Just . . . news.

(We're slightly bored already!)

There've been big changes in Paradise Gate over the past few hours, beginning with this morning's announcement of a not guilty verdict in the case of *Powers That Be v. Marianna Elena Novak*.

The ripples of this landmark decision were felt throughout the settlement. Literally. Because of all the stomping and hollering.

We caught up with Novak as she emerged from detention, appearing rather dazed.

"People are happy for me? Are you sure?"

"Yes, quite," we assured her.

We began to ask a second question, but Novak's bright smile turned into a soft yelp at the appearance of a woman we know as Faye Novak and who she referred to simply as "Mom."

WAIT, THOUGH, IT GETS BETTER

——————

Adding to the day's shockers, late this morning, Theodore L. Mervin and Susana Lululaymon announced their resignation as co-chairs of the Powers That Be.

When asked about the sudden decision, Mervin professed that he'd been in the role for eighty-one cycles and was ready for a change: "I've been glad to perform this service, and now I'm looking to focus more internally."

"Will that involve addressing the deep insecurities and rampant narcissism that were so evident in your tell-all memoir, *A Man, a Plan, a New Afterlife*?"

The (former) Chairman declined to answer.

Ooh! But hey, this just in: We've learned that Judge Maria Diego has stepped in as Interim Chair of the Powers, promising sweeping reforms, details to follow.

"As the first order of business, the detention facilities known as Limbo will be closed within a week," she proclaimed.

Mari,

I don't expect you to forgive me, but I want to clear up a few things like I promised I would.

I told you I'd been in trouble before we met, but I was too ashamed to tell you more. Things were bad when I first arrived in Paradise Gate. Really bad. I'd given up on everything, wasn't going to class, got kicked out of my dorm. The guy you know as Havel found me sleeping in the park. He found me a place to stay and brought me to some meetings. I was in no place to question his kindness.

I told Havel about my uncle—how he tried to save me, how he died, etc.—and Havel did some digging to see where my uncle had landed. He'd been sent to detention a few weeks before I arrived. Of course this upset me. I owed my uncle everything. Havel said he knew a guy who could help in exchange for a small favor. It didn't seem like a big deal, so I did the errand, carried a message to some guy on the outskirts of the grid. But then, of course, they asked for another favor. Havel said if I refused, they'd have to report me (turns out the first errand was very illegal). I was trapped. If I got arrested, there was no way I could help my uncle. So I agreed to more.

I'd been doing jobs like this for a while before you showed up. Things had escalated. At some point, I realized Havel wasn't on the side of the rebels. He was working for the PTB. And that meant so was I.

Honest, Mari, I didn't pull you in on purpose. The first

time you found me smoking was a total surprise. But then we started talking and you made me laugh and think about stuff. I had forgotten what it felt like to spend time with someone who wasn't trying to use me, who didn't have some big agenda. I started looking forward to our meetups. But then one of Havel's minions found out about us and started pressuring me.

I didn't tell him much at first. I didn't want to rat on you, Mari. I swear. I avoided check-ins with Havel whenever I could. Sometimes I avoided you. But then they'd send me a clip of my uncle or pics of you in places you didn't belong . . . and what could I do?

You weren't supposed to be on that mission, Mari. The whole thing was a trap we'd been setting up for months to catch the Transcendentalist leaders. There never was a transport. I wouldn't have agreed to any of it if I had known you'd be there.

Mari, I promise I didn't want to hurt you. I know that doesn't change the fact that I did, but I wanted you to know the truth. And that I'll be sorry for all eternity.

~J

AFTER

DAY ∞

LARISA LEANS OVER my shoulder and snorts. "Does he seriously expect you to feel sorry for him? What a dipwad."

"Yeah," I say. "Definitely a dipwad."

Because what Jethro did to me wasn't okay, no matter how you slice it. His letter makes me feel better in some ways (he *did* care about me, did try to protect me at times, did say he's sorry), but it makes things worse in others, brings up all sorts of *could'ves* and *should'ves* and *what-ifs*.

What if I'd listened to his warnings?

What if he'd told me the truth much sooner? Could we have found a way to break free together?

Larisa snakes an arm across my shoulder. "C'mon. Time to trash that thing, kid. You can't save every sad sack in the afterlife, you know."

I shove her back playfully, tossing the pages into the bin by my desk. I'll pull them out later, read his letter a few more times, try to make sense of it. Still, it's good practice. Throwing heartache where it belongs. Even if it's just for a moment.

If I've learned anything since I died, it's that healing is complicated. It doesn't follow anyone's prescription or timeline.

A FEW DAYS after the trial's conclusion, I run into Z near the building we used to call the Center. She's been having a rough time, she tells me. She watched the court proceedings, every minute of them, and hearing my story only made her feel more guilty.

"Guilty about what?"

"I lied to you too," she says. "I knew who the shooter was. I was just too ashamed to say it."

The shooter was her ex, she tells me, aka the reason she fled the group home she'd been in and landed on the streets. Somehow he'd tracked her.

"So, it was your ex I pushed? Not some rando bad guy?"

She nods.

I attempt to take it in—an explanation that is at once more banal and far sadder than the random shooter theory. And every bit as unfair to both of us. The PTB probably could have figured all of this out, if they'd bothered looking deeper into Z's archive. But it didn't occur to them that she was more than a witness; she was a person with her own story to tell. Z was just as invisible to them as she was to Brookline's commuters.

"I knew it was a bad idea, staying in one spot for so long," she tells me. "But I got used to seeing you and your mom. I never had that—a real mom, I mean—and it sounds hokey, but sometimes I imagined you were my family. The longer I stuck around, the more Brookline started to feel like home."

"That doesn't sound hokey at all," I say.

"But I should have kept moving. We'd both be alive right now if I'd been smarter."

"No. Don't say that. Your ex was the criminal, not you." Softening, I add, "What you've been through is awful. I'm so sorry." I mean it.

"HEY."

Back in the dormitories, Larisa whistles for my attention. "Do I look okay?"

She spins in the open doorway, modeling the outfit she's picked out for Ascension Day: a Day-Glo-yellow jumpsuit peppered in tiny black stars. She's spiked her hair and painted her nails with rainbow polish and goggly-eyed emojis. She presses them together now in a faux namaste. She looks completely ridiculous. And somehow even more herself.

"You're perfect," I say, "a model for clinically batshit zealots everywhere."

She attempts a scowl, fails, and then rams me with a hug. I squeeze her back, tight.

"I'm gonna miss you, kid," she whispers into my shoulder. "I wish you'd decided to come."

"Soon," I tell her. "I will soon."

I WASN'T SURPRISED when Larisa signed up for the first big ascension ceremony. With the PTB out, individuals can now choose their own time to move on. Turns out, the border between the In Between and the Ever After is more fluid than we'd been led to believe. When you're ready, you're ready. It's as simple as that. The PTB led us to believe that they held the key to actualization, that there was some sort of magic in the ninety days and that inner peace could be created with a certain series of steps. But our new leaders have opened up the glass elevators so that everyone can choose their moment. Turns out, we're each a better judge of our own readiness than anything a wrist device can track, and there are as many ways to find that readiness as there are people. Once Larisa learned that her dad was okay (he'd hopped a secret transport to a nearby settlement a few cycles back and has been in touch by email), she declared herself ready to move on.

Another leap of faith. Nobody can say for sure what happens after. Some say that every soul finds the Ever After they need. In Faye's version, people spend whole days doing the things that animate them: making art, building community, telling stories. In the evening they gather together to eat, dance, and sing.

"Sounds kinda hokey to me," I told her. "Don't they have any good TV?"

She laughed. "If that's what your soul wants, baby, then yes."

Faye has decided to ascend too. I was surprised when she first said it, but then I really looked at her—my beautiful, unconventional mother—at how focused she's become, how loyal and loving and determined to improve. She isn't perfect. No one is. They say that even in the Ever After, souls remain engaged in a process, evolving to become their fullest selves. Still, my mom's put in a lot of work already and faced up to her darkest truths. If she says she's ready to move on, I'm not going to hold her back. Not this time.

When I told her my own decision, her lips quivered and her eyes grew bright. "I can't leave you, baby. Not again."

I snatched her twirling hands from the air, caught them firmly in mine.

"Think of it as striking out ahead," I told her, "you saving a place for me. Anyway, someone needs to update Nonnie and Pop-Pop. You can tell them I just need a little more time to sort things out."

It took some convincing, but she finally gave in.

Now that my biggest hurdles are cleared—paparazzi off my back, Faye in a good place, the constant swirl of worry settled—I can finally, for the first time, focus on me. Figure out who I want to be, apart from responsibilities and self-doubt. Decide what it is that I need, to become my best me.

There's no Center anymore, no clear path forward. No rules. For someone like me, it's a little terrifying, to be honest. But also exhilarating.

Tomorrow I'll move into a new residence for teens in transition. Specialized programs are sprouting up everywhere since the Center went out of business. A few former Catherines have joined mine, including Catherine of Phoenix, who was released from detention with everyone else and now goes by Annabelle. They all go by their original names now and, released of the pressures of the Center, have become infinitely less annoying. Reenie is still around, too, working as a freelance counselor with her own curriculum. She and I have been talking about how I should use my time going forward, and I told her I'm not totally sure what to do next.

"That sounds pretty normal," she says. "Death turns everything sideways. It takes time to unpack it all, figure out what we each really want and need."

One thing I do know is I'm through with all the power poses and chanting (to each their own), but I tell Reenie that I might be up for giving meditation one more try. I might give yoga—actual yoga, not that *Youga* BS—a go too. I'm in a better place now. I feel like it wouldn't be such a bad thing to learn how to be still.

I'VE BEEN DIGGING around in my archive again. It's no longer forbidden, and Simone and crew have made their Frankenstein technology available to everyone. All sorts of folks show up at the newly expanded warehouse to explore their pasts, which maybe isn't 100 percent healthy but it's where we're at. I can't change where I've been, I've realized, but I can try to learn from it, to decide which bits of my old self are worth keeping and which I'm ready to let go.

I think a lot about my final days, how broken down I felt in the end, obsessed by money and test scores and my own sense of lack. I was desperate to build something better, terrified that I'd never get there, never find a moment's rest. I hate that life brought me to that place. I hate what life did to Faye too. But I'm able to see all of it in a different light now. I wasn't a hero or a victim; she wasn't a villain. We were just two people, doing the best we knew how with the gifts we were given in a world that wasn't always kind.

"You're not the only one who felt that way," says Simone, when I share my newest revelation. "That's why it's up to us now to build a better kind of world."

WITH THE PTB out, banished into some far corner of the In Between, it's not at all clear what comes next. The Left Hand have already made contact with two nearby settlements and believe there are more out there. The third founder has been in touch. He says he couldn't abide the direction Chairman Ted and Lady Lu were taking things and exiled himself rather than compromise his values. He feels bad about the state in which he left the grid, though, and has offered to help the Left Hand's tech pros repair the worst of the glitches.

Simone/Alisha is helping shape what she calls the New Beginning. Her vision is a community run by all of us, charged with holding up every soul—no exceptions. There will be more options available and few hard-and-fast rules. You can choose to focus on gratitude if you want, but there will also be storytelling circles where folks gather to make sense of shared pain, to repair harms, and to heal.

I've volunteered to help. I'm not a gifted leader like Simone, but I'm good at anticipating problems and tackling to-do lists. She says every movement needs folks with those skills. Rupi Patel is helping too (we've met; she's even funnier in person), and so are a few former Catherines.

Some are saying it's odd that so many young women are stepping up to lead the next phase of the afterlife, but I look around at all the souls I've met, all the brave things they've done already, and I don't think it's so strange at all.

NOW

ASCENSION DAY IS beautiful. The rooftop elevators have
been decked out in festive colors, and with the help of a few savvy
coders, for the first time in collective memory, the simulated sun
has broken through, painting the sky a glorious robin's-egg blue.

Rupi Patel is the MC. She invites each of the honored guests
up to share a few words and a joyful clip from their archive. When
Faye's favorite memory appears on the screen, my heart stops. It's
the first home I remember. I sit atop a big white bed. Sunlight dap-
ples the walls while music croons through the speakers. Faye sings
along, dancing with a mop, while a tiny me looks on, mesmerized.
Faye turns and sees me there, almost forgotten, and with a great
swoop, she catches me in her arms, twirls me up up up, into great
peals of laughter.

Faye squeezes my hand as we watch the scene together, and I
feel the thrill of what's coming coursing beneath her skin.

Rupi nudges the honorees toward the elevators, and Faye's fingers loosen.

"Today is your day, brave souls. You've discovered what every one of us knows in our heart: You are worthy. Enjoy this next phase. Relish every moment. We'll see you soon."

At that a trumpet blares and a thousand simulated doves crest across the sky. The applause is deafening.

ACKNOWLEDGMENTS

How do I begin to thank folks for a book that has lived in my imagination for fifteen-plus years? I will leave someone out certainly, so first, a big THANK-YOU to the many writers who've touched this manuscript in its various iterations and to the non-writer friends who've said, *We believe.*

First shout-outs go to Tim Wynne-Jones, Uma Krishnaswami, and my first-ever workshopmates at Vermont College of Fine Arts, who read the first pages of this wacky concept and said, *Yes.* Thank you to Elizabeth Bluemle, who awarded an early draft the VCFA/ Flying Pig Bookstore Humor Award. That gust of confidence has kept me going.

Liz Cook, Alicia Potter, and Adi Rule cracked this story wide open with their insightful questions. Jennifer De Leon, Desmond Hall, Rajani LaRocca, and Susan Tan listened to me howl toward the end. The Beverly Shores retreat crew has kept me going for twelve years (and counting) with their love and humor. Marianna

Baer got me through some especially messy drafts and moments— what would I do without you, dear friend?

To my Boston dance community (Masacote, J&L Studio, MetaMovements, Querencia): Thank you for giving this writer space to get out of her head and explore other creative vocabularies. I love grooving with all of you! To Naima Workman, Brandon Compagnone, and the Baptiste Brookline yoga community: You all are the real deal. I'm grateful for every moment I spend grounding down, reaching up, and becoming a better human in your studio.

To Erin Harris, my brilliant agent, who went from *let's talk* to *let's sign* when she saw this story and who has been the ally I needed, though thick and thin. To Stacey Barney, who pushed me to re-envision this story in the best possible way and then patiently probed every plot point and world-building detail. (Good gods, the tech!) To Chandra Wohleber, Aaron Burkholder, and Cindy Howle, copyediting dream team, Theresa Evangelista, jacket design goddess, and R. Kikuo Johnson for the gorgeous illustration (I'm still pinching myself). To Jenny Ly, Sarah Sather, Suki Boynton, Emily Rodriguez, Nicole Kiser, and the whole Penguin Random House team for their marketing savvy and support.

Lastly, thank you to my loving family, who puts up with my unusual life choices, corny jokes, and nonstop seeking. Especially special thanks to my beloved Uncle John and Grandpa George, who never let a good (or bad) pun get away. I'm not sure what the tech is like where you are, fellas, but if you're reading this, I hope it gives you a chuckle.

When KATIE BAYERL isn't penning stories, she can be found dancing, writing about social causes, or herding a trio of (mostly well-behaved) cats. Katie holds an MFA from Vermont College of Fine Arts and is on the creative writing faculty at Grub Street. Her previous young adult novel, *A Psalm for Lost Girls*, earned two starred reviews and was a Texas Library Association selection, among other honors. Katie lives in Boston, Massachusetts.